Loving Mother:

It is midnight. I have no wish to sleep. It is better by far to spend the long hours with you, talking with quill and ink.

We await only the trumpet's call to arouse the army to victory or defeat. A merry party supped with the King tonight. He was gay and filled with hope, and his sureness of our success was contagious. He jested with me. First, he said he would make me Governor of Virginia. I suggested Sir William and Sir John Berkeley would not like that. He laughed. He has the most infectious laugh, Mother.

But these are idle thoughts. What concerns me most is your plight if we lose tomorrow. You and Cook Ellie *must go at once to Devon*. I have arranged for your escort. John Prideaux will come with you. We are indeed in a great revolution, one that has gone deeper than you can possibly imagine.

Do not fear for me. I have a place of honour near the King, a good horse and my sword. The anxiety that besets us will soon be settled one way or the other. Any outcome is preferable to the long waiting of the past weeks! Will it be failure or glory? Who knows?

                                        Richard

BENNETT'S WELCOME

Inglis Fletcher

BANTAM BOOKS

TORONTO • NEW YORK • LONDON • SYDNEY • AUCKLAND

*This low-priced Bantam Book
has been completely reset in a type face
designed for easy reading, and was printed
from new plates. It contains the complete
text of the original hard-cover edition.*
NOT ONE WORD HAS BEEN OMITTED.

RL 8, IL 8-up

BENNETT'S WELCOME

*A Bantam Book / published by arrangement with
The Bobbs-Merrill Company, Inc.*

PRINTING HISTORY
Bobbs-Merrill edition published July 1950
4 printings through November 1950
Bantam edition / August 1972
2nd printing . . . July 1980
3rd printing . . . May 1986

ISBN 0-553-25650-5

Published simultaneously in the United States and Canada

---

*Bantam Books are published by Bantam Books, Inc. Its trade-
mark, consisting of the words "Bantam Books" and the por-
trayal of a rooster, is Registered in U.S. Patent and Trademark
Office and in other countries. Marca Registrada. Bantam
Books, Inc., 666 Fifth Avenue, New York, New York 10103.*

PRINTED IN THE UNITED STATES OF AMERICA

H   12 11 10 9 8 7 6 5 4 3

A HAPPY COUNTRY

"Your people military and obedient; fit for war, used to peace. Your church enlightened; your judges learned . . . just. The fields growing from desert to garden . . . the city growing from wood to brick . . . your merchants embracing the whole compass of the earth. . . ."

—FRANCIS BACON (1611)

INTRODUCTION

Bennett's Welcome has long been in my mind as a panel of
the Carolina series of historical novels of the Colonial and
Revolutionary period.

In chronological order they are *Roanoke Hundred*, 1585;
Bennett's Welcome, 1651; *Men of Albemarle*, 1710; *Lusty
Wind for Carolina*, 1720; *Raleigh's Eden* and *Toil of the
Brave*, the American Revolution.

This book is not a history. It is a story of the people who
lived in Virginia during the Cromwellian era. At that time
North Carolina was still a part of Virginia. The first colonists
of North Carolina were drifting southward by way of the
Blackwater and Chowan rivers to take up land along the
Chowan, the Roanoke (Moratuck) and the Great Sound of
Roanoke (the Albemarle Sound of today). These venturers,
from 1640 on, were independent trappers, explorers and
land-hungry men. They came from Jamestown and the counties on the south side of the James River—Norfolk, Isle of
Wight and Nansemond.

With the passing of the Cromwellian period in England,
and Charles the Second on the throne, Sir William Berkeley
was for the second time the Royal governor. Then the migration south became a steady flow—Quakers under the active
persecution of Berkeley; Puritans out of favour; Cavaliers
who wanted more acreage than was available on the James,
York and lesser Virginia waterways.

I have endeavoured to show, through the names of the
first colonists of Virginia and Carolina, the close alliance with
the Roanoke Island venture of 1585. Many of the names
given by Hakluyt in the various colonizations on Roanoke
Island appear in the lists of early Jamestown. Again, as early
as 1646, they appear as landholders in what was to become
North Carolina. It is assumed that some of these, on the

littoral, came by ship via Chesapeake Bay, for there were many Marylanders in the early groups; but for the most part they followed the rivers.

To me the most significant thing is the *continuation* of the early ventures of colonization. Out of the five failures of Roanoke Island came the successful Jamestown colony; out of Jamestown came the southward movement, until the sound and the waters about Roanoke Island became the waterways of the new and permanent colony. If one studies the map, one may see it as a circular movement, not a north-and-south migration.

Another interesting point is the persistence of names of the first expedition under Sir Richard Grenville, still present in the Albemarle to this day—not only names, but characteristics of Devon and Cornwall fisher-folk, yeomen and the county families, West Country-folk who love the sea and the land.

As I set down earlier, *Bennett's Welcome* is not a history. The happenings of the Cromwellian years in Virginia have been compressed to fit into the framework of the novel. However, I have drawn the historic incidents from the ten years of the Cromwell government up to the Restoration.

I have endeavoured to give the picture of a period of great change in England, reflected in the Virginia Colony. In 1652 a Stuart governor sits in his mansion at Green Spring, a stone's throw from Jamestown, while a Cromwellian governor administers the government through an elected Assembly.

Roger Greene's grant of ten thousand acres for one hundred persons (1653) was sixty-nine years after Amadas and Barlow landed on Roanoke Island, and the first Assembly in Perquimans was in 1665. By that time a number of families were well established along the rivers and creeks that flowed into the Great Sound of Roanoke.

The eastern end of the sound, near the Atlantic, is guarded by Roanoke Island where Sir Richard Grenville planted Sir Walter Raleigh's first colony (1585), and where a few years later John White's colony of men, women and children disappeared, leaving behind them the greatest unsolved mystery in American history, the tragedy of the Lost Colony of Roanoke Island.

These were fine substantial people, men and women of integrity, resolute and forthright. They had no thought of heroic deeds, but they had the moral stamina that builds nations. They went about the business of cutting fields from the forest, planting and harvesting; trading with their neighbours and the Old World. They lived frugally in the beginning, always striving to better their condition and the condition of their children, building a New World in the pattern and freedoms of the Old.

To these early colonists and their worthy descendants, who live today in the freedom their ancestors won, I dedicate this book.

INGLIS FLETCHER

Bandon Plantation
Edenton, North Carolina
June 20, 1950

ACKNOWLEDGEMENT

I ACKNOWLEDGE gratefully the assistance of librarians and staff members of the British Museum, of the Euston Street Meeting Society of Friends Library and the Victoria and Albert Museum in London.

I thank the Library of Congress, with emphasis on the Rare Book Division; the Folger Shakespeare Memorial Library in Washington; the Reference Library of Williamsburg Restoration, Inc.; the Library of the College of William and Mary, Williamsburg, Virginia; the National Park Service, Jamestown Island, Virginia; the Library of Guilford College, North Carolina; and the State Historical Commission, Raleigh, North Carolina, for maps of the period.

I have used King Charles's own journal for "The Flight" and Thomas Blount's *Boscobel*. The Blount name appears in all the early settlements, from Sir Richard Grenville's Roanoke Island colony on through the beginnings in Jamestown. It is still an important name in the Carolina of today. The only modern history I have used is John Buchan's excellent *Oliver Cromwell*.

The names of the principal characters (fictional) are taken from a deed of transfer of Coddington Court, Herefordshire, dated the Third Day of July, in the twenty-sixth year of the Reign of Henry VIII.

CONTENTS

Book One
ENGLAND

Book Two
THE VOYAGE

Book Three
VIRGINIA

EPILOGUE

BOOK ONE

England

CHAPTER 1

The Lady's Bower

THE August sun shone golden through the tall Lombardy poplars that circled Coddington Manor. It was near sundown and the wild marsh-hens fed in the meadows and on the greensward that ran from the stone terrace to the verge of the pool. Wild ducks winged their way through the evening sky, to rest on the dark waters among the lilies, squawking and quacking to attract the attention of the drake that still hung aloft, waiting to plummet downward.

The pool was lip-shaped and lay like a kiss of the gods in the green grass, reflecting the golden sky and the Lady's Bower. Pale roses bloomed on the pool's edge. The evening quiet lay across the landscape. The black-faced sheep grazed silently. On the horizon the church tower rose above the massed oaks, a black spire piercing the gold above.

The door of the rambling black and white house opened slowly and a young woman stepped out, lifting her wide blue saddle skirt to avoid the stones. A young maid of fourteen or fifteen, with the natural manner of a child, followed her, carrying a small spaniel in her arms. The dog barked and squirmed until the child released him. He ran barking toward the pool. The ducks rose swiftly, beating their wings toward the water. With frightened squeaks they flew away, leaving the water troubled.

"Naughty dog! Naughty dog!" the child cried. "Naughty, naughty Fifi!" She picked up her long skirts and sped around the hedge into the bower, where the puppy had taken refuge.

The bower, interlaced of yew and holly, had been hollowed out to make a little room. A white bench stood at one end, and an iron table on which lay a bit of crewel-work. The yellow light sifted dimly through the thickly interwoven boughs. The child stopped short, her mouth made round to utter a sharp cry. A tall man stood behind the bench, his

3

fingers on his lips. He wore jack-boots, dusty and soiled, as were his leather tunic and breeches. A wide hat with a bedraggled plume lay on the bench, with a Cavalier's jewelled C.R. pinned to the side.

"Sibyl," he whispered, his fingers to his lips, "come close."

"Master Richard! Master Richard, we thought you were in Scotland with the King's army."

"So I was, sweet child, but now I am here."

"But how did you get here?"

"On horseback. I turned the nag loose down the road. I'll want my own Saladin when I leave. Tell me, where are my mother and your sister?"

"Dame Margaret is working in the great room. Mathilda is walking in the grove with her guests, Master Nicholas Holder and Kathryn Audley. They came out when I did. Did you not see them?"

The man smothered an oath. "I wish Kathryn had come alone," he said. He moved so that he might look through the opening. He watched the three figures moving across the grass. Nicholas Holder, tall as he, fair as Richard Monington was dark, was bending over Kathryn as they walked, paying slight attention to the child's sister Mathilda.

Richard Monington, Lord of the Manor of Coddington, watched them, his dark brows drawn together.

The child said timidly, "We came here yesterday to visit with your mother—Mathilda and I. The others rode over today, on their way to Ledbury after the hunt." She paused. Richard was not listening. He had torn a blank page from a book and folded it into a tiny cockade.

"Do not call my mother. No one else must know I am here, for I come secretly on the King's business, but give this to Kathryn Audley," he whispered. "Be sure no one sees you. Do you think you can do that, Sibyl?"

The little maid nodded, her dark-brown curls bobbing. "Sir, yes, when we are drinking tea."

Richard lifted the child to the bench. She stood now, tall as he. He leaned forward and kissed her soft lips. "That for Mistress Kathryn Audley," he said, his voice low. "Tell her I'll wait until moonrise, but no longer. Can you remember?"

The girl nodded. She stood a moment looking at him, her dark eyes troubled. "Kathryn is for Oliver's men. I heard her tell Mathilda that her guardian Sir Robert also stands for

Oliver and the Parliament. 'The Stuarts have caused enough trouble.' " She repeated the words parrot-wise. The man's face darkened. The child shrank back and all but fell from the bench. Richard caught her. For a moment she lay against his rough leather tunic; then he kissed her lightly on the brow.

"That one is for you, sweet Sibyl, for being my little messenger." He swung her from the bench. "Whistle your puppy and scamper. Wait . . . the book and worsteds—carry them with you. I don't want anyone coming here."

"Yes, sir."

Richard's hand was on her shoulder. "What was the message I just gave you?" he asked.

"You will wait in the Lady's Bower until moonrise," she repeated.

He nodded. Sibyl lifted the yelping puppy from under the bench and tucked him under one arm. The book and trailing hanks of bright worsted under the other, she ran out of the yew bower through the open doorway.

Richard Monington drew farther back into the gloom, but stood so that he might look toward the pool. Kathryn had moved away from Nicholas Holder and was strolling slowly along the stones toward the house. How tall she was! He thought, as he had thought many times before, that she was the loveliest woman he had ever seen. How gracefully she moved, her blue skirt delicately lifted, so that the hem would not touch the green grass! Her pale-gold hair was wrapped in a silken scarf, but one braid fell loose across her shoulder. His heart beat swiftly. He would have liked to touch her hair, bury his face in its golden beauty. It had been so long since he had seen her—months now, months! Not since they had quarrelled on a midsummer eve last year, when he told her he must join the King's army in Scotland. It was soon after she had come to live at Audley Court.

"You are mad, Richard, mad!" she had said hotly. "Surely you know that the Stuarts exact loyalty from their subjects and give nothing in return. Can't you understand that Cromwell is the power of England? My guardian says he will be king before another year has passed."

Rage had come rushing through his veins. "Damn what your guardian says!"

She had stopped him. "Richard!" Her voice was brittle. "One does not curse Sir Robert Harley."

"I'm sorry, Kathryn. It's my wretched temper."

She had paid small heed to his words. She went on: "How can you expect to keep my friendship when you hang on the skirts of the Stuarts?"

He had caught her hands. "It is not your friendship that I want, Kathryn. I want your love, your passion. I want nights like last midsummer, when you lay in my arms and gave me kisses deep as my own. Kathryn, have you forgotten so soon?"

A faint color had risen to her creamy cheeks, her voice had softened. "Better to forget, Richard. It is like this in wars. It was like this in the War of the Roses, and in the Civil Wars. How can it be different now in this invasion?"

"Women have not part in wars. They think as their husbands and their lovers think. They follow the men they love. You swore you loved me, Kathryn."

She had passed over his last words as though he had not spoken them. "That is not true. I think as my guardian thinks. He has left the King's cause and gone over to Cromwell's side, because Cromwell believes in the people's cause —the Parliament is the voice of the people."

"Cromwell's men are of no merit. A few battles won . . ."

She had whirled on him. "How can you say that? Hampden and Pym—Cromwell's men of no merit?"

"Cranks and radicals . . ."

"What of Fleetwood, and Lord Fairfax and Lord Grey of Groby?"

"Misguided! They will turn to the King. When Charles rides this way and beats the drum, their swords will be at the service of the Stuarts. Mark my words."

She had shaken her head. As he now remembered it, she was a little sad. "It is you who are misguided, Richard. You are blinded by an old loyalty."

He had caught her in his arms and kissed her fiercely. "Must we quarrel, my sweet love? Let us go away to Virginia, to the lovely New World across the Western Ocean. Let us have a life of our own—not your guardian's life, but ours."

She had disengaged herself from his arms. There was scorn in her eyes and in her voice. "And so speaks the Lord of the Manor of Coddington! What is England coming to, when her men run to a New World while she is bleeding from her wounds? Is there no love of England save among the brave men of Oliver Cromwell?"

He was stung to unbridled anger. When only a young boy he had stood at his father's side at Naseby in the first Civil War. She had called him hero, for she had been Royalist then and hot for the King.

She stood facing him, her head erect, her body straight and taut as a bow of yew. Anger had died in him as he looked on her beauty. It was Sir Robert Harley who spoke, not his sweet girl. This was the new jargon, spoken by a man who was looking for quick rise to power. Richard had said bitterly, "Remember when Birch marched into Hereford? Remember when the Roundheads danced in the Cathedral to the music of the organ? Remember when Cromwell pulled down the cross at Coddington and denounced my people as pagans? Were those the acts of brave men?"

"You are insolent, sir!" she had said and walked away.

In his anger he had let her go, and those were the last bitter words he had heard from her lips. Now, months on months later, he waited for moonrise. Would she come to his signal, the scrap of paper twisted in a peculiar way, a sign they both knew?

In call of his own house, where his mother waited uneasily for news of him, Richard paced the gloomy cavern of the yew bower. A fool he was, to trust his safety to a child and a rebellious woman when Roundheads might be close by and his own troops still some way off on their march from Scotland. If by any chance the two armies met and engaged in the north, it would be bad for him, absent from his men. But that was hardly likely to happen. Richard had been delayed, first by a swollen stream and then by his horse going lame on the last relay. The main body of the Scottish army might well be not far behind him.

Charles Stuart, the young King, had been reluctant to send him by way of Coddington Manor with messages for Sir Edward Massey commanding the Royalist forces in these Midlands. But here he was, skulking on his own grounds, afraid to walk to his own door—for his mother's sake, he argued to himself. He must not bring the wrath of Oliver's men upon her because of her son, who rode for Charles Stuart.

The evening deepened. The yellow sky turned grey, the grey to darkness. A few stars shone. Church bells chimed, the sweet ring of the bells of Coddington Church; a faint tinkle echoed them as the cows moved homeward. The air was chill. He took up the thick cloak from the bench and spread it over his shoulders. Many a night he had slept on the ground, easy in its comforting warmth, on the march south after the army had been turned from Scotland.

He heard voices at the rear of the house, and the sound of horses' hoofs on the court-yard stones. Nicholas Holder's voice was speaking. "No, I've heard nothing of Richard. The Royalist army is in the north. General Monk defeated them at Stirling—a decisive defeat, rumour says."

His mother's clear sweet voice, troubled but without a tremor, came to him clearly. "Nicholas, I count on you to make me aware of any change. Can I trust you to do that?"

"Always, madam. Richard is my old friend and dear to me."

"Yes, yes." Her voice was hesitant now. "Yes, but some say you are wooing—and not a Royalist maid, Nicholas."

"They say! Let them say, and be damned to them! Pardon, Dame Margaret. I spoke without thought. Believe me, you shall have the first news that comes to my ear."

"Thank you, Nicholas. Give my remembrance to your dear mother. . . . It seems sometimes that the nights are too long to endure. . . . Good-bye, Nicholas. I am sorry you must leave before supper. I'll send a groom with Kathryn when she leaves."

There was the sound of a horse's impatient neigh, of leather creaking, as Nicholas flung himself into the saddle; of the clatter of gravel, as he trotted down the tree-lined drive to the road.

Richard moved to the archway in the interlaced yew bushes which made the entrance to the bower. It was not quite dark. He could hear Nicholas go cantering up the gentle slope to the top of the hill where the Holders had lived since the time of Great Harry. Just so long had the Moningtons lived at Coddington Manor. Just so long had the two families held the same loyalties. Now he felt a dislike for Nicholas. Why? Because he stayed safe at home? Or was it because he had bent loving glances on Kathryn Audley?

Richard paced back and forth in the bower, restless, uneasy, starting at each noise, waiting for the dark. Oliver's men—where were they? For days Charles's army had been on the march, knowing that Ironside was sending his men

southward toward London on a course that paralleled the
Royalists. The King's officers, his ministers and particularly
the Earl of Derby, had persuaded Charles that England was
waiting for him. He had only to show his standards, beat his
drums, and the countryside would rush to his colours. Oliver
and his New Model would go down in defeat. The King had
an army of sixteen thousand men. Richard was young and a
novice at soldiering, but he was uneasy at this decision. Oliver
had generals who didn't play the old war games, any more
than Oliver himself. Richard hoped that austere general of
Cromwell's, George Monk, had been left behind in Stirling.

No, the Roundheads did not fight fairly, Richard thought.
After a battle men must bivouac and rest. That was the way
wars were fought on the continent. But Ironside recognized
no customs. He sent his cavalry straight into the bivouacs,
cutting the resting army into lean strips, bisecting the lines,
forcing small groups to fight without hope of support. Richard
remembered how Oliver had passed his whole army across
Fife and taken his enemy in flank. A bitter turn for Charles
to face, with David Leslie and his sixteen thousand men cut
off from supplies, and no communication with the Gordon
Highlanders Middleton was bringing to the relief. No choice
for Charles but to march south.

Richard saw the country as a map; Charles's march from
Stirling to Carlisle, Kendal, Wigan, Warrington, where Richard had left him to ride ahead. Cromwell, with Harrison,
Lambert, Fairfax and Fleetwood, four great generals, was
hot on their parallel route. Where would the two armies meet
and engage? Would there be a general battle? He was not
happy at the thought. He did not share the Royal generals'
belief they had left Oliver far behind; he knew now how
futile had been the King's hope that they would raise an
army in the Midlands of England; he knew now that none of
the great Commonwealth leaders had any idea of coming over
to the King's side. Only Massey had changed colours.

Somehow, in his mind, Richard saw Ironside's army crossing the River Severn. This was Richard's county, Herefordshire, the scene of innumerable skirmishes in the Civil Wars.
He knew it from one line to the other, from north to south.
So far, Cromwell's men were on the eastern road. Would
they wait until both armies were down in the Midlands and
then endeavour to push the King back against the Malvern

Hills? Wales was enemy to them both—the Marches were
a death trap. Herefordshire people knew the temper of the
Welsh down through the centuries—raiding, fierce men, free
men who wanted no outsider to cross their border.

A twig snapped, dragging Richard out of his reverie. He
heard a horse galloping and the sound of men's voices. He
couldn't understand the words, but there was instantly excitement and the confusion of other voices. Men were running
for the stables. Doors opened and closed sharply.

Richard rose from the bench where he had been sitting,
retreated into the gloom, his hand on the hilt of his sword.
Across the lawn a figure moved silently. Slim, elegant, with
the faint moonlight on her, Kathryn came swiftly toward him.

"Oliver's men are coming!" she cried, not noticing his
outstretched hand. "You must go quickly, quickly! My brother
Roland is here. He says a troop of Oliver's men are marching this way!"

He caught her in his arms. She struggled to release herself,
beating her small white hand against the steel breast-plate.
"Let me go! Let me go!"

The words died as he pressed his lips against hers. For one
instant only she responded to his ardour. After that moment
he released her, for her lips had gone cold and unyielding.

"Fool!" she said, holding her voice low. "Fool! If you do
not care for yourself, think of your mother. They will punish
her for harbouring you." She began to cry. "I am a traitor
for even warning you. If Roland or Nicholas finds out . . ."
She turned, listening. He saw her white, troubled face as she
stood at the entrance of the bower, where the moonlight fell
on the dark mass of the trees.

"Tell me you love me," he said, not moving. "Tell me,
Kathryn! Give me some hope, some comfort to warm my
heart."

"Stand away!" she whispered fiercely. "Do not touch me.
I hate all Royalists. I despise you."

A trumpet sounded in the direction of Coddington village.
Bells rang from the church, swift strokes. It was the alarm.

His hands fell heavy on her shoulders as he turned her
toward him. "You don't hate me, my pretty Kate. You love
me."

A man's voice called, "Kathryn! Kathryn, where are you?"
She wrenched herself free and ran swiftly across the grass to

the house. It was her brother Roland crying impatiently, "Where is the girl?"

Richard heard Kathryn's even, calm reply: "Here I am, dear brother. Did you ever see anything as beautiful as the pool in the moonlight? Look at the shape of it—two lips, lovers' lips." Her laughter rang against Richard's heart. "I think the moon has kissed the sweet soft earth with a lover's kiss."

"You are moonstruck, my girl," Roland's heavy voice answered. "Come, it's very cool without. Tell Dame Monington farewell. I want to ride with you to Colwall before I join my men."

Kathryn lingered at the door. "Are the Roundheads close by?" she asked, her tone raised.

"At Coddington Church, at this moment. They'll be here soon. . . ." The voice died away. The door closed.

Richard moved back into the shadow, his heart beating swiftly. She had lingered to warn him. Some of Oliver's men were at Coddington. The pool was "a lover's lips, the kiss of the moon on the warm soft earth," she had said. Was she thinking of his lips on hers? She had said, "If Nicholas finds out." So Nick is turning recreant to the Stuart cause. "My dear old friend!" Judas!

He buckled on his sword, alive to his very present danger. She had spoken the truth. If the Roundheads found him here it would go hard with his mother. He must get away, cautiously. There might be scouts between here and Ledbury. He hoped General Massey would be at Ledbury or Estnor soon.

He moved out through the shadow, keeping close to the garden wall. The stables and a horse—by good luck he could manage.

When he came opposite the court-yard at the back of the house, he saw two grooms standing by the rack where the horses waited. Roland Audley's and Kathryn's mounts. He pressed back against the wall, hoping that he had not been seen. A gleam of light illuminated the terrace as the door was opened. One of the servants came out carrying a brass lanthorn which he held high to light the way for the riders, moving slowly ahead of them to the mounting block. Richard's mother stood in the open doorway. Near her were Mathilda Jordan and little Sibyl.

"Good night, Kathryn. Good night, Roland." He heard her dear voice distinctly. "Do have a care riding along the lane in the dark. I wish I could persuade you to stay the night; there are so many empty rooms. . . ." Her voice broke a little. "This terrible, terrible war!"

"It will not last much longer, madam." Roland's voice was confident. "A few months, no more." He bent to kiss her hand.

Kathryn said, "We will be quite safe, dear Dame Margaret, quite safe. These are Oliver's men, you know."

"Cromwell's or the King's," Madam Monington said, her voice firm again, "there are evil men in both armies. That I know."

Kathryn mounted. Roland lingered a moment to say his farewell to Dame Margaret. "You will be quite safe, madam. Long since I asked General Fleetwood to instruct his men that Coddington Manor is out of bounds."

"Thank you, Roland. You are kind to think of the welfare of defenceless women."

Mathilda said, "Farewell, Kathryn. Farewell, Roland. I hope you ride toward good fortune."

"No word from the little Sibyl?" Roland laughed as he laid his hand on the maid's brown head.

"Sir, I wish you good fortune."

The women moved inside and the door was closed. Roland swung onto his horse. To the stable-boy he said, "I'd advise you to move the horses to the far meadow. I've asked for protection, but you know how it is—a good mare is a temptation to a foot-sore man, or to a cavalryman riding a lame nag."

"Yes, sir. Thank you, sir. I'll lead them down to the pond tonight. It's no use, sir, to lay temptation across a man's path."

Roland and Kathryn trotted away. Richard had one full look at her as she rode through an open space where the moon lay like silver in the lane. She caught up her scarf as though to wrap it more closely about her throat, but the wind caught it. It fluttered for a moment. To the man crouched in the shadow of the wall it was a signal, a farewell.

Richard stood quite still, wondering what his next move would be. He wanted most earnestly to step inside his own doorway. He wanted to kneel before his dear mother, but he must not. If Parliament men should come, should say, "Madam, we are searching for your son," Dame Margaret must be able to answer in all truth. "I do not know where he is. I have not seen him this twelvemonth, when he rode away to Scotland." His mother was a brave woman and resourceful, but a poor liar. No, he must go without speaking to her. Best move to the stables, saddle that black devil Saladin, and be off to find the advance detachment of the King's army before the moon rose high in the sky.

He heard voices. He saw a lanthorn bobbing up and down, moving toward the kitchen wing. The groom would have his mouthful before he led the horses to the lower meadow for safety. Now was the time to cross the court-yard to the stables. The stable was quiet. Richard waited at the stall while Saladin ate his mash. The horse was saddled. Five minutes and he would be riding down the lane. "Hurry, my beauty! One last crunch before I slip the bit between your teeth. Now, no biting! Don't you know your master?" He paused, foot in the stirrup. The stable-boy was running across the court-yard. Others were at his heels.

The gardener was shouting, "Get the horses. Drive them down through the narrow path. Quick, lad, quick! Bean't you hear the soldiers galloping down the highway?"

Richard looked up toward the hills. The moonlight played on steel casques and breast-plates. He heard hoofs and a snatch of psalm-singing. God! He was caught. There was no time to get out of the lane that led to the coach road. With quick, sure fingers he unbuckled the girth and slipped the bridle, dropped them into an empty stall. For himself, the loft? No. If it happened to be a foraging party the stables would be searched first. The gardener's cottage, deep in the beech grove, would be his only hope.

He saw Sibyl running toward him in the moonlight. "They are here," she cried as she reached him, "turning into the lane! The loft?"

"No, they will go there first. There is no place to hide in here. Damme, I'm trapped! I'll go out to meet them." He unsheathed his dagger.

Sibyl tugged at his leather jerkin. "No, no! They will hang you as they did old Lunberry—at the roadside, with his legs all sprawled and his eyes ticking out. Quick! I know. The dovecote. There's room for you."

She caught his hand. Moving cautiously she slid out of the door and along the side of the building. Behind the stable was an open stretch of ground. She followed the garden wall until they were opposite the sheepfold.

"The dovecote!" He laughed. "By Gad, child, you're a quick one to think of the dovecote!"

"I've been playing house up there. It is all sweet and clean. When you're inside, I'll pull the ladder away and hide it as I always do. No one will know. We'll have to scamper across. I hope they don't see us."

They bent low and made a run for the sheepfold and fowl yard. On top of the long brick building was the great dovecote where he used to keep his pigeons. Many a time he and his older brother had hidden themselves there. . . . He laughed quietly. "Maybe my feet will hang out, little one."

"No, no. You can curl them under you." The child's voice was shaking; her hand was trembling. "Be careful, sir. Please . . ."

"That I will. I want to keep my body whole, so I can fight."

"Your sword—don't let it rattle."

"Not a rattle. I'll muffle it in my cape." He mounted the rickety ladder. "Can you manage the ladder?"

"Yes, yes, I always do it alone. I'll come to let you know when they have gone."

"Good night, sweet child!" She looked very tiny standing in the moonlight, her small triangular face, with great dark eyes, turned up to him. He watched her struggle with the unwieldly frame, slip it down and push it under the berry bushes that grew against the garden wall. Then she waved her hand and was gone.

Richard stretched himself on his stomach, so that he might look above the stable toward the house. The court-yard was plainly visible. He laid his dagger beside him and drew his sword from the scabbard. If they should discover him, he would do some damage before they took him.

He was no more than comfortably settled when he saw a dozen riders come up the winding lane into the court-yard. They were followed shortly by others, until the terrace and half the lane were filled with horsemen. Other sounds crowded the evening air: the clatter of armour, hoofs striking against

cobbles, the sharp crack of a sword hilt against the great
oaken door.

"Hallo the house! Hallo the house!" Below him a horse
whinnied. The stable-boy cursed and muffled the sound with
his coat. "That devil Saladin!" he moaned.

Richard turned his head slowly, until he could see the
cow barns. He saw stable-boys and grooms leading horses
across the field and into the beechwood plantation. That was
good. They would be safe for the moment in the dense wood.
He rolled back on his stomach, striving to look through the
open door into the great hall. Straining his neck, he had a
glimpse of his mother standing at the foot of the curving
stairs. An officer entered, his hat in his hand. She came forward, very tall, very stately. With a gesture she pointed the
way to the great room where a fire burned brightly. She
seated herself in his father's high-backed chair, her white
hand laid along the oaken arm. The officer stood, his hat
under his arm. His deferential attitude quieted Richard's
alarm. He thought it was like a play at the theatre in the old
days, which one watched from the high gallery, but could
not hear the words that were spoken by the actors.

Other riders arrived, among them someone of importance,
to judge from the conduct of the men. A murmur came from
the dragoons, who were standing stiffly at attention.

Merciful Lord! It was Cromwell, Old Noll himself, who
dismounted at the block! Impossible. Why, Cromwell was in
Yorkshire. But there he unmistakably stood. With a nod of
greeting to his men he strode across the terrace and entered the
house, two of his generals beside him.

Dame Margaret Monington arose, bowed slightly as Cromwell entered the room. Her white hair shone like a silvery
halo about her high-held head. If she had fear within her,
she would not show it.

Cromwell bowed as he stood before her. She waved him
to a seat by the fire opposite her and turned to call a servant.
Richard could almost hear her say, "Bring a hot punch, Graves.
The gentlemen have come a long way. The wind from the
Marches blows cold tonight."

Richard leaned out of the opening, trusting that the overhanging shadows would obscure him. By twisting about he
could look through the oriel window to where his mother
sat. After a time, he withdrew his head. It was no use. He

could not hear what was being said in the great room. For a moment he felt he must go and stand by her side; but he thought of the dispatches he carried from the King to General Massey. His presence would bring danger, not safety.

It was mid-August in the year 1651. The Parliament's Civil Wars had long since been won. Parliament had beheaded the King, but a new King Charles had arisen. Out of France he had come into Scotland and a new war had followed.

Now the young King, after the bitter defeat of Dunbar, was invading England itself—a bold if forced move. He marched his army of sixteen thousand men down the western road, as Hamilton had done in '45.

Richard Monington had been ordered ahead to make contact with General Massey, who commanded the British Royalists of the Midlands. By now he must have arrived in Richard's own country of Herefordshire. Ledbury, where he might be expected to encamp, was only three miles from Coddington Manor, Richard's ancestral home. Richard had chosen the road that would take him there. Now, besides his dispatches, he had news for Massey indeed. If some way he could get word to the general in time they might capture King Cromwell himself.

A voice rang out sharply. A trumpet sounded. The men mounted and rode across the court-yard, beyond the stables to the open fields. Richard watched them. They would bivouac in the open meadows, cutting off his chance of escape. Lying on his stomach, his chin on his folded arms, he watched familiar preparations for an evening meal. Horses were unsaddled and picketed. Men unlaced iron breast-and-backplates and let them clatter to the ground. Little fires sprang up, dotting the field, showing where two or three soldiers rested on the ground in the warmth of the fires.

Anger was strong in Richard Monington's breast, stronger than his anxiety for his own safety. The boards on which he was lying were hard, harder than the earth where Oliver's men lay. Damn them to eternal fire! He turned and twisted, wrapping his cape about him to fend off the chill wind.

He looked up at the rim of the hills that rose against the sky. The moon was climbing. All about him was moonlight, clear and cold. Trees and small farm buildings were black, without form. Poplar trees cast long black shadows, touching the pool. After a long time the voices of the soldiers were silent and they slept.

Richard knew he must make his endeavour soon. If he could creep through the meadows to the beechwood plantation undetected, there would be a chance to get to the horses. He looked at the rising moon. Two hours, perhaps three, and the soldiers would be in their deepest sleep. He folded his arms above his head, his face down. A few minutes' rest for himself before the try. Before he dozed off, he thought of the girl Sibyl. That little one had a quick, ready wit. The old dovecote was a proper hiding place, since the pigeons had been moved to the new one on the far side of the stables. But it smelled of feathers and manure. "Damn Oliver!" he muttered. Oliver would be sleeping in *his* bed, under linen sheets scented with lavender. He closed his eyes and napped, circled completely by Oliver's men.

CHAPTER 2

Roundheads at Coddington Manor

WITHIN the house Oliver Cromwell sat long at table. On one side of him was Lieutenant-General Monk, on the other Fleetwood. Aides stood behind them. Harrison and Lambert were still north, harrying the King's progress. Lord Fairfax had his army north of Ferrybridge, coming south in reserve, should the main army make contact with the Royalist troops. Cromwell had ridden at top speed ahead to make a quick and secret survey and test the temper of the people. Monk was to return immediately to his command in Scotland.

Oliver sat tall at the table, his stocky torso long, his shoulders broad, thick and powerful. His head was well set, and his neck strong. His large, brooding eyes under heavy brows were lowered on the map that lay on the table.

Dame Monington's fine Worcester dishes had been pushed aside, some lifted from the table and set on the hearth. A frightened footman peeped in the door that led to the pantry. Seeing the great ones were intent on their maps, he sidled in and hastily took up plates and cups from the hearth, before the heat of the oak logs cracked the precious China. A fork dropped from his trembling hand and fell to the marble hearth with a great clatter.

Fleetwood stormed at the awkward fellow, but Cromwell, without lifting his head, spoke kindly. "Let the lackey clear away the dishes. We will be long here, and want no interruptions, once we are started working." He turned his melancholy eyes directly on the servant. "And no eavesdropping!"

The man told it later in the servants' hall when they were washing up. "He is either a devil or a saint, I'd say. His eyes bore into one like a dagger, they do. He could strike you dead, I believe."

Cook Ellie, a strong, sturdy Devonshire woman, said, "More likely devil. 'Tis said he used to ride across the Fens

18

about Huntingdon on a great black charger, like old Beelzebub himself."

"Hist, woman!" warned old Graves the butler. "The walls
have ears. He'd gladly hang you to a gibbet, just as he's hung
others afore this. Mark you how he ordered the people of
Coddington to take down the cross from the church."

The scullery maid paled at the words. "Take down the
cross? Why, I thought he was a godly man."

"So he is," said one of the milkers, who had just entered
the kitchen from the scullery. "So he *is* a godly man. Why
don't you speak what he said when he had the cross taken
down?"

"I don't know what he said," the butler murmured. "I
only know what he did."

"Well, I know," the milker said, settling his shiny copper
pails on the table. They were filled to the brim with milk,
warm and foaming from the cows' udders. "What he said
was 'Don't worship images. Worship God.' "

No one spoke for a moment.

Cook broke the silence. "How late you are milking, Coscroft! The general wanted milk when others called for ale,
and I had to serve the great one morning's milk, because you
were sluggard and had brought none to the house. Sluggard
you are, and I'm telling you, you can't go down the lane at
nightfall with the girls, leaving your milking till midnight
again, lest I tell the mistress. Hear?"

The milker backed off from Cook Ellie's wrath. " 'Tain't
maids, mistress, 'tain't maids. 'Tis his soldiers that kept me
running—carrying wood for their fires, fetching water and
opening cider barrels."

Graves came into the room with some empty wine bottles.
He paused at Coscroft's last words, his thin face, with its
beak, working. "Damn you, Coscroft! What right have you
to open my cellar?" The old man's eyes blazed and he shook
his fist under the milker's nose.

Coscroft backed off as Graves advanced toward him. "The
right of a man with a sword at the seat of his britches, sir,
and that's *right* enough for me."

"You're a coward. Oliver's men wouldn't spear you." The
butler took a great key from a leather pouch and started for
a door that led to the cellar below the scullery where the ale
and cider were kept.

"Don't go, Mr. Graves," the milker pleaded. "Don't go. They're making merry down there, and there's goin's-on you wouldn't like to be seeing."

The butler paused. He was a Churchman and he had no desire to look on sin, even though it were the sinning of the Roundhead army.

"Get them out of there," he said to Coscroft.

"How can I?" whined the milker. "A feeble man am I, sir."

"Lure them out. Tell them there's better cider in the milkhouse. Tell them anything. There's only a thin door between the cider barrels and the wine cellar. Go, I say!" He advanced on Coscroft with such ferocity that the milker turned and bolted from the kitchen.

"You've put him atween the devil and the deep sea." Cook's smile was broad. "My, but you are a fierce one when aroused, Mr. Graves! I'm astonished at your boldness. Why, Coscroft is twenty years your junior."

"What matter if he is thirty years younger 'n me? What right had he to take my keys, open my cellar to soldier scum?" The butler's thin face flushed.

"Hist, man, don't play the part of the hawk, with your eyes burning! You'll have a seizure, you will. Besides it's not safe, shouting that we're for the Stuarts, with him and his men a-sitting in our dining-hall, eating our joint and burning our candles."

"Keeping us up till after the midnight bell's tolled at Coddington Church." The butler laid down the long iron spoon he had caught up when he advanced toward the milker. "You're right, Cook. I must control my anger, but it roils me to think of them drinking our good cider. Last year's press was the best we've had for years. Let them drink it green. Green wine and green cider—they don't know the difference. Only gentlemen know what they are drinking, for they have the palate."

He sat down at the head of the table, where the pantrymaid had laid a place. Cook fetched a well-filled plate and the butler fell to. Between mouthfuls of joint and a gulp of small beer, he said, "I'm a-minding what a palate Master Richard has for choice wine. 'Graves, my good fellow,' he says to me, 'Graves, be damned to you for serving this swill! Bring me the Madeira my father had laid down in '30.

That was a vintage year. Or bring me a bottle of Canary that has some age and body.' "

The scullery maid, Patsy, paused in her dish-drying and let her cloth fall on the table. "Oh, poor Master Richard! I wonder where he is now."

"Poor Master Richard indeed!" the butler said severely. "Glorious Master Richard, out fighting his battle for King and country!"

"Yes, sir, that I know, but my Jamie says there's times when one fights about glory and King and country and yearns to lay down in a comfortable bed for a good night's rest."

"And a wench between the sheets with him." The footman spoke up from his end of the table, a sly grin on his face.

"You're an evil-minded man." Patsy's cheeks were pink with anger. "You and your sly ways, coming up behind girls on the stair and pinching!"

Cook, arms akimbo, faced the footman. "Up to your old tricks again, Smolkins. I'll have to report you to the house-keeper; or maybe you'd like to go off with Old Noll's army."

"Merciful God, no," the footman said. "Pasty here doesn't mean me, surely. I have the greatest respect for her . . . ah . . . dignity."

"You're full of words, a regular gas-bag," Patsy said sullenly. She pulled up a chair and began to eat.

"Let's have a little peace," Graves said severely.

Cook laughed. "Peace in these times of war? We have a saying in the West County that peace is an unnatural, temporary condition between wars." She stacked the blue Worcester plates and placed them on the Welsh dresser. "Can't take them to the dish pantry, for it might disturb His Greatness in there." She nodded her smooth dark head in the direction of the dining-room. "List!" A rumble of sound without formed words came from the room where the generals conferred over their mysterious map.

Then one voice came clear. "I tell you, General, Charles Stuart isn't forty miles from where we sit at this moment! I know. I feel it. I smell his army as though I saw it with these two eyes." A laugh followed. "Laugh as you will, but you'll be laughing the other way. Where are they? Why, they may be as close as Leominster and on their way to Ledbury. I'll wager he has forces between us and London. Yes, I'll lay another wager: we'll battle before many suns have set."

"Now, Fleetwood—" a commanding voice sounded—"your nerves are on edge. There isn't a Royalist between here and the Marches of Wales, or between here and Worcester. Cease your talk. It's plans we are interested in, not conjecture. My couriers have not brought in a single dispatch from the north of any imminent danger."

"Look to the south and the east, sir, as well as to the north. I'll swear Charles has his sixteen thousand men drawing close. Sir, we do wrong to underestimate our enemy. We're in danger here."

"Fleetwood, there may be something in what you say."

In the kitchen the men and women looked from one to another. No one spoke. They had been a strong household of Royalists. But were they now, with Cromwell's men all about them? What of Coscroft, opening the door of the wine cellar to the riff-raff of the Roundhead army? They'd never believe that these were pious men.

A maid ran in. "The mistress wants you in the great hall," she said to Graves, who rose quickly.

"She should be abed long ago," the cook growled, helping Graves on with his livery coat.

"I'm afeard for her," Patsy said. "He's like to put her in the stocks, if she talks back to him."

"He wouldn't dare." The footman shifted his chair, his eyes on the disappearing back of the butler. "No one dares to lay hands on the mistress."

"No one, that's a fact. She's got the heart of a lion, has she, and even an enemy has respect for courage."

"Respect? Aye, that's a word that some folk don't know. I can't help wish Master Richard was near to give us comfort."

Cook sat down heavily. Her feet ached, and her legs. It was well after midnight, and no general had dismissed them for the night. "Step outdoors, Smolkins, and see what you see. I thought I heard the beat of hoofs on the upper road."

Smolkins set his pewter mug down and went out through the buttery door. The room was quiet. Cook looked about. Patsy washed the last of the dishes and wiped off the top of the long deal table. She placed a large platter on the tall Welsh dresser, amid the pewter dishes and bowls. The kettle steamed on the hob. The old hound slept on the hearth. It was a quiet, peaceful room, the heart of the house, Cook always maintained, the central heart. It was always clean and shining, cheerful with the glow of open fire on the hearth. Pots of blooming plants on the ledge reflected on the leaded panes of casement windows. Copper kettles shone on the hooks above the fire. Candles burned brightly. Madam was never stingy about candles.

For a long time the two women sat in silence. Cook looked up suddenly. Had she heard scratching on the window? She turned her head slowly. She did not wish to see the face of a crop-headed trooper peering into her kitchen. The sound was repeated, a stealthy, urgent sound. She got up and went to the window. There was no leering face or burly figure or the glint of moonlight on casque or body armour. Again the scratching sound.

Patsy came to Cook's side. "The cellar! The cellar! Don't open. 'Tis like to be a drunken soldier."

"Run upstairs, Patsy. Lock your door. A pretty maid like you isn't safe." Patsy fled at Cook's words, her candle flickering with her running steps.

Cook picked up an iron spider in one hand, with the other lifted the latch. Richard Monington, dishevelled and untidy, stood on the top step. He wore a stable-boy's leathern small-clothes and jerkin and he carried a bridle and saddle over his arm. In his right hand he had a dirk.

"Merciful God!" Cook whispered. "Merciful God!"

"Don't faint, Cook. Get me something to eat. I'm famished." He sank onto the settle by the fire, his head in his hands.

Cook stood for a moment looking at him, then moved swiftly to the larder. Better to be captured on a full stomach than an empty rumbling belly, was her thought as she set food on the table. When she turned, she saw he had fallen asleep, his head against the hard oak back of the fireside settle.

Poor soul! Poor young lad, worn out by wars and fighting! She hesitated about waking him. "Needs must," she muttered aloud. "Needs must. Who can tell what devils will be peering into my sweet kitchen?" Her heart beat briskly, for there were sounds from the dining-hall. A chair scraped. She snatched the food from the table and carried it to the little shed room off the buttery. She ran back and laid her strong hand on his shoulder. "Master, master, be quick!" Half awake he followed her without question, stooping to enter the shed. "Mind the step. Here's food and a hot cider cup on the bench. I'll fetch a candle. No telling, they might step from the dining-hall. "A voice called. She ran back to the kitchen.

Richard came into the shadow of the door. "Who is in the dining-hall?" he asked, catching her arm. "Who?"

"He himself," she whispered. "The accursed one." The voice called again. "I'll go. Mr. Graves is with the mistress."

"Wait," Richard said. "Wait." He snatched the serving-boy's apron from a hook. He slipped the halter over his neck, tied the strings about his waist. He set a tankard and mugs on a wooden tray and started for the dining-hall.

"For the love of God, don't!" the Devon woman pleaded.

"Leave be, woman. Who will see the master in the servant?" He passed from the room, assuming a slouching walk.

Richard stood inside the doorway and looked vacantly about the room. They were all there, Monk, Fleetwood and the lesser men. Cromwell's back was toward him.

Fleetwood spoke sharply. "Can't you answer the bell, lout?"

"Bein' goin' to my bed, zur. Butler he been gone, zur. Is it ale you're wantin', zur?"

"Ale and a bit of food. Some cheese. I understand Herefordshire dairies have sharp good cheese."

"They do say, zur." He slipped close to the table to set the tray down in front of Monk. In this way he faced Oliver, so close he could have touched the great wart on his lower lip. He looked hard, until Fleetwood shouted, "Stop staring and bring the cheese."

Richard did not move. "Is it the general hisself?" he whispered. "Hisself?"

Cromwell smiled, but scarcely took his eyes from the papers before him. "Himself, lad. Now do what you are told."

"That I will, zur. That I will." He moved away from the table. At the door he paused. "Cook, she makes a brave, fine rarebit—" he smacked his lips—"brave and tasty and sharp."

"An idea, lad. If Cook's awake, let's have a rarebit." It was Cromwell's warm, modulated voice that spoke. "Don't waken her."

"She's sittin' by the fire, zur, lessen you should want somethin'."

Cromwell turned to Fleetwood. "And you tell me this is a Stuart household."

The younger man looked sharply at Richard. "Whose colours do you wear, fellow?"

Richard stroked his leather tunic. "I be stable-boy, I be, and a rare good one." A laugh went up around the table. Richard stared at Fleetwood in a puzzled way. "Zur?"

"Begone, fellow, and don't come back until you have the brave, fine rarebit smoking hot. Begone!"

"Zur." Richard backed out. He stood at the door a second.

"Herefordshire, yokel, par excellence," Monk remarked.

Fleetwood said, "I'm not too sure." He rose from the table. Richard retreated quickly, kitchenward. He did not want the door closed against his face.

Cook had not moved from where she stood when he left the room. When she saw him her hands flew to her ample bosom. "Thank the good God!" she whispered.

Richard swung her around. "Quick, Cook, a brave, tasty rarebit, to show these rebels what you can do. Quick! 'Tis hunrgy they are for a bit of Herefordshire cookery. I'll get the cheese and the ale."

Cook, aided by Richard's encouraging words, set to work. "Never was so fine a bit of cookery on such short notice," he said, balancing the tray. "I know that Old King Harry himself stopped here for supper in fifteen hundred and—what year was it?"

" 'Tis set down on the king beam above the fire-place, 1535, plain as day."

"So it is. So it is. Now give me a cloth for my arm, so I won't burn my hands. And, Cook, keep everyone out of the kitchen but Graves. I want to talk to him."

"No one will come now. They've all gone to bed." Until Richard had left the room she forgot that Coscroft had gone out at the butler's orders to bring news of how the soldiers were bivouacked.

Just as the door swung shut Coscroft came in. "Where's Old Graves?"

"With Madam in the great hall."

Coscroft drew himself some ale from a keg on the buttery shelf. He began to talk. "They're all around—a close circle of fires from Bosbury Road along the River Ledden. But the folk at the tavern didn't know whether they be Oliver's

men or the King's." He took a big swallow of ale and yawned
mightily, rubbed his eyes with the back of his hand. "Is
Butler going to be all night dancing attention on Mistress?"

Cook saw her chance. She must get rid of Coscroft before
Master came back, without rousing his suspicions. She didn't
know how he stood, whether for King Charles or Oliver.
"It's one of her worrisome nights. Sometimes she sits till
sunrise in front of the fire, not moving a whit."

"What for, with a fine big bed to rest in?"

"It's Master Richard she worries for, him off and gone
this year past, fighting up Scotland way and all. You go to
bed Coscroft. I'll tell Butler, if he comes back."

Coscroft set his pewter mug on the table, stretched and
belched. He nodded toward the dining-hall. "They still there?"

"Yes. I'm waiting, if they should be wanting something
more."

Coscroft nodded. "So they might. You're a good cook, if
you do come from that foul West Country."

"I'll tell Graves what you said. Get along with you! I'll
have no talk out of your mouth about Devon. Get along."

Coscroft laughed and went away. Cook sat down quickly,
as though her knees would no longer hold her up. The Lord
be praised, he was gone! She watched the window for him to
pass on the way to the stables, where he slept in the loft above
the cow-sheds. She saw his lanthorn bobbing along the path
at the garden wall. After a time the tiny pin point of light
was lost in the shadows. The moon was covered with moving
clouds. 'Twould rain on the morrow. Water always followed
a mackerel sky.

In the dining-hall Richard served the rarebit and the ale,
slouching along, hoping to hear a word or two. At first the
talk was only of battles fought and marches made—the past,
not the future. It was the future he wanted, and soon his
ears were full of it. He was startled but must not show it. In
sudden awkwardness he spilled a little ale on Monk's sleeve
and got a sharp reproof. He felt Fleetwood's eyes on him
more than once.

Finally Fleetwood spoke. "The Moningtons must have
fallen on evil days that they have a fellow like you to serve
them." Richard met his eyes vacantly. "What's your name?"

"Silly Dick," Richard answered instantly. "And I be no

servant, I be stable-boy, but Cook says, 'Take the ale to the gentlemen.' "

"So you're stable-boy, are you? I hear Mr. Richard Monington has some fine stock."

"Yes, zur, that we have. Our cows are best."

"Bother cows! Horses I'm talking about."

Richard looked downcast. "Zur, we did have, and that's Gods' truth, but Master himself, Nigel Monington, took some away with him when he rode to the wars, and young Peter, his stepchild, took some when he went to wild Scotland. I don't rightly know what became of Peter. He got killed. They say a Roundhead killed him." He looked from one to the other. "Did you ever know Master Nigel? He was a rare one with horses."

"What about the present owner, Richard Monington? Is he a good horseman?"

"He is, but not like Master Nigel. Why, he could gentle any horse." A sly look came on his face. "Some say he could gentle women same as horses."

Monk, a tall man with a fine head and intelligent face, got up from the table and stood with his back to the fire.

Fleetwood said significantly, "So that's the man you duelled with, Monk?"

"I didn't kill him." General Monk spoke quickly. "He was like to get me once, but luck was with me. We called it quits. Each man had drawn blood."

Cromwell never took his eyes from the maps. He had eaten nothing, nor had he drunk the ale from his tankard. An abstemious man. The word went round through both armies that Old Ironside could ride all day and all night without a bite or a sup. Now he said, "Enough talk, my men. Let the lad get his rest." Without looking he tossed a coin, which Richard caught nimbly, bit, and put in a leather pouch that swung from his belt.

As he started to leave, Cromwell said, "Thank Cook for her kindness, and tell her to take a bit of rest. We will want breakfast early. Can you remember that?"

"Zur, that I can. Tell Cook to go to bed and make breakfast at six in the morning."

"No, at three o'clock."

Richard piled the dishes on a tray and moved toward the door.

Fleetwood called out, "I'll come to see your horses."

"Yes, zur, thank you."

As the door closed Cromwell was saying, "Yes, three o'clock is better. If there's anything in Fleetwood's apprehensions, we'd best cross to the west of the Ledden and ride some distance south, avoiding Ledbury and the possible neighbourhood of the enemy, before we strike due east. We'll go the way we came. It will take hard riding."

Once in the kitchen, Richard divested himself of his apron. Cook was waiting. "Thank God! You were gone so long, I was almost crazy with fear. Did they suspect anything?"

"I don't think so. General Fleetwood, the one with the long, thin nose, asked questions about horses. I must see Coscroft and send a message to General Massey."

Cook shook her head. "We don't . . . that is . . . we don't quite trust Coscroft. He talks strange these days. Wait. My nephew Cowley . . . he's been wanting to get into the King's army."

"Where is Cowley?"

"He's doing stable work, but he sleeps in the stable loft. I'll rouse him."

"Be quick, Cook. I'm not sure about Fleetwood . . ." But she was gone.

Richard wrapped some meat and a piece of bread in a napkin and put it into the leather pouch. By the time he had finished a glass of milk, she was back, followed by Cowley.

Richard liked the lad's looks. He had large dark eyes, frank and fearless, and reddish-brown hair. His olive skin and oval face showed his Norman blood. He stood almost as high as Richard and had the lithe movements of a fencer.

Richard said, "Cowley, I want you to do a bit of work for me, important work. Can you ride?"

"Yes, sir, I look after horses."

Richard smiled, thinking of his late masquerade.

"Good! We must get to the lower meadow near the beech plantation. Bring Saladin for me and get yourself a mount. Best we meet there. If anyone asks where you are going, say you are the shepherd and have to be in the hills by daybreak. Understand?"

The lad nodded.

"I've a saddle and bridle," Richard said. "I'll go down

below the garden. When we meet at the ponds, I'll give you your orders."

"God with you!" whispered Cook devoutly.

The two men left the room. Shadows were heavy; the clouds had covered the moon. She hoped they might get through the pickets; even soldiers slept sometimes. She moved about, tidying up. It was then she discovered the master's long cape, left where he had carelessly tossed it onto the back of the fireside chair. She must hide it. There was a priest's hole in the side of the great chimney, behind the glass cupboard, but it was long since it had been opened. There might be crickets or rats to bite into the fine wool, and that would be a great pity. Her own room would be best, where it might hang on a peg in the wall. She folded the cape over her arm. She was in the act of blowing the candles when the butler came in. He set the flagon of wine on the long stretcher table and, nodding toward the great hall, said, "She wants you, Cook."

"For what, Mr. Graves?"

"She didn't say, but I think she will sit the night by the fire. She can't rest easy with Cromwell beneath her roof, she says."

Cook hesitated a moment, wondering whether or not she should tell Graves about the master. Fewest to know, fewest to tell, she thought. She went through the door, shut it quietly, so she would not disturb the men seated at the dining-table, planning a campaign that would entrap the King's men and cut them off from London town.

Margaret Monington sat before the fire, where six-foot logs blazed, giving comfortable warmth to the great hall. Near her, on the faded Turkey carpet that had once been a lovely rose, lay her little spaniel, as evenly marked black and white as the blocked floor of Italian marble. Candles were lighted on the mantel-board, and on a stand. The long green tapestry curtains were open between the great room and the curved room beyond, where the moon was visible through the leaden-paned glass of the great oriel window.

Little Sibyl sat on the floor, looking at a book with pictures of great battles in history. Mathilda sat on the bench that followed the curve of the oriel, the red of the velvet bench in sharp but not unpleasant contrast to the purple dress which covered her yellow satin petticoat. She leaned against the

window, her head drooping. Perhaps she was sleeping, Sibyl
thought. Mathilda could sleep, for she had no deep worry
in her heart, as she, Sibyl, had.

Her gaze wandered from her sister to Dame Margaret.
Her eyes were open. She sat stiffly. She did not even lean
against the high back of the crewel-work chair. As always she
was attired in black. She was very old-fashioned, Sibyl
thought, for she still wore a white embroidered collar, starched
until it stood out as wide as her shoulders, and a little velvet
cap, held in place with wire, moulded to a peak over her
smooth white forehead, patterned after the Stuart Queen
Mary, the Martyr.

Her wide velvet skirts were spread to cover her feet, and the
Bible lay across her knees. Her long, fine hand turned the
pages slowly. Sibyl loved Dame Margaret. She loved Coddington Manor. Often she and her sister had stayed there for
months on end since their mother died five years before.
Now that her father, Hugh Jordan, was away on the continent, they would stay until his return. Her father's goings
and comings were mysterious. Some of the time he was at
the University of Oxford and sometimes abroad in the Low
Countries. When he was at home he kept himself shut up
in the quiet library, writing, always writing. She could not
keep her mind on the picture of Agincourt and the gallant
figure of the Soldier King, the Fifth Henry. Once she had
heard her father say to a visitor, "If Charles were the warrior
that Henry was, there would be no chance for a Cromwell."

For the moment she had forgotten the terror of Cromwell
and his monstrous generals, who sat in the dining-hall this
very moment. In the soft light of the ancient panelled room
there was quiet and peace. When she looked at the proud
figure of Dame Margaret she felt reassured. Surely Richard
was safe. He was proud, too, and brave as a lion. He was
like an earlier Sir Richard, whose portrait hung behind her
on the mellowed oak-panelled wall. She had often heard his
story, how he followed his King to France, fought bravely
at Agincourt, and won a knighthood on the battlefield. He
had followed his King even farther, and he, too, had married
a lady of France.

Richard had been her idol ever since she could remember,
with always a sweet word for her, a toy or a present, like the
little spaniel at her side, which he had brought to her for a

birthday present. "From the Royal Kennels," he had said. "What will you name her?"

"Prince Charley," she had cried.

He had laughed, a great rolling laugh. "Embarrassing when she drops her first litter." She didn't know quite what he meant, but her sister had blushed a bright red.

Sibyl's eyes roved to the carving over the fire-place. Another Monington in one panel, and his King, Good Harry, in the second. The date was there, 1535, the year Coddington Manor was built and the year Henry VIII had paid his visit. The same date was on the king beam that ran the whole length of the old kitchen, the buttery and the little room beyond—eighty feet in all, hewn out of one mighty oak. That was Graves's boast. He boasted too of the age of the black and white manor-house and the portraits in the hall of long-gone Moningtons, for Moningtons had lived here since the ancient Kingdom of Mercia—Lords of the Marches they were called later.

Her governess had taught her nothing about Mercia, the Ancient Kingdom. She had told her about the Romans, who built their camp in the Malvern Hills. The butler was a learned man. He could not read, but he had a grand memory. He remembered and told great tales of the Welsh raiding over the borders into the rich red orchard country and driving off the yeomen's cattle to the hills. Some stayed in the Marches and built churches to their saints. David was a Welshman's saint.

She recalled a story Graves had told her about the oak tree planted over a Welshman's grave, how some of the branches turned down and rooted in the earth to form an arch. A Welshman could pass under it in all safety, but if an Englishman stepped between the branches and the trunk, he died instantly.

At this point in his story Graves had looked at her severely. "You, miss, being English, had best have a care about walking under oak branches, if they touch the earth."

How terrible the thought! Sibyl could feel herself struggling against the steady pressure of the oak limb, which pinned her to the rough bark of the giant trunk. "I will never, never run under the oak branches again," she had vowed.

" 'Tis not all oaks that have vengeance within them," Graves had said softly; "only Herefordshire oaks that grow near the Marches, and then only those whose branches trail the ground. The oaks protect our Lords of the Marches." The calling of a man's voice had interrupted the butler's tale and he had gone away to answer the summons. . . .

Sibyl's thoughts were interrupted by the entrance of the cook.

Dame Margaret looked up from her reading. "Cook, bring your stool and sit by me. I am weary with reading, and to think brings sombre visions of danger. Sit beside me this night as you have sat beside me through other black nights. Bring your stool and sit close to the fire. I have a desire for a strong Devon woman beside me."

"Yes, ma'am." Cook lifted a sturdy bench and placed it near the fire by her lady. She stirred the fire and laid a fresh log across the low irons.

"Sit down." Dame Margaret spoke again. "Sit down, Cook Ellie."

"Ma'am, if you are to sit up the night, 'tis a hot posset you must drink, and perhaps eat a bit of cheese."

"I can't eat," she said impatiently. But after a moment she changed her mind. "Yes, perhaps a hot brew, and warm some milk for Mistress Sibyl."

"The child should be in her bed."

"I want her near me," Dame Margaret said. "I don't trust our unwelcome visitors, for all they prate of godliness."

Cook glanced at Sibyl. "I could make her a bed on the long bench yonder and cover her well from the draughts."

"Yes, of course. I didn't think. Sibyl, put the book away and lie down on the bench. Cook will fetch a chair to put beside you so you won't fall to the floor."

"Ma'am, I'm not sleepy."

"Do as I request. It is near midnight. Where is Mathilda?"

"Sleeping by the window," Cook said, "with her face in the bright of the moon." She shook her head. "No good will come of that. The moon madness will enter her soul as she sleeps, all unguarded."

"Nonsense, Cook! An old wives' tale."

" 'Tis true, Dame Margaret. All my life I've heard it. We Devon folk don't scoff at old tales. Mistress, have you so soon forgot your West Country ways? Some grow soft in a soft country," Cook muttered.

"A West-Countryman does not lack strength or loyalty. Get me the drink, Cook."

The woman moved lightly on her feet, unhampered by her height and strong, big frame.

Sibyl protested only once.

"Loosen your collar and remove your shoes, child." Dame Margaret said. "Stretch yourself on the long bench. The velvet cushions will be soft beneath you. Cover yourself with the cape Cook left on the chair."

Sibyl took up the cape. She stood very still. It was Richard's cape! What did this mean? Was he no longer hidden in the dovecote?

"Why do you tarry, child? Why do you look at the cape so earnestly?"

For one wild moment Sibyl thought she must tell Dame Margaret that her son, her beloved son, was here near her, in danger. O Lord God of Kindness, help me! she prayed silently.

"Are you rooted to the floor?"

"Nothing. Nothing, Dame Margaret. I was looking at the cape."

"What is wrong with the cape?"

"Nothing. I . . . I mean nothing except that it has feathers on it. Dove feathers."

"Silly child. Go lie down."

Sibyl crowded the cape into a bundle. Dame Margaret must not see it. She must not know.

"Wait a moment. Let me see that cape." Dame Margaret's voice was sharp.

Sibyl moved slowly toward her, hoping that fear did not leap from her eyes.

Dame Margaret put her hands on the cloth. The room was very quiet. In the silence Mathilda's gentle, rhythmic breathing could be plainly heard.

Sibyl looked at the floor. She did not want to meet Dame Margaret's questing eyes.

There were footsteps in the entry. Dame Margaret said quietly, "Roll youself in the cloak and try to sleep, like a good child. . . . Wait—Cook is here. Drink your hot milk first."

Sibyl drew a deep breath. She didn't recognize the cloak, she thought. She sat on the long bench swinging her feet, sipping the scalded milk while Cook served Dame Margaret a drink of mulled cider. When she had finished, Cook took the mug from Sibyl. "Swing your feet up on the cushion and fold your silk skirts smoothly so they won't wrinkle."

"Dame Margaret said to cover me with your cloak." There was no change in the impassive face that bent over her. Perhaps she was wrong. Perhaps the cape really belonged to Cook . . . but the feathers . . . and the pleasant, crusty smell of tobacco smoke . . . surely . . . Her eyes closed.

Cook took the silver cup from her mistress' hand; she covered it with a cloth and put the tray on a small table in the alcove. After giving the log a strong push with her stout shoe, she sat down on the bench and leaned her back against the wall. The day had been long, and she must have breakfast for these Roundheads by three. What an hour! Her eyelids drooped. Mistress wanted nothing of her but her nearness and her silence. . . .

Her eyelids opened at the sound of Dame Margaret's voice. "Is he safe?"

"God knows, ma'am. How did you know?"

"His cape, of course."

"He came——"

Dame Margaret interrupted. "No, don't tell me. They may question me later. . . . All we can do is to pray."

"All, ma'am? Surely you know that God is close to a mother who grieves for her child."

"Oh, Cook, if I only had your simple eternal faith! . . . But I know he is safe. I know. I have a certain faith."

"Surely, ma'am. Surely when you kneel before His altar and let your heart speak, He will answer. Don't you remember how all the women knelt by the cliff at Hartland when the great ship was beating herself to death on the rocks below? Don't you remember how the bell rang out for each man our fisher-lads saved? Don't you remember the beautiful faces of the women who prayed when the first dawn came? You said the words with your own lips, ma'am: 'Faith makes all things possible.' "

The green log on the fire made a sizzling sound; a green flame suddenly blazed.

Dame Margaret's voice was low. "I remember. Yes, how could I forget the bravery of those women, while their men fought the cruel, wild Atlantic!"

"Your man, too. He was there. It was his voice that urged the poor, tired lads. 'Let no foreign man drown on our shore. On, my lads! We'll beat the sea yet, God helping.'"

"God helping," Margaret whispered. His voice . . . she could almost hear it, strong, vibrant, confident. "Richard is safe," she said with conviction. "Thank you, Cook. You have helped me."

"Not I. It is your own blood, Prideaux blood, which beats strong in your veins. West Country womenfolk be strong as their men are valiant. It's our way, ma'am. We are conceived in strength . . . and that way we will live."

Sleep, Cook, sleep for a little while. You have comforted me and renewed my spirit. I will be strong to meet what comes . . . The words were not spoken aloud. War, the cruel anxiety of war beat down on a woman's heart and soul . . . Oh, Richard, Richard, live to manhood, to middle years, to venerable age, in spite of wars and battles and men's hatred!

She must have dozed. Some sound wakened her abruptly. She glanced quickly around the room. The child Sibyl slept, wrapped in Richard's cloak. Mathilda had stretched herself on the window-seat in the far room. There was no movement to show that she was awake. Cook slept loudly, her head drooped forward, her chin resting on her full bosom, the white part in her hair showing; a dark strand, loosened from the smooth knot at the nape of her neck, lay across her shoulder, another strand on her apple-red cheek.

Some noise must have brought her thus quickly to consciousness. A little sound behind her made her turn. Mathilda was moving quietly across the long room toward her. In a moment she bent her lips close to Dame Margaret's ear. "Riders have just come into the court-yard—young officers. The sentry took them straight to the dining-hall, I think. I heard only a few words . . . a prisoner taken by the pond, a country yokel. Then another officer came up with a man wearing a smock. I did not see his face. He walked clumsily, slouching, but I thought of Richard as I looked at him in the moonlight."

Dame Margaret's grasp was heavy on the girl's arm. "No names. We must be watchful. Let no one cause you to reveal your thoughts. He is in Scotland for the King. Remember that:

in Scotland. Go back to the window-seat. Watch. Listen. We must meet guile with guile."

The girl moved away as quickly as she had come. When the door opened and Cromwell entered the room, he saw a stately figure of a woman dozing by the fire. The servant at her side was sleeping, too. A small spaniel slept at their feet. An officer was with Cromwell, tall, heavy-featured, with a strong, arrogant face, a large nose and a thick neck. As they came forward the dog rose lazily, then uttered a short, sharp bark, backing against the woman's velvet skirts.

Dame Margaret opened her eyes and lifted her head proudly. "Yes?" she said and paused as though waiting for an explanation of the intrusion on her privacy.

Oliver's manner was courteous. "Pardon me for coming into your room so noisily as to waken you. I thought you had retired to your bedchamber long since."

"It is not the custom in our house to retire while the guests are still awake, even though the guests are . . ."

A wry smile crossed Cromwell's firm, full lips, ". . . are not of your choosing?"

"Guests who are strangers to us."

"And enemies, no doubt you wish to say?"

"Since you force me, yes enemies."

"We do not war on women." Cromwell spoke quietly.

Dame Margaret said, "Will you sit, sir? You and your officer? Cook, draw chairs to the fire." Mathilda had come to Dame Margaret's side.

"If I may venture a remark," Oliver said, as he sat facing her from the far side of the fire, "if I may venture a remark, you seem very like a queen surrounded by her maids in waiting."

Dame Margaret did not smile. She said, "Every woman is a queen by her own hearth. May I inquire why you are here?"

"I thought the room was empty, Dame Monington. I wished to consult with my . . . with General Monk privately. Pardon me. Allow me to present General George Monk."

Dame Margaret did not look at the general. She said, "The name of the Monks of Monkleigh is well known to me."

General Monk advanced a step toward her and bowed. "The name of Prideaux is well known to all West Country folk."

"You are far from Devon, sir, very far." She paused, looking him straight in the eye. "A long distance and not measured by miles."

"Prideaux has been a strong family since the days of the Conqueror, great in war and in peace," Monk said politely, but the red from her words still flushed his cheeks.

"And always loyal," she finished.

Cromwell smiled slightly. "Perhaps, ma'am, you can assist us in the matter about which I intended to consult General Monk. It is about a prisoner that my men have brought in. They found him in the lower meadow. He says he lives on the place, a tenant of sorts. My young men do not believe his story." His eyes were piercing in the black insistence. "There is a rumour about, that your son Richard was seen riding this way. A horse was found . . ."

She met his eyes, a look of incredulous surprise on her face. "Richard? My son Richard? You must be mistaken. My son is in the army of his king, in Scotland."

"All the King's army is not in Scotland," General Monk said.

She raised her brows. "Not in Scotland? Then where are they?"

Monk grinned. His face was pleasing then, in spite of the one squinting eye. "I wish we knew just where they are."

Cromwell looked at him. He was not pleased. He addressed Dame Margaret: "These young men of mine think the yokel is no yokel . . . one of Charles's intelligence, perhaps. They want to hang him at once."

The room was silent. Cromwell's eyes never left her face. A look of incredulity, horror, then anger crossed her features in quick succession. "I will not have it!" she said. "There has never been a man hanged at Coddington Manor, and there will be none now. Is it not enough, sir, that I allow your motley crew of vagabonds and riff-raff to encamp on my meadow, and house you and your officers under my roof? There'll be no further talk of hanging, sir! Take your prisoner off to the Bosbury or the Colwall Road to do your murdering."

She had risen as she spoke, and stood tall, very erect, with her fine head thrown back defiantly.

A look of surprise and a certain reluctant admiration crossed Cromwell's face. He was used to respect, subservience even, due to his great position; here he met courage and defiance. Like all strong men, he admired bravery and strength in others, particularly in women.

Surprisingly he said, "My mother was a woman of strong opinions also. Madam, please, I have no present intention of hanging a man on one of your trees."

"If you did, the tree would fall and strangle you," she said fiercely.

He made a conciliatory gesture. "Please sit down, madam. All we want of you is to see this fellow and tell us if his story be true. Is he, as he says, a sort of tenant on your place?"

Margaret sat down, her hands lying on the arms of her chair; quiet, gentle hands, not clenched, not nervously tapping the oak; quiet.

She bowed her head slightly. "You may bring the prisoner in."

General Monk stepped to the door. A moment later Fleetwood entered, followed by Richard dressed in rough breeches, heavy brogans covered with earth. A faded blue smock, such as hop-pickers wear, covered him from shoulder to knee. His hair was tousled, his face smudged. He held a cap, which he turned nervously in dirty hands.

His mother looked at him, displeasure in her eyes and in her voice "Well, Willie, you're in again, I see."

Richard opened his mouth to say something, but Cook interrupted. "Stand over by the hearth, and don't be messin' up the madam's best carpet with your manure-covered feet —over here. where I can whisk the dirt into the fire-place."

"That will do, Cook. Go out and heat some good cider for the gentlemen. They'll want something after their investigation." She turned back to Richard. "Now, Willie, what's the tale you've been telling these gentlemen? That you're a sort of tenant on my land?"

Richard looked down at his feet. "Well, ma'am, ain't I just that? Sort of . . . livin' under your haystacks . . . and helpin' with the pickin' and the hayin'?"

"Did you tell the general I'd had you up for poaching more than once?"

"Noa, I never said the word. 'Tis an ugly, bad word, it is. Noa, I didn't." He took a step forward. "Naething but a hare, once and so often, to make a good stew. You won't abide snaring the wild marshhens and fowl."

His tale was interrupted by Fleetwood, who had until this

moment stood silently by. Now he addressed Cromwell. "Sir, do you see resemblance to the yokel who brought our ale at table?"

Cromwell said, "I didn't look at him. My eyes were on maps, and, as you know, I drink no ale."

Fleetwood turned to General Monk. "Did you take notice of the fellow?"

Monk shook his head. "Only that he was deuced awkward pouring the ale from the tankard. What did he say his name was?"

"I'm not sure. Silly Dick, or something like that. Said he was the stable-boy."

The poacher began to laugh silently, his body shaking.

"This is no occasion for levity," Fleetwood said. "You're lucky you're not hanging from the limb of a tree this very moment."

Dame Margaret half rose. "General," she appealed to Cromwell, "will you inform this man that I'll not have talk of hanging at Coddington Manor."

Cromwell frowned at Charles Fleetwood.

The fox-like general was persistent. "I swear it's the same man disguised, dressed differently."

"Why do you laugh, fellow?" George Monk spoke severely.

Richard's face straightened. "I been laughin' when I think of my brother, Silly Dick, servin' ale to General Cromwell. That's why I'm laughin'."

Cromwell's piercing glance went from the poacher to the aristocratic woman seated in the fireside chair. "Is this man what he says he is, madam?" There was cold authority in his voice now; his brilliant, dark eyes were as hard as granite.

"Willie is a liar. He *is* a poacher." Her answer was short.

Richard answered her as though there was no one else in the room. "My lady, I swear by Coddington Church cross, that on your land I do not poach. Perhaps on the Holders' land and old man Harley's I snare a rabbit or two, but not on your land. I'm a poor fellow with no gift of words, but Will Pooley don't forget how kind you were to a little boy whose father had been killed in the war." He turned to Cromwell. "Take me away, please, good sir. There is no need to trouble the lady if——"

He did not finish the sentence. The thud of something dropping to the floor caused every eye in the room to turn.

Sibyl had kicked the book with the battle pictures off the bench in her effort to sit up. She stretched her arms above her head, yawned and struggled out of the folds of the cape, swinging her stockinged feet to the floor. It was then that she looked in the direction of the fire-place.

She let out a shrill squeal. "Oh, Willie, Willie, did you snare the drake for me?" She ran across the room toward Richard. Half-way across she stopped as her eyes fell on Cromwell and his generals. She put up her hand to cover her mouth, made a little awkward curtsy. Falling on her knees, she hid her face in Dame Margaret's skirts.

Cromwell took a step forward; his voice was gentle; he loved children, for he was an indulgent and understanding father. "Little maid. don't cry. Come, look up. Tell me about the drake. Did—" he paused, then went on smoothly—"did Willie promise to snare a drake for you? Tell me."

Sibyl lifted her hair. One dark eye was visible under her mop of falling hair. "Sir, he promised. It is the big fellow that squawks and quacks every night on the little pond." She sat up. "A big drake, all bronzy-green and black. Haven't you heard him making a great love racket to attract my four ducks?"

Monk lifted his hand to his lip to hide a smile. Cromwell patted her shoulder. "Perhaps Willie will snare your drake for you little maid—in gratitude."

"Gratitude? Sir, I don't understand."

"Willie does. I now sentence him to snare the love-making drake. Gentlemen, shall we leave and allow Dame Monington and her ladies to retire?"

Fleetwood alone appeared disgruntled. "Step lively, fellow! The maid saved your skin . . . but I'm not sure of you."

Willie pulled his forelock, made a bow in the direction of Dame Margaret. "Lor' love ye, ye'll have your drake, miss." He followed Fleetwood and Monk from the room. Before the door swung shut a soldier stepped up beside him. Cromwell lingered for a moment to express to Dame Margaret his thanks for her enforced hospitality—and just then his eyes fell on the unfortunate cape.

He pointed to the bench where Sibyl had left it. "That cape looks as though it belonged to a soldier," he said, "very much like a soldier's cape."

"So it is, General Cromwell," said Dame Monington calmly. "The cape belonged to my husband. He was a good soldier."

Cromwell stood in silence for a moment. There was a cold light in his eye. Then he said briefly, "Madam, I am obliged to you for your courtesy to my officers and to me." He bowed and followed his subordinates from the room.

Mathilda picked up her skirts and ran to the window. She knelt on the window-seat looking out on the court. Cook blew the candles. The moonlight flooded the room, as Dame Margaret, her arm over Sibyl's shoulder, moved silently to the window and joined Mathilda.

Cook came after. "You're a bold little liar, and I don't know but the Lord will sizzle your tongue in your mouth. Liar," she repeated, a sort of gay pride in her voice.

Mathilda kissed her sister's smooth young forehead. "I don't see how you ever thought of it."

Sibyl grinned. "It was a game of riddles . . . just like a riddle. One must play a part and confuse the other side, don't you see?" She began to sob softly. "I'm not a liar. Lying is a sin. I don't want to be a sinner."

Dame Margaret kissed her gently. "Lies can be noble, my child. . . . Let us ask the good Lord to protect . . ."

Mathilda touched her arm. "Richard is being escorted toward the stables. One man is walking behind him—a guard, I think."

"They'll never hang him," Sibyl said confidently. "He'll get away."

"Fleetwood," Mathilda said slowly. "I'm afraid of Fleetwood. He wasn't convinced."

"Richard will get away," Sibyl repeated. "I feel it in my joints and here in my heart." She laid her hand on her flat chest. "Here, I feel it right here."

Dame Margaret said, "I pray God you are right."

As dawn broke Richard heard the faint sound of Ledbury bells. He had eased himself through Cromwell's strong patrol in the darkest hours of the late night. Twice he all but stumbled over sleeping men, but the glow of embers of a dying camp-fire warned him. Through fields and vineyards he had circled, after he left his horse tied up in Yeoman Winny's cow shelter. The old man would recognize Saladin and somehow manage to get the horse back when the danger was past.

He hoped Cook's nephew, following the east side of the River Ledden, would by now have made his way to the Royalist forces and alerted General Massey that Cromwell and his high generals might be caught in a trap at Coddington Manor. The lad looked sharp enough, and he hoped that he knew the countryside.

Richard wondered whether he had killed the guard Fleetwood had set to watch when they locked him in the tack room of the stable. Fleetwood was a shrewd, suspicious devil, only half convinced the poacher story was true. The guard had sat with his back to the tack-room door, leaning forward, his knees drawn up to his chin. He was sleepy, and this had given Richard his chance. Evidently the guard did not realize that the door was a Dutch one, cut through the middle. Certainly the ropes that tied Richard's hands seemed well knotted, but he had managed to pull the ends free with his teeth. Lucky for him, they had not tied his hands behind him. He found an iron horseshoe on the floor. A blow with it on the back of the head, and the sentry had slumped over without a sound. Gagging him with a maize cob was rough but necessary. Richard hadn't wanted to kill the fellow. He hoped he hadn't. He loathed taking life. Standing up and fighting was one thing, but sneaking up behind was a coward's way.

Well, as he thought it over now, perhaps he was a coward; certainly the brutality of war sickened him. If he could get away, he would make for Bristol and take ship for Virginia in the New World. There would be opportunity.

Richard was a man who looked straight at facts, with no side turning. The Royalist army would not win. Men had been deserting every day of the long march down from Scotland. Loyalty to a King was not enough to hold men when they were not fighting in self-interest. Old Ironside, he thought with reluctant admiration, has a cause. He has convinced his soldiers that he thinks only of their good. He feeds them, gives them their pay; every man is made to feel that he is fighting a holy fight for the good of the people of England. Damn him, he had unleashed a power he won't be able to control! It takes a King to be the true symbol of sovereignty. Would to God England had a King with the strength to lead! Not a young boy no older than himself. Men won't follow Charles. The nobility, yes, for the favours he has bestowed or will bestow. But the gentry and county families are divided in my own county. The Harleys, the Holders and a dozen other families have gone over to the side of Parliament—which means Cromwell, for Cromwell *is* Parliament.

If we don't capture him now, he will win, for he has the habit of winning. He believes the Lord is on his side . . . and indeed may He not be?

So deep in these disturbing thoughts was Richard Monington that he all but stumbled into a camp of soldiers when he reached the rise in the hill. An open field lay ahead, bare and naked, with rows of hop poles in uneven lines. In the hazy light of false dawn they looked like ragged lines of soldiers. For a moment he paused, heart beating heavily, then he moved on, following down the rows. Some withered vines, swaying in the wind, caught the button of his smock. He paused to untangle the clutching tendrils.

A sleepy voice broke the stillness. "Trumpeter, wake! Wake! It is time to blow." A horse whinnied, followed by the restless sound of horses tramping, pawing the hard earth.

Richard backed away cautiously, until a thicket of wild plum stood between him and the camp. It was still too dark to discern more than the shadows of men moving about. Cromwell's soldiers or King Charles's? He did not know. Surely by now Cromwell had no horse within the near sound of Ledbury bells.

Someone threw wood on the embers and a blaze sprang up that lighted the faces of men huddled close for warmth. One man stooped and spread his hands to the blaze.

A voice asked, "What of the prisoner? Has the lad accounted for himself?"

"He won't talk. Says he came from Bosbury way. He asked to speak to an officer." A gruff laugh followed. "The louder he insisted the louder I laughed."

"Officer be damned! These country-folk think themselves so fine that they won't talk to a corporal of the King's Dragoons."

King's Dragoons! Then they were his men. Richard's joy at the soldier's words was dampened by another thought: "the prisoner" must be Cowley, the cook's nephew. Damn the men for fools! As he neared the fire, he caught sight of Cowley, bound to a tree at the left. The sight of the lad's woe-begone face, his painful position, like a trussed-up fowl, filled him with bitter rage. All the late night he had prayed that Cowley had got through, and Massey had received in time the word that Cromwell, Monk and Fleetwood might be caught in one sharp trap. It was too late now. The Roundheads were galloping away. No chance now to take hostages that would have ensured the disorganization of the Roundheads, Charles's safety at the very least, and at the best a marvelous victory, Charles on the throne and the regicides punished. His anger and cruel disappointment were in his voice. He railed at the world, at fate and at himself. He walked out of his hiding place and as he approached the camp-fire, he had no thought of the appearance he made, and with his tousled hair, his di-shevelled clothes, the blue smock.

"What unit is this?" he demanded of the first man he met. "Where are your officers?"

A stocky dragoon barred the path. Two others sprang from the fire and stood at his elbow.

"And who may you be, yokel, making demands of honest soldiers?" The stocky one mimicked Richard's words. " 'What unit is this? Where are your officers?' says he, so high and mighty. Hallo, Digby!"

An older man with a thin grey beard came forward. He looked searchingly at Richard. "Have done, Sanders. Don't you know a gentleman when you see one? Zur, there are no proper officers nearer than Ledbury."

"Thank you, my man. Will you have the lad there cut free?"

Digby hesitated. Sanders protested. "Now he wants our prisoner freed. Who are you? What do you want?"

"I want two horses," Richard said shortly. He unbuttoned the blue smock and tossed it to the ground. In his belted leather tunic and breeches he was a more commanding figure.

Several soldiers, hearing the argument, gathered round. One of them, a tall, red-faced trooper, with a sword slash along his neck from ear to thorax, Richard had seen before. The fellow recognized him.

" 'Tis Captain Monington, him that's courier for the King," he told the grey-haired Digby. "I've seen him often enough in Scotland with Sir John Brown's command. That's so."

"We'll have the horses in a jiffy, zur. Coles, untruss the prisoner, since he is a friend of the captain's."

The heavy-set Sanders was still truculent. "Like as not they be some of Cromwell's fellows. We've got no call to let them through."

Richard mounted his horse. "You have not told me what unit this is."

"Scudamore's Horse, Captain," said Digby, "out scouting for cattle for the army."

"Ah, I see. Well, I advise you to post sentries when you camp. I found it very easy to come upon you this morning. I should report you for negligence." He lifted the reins. Two men were helping Cowley onto the second horse.

Digby stood at Richard's bridle. "Zur, Lord Biddulph's here at his mansion. He arrived from Leominster yesterday. Might be the King's on the other side of the Ledden. He's marching from Leominster. There's talk that General Massey is close to Ledbury."

"Thank you. You look a knowledgeable fellow. See that your men keep a sharp lookout for scouting, recruiting or foraging parties. It won't do to be caught."

A grin spread on the man's face. "With our britches half-way? Excuse an old dragoon for rough talking, zur. Some of these young'uns know too much about dicing and not enough about soldiering, I'm a-thinking. Thank you, zur, we'll be on the lookout."

CHAPTER 3

A Prideaux of Cornwall

DAME MARGARET went into the walled kitchen garden before she broke fast. She had not slept. Worry for the welfare of her son was too deep-seated to allow her to rest. After a vain effort she had lighted a candle and opened her Bible. As she read, she gained reassurance and tranquillity, for her faith was strong. While she read she had heard from time to time Cromwell's scouts gallop into the stable-yard. Thus she read until after the Roundheads had all ridden away, read on until sun-up.

The earth had been turned over in the flower-beds, ready for winter garden planting. Biggor, the gardener, was examining a late pear which he had picked from the espaliered tree against the south wall. He greeted Dame Margaret, lifting his cap and pulling at a grizzled forelock.

She noticed that the hand in which he held the pear was shaking as though he had a palsy. Biggor's getting old, she thought. She scanned his face more closely. Fine wrinkles gave the parchment-like, weathered skin the look of an old apple, his cheeks were red from wind and sun. Yes, the gardener was old, old and garrulous and wise. He told tales of the wee ones, the faries, as glibly as he made conversation about the roses and lilies in his borders. He had a broad speech. At first Dame Margaret, whose ear was attuned to the softer Devon tongue, could not understand the harsher Herefordshire dialect. Now she understood him very well.

As she walked about her rose garden she was always inclined to pause when she found him on his knees clipping his borders, or pursuing some pest that ate the leaves of his roses, or clipping his hedges into figures, strange birds and animals. Like all gardeners he was resentful when one came with shears and basket to cut roses. He would take the shears from her hand. "I'll be doing that myself, Dame Margaret. The thorns be stiff and filled with a kind of poison. Ye wouldn't want your pretty fingers all bitten by thorns, now would you?" She always yielded the shears without protest, knowing his guile was because he could not abide anyone snipping the tiniest bud of his precious roses.

"Why not let him grow to old age on his stem?" he muttered one day. "Cut him down in his youth! 'Tis against Nature, it is, to take a rose before it comes to full bloom. Just like wars cutting down the young before their time."

The gardener moved closer and put his hand before his lips, in a gesture which was reminiscent of one of Will Shakespeare's conspirators. "Old Noll's gone. Before the dawn broke they clattered their horses across my court-yard. Lucky I had driven the kine away to a hiding place. I saw him plain as day, with the moonlight on him, old Oliver himself. He's got a gloomy face, like he'd et something bitter."

"Yes, I heard them go." Dame Margaret unconsciously lowered her voice. "General Fleetwood informed me that Willie the poacher got away."

The gardener looked up at her. "Did he that?" There was a little gleam in his faded old eyes. "Did he that?"

Dame Margaret asked, "Do you know how he escaped? Fleetwood was very angry about it."

Biggor took up his rake, which was propped against the garden wall. "Well, might be someone hit the sentry over the skull with a horse's shoe. . . . Fellow like to ha' died."

"Oh!"

"But he didn't. Parl'ment soldiers have thick skulls, that they have."

"Do you think he got away safely?"

"Dunno, mistress, I dunno, but the young master he be well able to make his way about Herefordshire. Wouldn' no one say no to him if he hid in a barn or a hayrick or a hop field—no one."

A faint colour came to Dame Margaret's cheek. It was intolerable that her son, the Lord of the Manor of Coddington, should be slinking about the countryside, hiding in barns and hayricks.

"Mayhap he fared no so bad. Stacy, the hostler, he says Saladin is gone." Biggor glanced sideways at Dame Margaret.

"Oh!" she said. A smile came to her lips.

"Might be the master enjoys hisself. Not so long ago as

how he was always runnin' off to the hills, hiding, in the
Roman Camp or up Langland's fields, pretendin' 'e was Piers
Plowman in the Malvern Hills. . . . Recollect how he loved
to make heself into Dick Whittington and build a bonfire of
the King's paper debts in front of the Queen, that was a-
feasting in his house. 'Whittington,' he says. 'Whittington
was borned in Sollers 'ope, a Herefordshire lad.' That's a story
they tell around here. One day Master Richard axed me, 'Do
you think I'll ever banquet the Queen, Biggor?' I said,
'May can. There's been a greater Queen banqueted in this
very housen.' Ma'am, don't be a-worryin'; 'e's gone to get hisself outa trouble like 'e always done. He has a good smart way
with his tongue, has Master Richard."

Biggor cut a full red rose and handed it to her. "I've
heard the old master say that your folk paid a red rose
every year to the Grenvilles of Bideford."

Dame Margaret's face brightened. "How kind you are,
Biggor! Well I remember how hard the gardener at Portledge
worked to have a perfect red rose for that occasion. Thank
you." She walked away down the path toward the lily pool.

Biggor stood looking after her. Poor lady! Poor, poor lady!
God knows whether I spoke the truth or a lie, but it brought
her comfort. He did not tell her what he had heard the
long-nosed officer say when they rode past his cottage early
in the morning: "That was no poacher, General Monk.
That fellow was Richard Monington, sure as I sit this saddle."
The other had answered, "Our Lord General believed Dame
Margaret. Let it rest at that, Fleetwood." And the nosey one
had said, "He is too tender where women are concerned;
tender and easily fooled."

No need to tell her that, Biggor thought. He watched her
move her stately way across the greensward to the flagging at
the edge of the pool.

Young Sibyl came skipping down the path to join her. "He
got away! He got away! Cook told me. God had his arms
about Richard."

"Yes, dear child, God had his arms about him."

"But we helped too, with our riddle."

"Yes. Yes, you helped most of all. You love Richard, don't
you?"

"I do, I do. I wish Mathilda would marry him, instead
of mooning over Nicholas Holder. Isn't it strange, Dame

Margaret? Richard yearns for Kathryn Audley, and so does Nicholas Holder; and Mathilda is beset for love of Nick; and I love Richard; and Kathryn loves herself. I think she has in mind to marry one of the Berkeleys. She wants to marry a Sir, so she may be Lady Something-or-other."

"You see too much, sweet child. How old are you?"

"Fourteen and over. I'll be marriageable at fifteen, don't you think? I'm tall."

Dame Margaret laughed. "Not for a long time, my dear. Why not have Richard wait for you?"

The child's laugh rang out clear and sweet and young. "Richard hardly knows I'm living. Besides, I want him to be my brother. But Mathilda doesn't yearn for him, nor does he yearn for Mathilda. Don't you think everything is very confused, Dame Margaret?"

Very. But I see Mathilda beckoning to you. Perhaps it is time for your lessons."

Sibyl made a little face. "It's always time for lessons. I thought when Father sent Mademoiselle away, I would never have lessons again, but Mathilda is more strict than Mademoiselle. She feels so superior because she reads Mr. Shakespeare's plays."

Sibyl started to run in the direction of the house, then turned and darted back. "I heard her say Mr. Shakespeare was a poacher, and Sir Thomas Lucy sentenced him to gaol. Perhaps our poacher Willie may write plays." There was an impish look in her dark eyes.

Her words brought a smile to Dame Margaret's lips. "Let us hope our poacher Willie doesn't get into gaol."

"Ah! There you are laughing." The child caught Dame Margaret's hand and kissed it lightly. She ran away toward the house, singing at the top of her voice:

> "Taffy was a Welshman,
>   Taffy was a thief,
> Taffy came to my house,
>   And stole a piece of beef.
>
> "I went to Taffy's house;
>   Taffy was in bed;
> I picked up the marrow-bone,
>   And struck him on the head."

She stopped in front of the door to the morning room, where Mathilda stood regarding her with disapproving eyes.

"Stop capering around like a puppy and mind your manners," Mathilda said severely.

"Oh, Sis, how can you stand there looking so serious? See how the sun shines, and hear the birds sing, and Richard is got away."

"*Has*, not *is*," Mathilda corrected.

"I don't care. That's exactly what Biggor told me: 'Master Richard is got clean away.' " She slipped her hand through Mathilda's arm. "Come, Sis, be kind this morning when the world's so gay. If I have to read aloud, why can't I read Mr. Chapman's play *Eastward Ho?*"

"No. You will do your Latin."

"Oh, Sis. I loathe my Latin!"

"Behave! Think how young Princess Elizabeth studied Latin. Her tutor, Mr. Ascham, never had to urge her to study, and she became a queen."

"But I'm not a princess, so I can't be a queen." The dimples hovered about the corners of her mouth. "And you are not Roger Ascham." She saw the frown appearing on her sister's forehead. "You are much too pretty, Sis. Richard said you are pretty."

"Stop talking nonsense, Sibyl!" But Mathilda couldn't hide the look of pleasure. She turned away, so that Sibyl might not see her face, and picked up a ruler made of ivory. "Now to work! I do not want to slap your hand with this. No, we are not going to read a play, not *Eastward Ho*, or Shakespeare. Twenty pages of Latin."

Sibyl let out a wail. "Twenty pages, Sis! That's more than the boys at the college have to do. Listen: did you know, Sis, that the Little People were abroad last night? Biggor saw one no higher than a toadstool, sitting on the paddock fence. A dové flew over and sat right beside the little one, and he never jumped down or anything. Biggor says that's a sign of good fortune, but I think Richard frightened my doves when they came back to the cote."

"Whatever are you saying, you silly child?"

Sibyl clapped her hand to her mouth. "Oh, I forgot."

Mathilda caught her shoulder and gave her a little shake. "Now, miss, tell me what you are talking about."

"Nothing, nothing. . . . I promised. But so much happened after that, perhaps it can make no difference now."

"Tell me instantly."

"Well, nothing really, only I hid Richard in the dovecote, when Cromwell's soldiers came last night."

Dame Margaret stepped in from the terrace to the morning room at that moment. She crossed the room and sat down near the desk where Sibyl was seated. "Sibyl, will you repeat what you just said? Perhaps I did not hear aright. I *thought* you said that you hid my son in the dovecote."

Mathilda said, "Madam, it is one of her stories. She is always making up little tales, with herself the heroine."

Sibyl faced her. "I did not make a tale. It was true. I shouldn't tell, because I promised." She turned to Dame Margaret. "Should I break a promise, madam?"

"One honours confidence, Sibyl, but perhaps since the urgency is past, one might be released . . . especially since you seem to have known something of my son's presence here before I, his mother, knew anything."

"He told me not to tell you. He was afraid if you knew you might not be able to answer questions honestly. You see, madam, Richard knew Cromwell's men were on the way. He was sure they would question you about him, since it's well known he's in the King's service."

Dame Margaret's eyes did not leave Sibyl's face. The child was frightened at her silence, not knowing what she was thinking. "I ran into him, ma'am quite by accident. I was chasing after puppy into the Lady's Bower, and there he was."

A slight sound escaped Dame Margaret. "The Lady's Bower! He was as close to me as that, and I . . ."

"Yes, ma'am, but the soldiers came." She hesitated. Somehow she must say nothing about Kathryn Audley before Mathilda. "They came and I said the dovecote was empty and clean, for I had been playing in it. It's my play house, where I can go to play and look at the meadows and the Malvern Hills and . . ."

"My son hiding in a dovecote! It's preposterous!"

"Yes, ma'am. Then when they placed a sentry right near, I feared they might think it strange that there were no doves there, so I ran to the new cote and released two or three. They flew right away to their old home."

"You went out in the dark, with soldiers camped all around?"

"Yes, ma'am. Don't you think it was best to have doves in the cote, along with Richard?"

Dame Margaret sat silent for a little time. Then she rose from her chair and walked out of the room. Sibyl looked at Mathilda, her eyes round and frightened. "Is she angry with me? I only wanted to help Richard."

Mathilda put an arm about Sibyl's shoulder. "No, I don't think she is angry. She is disturbed by Richard's danger. How could she be angry with such a brave little girl?" Mathilda kissed Sibyl on the cheek. "Run up to my room and get the book. Perhaps we will read an act from *Eastward Ho*, instead of Latin."

"Oh, Sis! The part about Virginia! . . . Virginia—isn't it a beautiful name!" She flew out of the room.

Mathilda watched her run joyously up the spiral stairway. What an extraordinary thing for a child, to think so quickly about the dovecote as a hiding place! She laughed softly. Now that he was away, one could laugh about the elegant, fastidious Richard reposing in a dovecote.

Dame Margaret went into the dining-hall and called for Graves. "Send Cook in to me, and come back with her. I want to talk to you both."

While she waited, sitting in the chair lately occupied by Cromwell, she thought of the two good people. They had been faithful servants through the years, ever since she brought them from her home in Devon north to Herefordshire, when she married Nigel Monington. Cook had nursed at the breast Margaret's child by her brief, earlier marriage. Cook had been young and strong, with abundant milk, abundant as that of the strong red Devon cows that grazed in the lush green meadows.

Her mind turned for a moment to that short marriage to Edward Coffyn. Poignant memories of their youthful love . . . his tragic, heroic death the night the great French ship sailed to disaster at Hartland Point . . . the dark turbulent sea, the wild pounding waves. Even now, after nearly thirty years, she could not think of that night without hearing the melancholy tolling of the bell and the measured tread of rough fishermen carrying the body of her husband up the narrow rocky path. What were the lives of the few foreigners he had rescued, against his own dear life?

When Nigel Monington asked her to be his wife three years later, she came north to Herefordshire gladly. He was older than she by ten years. As Lord of the Manor, he had many duties in his county and in London, where he sat in Parliament. She went with him to London, for there was entertaining to be done, and a beautiful hostess wielded some power. She loved her new home with its old black timbered walls, plastered with white fabric, of the time of the great King Harry. She loved the Malvern Hills against the sky. The apple orchards became as familiar friends as the apple orchards of Devon. She loved the hills and valleys and the gentle meadows where cattle grazed peacefully in the long grass; the placid streams; the clouds hanging over the hills that set the boundary of rugged, unruly Wales.

Peace was here, and sanctuary. She had never seen the sea again. Yes, peace in the hills and valleys of mid-England, until Cromwell came with his rough-footed army to trample and destroy and drench the good red earth with redder blood. Bathed in blood, she thought bitterly. Her dear husbands and one son gone, their bodies deep in the earth; her other son fleeing like a hunted fox before the baying hounds.

Cook spoke, rousing her from her sombre thoughts. "Madam? You want to speak to me?" She stood before her mistress, strong and competent, her round face flushed from cooking at an open fire-place.

"Yes. I want to thank both you and Graves for behaving well in the distressing circumstances of last night. I never thought I would be forced to ask any of my people to cook for or serve rebels to the King."

"Don't you be worryin', Mistress Margaret. We served them enough, just as we serve farmers in harvest-time, or the pressmen who make the cider. We gave them no frills, liken we would give the gentry."

The old butler chuckled. "They made a great fuss over the wine, madam. 'Twas the Moselle Master always said was fit only for the swine."

Dame Margaret smiled.

Cook straightened a dish on the sideboard. "I told him this morning his father would fair turn in his grave, if he knew he was consorting with rebels. And so he would. Many's the time I've been to Monkleigh when the ancient ones were living. I told him he was takin' up with lesser folk."

"What are you talking about? Who is taking up with lesser folk?"

"Why, the one they call General Monk, who else? A fine Devon name it is, and him running about, following that Cromwell. Why, he's heathen, he is, standing straight up at Coddington and shouting to his soldiers to tear down the cross on the church tower. He's Antichrist, he is. Talk about the Papists—why, he's worse than any monk who ran hiding in the priest holes, in the old days."

Dame Margaret leaned forward. "So you knew he belonged to the Devon family."

"That I did, and it's he that told me hisself. 'Cook,' he says, putting his head in the door, ' 'twas a good meal you served us last night, and thanks to you.' He tossed me one of Cromwell's coins. I says, 'Thank you, but you can keep the shillin'. My mistress wouldn't like for me to be taking coins for doing my work.' Says he, 'You are bold to talk so.' I says, 'Sir, no bolder than other Devon folk who say what they think, to king or plough-boy.' 'Devon—where?' he wants to know. 'Nigh onto Bideford,' I says. 'The Grenville stronghold,' says he. 'What would you say if I told you I was a Devon man? I live at Monkleigh.' I says, quick as anything, 'If you are Master George Monk who used to ride down the lanes like Satan on a black horse, I'd be astonished.' He laughed and clapped his hand to his thigh, and that skinny one they called Fleetwood, he laughed. 'I'm the one, Cook,' says Monk. 'What do you say to that?' 'I'd say you were in poor company. You should be riding for your King, instead of *him*. The Monks was always right loyal to their Kings.' "

Dame Margaret turned to Graves. "Did you hear her say that?"

"Indeed, madam, and I was shakin' in my poor old knees, so I could scarcely stand. I all but dropped a dish to the floor."

Cook smiled. "And what did you hear him say, Graves? Like I said, the way to treat that kind is to look at them above the eyes and don't unstiffen your neck. The general laughed and laughed. He sat himself down at my kitchen table, right beside the fire. Says he, 'Spoken like a sturdy soul. I'll eat my meal right here. Many's the breakfast I've had in Monkleigh kitchen when I was a lad.' I answered him, 'Sir, you're nothing but a lad now, a wilful, strong-headed, misguided lad, but you're welcome in my kitchen, and I'll cook you a rasher and four fresh eggs and warm up the scones. I'm sorry that it's too late for fine strawberries.' 'Not Devon strawberries?' he asks. 'As good, and our cows give as good milk to clot.' He smiled. 'Woman, woman, you're false to Devon, I'm thinking.' ''Tis not so, sir,' I told him. 'But where the body is, let the heart be free.' Says he, 'Ah, yes, 'tis true,' and he applies himself with vigor to his meal. The Monks are good trenchermen, strong, lusty people, and headstrong. I could see he was the spit of his father."

Dame Margaret settled back in her chair, a smile on her face.

"Then you're not angry, mistress, for me bein' so bold with the rebel general?"

"No, since it turned out well. But don't let your unruly tongue run away with you again. You might be hung for treason."

"You wouldn't dare talk that way to General Cromwell," the butler observed, his eyes on the tankard he was polishing.

Cooks face grew thoughtful. "No," she said, "no. I'm afeard of those frantic men. They talk like they was Jesus Christ Himself, or God Almighty, come to earth. Solemn faces, burning eyes, mouths wrapped in a great cover of Bible words. I'm afraid of them."

The butler said, "Master Richard wasn't afraid when he took to serving them last night." His shoulders shook with laughter. "He was enjoying hisself. He was a-baitin' those men something awful."

Dame Margaret rose. "I hope my son will not find himself in trouble because of his masquerading, if he should get caught."

"Never fear, madam. Master Richard never get hisself caught more than Old Giant Red Fox hisself." She knew he referred to the mythical fox of extreme size and cunning that had evaded the hounds for these many generations. "Old Great Red hisself—that's Master Richard."

"I hope you are right, Graves. It is a time of deep anxiety. I want you and Cook Ellie to know that I value you both for your loyalty to my dear son, and to me through the long years."

Cook bobbed. Graves opened the door for Dame Margaret to pass through. After she had crossed the hall and mounted the narrow spiral stair, he turned to Cook. "Her's fair worried out of her wits, for all she keeps her face and her body still and quiet."

"She's been quiet like that from a child." Cook moved across the room on her way to her kitchen. "But she's stormy enough within herself." She ran her fingers over the long side table. "Dust," she said, "dust. I venture to say it's a two-day dust. That girl Patsy is as lazy as a hound."

"She's got the lads on her mind," the butler observed as he rubbed his polishing cloth over the offending board. "Last week I saw her walking along under the hedge in the moon-shine with that daffy stable-boy Silly Dick. They was twining arms like ivy on the walls, clinging. Mark my words, Cook, we'll be having another squalling hedgerow babe before long."

Cook said, "I'll talk to that young person." The grim turn of her lips boded no good for pretty Patsy, who couldn't resist a questing lad with glib promises of wedlock on his tongue.

Dame Margaret paused for a moment at the door of Richard's bed-chamber. Cromwell's officers had not been allowed to occupy the room. She had given orders to lock the door and it had been opened only when Graves came asking her for the key. That was when they were searching for Richard. They had been satisfied, he told her when he returned the key. "It's the Lord's blessing that no one had entered the room since the master went away, ma'am. The dust lay thick on the wood of the chests, and the bed was stripped, with only a coverlid over it."

They had examined everything, opened the clothes-press and peered into drawers, but they found nothing to prove that he had been there or laid his head on the pillow. They had left reluctantly, Graves reported, and gone on up to the third floor where they examined every nook, opened boxes and chests, but of course discovered nothing. " 'Tis a pity our ghost, old Sir Richard, didn't walk among them clattering his sword. If he's a good ghost, as they say he is, surely he would choose to befuddle our enemies."

Now inside Richard's room, Dame Margaret looked about. To her it was not an empty room. It was alive, peopled by her two sons playing with their dogs, or the pigeons outside the casement, old birds' nests and birds' eggs, bottles of insects, frogs, even little garden snakes. She saw herself seated by the hearth, telling them stories or reading to them from the Bible —Richard always attentive, his eyes dreamy, listening; Peter, four years the older, fidgeting, wandering away to master a horse or teach his dog a new trick.

She thought of the empty room when they went away to school; the first holidays when they came home filled with talk that showed their interest in new things, new people. Peter had gone first to the wars. She had buckled his sword and tied the gay ribbon knot at the hilt. Laughing he had gone. Laughing he had died, they told her afterward, just as his stepfather had gone to death, his naked sword in his hand.

Richard went next to war, not laughing, a little serious, a little sad as he kissed her cheek. She remembered now how he had stood at the window, how his eyes had looked at the purple hills and the long meadow. Richard's feet were deep in the soil. He loved the land. Things grew for him and flourished. Vineyard and orchard became fruitful under his care.

"Keep the land rich, Mother. Plant well, manure well, and the earth will make us rich."

She had shut her lips together. No tears. Her sons had never seen her shed tears. The duty of men was to go forth, to defend the land and the King. And the duty of women was to stay at home and hold the hearth against enemies.

Dear Richard! Last night he had been as gay as his half-brother, who loved bright danger. He had parried and thrust and defended as though he played a game. So he had—a game for his home. What comfort he had brought to her troubled heart when he spoke the quick message in terms of gratitude to the Lady of the Manor from a humble poacher! She alone had known what his words meant—his gratitude to her, his mother, for the comfort she had given him when he grieved for his dead father.

Her thoughts went to Kathryn Audley. How perceptive little Sibyl was, how keenly observant! "She wants to marry a Sir, so she may be 'My Lady.'" Let Kathryn Audley find a husband among the lesser nobility. There were plenty of young men with broad acres who would be enchanted by beauty and look no further.

Richard did not know, nor would she be the one to tell

him, of Kathryn's near relationship to Bradshaw the regicide, that violent judge, traitor to his King and his country. She would not tell him, unless . . . But no, Kathryn's eyes were turned to Nicholas Holder for the moment.

She stood for a moment glancing about the room before she closed and locked the door, shutting out poignant memories of two laughing, carefree children.

Sibyl took her lesson book and sought Cook in her bright, cheery kitchen. She liked to perch on a little three-legged stool close by the great fire, while Cook, with her crocks in her lap, mixed dough for pasties, or wrapped delicate, flaky crust about a fine apple to make a dumpling, or mixed currants and suet for a pudding. She liked the warmth of the fire, the crackling of the drippings from the joint on the spit. Sometimes she was allowed to crank the jack so the joint would be evenly cooked, or roll out the dough on the board. She liked the snatches of song and laughter from the girls in the milk-house. Some of the chatter with the lads, when they brought the fresh, foaming pails of milk from the cow-sheds, was rough for young ears, but Sibyl, keeping very quiet in her corner, was often forgotten.

She liked the large, low-ceilinged room with the casements open to the garden. She liked the shining rows of copper pots and kettles hung on a rack above the fire. She loved the cat sleeping on one side of the fire and the dog on the other; the sweet, pungent smell of dried herbs that hung from the great oaken beams; the rows on rows of crocks and jugs of Worcester pottery. She saw through the open door the shelves in the buttery, with apple butter, pear and quince. A red ear of corn from last year's harvest frolic hung over the door. There were shallow pans of milk on the back of the great iron oven which was embedded in the side of the chimney-breast. The cream would rise as the milk grew warm. One could skim off a solid tablecloth of cream after it had clotted, if one were skilful like Cook. Clotted cream was something one learned in Devon, not in Cornwall, nor Somerset, nor Gloucester, nor even Herefordshire. One had to make this delectable cream the Devon way if one wanted perfection. If only it were strawberry time! Sibyl grew hungry at the idea.

"What clouds your thoughts, young miss?" Cook inquired, looking up from her apple-peeling.

Sibyl said, "You have dashes of flour under one eye and right on your chin. You look very comical, Cook."

"I don't feel comical, and that's the truth. What with having to air out my dining-room and my kitchen to get shed of the odour of disloyalty, I'm behind in my work. You know well that our lady likes her meals on time."

There was a moment's silence in the kitchen. The gruff voice of Smolkins came through quite clearly. He was in the buttery. He had just placed a pail of milk on the long bench and was waiting for the maids to pan it into the crocks. "The story is that men are coming from Lemster, King's men marching fast toward Worcester, and Cromwell's soldiers will catch up with them on the Severn."

"How can that be?" the girl asked. "The King's army marches the faster, doesn't it? Haven't they the better horses?"

"The King and his men aren't running away. They're itching to fight. I heard Mr. Nicholas Holder telling our madam that there'd be a battle. They say . . ."

Cook raised her voice. "You're a great one to repeat tales you hear. Always the one to carry a tale. Let talk of battle come from your betters."

"Yes, ma'am." Smolkins spoke meekly enough, but he was bursting with importance. "I did listen to my betters. Your nephew, Cook, told me . . ."

"Cowley? Where is he?"

"Changing his dirty garments and washing his face and hands at the pump. It's a pretty sight he is, Cook, if you don't mind dirt. He says he slept in a ditch, and the soldiers caught him and tied him up to a tree."

Cook got to her feet with such haste that a dozen bright-red apples fell from her ample lap onto the brick hearth. Sibyl stooped to gather them up and missed the entrance of Cook's nephew into the kitchen. When she raised her head, he was there, a tall lad with a thatch of waving reddish hair and eyes as blue as corn-flowers. His face was scratched but it looked fresh-washed. His leather small-clothes were muddy and his tunic had a cut across the arm, as though it had been slashed by a hunting dirk.

Everyone gathered around him, the maids from the dairy and the buttery, Smolkins and the butler. Cook hovered about.

"Sit you down, Nephew. Patsy, fetch a jug of cider. Cut some meat off the joint, to eat with the fresh-baked bread.

You must be aweary, si—" Cook caught herself and changed the "sir" that she was about to say, to "nephew."

"There'll be fightin'," the lad said, "before a fortnight has passed. The armies are moving toward each other. Mayhap they'll meet at Ledbury, for Cromwell's a-marching fast."

"Was you caught prisoner by Old Ironside?" Patsy asked. She had edged up until she stood almost touching Cowley's elbow.

"Nay, I be caught by King Charles's men. They wouldn't believe me. They said I was a Roundhead spy and should be strung up right there."

"Laws-a-mercy!" Cook gasped. "Laws-a-mercy! Whatever are they thinking about, not knowing a King's man when they saw one."

Her nephew laughed. "Fancy I was a sight, having hid in a ditch half full of mud and water. So they tied me to a tree and they went on dicing and quarrelling half the night. Dicing away the young King's shilling before they got it—that's what they were doin'."

"How did you escape?" the butler asked, pouring a fresh mug of cider.

"I didn't escape. Master Richard came and made them let me go free."

"Master Richard?"

"Yes, and blast me, he looked no better than me, a-walking out of the hop vines! He surprised them like. 'Bring me to your officer,' says he. 'What do you mean by not posting sentries, and Cromwell no more than twenty miles away?' says he." The lad laughed again. "You sould have seen the corporal's phiz, he was that mad. But Master Richard gave him no mind. 'Bring me two horses and cut the bonds of the lad yonder that you've got trussed up like a fowl.' The corporal fussed and spoke back sarcastic-like, until one old trooper said, ' 'Tis Captain Monington, of the King's army.' "

"And then? What then?"

The lad took a gulp of cider and set the pewter tankard on the table. "And then? Why, we got on the horses and off we rode. We met a scouting party from General Massey's Royalists a few miles up the road, and they told us where the general was resting."

"Where was that?" Sibyl asked, edging near to the table. "Where was the general's army?"

The lad looked down at the girl, his blue eyes smiling. "That would be telling, wouldn't it?"

Cook interrupted. "Better wash up there in the pantry. I'll take you to Dame Monington. You must tell her about her son. She's been anxious, very anxious."

Cowley got up and stretched his arms above his head. The tips of his fingers touched the king beam. He yawned. "A man gets no sleep at all, bound to a tree," he muttered.

Cook said, "After you talk with the mistress, you can sleep till dark night."

Sibyl caught Cowley's hand. "I'll take him to Dame Monington. She's in the morning room. My sister is helping her make up accounts."

Cook nodded. "Go along with the child. Be sure you forget nothing concerning Master Richard, Nephew."

Sibyl walked beside the tall lad, skipping every now and then, for his stride was long. He laughed and walked more slowly.

"I can take two steps to one and keep up," she cried.

"And I can cut down half and match you, girl. Your name is Sibyl, isn't it?"

"Yes, Sibyl Jordan. I live in Gloucestershire not far from Bristol. I'm a visitor here. I've seen you in the kitchen and at the stables."

"I am a visitor, too. I'm visiting Cook Ellie."

"If you're Cook's nephew, you must live in Devon."

"That's right, so I do. But sometimes I live in Cornwall."

"By the sea? I'd love to see the ocean."

"Perhaps you will some day. Would you like me to take you to Tintagel, where King Arthur and his knights dwelt?"

"Ah, yes. Yes, I would. When will you take me?"

The lad's face sobered. "God knows, child." He was silent. Sibyl sensed his sadness and did not speak until they reached the morning room.

Dame Monington was bending over her embroidery; on a stool beside her was a pile of coloured yarns. Mathilda sat on the window-seat. She was reading from a book. As the door opened, her voice reached them: " 'Egad, sir, I think the whole world is speaking of this fabulous land of Virginia!' "

Sibyl sat down across the room and caught Dame Monington's hand in both of hers. "Oh, madam, madam, Cook's nephew is here. He has seen Richard."

Dame Margaret's long white hand flew to her heart. She leaned against the high back of the chair. She breathed rapidly.

"Sibyl!" Mathilda spoke sharply. "Mind your manners. See, you have frightened Dame Margaret."

"Ah, no. I only want to make her happy. Richard is safe." The small, sensitive mouth quivered. "Tell her. Reassure her," she cried, turning her head to look over her shoulder toward the tall figure in the doorway.

Dame Margaret had recovered herself. "Step in, young man. What news have you brought of my son?"

The lad advanced. He made a short bow in the direction of Mathilda as though to acknowledge her presence, a more ceremonious one to Dame Margaret.

"This morning I left Master Richard. At his request I rode to Coddington Manor to bring a message to you, ma'am, and to get his horse, which he left last night at Yeoman Winny's stable."

"Give me the message."

The young man glanced at Mathilda. "Please, the master's orders were to speak to you in private."

Dame Margaret said, "Mathilda, will you and Sibyl go into a guest room until I call?"

Mathilda stood up, straightened her full-skirted dress, drew it close and walked past the messenger, her head high, her look slightly supercilious. Sibyl followed, walking slowly, showing her reluctance to leave without hearing the great news. She left the door open a crack.

"Close the door, Sibyl," Dame Margaret called. "If there's anything you should know, I'll send for you." She turned to the lad. "Your message, young man! I do not know your name."

"John." He paused a moment. "Your son asked me to say to you, 'I am well, in the best of spirits. The King's army will soon be in this district. Cromwell's full army is not far northeast of Worcester. He rides to join it after scouting this country. General Massey has a strong force, some two thousand men, waiting near Ledbury for King Charles.' Your son says to put no confidence in Nicholas Holder, for his loyalty will be with the Harley family and they, as you know, have now espoused the cause of Parliament and Cromwell." He paused. "I think I have repeated all the message, ma'am."

"Thank you." She sat quiet, her eyes on the fire. After a moment she looked at him. "You say you are Cook's nephew? Your name is Cowley?"

The lad's face flushed. He took a step forward, turning his hat nervously in his hand. "Ma'am, my name is John Prideaux. I am from New Place in Cornwall. I fled from Cromwell's men and came north, hoping to reach King Charles's army. I found work here at your stables as a groom. One day in the kitchen Ellie recognized me." He smiled a little. "I look like my father, they say."

"Then your father is Sir Richard Prideaux, my cousin?"

"Yes, ma'am."

"Why didn't you come directly to me?"

"I did not want to burden you with my presence, ma'am. You see, I killed one of Cromwell's officers in the West Country. A fair fight," he added quickly. "The county folk hid me and got me away to Bideford, where I found a smuggler's ship going out to Lundy Isle. From there I found another ship sailing up the channel to Bristol. There I hid for three days, then made my way up the Severn and into Herefordshire."

"Why did you come here?"

"I heard that King Charles's army was marching south from Scotland. I thought somehow I might find it."

"And you came here?"

"Yes. I was hungry. A man has to eat. The stableman boasted that the best cook in the county was right here—a Devon woman, he told me." An engaging smile lighted up his face. "I knew I was safe. A Devon woman wouldn't betray me. So I told Ellie who I was. She arranged the rest. I think Cook Ellie enjoys intrigue, ma'am. I was to stay here, saying nothing until the young master returned out of the north, and . . ."

"Did you tell this story to my son?"

"That I did, ma'am."

"What did he say?"

"He asked me questions by the score. When he was satisfied, he called me 'Coz,' and sent me here to you."

"Did he ask you to tell me your name and your story?"

"Ma'am, yes."

"Why didn't he write his message?"

"He feared that some of Cromwell's men might still be near the bank of the Ledden, ma'am."

She smiled. "Then the journey was dangerous."

"Well, there was one burly straggler. . . . Written messages are always dangerous in war," he answered quietly.

"Sit down, John. I must think what to do with you. You might take Richard's room."

He took a step in her direction, alarm in his long thin face. "Please, ma'am, do nothing. Tonight I sleep here, in the stable loft as usual. Believe me, it is best to continue as I am. One does not know who is loyal and who is not. No attention will be paid to a stable-boy or a groom. I can ride Saladin to the army without comment, going to the market at Ledbury. Tuesday being market day, I had best go tomorrow."

"I suppose you are right. It seems a pity that Richard Prideaux's son should sleep in a loft." She was smiling now. "Yet my son Richard housed himself in the dovecote."

Young John burst out laughing. "He told me. What he did with those long legs of his, I cannot imagine."

"Yes, 'tis a pity that Mathilda and Sibyl should not know who you are."

"Pray don't acquaint them. A secret remains a secret with a few, but never with many."

Dame Monington nodded. "Yes, that is true. Mathilda is a very nice young person, and she's not blood-kin."

Again John grinned. "She's quite a high-headed maid. I fancied, from the angle of her tilted nose when she passed me, that she smelled the stables."

"Mathilda is young. Just now she is taking the responsibility for a young sister very much to heart."

John said, "The little one is very warm and friendly. Every man and woman on the place loves her." He rose from the bench. "I must be going now. It's a far piece to Yeoman Winny's, where your son hid Saladin, and I must be with him by midnight."

"You have joined the King's army?"

"Your son was kind enough to speak to General Massey for me. Now I am attached to his regiment."

Dame Margaret extended her hand. John dropped easily to one knee and kissed her fingers. "God go with you, John Prideaux." Her voice was low. "Stay close to my son. Guard him."

John smiled. "Your son is a strong man and very wise. He leans on no one, but I will stay near to him. Already I feel a deep affection. Perhaps it is blood drawing blood, but I have ever held admiration for boldness and courage in a man. I only hope I may be worthy of his friendship."

Dame Margaret was silent for a long time after John Prideaux had gone. How strange life was! Here was a little leaf of the past, turned in the book. Richard Prideaux, the lad's father, had loved her long ago; now he was gone and his son stood before her, an engaging, manly youth, built in the image of his father.

That night at supper she gave a little homily for Mathilda's benefit. One may discern a true gentleman, or lady, by the treatment of inferiors. A lady never, never willingly hurts anyone, particularly anyone beneath her in station.

Mathilda ate her meal in silence, vaguely uneasy. She wondered what she had done that caused Dame Margaret to talk as she did. Surely she had been polite to the groom. She had even thought him comely and noticed that he held himself like a gentleman.

After dinner Cook was closeted with Dame Margaret so long that there was no opportunity before bedtime for Mathilda to continue reading the exciting play.

Sibyl wondered what Dame Margaret and Cook's nephew talked about. Richard, of course, and perhaps about the Roundheads. She sat so long at the window, looking out into the night, that Mathilda called to her to put out her candle and get into bed, or she'd have an ague before morning.

CHAPTER 4

King's Men at Coddington Manor

AT DAYBREAK Sibyl woke to the bay of the hounds. The hunt
was on. She jumped from her bed and ran to the window. Far
down across the meadow she saw it. She counted twenty
horses bunched, leaping the low hedge. Stragglers followed,
a smaller group. It was beautiful to see, but she hoped the
hounds wouldn't come upon the vixen. . . . She wished they
would let her hunt. She could ride well enough. She had
jumped the high gate that led to the field, and that was a good
jump. She had put her mare, Darling Bit, over more than one
stream, but Dame Margaret said she was too young, and so
her father forbade her to hunt. He allowed himself to be
influenced by anything Dame Margaret said about her.

Mathilda still slept, her hand under her cheek, a smile on
her lips as though her dreams were happy. Sibyl dressed
hurriedly but it took time. There was so much to go onto
her slender body—the tight little muslin waist about her middle; the little embroidered modesty that showed under the
rounded neck of her frock; petticoats, wool and muslin; reeded
panniers; and then her light wool dress.

She liked the dress. Its sand colour was so pretty, with the
brown braid trimming.

She flew down the winding stairs. She loved to slide the
dark walnut rail from the third floor to the first, but that was
forbidden this year. Last year she had had fun and run like a
boy all over the place. This year she must learn deportment.
"Mind your manners." . . . "Curtsy with grace." . . . "Sit with
your feet close together, only the toes of your little soft shoes
showing from under your wide-spread skirts." Although she
was allowed to eat at table with the elders, she could not
speak unless she was spoken to. It was fun eating in the
nursery. Still, growing up had its pleasures—listening to
grown-up talk for one.

She ran to the kitchen as fast as she could go. Cook was making breakfast for the dairymaids and the stablemen. The butler sat at the head of the long table. There was rank in the kitchen as well as in the dining-hall, and those who sat below the salt did not speak until they were addressed.

Everyone at the table rose and bobbed as she came in. Cook brought a little gate-legged table and put it in front of the fire so she might have her early meal. Sibyl loved to eat by the fire. After a moment the servants resumed their talk as though she were not in the room. Cook brought her a rasher of bacon and an egg and a jug of milk.

Graves said, "He got away toward morning, Cook." Everyone understood whom he meant. "I gave him a hunk of bread and cheese, for God knows what he'll find on the road this day."

"Plenty," Smolkins said, "plenty. They told me at the tavern last night that there are little skirmishes going on between recruiting parties; that the King's army is coming along the Leominster Road, or the Worcester Road, or the Hereford Road, or the road from Wales."

"They can't be coming on all the roads in Middle England."

"That's God's truth, they can't. I'm just telling you what they said at the village, when I went this morning to carry in a dozen sheep to be sold before the army took them without by-your-leave." Smolkins grinned, well satisfied with his strategy.

Sibyl said to Cook, "Is the hunt breakfasting with us?"

"Good Lord Almighty, I clean forgot! With all this coming and going of armies, how can a body remember everything? Get up from the table, Smolkins, and bring in a ham from the smokehouse. Patsy, run to the hennery and fetch eggs. You men get out of here. You've lingered long enough in my kitchen." Standing in the middle of the floor, Cook gave orders, marshalling her forces like a general about to give battle. "Miss Sibyl, you run and see if the mistress knows the hunt will stop here instead of at the inn. They sent word last night, but for my life I don't remember if I gave the message."

Sibyl ran out of the kitchen. She loved to see Cook make things move. She looked so big and strong and competent, her eyes shining, her cheeks red, her hand waving her wooden stirring spoon like a baton. Everybody jumped when she spoke, even the butler. Though he was too dignified to jump, he paid heed to her and moved a little bit faster than he usually did.

Sibyl knocked lightly at Dame Margaret's door, very lightly, so she would not disturb her if she were asleep, or at her devotions, kneeling at the little desk near the window.

Dame Margaret called, "Come in." She was up and dressed. The bed where she slept all alone was as big as the great bed of Ware which everyone knew was almost ten feet wide. It was built for a whole family, not just for one narrow woman.

"Cook asked did she tell you about the hunt?"

"Kathryn and Nicholas told me yesterday that they would be here for breakfast. The inn is crowded with soldiers, it seems, and there is no place for the hunters." Dame Margaret fastened a brooch on her square-cut bodice and tucked an embroidered handkerchief into the cuff of her long black sleeve. She stood for a moment before the reflecting glass, adjusting her little "Marie" cap. "Perhaps they won't hunt this morning, since the army is so near."

"Oh, yes, ma'am. I saw them from my window. I counted twenty-eight, though I couldn't see all for the trees."

"You saw twenty-eight riders? We had best be prepared for at least ten more. Run out and tell the new groom to be ready to take care of the horses."

"The new groom has gone, Dame Margaret. He went away before daybreak. Graves gave him some food, for God knows what he'll run into," Sibyl parroted.

Dame Margaret did not speak. She looked very serious, so serious was she that she didn't notice Sibyl had taken the Lord's name in vain.

"Went before daylight," she echoed softly. After a moment she held out her hand. "Let us go down to the dining-hall, Sibyl, to see that everything is prepared for our guests."

The riders came in after ten. Sibyl laid her lesson books aside when she heard the thud of horses' hoofs in the lane. She ran downstairs and out the door that led to the cobbled court-yard. Dame Margaret was on the terrace. Mathilda, dressed in a new blue woollen, was standing beside her. Stable-boys and grooms were on hand to lead the tired, sweaty horses to the paddock. As the riders dismounted, they came to the terrace to greet Dame Margaret; the women to curtsy, the men to kiss her hand.

The countryside was well represented, the Skynners and the Tate brothers, and riders from Cameron, Munsley and Frome Court.

Twenty or more had trooped into the dining-hall at Dame Margaret's invitation before Kathryn Audley and Nicholas Holder rode down the lane and dismounted at the block. With them was a strange young man whom Nicholas introduced as Stephen Bennett, a relative, he told his hostess, of Edward Bennett, the great merchant prince of London.

Sibyl thought Mr. Stephen Bennett looked nice. His skin was a warm brown, his cheek-bones were ruddy, and his hair was dark brown. His eyes were grey and wide apart. He had a straight nose and his chin was square. His mouth was wide, with laughter in the corners. He had a nice manner and moved easily. She liked him at once, and she was pleased when he bent low and kissed her hand and smiled at her. He lingered over kissing Mathilda's hand and looked at her with admiration in his eyes.

Kathryn called him to her side at once. "Come, Stephen. Before we breakfast, I want to show you the lily pond. It is so lovely, crescent-shaped, exactly like a woman's lips."

With a lingering glance at Mathilda he followed Kathryn through the hall and out onto the front terrace. Mathilda did not see the glance. Sibyl thought she had not really seen the nice young man from Virginia. She had eyes only for Nicholas Holder, a silly young fellow, Sibyl thought him, a fop, a cockscomb, with his elegances and his court mannerisms and his little blond moustache.

Nicholas was talking with Dame Margaret. He said young Bennett had just returned from Virginia, where he had a plantation called Bennett's Choice. "He came across on one of Edward Bennett's ships. He has a score of ships—Edward, I mean, not Stephen, who is a poor cousin from Gloucester."

"I once was well acquainted with Edward Bennett and his wife Mary Bourne," Dame Margaret said. "I visited her in Somerset more than once when I used to go to Bath to take the waters. I notice you call him the merchant prince like everyone else. He is a good man, although much of his wealth comes from selling indentured servants to the colonists in Virginia. I'm not sure I approve of selling white men into bondage."

Nicholas said, "Dear lady, what does it matter? Seven years' servitude for the scum of London. They are better off than in debtors' prison or Newgate."

"But they are not all from prisons, I hear. Some of our political exiles also are sold."

Holder laughed. "Even they are better off than in prison here. From what Bennett tells me, Virginia is a Utopia, an Elysium, a paradise where beautiful birds sing all day, and nightingales by night. One has only to stick a seed in the ground and behold, a plant springs up! There are great forests and wonderful wild grapes and glorious rivers, five times as wide as the Severn. To hear him talk, the Wye and the Ledden are little brooks. Jamestown is a flourishing town and the plantations on either side of the James River are fabulous. Why, the James itself is as wide as the English Channel—majestic, he says."

Dame Margaret smiled. "You are making a case for the Virginia Colony."

Nicholas Holder laughed again. "Am I? Perhaps I have caught the fever. Stephen is going back. He says there is talk that a cousin, Richard Bennett, is to be named a Commissioner for Maryland and Virginia by Cromwell's Council of State. Perhaps I may go out. I think Virginia might prove interesting for a younger son. They say tobacco growing is very profitable."

"If you are not in the war," Dame Margaret commented without a smile. "Come, let us go inside."

Sibyl listened, her mouth slightly open, her eyes wide and shining. She must talk with the young man from Virginia. It all sounded enchanting.

Mathilda had been listening to Nicholas, her eyes never leaving his face. Sibyl wished that she did not show her preference for his company so plainly. Now she followed him into the dining-hall, eager to be near him, to serve him food from the long oak side-table—partridge pie, veal and ham pie, cold sliced bacon, cheese and Cook's good dark bread.

The butler and two men were carrying tankards of ale. Some of the hunters sat down on the benches on either side of the long stretcher table. Others walked about, plates in hand.

Sibyl hoped no one would break a plate of Dame Margaret's fine Worcester ware. Men were so careless, leaving a plate on the edge of the mantel, or on the window-box among the flowers!

After she had filled a plate, she looked about. Kathryn Audley and the man from Virginia had not come inside. She went out into the hall and onto the terrace. She saw Kathryn standing at the entrance to the Lady's Bower, looking up at Stephen Bennett as though she were a lovesick serving-girl.

Something rose in Sibyl's throat, making it tight. She thought of Richard standing there waiting for Kathryn, only yesterday. She walked across the lawn. "I've brought you some breakfast," she said, holding out a well-filled plate.

Kathryn frowned, but Stephen Bennett smiled. "What a thoughtful little maid! Here, Kathryn, sit down at the table and take this plate. Perhaps, little Sibyl, you will show me the way, and I will bring out two more. Would you like to breakfast with us?"

Before Sibyl could answer, Kathryn interposed. "Nonsense, Stephen! Little Sibyl can send a servant with plates." Kathryn was not pleased with the idea of a third interrupting their tête-à-tête.

Stephen took Sibyl's hand. He did not appear to have heard Kathryn. They started for the house. Half-way across the lawn Kathryn joined them. "I find the wind a trifle cold. Perhaps it would be better to have breakfast in the dining-hall."

Sibyl dropped behind. She turned to look back and saw that her little dog, Prince Charley, was on the table, eating voraciously from the forgotten plate. Partridge was quite a treat to a spaniel.

Stephen did not stay at Kathryn's side. Instead, he took a plate of food and walked over to Dame Margaret, who sat at the head of the table. He sat down on the bench beside Mathilda.

The company was scattered about the room and the hall. The Master of Hounds, Richard Brooke, had hung his horn over the back of a chair. Two men of Colwall, John Mathern and the rector of the parish church, Thomas Taylor, were standing beside the fire.

"They have marched from Perth in three weeks," John

Mathern said. "The Royalist army is weary. Would it not be strange if Cromwell's men intercepted it at Ledbury, and a battle should be fought there, as in '45 when Scudamore's Horse was pursued by Major Hopton? Perhaps the King will win at Ledbury as Prince Rupert did when he beat Massey and his men. Massey was fighting for the Parliament then."

The rector said wryly, "This time the Cavaliers lack Prince Rupert. The prince had genius in his cavalry attacks. Now I fear the genius is on the other side. Rupert surprised the Roundheads, and he had Lord Loughborough at the head of his Cavaliers. I hope there isn't another battle at Ledbury, with fighting in the market-place, bloody mêlée in Homend and the Church Lane, the churchyard contested as a vital point to fight over. We've picked many a slug out of the church door."

Holder came up. "Cromwell has led the King into a pocket, is what I think." He walked away and sat down beside Kathryn Audley.

The rector lowered his voice. "I wish Holder would declare himself. One doesn't know which side he is on."

Brook, who was recovering from a wound he had got in Scotland in the King's service, said, "As long as he courts Kathryn Audley, he's bound to follow the Harleys, who are staunch for Cromwell."

The rector's thin, sensitive face was sad. "As a man of the Church I must not take part in war or talk of war. This civil strife is so tragic, so unnecessary—brother against brother ... households broken ..." He ceased as others joined them.

Sibyl heard no more. She slipped into an empty seat on the bench near Stephen Bennett. He was addressing Dame Margaret, but his lively grey eyes turned toward the silent Mathilda time after time, as though to draw her into the orbit of his interests.

"Virginia is not like any place in England. The river is so great all the navies of Britain could rest in its broad water. From the Capes and the Point of Comfort, past Mr. Sewell's Point, on up to Jamestown, there is great beauty, and the opportunity for great shipping."

"Is the James River as large as the Severn?" Sibyl asked.

Bennett laughed. "Much, much larger, and longer too."

Dame Margaret asked, "Do our people live well there? Do they all prosper?"

Stephen hesitated. "Not all are prosperous. Some very

wealthy planters along the lower James, and the upper, too. But I do not think, in all honesty, that the average colonist is better off than he was at home."

Mathilda spoke then. "I've been told that only thieves and rogues from the prisons went to Virginia."

For an instant a flash of something like anger shone in Stephen's eyes. "That is a story noised about by people of ill will. There are men here in England who want the colony to fail."

"Who could want failure for a great enterprise?" Dame Margaret asked.

"At first under the old London Company there was a division in the shareholders, a struggle for supremacy between the Earl of Warwick's group and those who sided with Sir Edwin Sandys." He hesitated a moment. "It's a long story. Some say King James sided with Warwick while he was thinking of marrying the Spanish Infanta."

"I suppose the Spanish would not want it to succeed," Dame Margaret said with a tone of inquiry.

Stephen nodded. "A permanent colony on the James and the Chesapeake threatens their supremacy in America. They plan to extend their holding in Florida, and the rich country is to the north."

Mathilda saw Nicholas crossing the room. She turned to Stephen Bennett, assuming great animation and interest. "Mr. Bennett, you haven't answered my question."

"About thieves and rogues? I thought I had when I said the story had been spread in England by persons who did not want the settlement to succeed. At first, there were men from prisons sent over. That was some years ago. Political prisoners we have, who come as indenturers." He was interrupted by a commotion in the court-yard.

The butler came in. "Madam, there's two officers and a small troop. A message has come. The King's army is marching this way. They want food, mutton and beef, and forage for their horses. What shall we do?"

Dame Margaret rose. "What shall we do? Why, feed them, of course. Send the herd-boys to the meadows and drive in the sheep. Let the kine be slaughtered. The King's army is the King. Go quickly and tell Cook to begin baking. Tell the maids to make the rooms ready. Open all the windows and let

fresh air blow through. I do not want the scent of Roundheads to greet the King's men."

The guests bestirred themselves. Kathryn and Nicholas
and others of the Parliamentary party made swift adieux
and as quickly mounted and rode away.

Sibyl ran alongside Stephen Bennett. "Come again, please.
Tell me more and still more about your wonderful Virginia.
Promise me, please."

He stayed his mounting long enough to kiss her hand. "I
will. I will come again. Will you make my farewells to your
lovely sister? I see my host, Holder, is half-way down the
lane. I must follow, for I do not want to fall afoul of the
King's army."

"I wish you were a Cavalier. You act just like one," she
cried, clinging to his hand.

"I wish you were a Roundhead," he called out. Sibyl
watched him gallop down the lane in swift pursuit of Nicholas
Holder and Kathryn Audley. He was gay, singing at the top
of his voice:

> ". . . to war and arms I fly.
>
> True: a new mistress now I chase,
>   A first foe in the field;
> And with a stronger faith embrace
>   A sword, a horse, a shield."

Young gentlemen like Stephen might embrace a Parliament
sword, horse and shield, but they hadn't embraced psalm-
singing. Sibyl knew the song. Mathilda often sang it to her
lute. She ran into the house and overtook Mathilda going up
the stairs. "Isn't he nice? *Isn't* he? Almost as nice as Richard."

Mathilda answered listlessly, "Who is nice?"

"Why, Stephen Bennett, of course. Don't you think so?"

"I didn't notice. Hurry! Dame Margaret wants all the
rooms opened, even the great bedroom."

"Oh, Mathilda! Is the King coming?"

"Don't chatter so much. I don't know whether the King is
coming or not."

Sibyl's excitement was not to be dampened by Mathilda's
apathy. "It's wonderful! One night Cromwell, next night the
King."

Mathilda did not answer, and after a time Sibyl too was

silent, as they helped the maids dress the beds for whoever
came to Coddington Manor that night.

It was dusk when they came, with much noise and clatter
of armour, and neighing and stamping of horses.

Dame Margaret met them at the door. Serving-men with
torches stood in the court-yard to light the way. Scots marched
to skirl of pipes behind the riders.

Tired as they were and foot-sore, weary with the long
march, yet the Scots stood straight and soldierly at salute
as the three officers dismounted and passed through the ranks
and across the terrace to the door.

The tallest officer, with a long face, stern and lined, approached Dame Margaret. He made a courteous bow. "My
name is David Leslie. I met your son by the river. He assured
me that I would find hospitality and welcome here, for myself and my men."

"You are thrice welcome, General Leslie. My people have
already prepared for your men." She turned toward the
others. "There is no need of an introduction to my Lord of
Lauderdale. We have met often at Court." She extended her
hand.

"May I present the Earl of Derby?"

"I did not see you in the dark, my lord. I thought for a moment you were the Duke of Buckingham."

Derby laughed. "You give me youth that I do not possess,
Dame Margaret. It is pleasurable to be here in Herefordshire
once again. Buckingham is with the King, who rides some distance behind us. We are scouts, as you see, seeking out a safe
road for His Majesty. Since some of the enemy may not
be far away, we must move with caution."

They walked toward the great hall, while men-servants, led
by the butler, bowed low and maids curtsied. The lackeys
assisted the guests in unbuckling the clanking backs and
breasters which they laid in the tall carved armories.

Dame Margaret said, "Show the gentlemen to their rooms.
Perhaps a rest will be more welcome than conversation."

The three officers looked at one another and laughed. "Ah,
well spoken, ma'am!" Lauderdale exclaimed. "A bath, a
sleep . . ."

"And then refreshment." Dame Margaret smiled.

Sibyl watched the weary men walk up the stairs, the spurs
on their heavy, dusty boots clattering against the oaken

treads. She nudged Mathilda. "Is the red-haired one the great Duke of Lauderdale? How ugly he is!"

"Well, he *is* ugly. He has a nice laugh, but his sharp eyes frighten me. Are all Scots so ferocious?"

"General Leslie wasn't ferocious. No, he was only tired. Oh, Mat, didn't the Scots look grand, the way they swung along at the cry of the wild bagpipes when they marched off to the stables? Cook says that the men have five whole sheep roasting on the big spits. I'd like to go down to the meadow to see them eat."

"Well, you can't go to the meadow, my girl. Run into the kitchen; perhaps you can be useful. Cook must be in a pet, with the maids off dressing beds."

"Are more officers coming? Perhaps King Charles himself? Wouldn't you love to see the King?"

"I've seen the King, in London, silly."

"What is he like, Mathilda? I've never seen a king."

"He's a dark young man, not more than two yards high. He was a Prince then. Now he's a Scottish King. That's why the country-folk won't rally to him. They don't like Cromwell about here, but they don't like the Scots, either."

"Did Nicholas Holder tell you that?" Sibyl asked shrewdly. "I wouldn't believe what Nicholas Holder says. I think he's a two-face."

"Sibyl!"

"I do. I do indeed. He's two-faced to ladies. First it's Kathryn Audley, then it's you he's saying sweet things to. Oh, just the same things to each of you! I've heard him saying poetry, and singing 'Go, lovely Rose,' and looking like a calf."

Mathilda's lips trembled. She turned and ran through the great room to the darker sanctuary of the alcove. Sibyl started to follow, but Dame Margaret, who had come in from the hall, stopped her. "You should not tease your sister. See, you have made her shed tears."

"I didn't mean to make her cry, Dame Margaret. I only wanted to make her realize what kind of man she is foolish about."

Dame Margaret lifted Sibyl's little pointed chin with her slim hand. Sibyl thought she was about to scold her. "What makes you so wise, child?" she said. "But don't tease her. It does not help to be unkind. Mathilda has been blinded by

Cupid. Her eyes will open, but just now words from you won't help. Let her find out for herself, Sibyl."

Before sun-up the guests departed. When Sibyl ran downstairs and into the kitchen, Cook told her that the meadow had been "shed" of Scots this long time. "They went off without those devil's pipes scritching. The big red-haired gentleman had given the orders, him they say is the King's favourite." She put two milk pans in front of Patsy the scullery maid, indicating with an index finger a spot that was not shining enough to suit her.

"If you'd keep your mind on your work, instead of on the lads, you'd get along better. And have a care about the soldiers! They look brave in their fine scarlet capes, but they'd make a scarlet woman of ye without givin' ye another thought."

Patsy blushed, but her blue eyes and her stubborn mouth showed mutiny. "Weren't ye ever a young lass, Cook?" she asked pertly.

"That I was, and many a Devon lad came a-courtin', or chasing me at the harvest festival, but I fended them off, and when I had my child, it was a proper child, born of wedlock, and not of hedgerow courtin'. . . . Now off with you and be about your work in the buttery." She went over and stirred a pot that hung on a crane over the fire.

"It's a good hundred head we've fed here these two days," she remarked to no one in particular. "I'm bound I don't like armies tramping across our land—first one, then t'other. It's like Devon in '45—first your side wins, then, before you know it, there's the enemy on your stoop."

Smolkins came to the fire. "Looks to me you can't tell t'other from which," he said as he warmed his hands. "They both want one thing—food. Your own side is just as like to clean you out of stock, drivin' off cattle and sheep, slaughterin' kine. Why, market day won't be nothing in Ledbury, come Tuesday. I heard one party of scouters, thereabout Colwall, drove off one hundred cattle. What we're to do without cattle and sheep, I don't know."

" 'Twas the Scots. They're a hungry lot."

"The Scots are King's men." Sibyl joined in the conversation.

"Are they now? I thought they were our enemy, miss, as

they've always been. Perhaps I wouldn't rightly know the difference."

No one answered Smolkins. The country-folk were suspicious of the Scots, as they were of the Welsh, or of any folk
who came from beyond county borders.

Cook said, "Those who tabled here, enemies or friends,
behaved like gentlemen."

The scullery maid put her head in the door. "How could
the enemies do otherwise when our lady stood up to them so
grand-like?"

Smolkins had the last word: "And did you hear what they
done at Ross, now? Made a great effigy of Oliver and fixed
a wooden face on it. They even had a big wart on the nether
lip. Ross men and women went parading the ugly figure
through the streets. And then they made a bonfire of Oliver,
all the time singin':

> " 'Who set three kingdoms on a flame
> 'Tis just should perish by the same.' "

" 'Tis a heathen thing to burn a man, even a straw man."

"No more heathen than making twelve little straw fires and
one big one to burn the witches."

"That's just burning the brush, as on Christmas-day. Or
the farm people toasting an ox on the new day of the year.
'Tis a waste of good ale to toast a whole ox in it," the milker
remarked, hoisting his yoke over his shoulder. He went out
the door, his shiny milk pails banging against his legs as he
walked, and they heard him singing:

> "Here's to you, Champion, with your white horn!
> God send our master a good crop of corn."

"He's purely a fool," Cook said.

But the scullery maid followed him with her eyes. "He has
the second vision, he has. The gardener, now, can see the
wee ones, but they are little folk who do no harm. Biggor
told me he had once seen the great house in the valley
meadow. Everyone knows there is no house at all, only a place
where the ghosts of a family gather that was murdered during the time of Great Harry.

"And he has seen the devil on New Year's Eve when he
passed the churchyard at Coddington. There was evil things

taking place inside, with the devil reading out names. Once he walked seven times around the preaching cross in the church, and repeated backward a long prayer, and the devil came out of the ground, all covered with smoke and fire. Biggor fell in a faint, and when he woke in the morning, there was the mark of a cloven hoof on his thigh."

Sibyl shivered and moved closer to Cook's side. It was a bright day, with sun shining through the leaded panes of the bow-window, but she felt an icy hand laid between her shoulders. "Did he see the devil under the cross that Oliver pulled down?" she asked in a thin, high voice.

"Get you gone, and close your mouth over your loose tongue!" Cook's voice was raised angrily. "Patsy, can't you see you're scaring the child out of her wits? Have done with these tales of witches and wee men and ghosts. Have done or I'll beat your fat buttocks with the poker."

The girl fled. Cook patted Sibyl's shoulder. "Pay no mind to these Herefordshire tales of badgers changed into friars, and demons sitting in the robes of the canon in the Cathedral church. Little tales! Some day I'll tell you about the witch of Devon, and the furies that ride the storm waves on the rocks of Arthur's Castle. We have proper ghosties, we have."

"We have Arthur's Stone, where the King lies buried in the Golden Valley," Sibyl said.

Patsy put her head in the door again to add a little more to the Herefordshire legend. "And *we* have the great stone at Colwall, that turns round in the night when the clock strikes twelve."

"How can a great stone turn round in the night?" Sibyl cried, her eyes very bright.

"Hist! There's Dame Margaret's call. Run and find what she wants, that's a good girl."

Sibyl ran swiftly through the darkened dining-hall. In the oriel window of the great hall Dame Margaret sat, stitching her tapestry. Mathilda, seated on a bench, was reading from a little book of devotions. The window was open to let in the sweet, warm air. Tranquillity and peace painted the picture. Evil things, such as ghosts, turbulence and war, were far away.

CHAPTER 5

A Love Philtre

THE gatherers were in the lower field, picking up the stones brought to the surface by the past spring ploughing. A penny a bushel was the wage. Men and women worked gaily, while the children played at games by the hedges, making patterns of the small stones. The girls formed little houses, while the small boys made forts, drawing sides for offensive and defensive warfare. Some children tended pigs and sheep, their broad hats decorated with the drooping bronze and green feathers of a cock.

Although it was not Oak-apple day, celebrated on the twenty-ninth of May, plough-boys wore oak leaves in their caps, for it showed their allegiance to the King.

In a far field the hop-pickers were at work. They moved about the vines in groups, so they might gossip. One wag sang an old drinking song at the top of his lungs, thinking of the pint he would have at the tavern when the day's work was over.

> "Back and side go bare, go bare;
>   Both foot and hand go cold;
> But, belly, God send thee good ale enough,
>   Whether it be new or old."

Sibyl rode down to the field on her little dun pony. She wanted to watch the men on wooden stilts who picked the highest vines. It was fun to see men working on platforms which had been set atop the carts, drawn by the fat old horses. As the men worked, the troughs of sacking filled up; then lads would stuff the hops into pokes and carry them to the oast-house to dry. It was fun to be at Coddington now, when the autumn was coming. The harvest festival was talked of for days in the kitchen and on the farm. This year would be good: apples aplenty to be crushed into cider or apple wine; apple culls to feed the hogs, so their meat would have a sweet, fine taste; but most of all, good cider for good palates.

Sibyl sat on her pony where the hedgers and ditchers were at work, and looked across the fields to the thatched roofs of the hamlet at the cross-road. These folk were happy and content. They had little interest in the long war except when it took their food away. Close to the earth, they drew strength from it, as their fathers and fathers' fathers had done before, back in an unbroken line to the Normans, and before that to the Romans and the Saxons. Other folk, foreign to the land, had come from time to time, and gone their ways or been absorbed. Each invader had left his mark. The Romans had built the camp on the hill and roads that were still used, and they had put Latin names on places, names that still might be traced.

Cherry Norman was now an apple, with no thought given to the conquerors from across the Channel. All was English as the rich red earth and the green pastures where sheep and cattle grazed, as English as the men and women who carried stones or clipped hedges or herded flocks.

And yet two armies marched only a few days' distance from each other. Dame Margaret had cautioned Sibyl that morning to keep inside the gate and not ride in the Ledbury Road. "It is not safe for you to be out of sight of the house," she had cautioned. All through the Great Rebellion, armies had trampled over Herefordshire, King's men and Parliament men, first the one and then the other taking their toll. And now, somewhere near, they would be at each others' throats again.

Sibyl had encountered no soldiers. For three days it had been as quiet, as peaceful, as it was this dazzling morning. No one had come to call. No one had hunted. No one had galloped up the road or turned into the long avenue lined with tall cypress of Italy. This morning Cook had commented that she had no one to cook for except the family—three lone women, with no man to liven them. "Women without men about are dull things" was her comment as she stirred the pot of pea-soup. " 'Tis not good for Madam or your pretty sister."

"If you ask me," Patsy had said, "I think it would be well if the young maid drank a philtre to get her out of love with Master Holder and into love with Master Richard."

"What is a love philtre?" Sibyl had asked the rosy-cheeked maid.

Cook had interfered. "Hush yourself, Patsy. No use putting ideas into the lass's head."

Now Sibyl thought of what Patsy had said, turning the idea over in her mind. . . . O love philtre. . . . She turned her pony's head down the path that led to the wood. She knew where old Granny Heskett lived. Folk said she was good at witching. Perhaps she knew of a love philtre—not to make love come, but to make love go away.

Sibyl entered the wood. A red fox crossed the path, his bushy tail carried low, and disappeared into the shadows. The pony shied and refused to budge. He stood shivering. Sibyl felt a damp coldness down her back. A fox might be a fox, but then again it might be a witch woman who turned to fox at her own will. After a moment the pony lifted its head and sniffed the air; then it moved into the wood path. For a long time the sickening acrid smell of the fox was in Sibyl's nostrils.

She rode deeper and deeper into the wood. She knew the sun shone brightly outside, but the wood was heavy in shadow. The path grew narrower. Brambles and vines and overhanging boughs caught at her hair and scratched her cheeks and hands. She was afraid to venture farther. To turn back was not to be considered; only a coward ran. The pony plunged steadily forward, breaking vines and branches in the effort.

Sibyl's heart pounded. It was not fear, it was sheer terror that made her palms clammy, her mouth dry. Presently she came to a small clearing. She saw smoke rising from the chimney of a small thatched cottage. The thin spiral of white smoke against the dark trees of the forest encouraged her. Smoke was real. Real people made fires to cook by or to warm themselves; not witches. She rode closer and called, "Hallo the house! Hallo the house!" as she had heard her father call more than once, when they travelled through a strange countryside.

The door opened. A girl stood in the door. She did not look like a witch, Sibyl thought. She was young and willowy. Her hair was black as a rook's wing. Her brows were so heavy that they seemed to meet across the bridge of her nose, giving her a fierce look.

She did not answer Sibyl's timorous smile with a smile; instead she scowled. "What do you want?" she said. Her voice was harsh.

"I want to see Goody Heskett," Sibyl managed to say. "I want to see Goody Heskett."

"Well, you can't see her. She's in the forest picking up faggots." The dark girl came closer. Sibyl caught a glimpse of the room, poor and mean, but very neat. A little fire burned on the hearth. Something moved—a dog? or was it a man? Surely a man stood near the window, his back to the door— and there was something familiar about him. The girl had stepped down from the stoop, pulling the door shut behind her. Sibyl was alarmed at the fierce, angry face. She lifted the reins and turned the pony quickly.

"Thank you," she said over her shoulder. "Thank you very much." She was in a panic. What if the girl snatched her from her pony, and the man beat her head with a stone? How foolish she had been to come to the forest! How very foolish!

The girl's voice rang out harshly. "I suppose you are after a love potion like the rest!" The laugh that followed was as wild as Old Billy who wandered about the countryside talking to himself. Sibyl urged her pony on. She wanted to get away as quickly as possible.

At the edge of the forest she saw an old woman. She was stooping, picking up faggots. The pony began to tremble as he had trembled when they encountered the fox. It raised its head and snuffed the air, snorting through its nostrils. Sibyl too began to tremble. Her hands were cold; her heart beat violently. She looked again into the thicket, but the woman was not there. Instead, she saw a red fox sliding into the shadows!

Sibyl clamped her teeth to keep from screaming. She kicked the pony in the ribs. It broke into a gallop. She did not pull rein until she heard the hop-pickers singing their lusty drinking song:

> "Though I go bare, take ye no care,
>   I nothing am a-cold;
> I stuff my skin so full within
>   Of jolly ale and old, old, old,
>   Of jolly ale and old."

Sibyl dismounted at the stable-yard and ran to the house. She wanted to get to her room without encountering Dame Margaret. She couldn't tell her about the fox and the old woman in the wood. She would laugh, and so would Mathilda. Cook would listen without laughter, but she would scold and tell her that she must not ride without a groom. It would be a secret that she would not tell anyone—certainly not to Mathilda, for the more she thought of it, the more she was convinced that the man in the thatched cottage was Nicholas Holder. Why he was there she could not fathom. Perhaps he had gone on the same errand, for a love philtre.

Sibyl met no one on the way to her room. Inside, with the door closed, she was glad to see the sun shine brightly through the leaded panes of the oriel window. She lost her fears amid familiar surroundings. How silly she was to be frightened by a rude girl and an old woman picking up faggots! A girl of her age should have more courage. What would Richard think of her if he knew she had run away?

She sat down on the window-seat and took up her Latin book. There was something steadying about Latin translation. It took all of one's attention.

The August moon was high, flooding the earth with silvery glow. Mathilda stood quietly looking out the window into the magic of the garden. Dame Margaret sat in her high-back chair at the edge of the hearth. The oak logs burned brightly, for the evening was cool. Sibyl lay on her stomach near Dame Margaret, her little spaniel close beside her. She was reading from a book by the light of a candle.

"You will ruin your eyes, child," Dame Margaret said. "Put the book away. Besides, you are quite too old to lie on your stomach. It is not seemly in a young maid to act the hoyden."

Sibyl glanced up, her finger marking the line where she had left off reading. "Oh, Dame Margaret, please. I can see quite clearly. Listen to these words about Virginia:

"'. . . we viewed the land about us, being very sandie and low towards the water's side, but so full of grapes as the very beating and surge of the Sea overflowed them, of which we found such plentie, as well there as in all places else, both on the sand and on the greene soile on the hills, as in the plaines, as well on every little shrubbe, as also climbing towardes the tops of high Cedars, that I thinke in all the world the like abundance is not to be found: and my selfe having seene those parts of Europe that most abound, find such difference as were incredible to be written.' "

"What is that book you are reading?" Dame Margaret asked.

"It is Sir Walter Raleigh's. There are things in it about Virginia. I found it in the library."

Dame Margaret sighed. "Yes, yes. I remember when my dear Edward purchased Raleigh's book. He was deeply interested in Virginia. He always thought he would go out some day." She sighed again. "But he never went." She was silent for a moment. "Virginia." She repeated the word slowly. "All Devon knew Virginia. Virginia was the goal of all the young adventurous lads. That was before I was born, Sibyl. From the nursery up I listened to tales of Sir Richard Grenville's great venture to Roanoke Island. Men were alive still who had sailed with him and had lived on that island for a full year before Sir Francis Drake took them off and brought them safe home to Devon."

"Was Sir Richard a Devon man like Sir Walter Raleigh and Sir Humphrey Gilbert?" Sibyl asked.

"The Grenvilles were overlords of Bideford, but their home was across the border in Cornwall. Many times I have visited at Stowe Barton, the seat of the Grenville family near Kilkhampton, a great house for a great family, famed for hospitality."

Mathilda left the window and took a seat on a low stool near the hearth.

"Tell us about the Hundred Men of Devon." Sibyl sat up, close to Dame Margaret's skirts.

"I've told you the story over and over." Dame Margaret smiled, but Sibyl knew she loved to talk of Devon and Devon folk.

Mathilda said, "I've often wondered why Sir Walter Raleigh got all the credit of the Virginia colonies. He never went out, did he?"

"Never. Sir Walter was a courtier. He could not leave London for fear some other nobleman would become the Queen's favourite, so he sent his cousin, Sir Richard Grenville.

There was a brave nobleman, strong and courageous, with life flowing warm and adventurous in his veins. Some say he was the greatest man Devon ever produced."

"Greater than Sir Francis Drake?"

"Greater than Drake to my thinking. But Drake walked with Destiny, or Luck, or Fortune. He was a shrewd man who built for Drake. Money from Spanish ships he captured he gave to Queen Elizabeth, but he kept his full share. A pirate he was at heart, a man of mean birth. But Richard, ah, he cared nothing for riches! His mind was set on the glory of England."

"Please tell us about the brave young men who sailed with him. Were they all from Devon?"

"Devon and Cornwall for the most part. Why not put your question to John Prideaux when he comes back? His grandfather sailed with Richard Grenville."

Mathilda asked, "John Prideaux?"

Dame Margaret smiled. "Yes, miss. John Prideaux, whom you passed by without seeing a few days ago."

Mathilda's puzzled look made Sibyl laugh delightedly. Dame Margaret held up an admonishing hand. "You will remember, if you think back, that you saw a stable-boy talking to me. You passed him by as though the smell of manure were in your nostrils. This was John Prideaux, of a very old county family of the West Country, a distant connection of my own, whom Cook protected."

Mathilda's cheeks reddened. She was proud, very proud. She could not bear to be in the wrong, nor could she bear to be laughed at. "Dame Margaret, how was I to know that the stable-boy was a prince?"

"Not a prince, my dear, a son of a county family. You do not get the point. Politeness is not simply for one's equals; it is a blanket that covers all classes. One should show courtesy and kindness to one's inferiors, as well as to one's friends."

Tears came to the young maiden's eyes. Rebuke from Dame Margaret, though gentle, hurt her, touched her deeply.

Sibyl caught her sister's hand. "You didn't really look at him, Mathilda. I did. I saw him more than once in the kitchen and at the stables. He was always polite to everyone, even to old Smolkins when the others laughed. I liked him."

Mathilda said nothing. She was ashamed of her behaviour, but she would not admit it.

Dame Margaret spoke of something else. "Virginia is still a magic word in Devon, handed down from father to son. I should not be surprised to find that many of the present settlers at Jamestown are come from the West Country. I must ask the young gentleman who was here at breakfast that morning whether there are Devon and Cornish names among the people of Jamestown." She turned to Mathilda. "Young Mr. Bennett, I mean. I know his people in London. Rather engaging, I thought him." Her voice rose as though asking a question.

Sibyl spoke quickly. "He is nice, even though he is a rebel. I told him it is too bad that he is a Cromwell man."

"What did Mr. Bennett say to that?"

"He laughed, Dame Margaret, and said he was thinking it is too bad we are for the King." To cover Mathilda's continued silence, she hurried on. "Mr. Bennett looked at Mathilda all the time. Did you notice, Dame Margaret? Does it really make such a difference, one being a rebel and one a Royalist? Men and maids, I mean."

A shadow crossed Dame Margaret's serene brow. She thought of Richard, of Kathryn Audley. "I'm afraid it is sometimes a barrier, Sibyl, even when young folk love each other."

"How silly! How can a King stand between lovers? Isn't he just a man, too?"

Mathilda turned on her sister. Her eyes shone angrily. "The King is the King by divine right. How can you say such a disloyal thing?"

"Oh, oh, I didn't mean that!" Sibyl ran to Dame Margaret's side. "I am not disloyal. I love the King. I meant only that he must sometimes be as other men."

"Mathilda said words she did not mean. I am afraid she is striking out to hurt someone else, even as she has been hurt, herself."

Mathilda raised her head proudly. "I do not want to hurt anyone. I do not understand what you mean, Dame Margaret. No one has hurt me."

"I am very glad to hear you say that, Mathilda, very glad indeed. You are so young, too young to think seriously about any young man. Your father will soon make plans for a suitable marriage for you. Until then it is well for you not to allow your affections to become engaged."

"I do not want my father to make plans for me. I don't want to marry anyone. I am going to be a spinster all my life, like Queen Elizabeth."

"What nonsense! I shall tell our father that you should marry Richard or that nice Mr. Bennett," Sibyl said thoughtfully. "Mr. Bennett would be better, I think, for then I could go out to Virginia and live with you. That would be wonderful, Sis."

Mathilda turned on Sibyl, her eyes blazing. "I've a mind to box your ears." Instead, she began to cry and ran from the room.

Sibyl looked at Dame Margaret in amazement. "Why, whatever is wrong with Mathilda? What did I say to make her weep?"

"Nothing. But don't tease her, my dear. Young girls have moods, which one overlooks."

"I shan't have moods when I grow up. I don't think they're nice. They make everyone else feel uncomfortable." Sibyl sat down on the stool, took up the book from the floor and began to read.

After a time Mathilda came back into the room. Her eyes were red, and she had a little handkerchief in her hand. She kissed the back of Sibyl's neck. "I'm sorry I lost my temper, Sib. Please forgive me, Dame Margaret. I do not know why I spoke so rudely."

Dame Margaret smiled and patted the girl's outstretched hand. "Bring your lute. I have a mind to hear you sing. Your voice is lovely and sweet."

Mathilda crossed the room and touched a spring in the oak panelling. A door opened. She took out her lute and fetched a stool close to the fire, ran her fingers across the strings.

> "When (like committed linnets) I
>   With shriller throat shall sing
> The sweetness, mercy, majesty
>   And glories of my king.
> When I shall voice aloud, how good
>   He is . . ."

She paused a moment, as though trying to recall the verse, then took up the song.

> "If I have freedom in my love,
>   And in my soul am free,

> Angels alone that soar above
> Enjoy such liberty."

"That is as doleful as a Scottish Lament, Sis. Can't you think of something bright and very gay?"

Mathilda smiled, and a tinkling ripple came from the strings.

> "No tears, Celia, now shall win
>   My resolved heart to return;
> I have searched thy soul within,
>   And find naught but pride and scorn;
> I have learned thy arts, and now
>   Can disdain as much as thou."

Her voice rose a little higher, with more vigor, as she finished.

> "Some power, in my revenge, convey
>   That love to her I cast away."

A string broke with a twanging sound.

A strong masculine voice came from the doorway. "Whom will you cast away, sweet Mathilda? Not me, I hope."

"Richard!" Sibyl and Dame Margaret spoke at once. Richard strode across the room to his mother's side, dropped on one knee and kissed her hands, first one, then the other.

"My dear son—" Dame Margaret's voice trembled a little— "I am so glad, so glad! Rumours of battle filled the air. We did not know."

"No fighting yet, Mother." He rose and turned to Sibyl, who was hopping from one foot to the other in her delight. He held his arms wide. "Come, my little conspirator! An accolade for a little miss who can keep a secret."

Sibyl pouted as she slipped from his arms. "I'm not a little miss. I'm growing taller every day. Soon I'll be as high as Mathilda."

Richard kissed Mathilda's fingers lightly. "Let me get off this heavy stuff and I'll call John Prideaux. He is waiting to pay his respects to you, Mother, but he hesitates to intrude on such a charming party or to interrupt Mathilda's 'Disdain Returned.' "

"How long were you standing behind the tapestry?" Mathilda demanded, her cheeks red. "How long, sir?"

"From 'No tears, Celia.' " He sang the first line of the song. "I wonder just whom you disdain, my sweet coz?"

"Stop teasing Mathilda and fetch John Prideaux. Call the servants, Sibyl. We must have food and some ale at once." Dame Margaret rose. Sibyl thought she had dropped years of worry and sadness from her face since Richard entered the room.

He strode to the door, his spurs clanking, armour rattling. "John, John, come in. Here are three lovely women waiting to make you welcome."

John Prideaux came to the door. A different figure he was from the stable-boy, tall as Richard, slimmer, younger, showing his Norman ancestry in his olive skin and full, dark eyes. His reddish-brown hair was square-cut as a Parliamentarian's, for it had not had time to grow since he had cut it as part of his disguise. He wore the light armour and high boots of a dragoon. He crossed the room with lithe, quick movements and bowed over Dame Margaret's hand with easy grace.

Mathilda stared at him as though she had never seen him, as indeed she had not, really, seen the gentleman before, but only the stable-boy. She curtsied as he bowed low before her.

Sibyl clapped her hands joyously as she looked at him, her head cocked on one side, her lips laughing. "The cuirass becomes you well, sir," she said, remembering her manners.

"Better than the old stable jacket?"

"Yes, yes, far better. But you were nice. I wish when you were a stable-boy you had taught me to jump. I'm sure you would have been patient with my poor efforts."

"Indeed, no patience would have been needed. I've watched you. You have a light hand with a horse, and that is something no one can teach. You have an instinct."

Sibyl looked first at Dame Margaret, then at Mathilda. "See? I told you he was nice."

"Come, help me with these buckles, John." Richard was struggling to unfasten the cuirass.

"Oh, let me help," Sibyl cried. "I can do it. I know I can."

Mathilda said to John, "Perhaps you will allow me."

"Thank you. Thank you very much."

Dame Margaret watched them with eyes that saw another scene. How often, with sorrow in her heart, she had buckled on armour for Nigel before he rode off to the wars! How often she had unbuckled armour with wild joy, on his return!

. . . The last time . . . she tried to close her mind to the last time.

The clatter of steel falling to the floor brought her back to the present. Richard, free from the weight, stretched and turned his body, his arms held high above his head. "What a barbarous custom this is, this wearing heavy metal, squeezing one's frame!"

"How barbarous is war!" his mother murmured.

"There will always be wars," Richard said seriously.

"I hope there will never again be wars between our own, brother against brother, father against son. Every night I pray God that never this agony may come again. If men must fight, let it be against a foreign foe, not one's own."

Richard laid a hand on her shoulder. She had spoken with a vehemence that seemed not part of the quiet, contained woman. For a moment he had a swift vision of his mother as she was in her youth, before life had caught her and moulded her into its pattern, before life had given her wisdom.

Later, when she was in bed reading her Bible by the light of one candle, Richard came into Dame Margaret's room. He sat on the foot of the bed, as he used to do when he was a wee lad with some problem to be solved. He had lost the gay, bantering tone of his voice, and his face was serious.

"We must be off shortly," he said, and not pausing for her surprised "Oh, my son, not now!" went on: "We have a long ride before daybreak, and a long ride to follow."

"Where are you going? Why must you leave so soon?" But she knew the answer before he spoke. There would be a battle.

"When I got up with our troops near Ledbury, I encountered General Massey. I told him that Cromwell, Monk and Fleetwood had been here. He was so surprised that I knew our couriers had not reported that a platoon of Cromwell's army, with the great leaders, had criss-crossed the countryside to spy out the land, learn the temper of the people and locate the King's main army. The very fact that Cromwell himself came this way shows how anxious the Roundheads were to get sure knowledge of where the King is. General Massey could not fathom how General Monk could be here. He is supposed to be in Scotland. Are you sure, Mother, that it was General Monk?"

"Don't be foolish. Of course I am sure. Isn't George Monk a Devon man?"

The shadow of a smile crossed her son's lips, but it soon faded. "General Massey can't account for his presence here, unless he and Cromwell are continuing their arguments. We have the story from Scotland that they are not the best of friends. That is understandable—two strong, violent men, each with his own ideas of fighting a war."

Dame Margaret asked, "Did you see the King?"

"Yes, Mother." Richard got up and paced about the room into deep shadow and out into the moonlight that fell brightly through the oriel window. "I wish I hadn't seen him. Massey insisted that I must report to him. We had the devil's own time getting past the guard. No wonder. He had a wench with him, who scuttled away, rolling under the bed in an adjoining room. She was too fat and got stuck. It would have been ludicrous, if it hadn't been tragic. Here we are on the eve of what may be a decisive battle. He hunts all morning and disports himself all afternoon. A country wench she was. It would seem that there aren't enough fine ladies following our army to give him pleasure! Pardon me, Mother, but I lose confidence in a leader who hasn't the wit to know that disaster may arrive tomorrow or the day after or the day after that."

"The Stuarts are feckless folk, Richard, but somehow they exact blind loyalty from their people."

"Not any more. The Scots are deserting every day. Here, in mid-England where the King expected recruits by the thousands, Lord Derby has gained only a few hundred. The militia of our own county are overwhelmingly for Cromwell." He sat down on a stool, his hands hanging between his knees, his head bowed.

"Surely you don't expect defeat, Richard. London is for the King."

"Since when? Cromwell and his army have London and they will hold it. The people who filled the streets huzzaing for the King will do the same for Cromwell, the people's Cromwell. Let us face it, Mother; *we* are done. A new thing is rising. This is no ordinary war, like the War of the Roses, or the First Civil War. It is a revolt of the commoners, the commoners against the Stuarts' favourites. Cromwell will have Parliament supreme."

Dame Margaret watched him as he talked, now sitting on

the fire-bench, now moving restlessly about the room. A dagger in her heart was his likeness to his father in countenance and voice; now, for the first time, in thought also. She did not speak of this. No man wants to be another. "Each man his own man" is a part of masculine pride. What she said was "You are observant, my son."

"Only a listener. We have men in our platoon who straggled in from Cromwell's army while we fought in Scotland. What they say is reported to me. We are fighting a wise general, skilled in warfare, courageous and daring. He is surrounded by skilled generals. The greatest is General Monk. Monk is against Cromwell's marching to London without him. If he was here, it must have been to get permission to take his army into London. He knows he has loyal men who can hold the city—he does not want to rot in Scotland. That's what General Massey says. Then there are Harrison, Lord Fairfax, Lambert, Fleetwood, others, all trained now in Ironside's way, which is the Swedish way of battle. Rupert taught them that. From Stirling, through Carlisle, Kendal and Wigan, we have lost vitality out of our original twenty thousand men."

"Derby has recruited for you from Lancaster and Wales?"

"A handful, not a drop in the pail to take the place of the Scots who have deserted and gone home. Massey hopes some Presbyterians may be enlisted in Gloucester. I say it is a false hope."

"This is melancholy news, my son. Surely you are too pessimistic."

"Only honest, dear Mother. I face facts. The army that once numbered a full score thousand is dwindling away. The King no longer thinks of London as his certain goal. There will be a battle before many days, as I said before. In my mind I have set September third."

"Why do you set that date?"

Richard laughed a little. "I am trying to put myself in Cromwell's place. He won the battle at Dunbar on the third of September. He believes in portents and signs, in spite of his deep religious convictions. The seers have forecast that the third of September will be an important day for him three times in his life, including his death on that date. He is in a position, now, to choose his own battle-ground for a decisive engagement. Playing the seer, I foretell it will be in Worcester on the third of September."

Surprise and anxiety crowded her voice. "September third is less than a fortnight away."

"I know that, and I have grave fears for the outcome." He was silent a long time. Then he turned from the window and faced her. He looked very tall, very strong.

She thought, Youth has grown to manhood without my being aware. War has done it. War with its hatreds, its spent blood. O God, if a time would come when there would be no wars and our men could come back to their homes and the land that needs them!

"Mother, you are wise. You have the heart of a lion in your woman's frame. You must be prepared for a lasting change in England. The King does not realize what is happening. He does not hear the truth. Those under his command have grown insensibly into all license, disorder and impiety."

He came to her, sat again at her side and took her hand in his, as though to soften his words by the warm contact of his strong grasp. "Let us not underestimate our enemy. He is very resolute and crafty, and carried forward by a strength that comes from the faith that God is on his side."

"But Cromwell's troopers are decayed old serving-men, tapsters and base fellows, while ours are gentlemen's sons and persons of quality—as you are, my son. Can their spirit equal our spirit, the spirit of honour and courage born of generations of gallantry?" Dame Margaret asked the question, hoping for an answer that would bolster her confidence.

A wry smile crossed Richard's firm lips. In the flickering light of the candle, she saw a disillusioned face. "That is what *we* want to believe, Mother. But it is not the truth. All armies have some tavern tipsters, some decayed serving-men, some drunkards, some mercenaries attracted by the army shilling. The enemy's soldiers are no different, but the spirit behind them is Cromwell. It is his will to have an army like Gideon's. He has welded his men into a unit. Religion plays a strong part with them. He has inspired in them a passionate creed. They have a greater understanding than ordinary soldiers. They are not after land or glory. They believe. Do we? I doubt it. Oliver says he wants a few honest men of conscience, that he owes everything to men who are godly. He has such men, but he has also chosen fighting men. Some are rogues no doubt, but they are whole-heartedly devoted to a cause. He welcomes separatists, Anabaptists, Baptists, schismatics and wild sects of all sorts, because they all believe. They are dour Old Testament warriors come back to life. They hate all opposed to them with a bitter hatred. 'Independents' they are called, and fiercely independent they are.

"Mother, can we defeat these people who are so determined to win, who have so much to gain and nothing to lose?"

"I don't know. You are making me doubt. I was so sure . . ."

He pressed her hands. "Don't lose faith, I beg of you. We need, more than anything, faith in *our* leaders and in our cause. Let us look the thing squarely in the face. Oliver's troops resent our higher social order. They would wreck it if they could, but they are *not* misfits, for among them are young students of Cambridge and Oxford, young yeoman farmers, freeholders' sons from his own county.

"Did you hear what he said in a talk to his officers and men? 'I would rather have a plain russet-coated countryman that knows what he fights for, and loves what he knows, than that which you call a gentleman and is nothing else.' "

"But he has gentle-born captains and followers, my son. Here among our neighbours are the Harleys and the Holders. Henry Ireton is of an ancient family. There is Lord Fairfax. John Hampden was a gentleman. And Oliver Cromwell himself and his wife came from gentle families."

"And what does that mean, Mother? Surely you can't call them 'decayed.' "

"I don't know what it means unless that this infection is spreading. But you, Richard—surely you are not turning . . ."

"No fear. I am my father's son, but I do not give blindly, nor do I close my eyes to our danger. This I perceive plainly: Oliver's regiments are his family; their courage is his. He looks to their welfare, which is his first interest. They get their pay and their food. He makes them believe that he has no interest beyond their welfare and the glory of God and England."

Margaret was silent. These were new thoughts exposed to her through her son's deep concern. She had no words to express her newly arisen anxiety. After a time she asked, "What does the King do to hold his men together, to encourage loyalty to him and the Crown?"

Richard's voice was bitter. "Nothing, nothing at all. Young as he is, new in his Kingship, *he* is the Crown, like his father before him. He is absolute—all might, majesty and power."

"Richard! These are words that belong to our Blessed Lord!"

"I cannot help it. I am only trying to show you the force of two leaders. I tell you a new fighting power has been born in England. A great commander has risen and he will sweep all England again, if we do not stop him."

"Are you telling me that the battle is already lost, lost from inertia, disbelief, indifference?"

"No. No. Whatever happens, we will fight with all the courage that is in us. It is best, is it not, to know what we are fighting? Cromwell has risen slowly, but if one looks back, the rise has been steady, increasingly strong, until it is almost at flood." He took up his cloak and threw it over his shoulders. "One more battle, and we will know who marches triumphant into London."

He leaned over and kissed her brow. She put her arms about his neck. "God with you, my son! In victory or in defeat, whichever God wills, you will stand strong and faithful, as your father did at Naseby."

He was gone. She thought of Nigel and the words he had said when he bade her farewell the last time: "Let the break be swift, dear one, swift and clean as the blade of a man's sword. No looking back, only forward to what the future holds." For him, her husband, and for her first-born son, the future had held death, but death in courage and honour.

CHAPTER 6

Richard Reports to the King

RIDING in a cuirass for six hours over rough and rutty roads was difficult even for a good horseman. John Prideaux was as uncomfortable as any tyro. His armour was a misfit. The back-plates had been forged for a broader, longer-backed man, and they rubbed a raw place. The breast-plates were too small and pinched his sides if he leaned in his saddle. The long jack-boots were heavy, so loose that they rubbed heel and toe. John had been wearing a stable-boy's leather breeks and loose, comfortable jerkin. He suffered under the weight of a dragoon's equipment. Being a soldier and riding to the wars was not all glory. Physical discomforts should be put aside, but they were ever present.

It had been raining for two days, and whenever they passed under overhanging trees, the water slid from his casque and dribbled down the back of his neck. But the sun came out, and the clean-washed air was pleasant to the nostrils. He found that by sitting very tall in the saddle he could avoid the side pinching of his corselet. Presently he caught the spirit of the troop who were singing a rollicking marching song. He did not know the words, but he hummed along with the others. Heigho, it was a wonderful day! The copper beeches gave the woods the look of sunshine.

John liked the old dragoon who rode with him. Thin almost to emaciation, he had the biting wit of a Devon countryman. After some conversation, John found that the fellow, whose name was Digby, came from Tiverton. He had fought in the First Civil War. Cromwell, the dragoon said, was a brave, bad man. He was a soldier, not a saint. Certainly he had not acted the saint in Ireland or Scotland, or in Devon for that matter. He had God on his lips from morning until night, yet he fought and slaughtered as cruel as any heathen or Saracen.

" 'Let God arise! Let His enemies be scattered!' That's what

Cromwell shouted above the roar of battle, and the Scots fled. I'm talking about Dunbar. He had for a watchword 'The Lord of Hosts.' Three thousand Scots were cut down that day, and ten thousand taken prisoner. I was there, and I galloped for Cockburnspath as fast as my nag would carry me, cursing myself for a fool to have gone to Scotland where I didn't belong."

The dragoon continued: "We had cut Cromwell off from England. We had two men for his one. He was in a devil of a fix, zur. We were on a hill—Doon Hill it were called. All we had to do was stay there and watch him a-twisting and a-turning. But, oh, no, the Scots dominies cried to Leslie that we must go down and smite the Sassenach hip and thigh.

"Well, it was Cromwell who did the hipping and thighing. He crept around to our right in the misty moonlight before dawn and crashed in upon us. It was fair awful, zur. We were driven back on the Foot, who weren't half awake, and all caught in a ravine with a burn in it. Cromwell hit us like a sledge-axe, he did, zur.

"That was when he shouted the words I'm telling you: 'Let God arise! Let His enemies be scattered!' While the fighting was on they say he laughed like a zany and bit his lip till the red blood spurted. But when the Scots fled—and me with them!—they say he halted his old troopers while he sang a psalm in his great roaring voice, 'O praise the Lord, all ye nations!' "

The dragoons spat disgustedly. "He might as well have sung, 'O praise Cromwell, all ye nations!' "

They rode in silence for a time, the dragoon's mind still on the Battle of Dunbar. "Leslie's army was crushed in an hour or less. Blood has gone to Cromwell's head, I tell you, young zur, blood and power. That's the man ye have to face between here and London. He has an army, he has, not tired, dispirited stragglers such as we. Look ye, the Scots are terrified by such a hazardous adventure. They're peeling off, every mile we march. And our English Presbyterians, well, they've heeded no warning that the King is approaching. They'll not join us."

"You think we are in bad case, Digby?"

"Aye, desperate, zur, most desperate. Have ye not heard that Oliver ordered Colonel Lilburne to hang onto our rear and harass our fagged men?"

John asked, "Digby, how do you know so much of what goes on?"

"I? Well, zur, my ears be very long and my mouth shut, save to the right ones. When I sit in the tavern, I listen to country-folk. I'm a countryman my own self. Then I stay close to our captain. He knows as much as most." He nodded toward the front of the line where Richard Monington rode. "If some of them listened to countrymen as our captain does, they wouldn't make mistakes, like taking the Worcester Road."

"Which road would you take?"

"I'd take a track through the hills to the Marches and Wales and turn to the sea, that I would. I'd keep away from the Severn. But the great one thinks of London, and only London. And to get there he thinks to find the most followers in the Severn Valley, like his father in the first war."

The troop entered Ledbury, clattered over the cobbles through Butchers Lane. They found a great body of troops around the Market House, overflowing into Church Lane. A press of men stood in each side street that bisected High. Women and children leaned from the windows of the many-gabled, timbered, black and white houses. Country-folk were gathered at the Feathers and the ancient Tabard Inn, and the men left their tankards of ale on the worn oak tables to join the throng of onlookers in the streets. For the most part they were silent, with blank, unreadable faces.

On the hill at the end of High Street stood Lord Biddulph's great mansion, which had housed the dashing Prince Rupert and his officers during the Battle of Ledbury in '45. Here were gathered the townspeople who were declared Royalists. They welcomed the King's men with joy. But they were not many. The market-day crowd of countryfolk was as absorbed in the business of buying and selling as though war were a thousand miles away.

"We seem to be among Parliament people," John Prideaux said to Richard, who had joined him when they dismounted at Biddulph Park.

"Not necessarily. Our people are cautious. They will wait to see which side wins. Most of them are not firm for Parliament, but they resent a Scottish army that comes invading England, even if the King leads it."

Richard threw the reins to Digby. "Mr. Prideaux has been made a cornet. You are to ride with him and instruct him about the roads and paths. We rest here for an hour, then take the short path to Estnor, where the King rests. You understand which path?"

The dragoon saluted. "Yes, zur, through the Conygree woods and Deadyman's Thorn."

"Yes. You will rest at Home Farm near Castleditch. You know the place?"

"Yes, zur, that I do. I was there when Cromwell's army fired down on Estnor in '44 and surrounded Castleditch. They shot their cannon into the house time a'ter time, but they didn't ha' enough men to cross the moat. The family escaped that night. Colonel Birch, he took the place, but the King's men came down on the Roundheads next day and made them all prisoners. That's when I joined the King's army. That's how well I know the countryside."

Richard interrupted the garrulous flow. "Good! We need men who know the old paths and the countryside." He turned to Prideaux. "John, you will have a detail. Digby will be your guide. One hour's rest for men and horses, then on to Estnor for the night."

John saluted. "Yes, sir."

After Richard Monington rode away, Digby addressed John Prideaux. "An hour is sixty minutes, zur. Five minutes to tether the horses and let them eat grass, five minutes to groom, five minutes to walk to an inn, five minutes to return —twenty in all, zur. That leaves out of sixty, forty full minutes when a man can seat himself at a tavern table and have his pint or two." His bright, sharp eyes rested on John. "Forty minutes," he repeated.

Cornet Prideaux' eyes had a hint of laughter in them, but his expression was solemn. "Is this a traditional procedure, Digby?"

"That it is, zur, traditional. Cider or ale. A man rides more cheerful for a bit of rest and a swallow. The captain has already distributed Ledbury tokens to give to the innkeeper."

John watched the men walk down the hill, swaggering a little as became dragoons before gaping country-folk. Some were singing a local song, "Content and good cheese are the comforts of Herefordshire." By contrast the Scots were quiet, marching two and two. Children ran after them, but not too close. Did not the Scots grab little children and carry them away? Some headed for the Old Talbot, where Prince Rupert was said to have had a brush with a party of Cromwell's men four years past. Some stopped at the Vine brewery, and others walked down to the Royal Oak in the south end, while the officers forgathered at the Feathers and stabled their horses in the coaching yard.

Richard, having seen that his men were cared for, made his way up Church Lane. It was so narrow that one could almost touch the houses on either side. Opposite the church he met General Massey and his aide. They had come from the old Norman church. Richard saluted and stood aside to allow them to pass by. He thought the general's face showed worry. He was not so sanguine as some of the others who surrounded the King. As Richard entered the church, bells sounded the hour of five.

He walked through the church and entered St. Kathryn's Chapel. The old tumult stirred within him as he knelt in the chantry dedicated to the worship of another Kathryn Audley. A saint she was, the older Kathryn, who had lived in the days of the second Edward. No saint was the Kathryn of his devotion.

His attention was caught by the figures of Edward Skynner, his hatted wife and their eleven small children, sculptured in alabaster on a tomb.

Something within him stirred at the thought of a man and woman who might now in this year of disgrace 1651 have given eleven children to the world. What would happen to them? What would the future hold in store for the children, born into a new world in which there might be no King on his throne, no grace, no pageantry, only dull, drab, uneasy living without gaiety and laughter?

Richard believed in God the Father who made the world, and in His only begotten son Jesus Christ. The creed of his fathers was born in him as deep-rooted as his love of land. But his beliefs gave time for gaiety in life. Cromwell, without a doubt, was a man of deep religious fervour, a Christian, but he was as dour as a Scot. Must love of God be a belief that saw no good in pleasure or love of life? Was love something not of the soul and the spirit, but solely an act to reproduce young?

Did the strong emotion between lovers consist of nothing of the soul, of the ecstatic poetry of the earth in her young beauty in the spring, or her more mature beauty in the autumn? Without this beauty was love between man and woman more than the mating of animals? The thought brought disgust. He wanted to believe that the irresponsible gaiety of the young King and his Court had back of it a healthy joyousness that came from untroubled spirits.

He sat down in one of the miserere seats, for it suited his mood. He leaned forward, his face in his hands. How had these thoughts found lodgement in his mind? For a long time he sat, his lithe strong body without movement. One image was in his mind—Kathryn, beautiful Kathryn Audley, so proud in her cool beauty, as cool, as chaste, as the sculptured figures on the alabaster tomb. He remembered, then, something else: the swift touch of her lips against his, a brief moment filled with passionate questing, the soft intake of her breath, the yielding of her body against his.

The blood beat strongly against his temples when he thought of the long kiss in the darkened mystery of the Lady's Bower. She had been his, for an instant, but he lacked the power to hold her. By Gad, he would not give her up, ever! "The devil is in me," he mumbled. He got to his feet slowly. "The devil himself gives me these thoughts even in the sanctuary of church."

He walked slowly down the aisle. As he neared the ancient effigy of the ecclesiastic he saw dimly in the dusk the kneeling figure of a woman, wrapped in a dark cloak, her hair covered with a hood. Her head was bowed, her face obscured. She was as motionless as the black marble statue. Timeless and still, she might be the symbol of all women at God's altar, praying for husband or son or lover, caught in the turmoil and death-struggle of war. As he watched her from the shadows, a feeling of the hopelessness of the contest came depressingly over him.

The woman rose, a quiet, fluid movement of a shadow seeking other shadows.

A new feeling came to him, mystic and strange. He thought of the old tales in which Saint Kathryn had appeared to a few devout in times of danger and stress. Out of her tomb, made for her centuries ago, she came to aid the people of Ledbury. Their own patron saint, she watched over them. The figure which had moved deep into the shadows of the altar turned. The light from a window fell on her profile, white as the alabaster. The bells sounded, St. Kathryn's bells. Did she make a sign of benediction, or was it the wavering altar lights that flickered?

He stood, powerless to move, awed by a benign presence. After a time he left the church and walked through the churchyard, where once men of Prince Rupert's Royal army had engaged and defeated the Parliamentarians, and so cleared Ledbury of the enemy. Since that not so distant day Cromwell had learned much and won many battles. Now the Cavaliers had no daring Prince Rupert to lead them.

At the foot of Church Lane he encountered dragoons walking up High Street toward the encampment at Biddulph Park. A group of Highland Scots, led by a piper, were singing a lament.

> "Why does your brand sae drap wi' bluid,
> Edward, Edward?"

Richard moved along the rough cobbles. A dirge fitted his mood. He must throw off depression. Battles were not won by men without hope. Victory came with confidence, was snatched by soldiers who believed that they fought a holy war, backed by a righteous cause.

At the entrance of the park he encountered John Prideaux already mounted. Digby led up Richard's horse. Part of his company took the Worcester Road, a lieutenant leading. He himself determined to ride direct to Estnor, with Digby to show the way by the old track.

The King held Court at Estnor. Twenty or more Court ladies, wives of officers, followed the army, enlivening the dull days of waiting. Richard Monington stood in a doorway that overlooked an inner grassy court-yard, and watched the gay dancing. Carefree they were, laughing as they circled first one way then the other in a lively contradance. Broad silken skirts of blue and yellow and scarlet fluttered and swirled to the turning. Officers in long hosen and trunks, with velvet tunics of various colours, caught and held his attention. These merry insouciant people gave little heed to the gravity of tomorrow. Three musicians sat on a stone bench under the leaded window of the timbered house, a house ancient, weathered, as sturdy as English oak and strong fabric could make it.

As Richard advanced beyond the corner and stood beneath a tree, he saw the King. Charles was seated near the archway that led to an outer court. He alone wore black, sombre and funereal. Near him stood as a lovely young girl, wearing a silk gown the colour of the daffodils of the spring fields. An old woman, in a blue dress over a frothy lace petticoat, and three gentlemen lounged, carelessly near. Richard recognized the heavy auburn head of the Duke of Lauderdale. The others he did not know. A footman in livery placed a small table at the King's side, another brought silver tankards, while a third poured wine into silver goblets.

No man wore the accoutrements of the King's army. It would almost seem that by changing their habits they had determined to cast aside all thought of war and the danger that surrounded them.

Two women strolled past him, casting curious glances at the tall, grave-faced young man in worn corselet, holding his battered casque. In clear, high voices they gossiped of the hunt and the King's pleasure in being in at the kill. Making no effort to lower her voice, the tall woman with taffy-coloured hair said to her companion, "A dour young gentleman! Is he a Scot?"

The other laughed. "Mayhap, but how handsome! I wonder who he can be, coming to the festival in dragoon boots and shabby armour."

"No doubt he is an uninvited guest, unaware that the King holds revel tonight, before he banquets in the castle yonder."

Richard felt the blood rising to his bronzed face. He was of a mind to back out the door and make his way to the camp. But the King had sent a summons to appear, so he must stand waiting until he was seen, recognized and asked to come forward. Waiting, Richard had time to study the King. He had the same look of discouragement he had worn in Scotland when he was overtaken at South Esk, wearied and very fearful—the night when he had said in great despair, "I must repent, too, that ever I was born."

Not much older than he himself was, Charles II now appeared to Richard a desperate and hunted boy, with no way to turn that would not lead to disaster. All Richard Monington's heart and loyalty went out to his King. Whatever came, he would be loyal to the end. Right or wrong, in glory or defeat, Charles would have his soul's devotion.

If only after Naseby Montrose had been victorious in winning back Scotland for the King, all would have been well, and the second Stuart King of England seated firmly on the throne. Instead he was in his martyr's grave, and . . .

In spite of the vapid and stupid frivolities about him, Charles II was not vapid or stupid. He was the wiliest of men. But he must be weary of the eternal admonitions of his generals. He must be heartsick over the failure of Derby and Massey to build up his army. Two hundred miles of marching in two weeks, and no beacons flaring along the march to bring encouragement, no drums or trumpets sounding to welcome him!

The only time Richard had heard the King laugh on the long way was when a soldier got his head jammed in a churn. Then he had laughed until the tears ran down his thin cheeks.

Many a Briton felt that Charles was more French than English or Scot. A pleasure-loving boy, the country people declared him. He would never satisfy the middle-class folk. Yet he had the charm of the Stuarts and captured the loyalty of many who disapproved his French ways. At the moment he was not the gay French Charles, but the sombre Scot.

The little crowd about him moved away, all save the Duke of Lauderdale, whose countenance was as sober as the King's. After a time Charles raised his eyes. He recognized Richard, standing alone, apart from the gay revellers. He spoke a word to a page, who came to Richard. "Sir, His Majesty will speak with you. Will you step forward?"

Half the company turned to look as Richard strode across the court, wondering who he was to be summoned into the presence. He knelt and kissed Charles's hand.

"You are welcome, Richard Monington. Sir Edward Massey has told me that you have been through the countryside. Have you raised an army of loyal Herefordshire men for me?"

"Alas, Sire, no."

The King turned to Lauderdale. "Why did my generals and my ministers not warn me? Why did they tell me that all the country-folk from the Border to Gloucestershire would rally to our banner? Derby promised me an army. Now he reports a few hundred." He glared at the unfortunate Lauderdale. "What is wrong? I am a king, yet not a king. Being crowned at Scone does not make me King of England." He spoke bitterly. "No Stuart is a king while that arch-villain Oliver Cromwell lives."

"Your Majesty must not be impatient. It takes time . . . patience."

"Must I always be on the run, no better than a fox seeking covert before the baying hounds?"

Lauderdale did not answer for a moment. His large heavy-featured face gave no encouragement, although his words were soothing. "Sire, at present you are not the fox. Oliver is far behind us on the east side of the Midlands."

Richard started to speak, then held his peace.

Charles gave him swift scrutiny. "Speak up, Monington! Speak up! That is the trouble—no one tells me what is going on. I am not a child. I can stand the truth as well as my sainted father could."

Richard said, "Sire, Cromwell was on the west side four nights ago."

Lauderdale turned to him quickly, angrily. "That is not so. I have read a dispatch that has just come into camp which says he is far to the north-east."

"My lord, I saw Cromwell with my own eyes. He stayed the night at my own home, Coddington Manor. He came with his generals, Fleetwood and Monk, and a small guard. They commandeered my house, killed sheep and cattle. He demanded lodging of my mother late one evening and departed ere daybreak."

The King leaned forward, his face alive with interest. "How does it happen that you are not a prisoner?"

"Sire, I was for a time not Richard Monington, but first Silly Dick, a half-wit stable-boy, and then Willie his brother, a poacher, whom his men captured and brought before the general."

The King's interest was lively. "Tell us the story, sir. It would pleasure me to hear how the wily Oliver has been outwitted by a half-wit stable-boy and poacher combined."

Richard told the story. The King and Lauderdale listened. Presently the King laughed aloud and slapped his knee. "Excellent! Excellent, my good Richard! We are pleased to have such a tale to brighten our dull spirits." Then he said, "We would be pleased to compliment your lady mother, and the little girl who showed such wit and daring." His eyes measured Richard from head to foot. "You are over-long to rest in a dovecote, my good Captain, over-long."

"Sire, surely no legs were as cramped as mine, but they unlimbered in time to serve the generals, and my ears were long to listen to their plans. General Massey has the information, Sire."

The King nodded. He rose from his chair and stood for a moment, watching the merry-makers. Their song rang out, airy and blithesome:

> "Come, merry men and lassies gay,
> Dance the laggard hours away.
> War and battles are far away.
> Come, merry men and lassies gay."

A frown furrowed his smooth brow. His large dark eyes held smouldering fire. He thrust out his lower lip, a habit he had when stubborn anger came over him. "Come, Lauderdale, let us go into my cabinet. This young man should tell us just what he thinks our enemy is planning, while we study the maps. You believe he is ready to give battle?"

"Sire, I am sure of that—and at a place of his choosing."

The King led the way through the timbered arch that led to the old part of the castle where he had lodgement. General Massey joined them with two of his aides. They unrolled maps and placed them on a long stretcher table.

The King sat down and motioned Richard to his side. "Please explain. Show me the spot where we are; where you believe Cromwell to be. Do you know the countryside, sir?"

"From the Marches east like the palm of my hand."

"Where is Cromwell then?"

"Sire, his armies are moving down toward the opposite side of the Severn. See—this is our route from Scotland, the western route—Carlisle, Kendal, Wigan, Warrington, and so here. The Roundheads took the eastern road. What Silly Dick picked up at Coddington Manor is this: Cromwell has ordered a general concentration at Warwick. By now it must almost have been effected. Lambert, Harrison, Lord Grey of Groby, Desborough, all are joining him there. At Warwick he is across our path to London, but he does not mean to wait for us.

"Fleetwood will report to him from Banbury, where, General Massey tells me, he has assembled a large Midland contingent." Richard turned to Massey, who nodded. "Preceded by Lambert, Fleetwood will march west. It is these forces we will encounter first."

General Massey raised his tired eyes from the map. His face was drawn and thin. He could not keep his desperate weariness from creeping into his voice. "I think you are right, Monington. But Lambert and Fleetwood are on the east side of the Severn and we are on the west side, and the river will lie between us."

"The river has bridges, General. Can't we hold them at the bridges?" the King asked.

"Sire, we can hold the bridgeheads. We can entrench at Worcester on the east bank and dispose the rest of our army south of the city on the west side in a strong position."

A merry-eyed young woman with a mass of corn-coloured hair came to the doorway, her flame-red gown making sunshine against the dark oak panelling of the room. She was a pleasing contrast to the blowzy wench of yesterday. She stood quietly, looking at the King.

He raised his eyes from the maps. "Ah, Dierdre, my lovely, do I see an invitation in your bright eyes and pouting red lips?"

"As Your Majesty desires."

The King pushed his chair from the table and stood up. "I have had enough of maps and battle plans. Let us go to our city of Worcester and defend ourselves there." He turned to Richard. "Good lad, we thank you for what you have told us of our enemy's intent. When I am King, and so crowned at St. James's, I shall appoint you Governor of Virginia."

Richard bent his knee. "I ask nothing of Your Majesty but the life of a countryman at my own manor-house at Coddington."

"Tut, tut! Governorship of Virginia is not too bad. At least Sir William Berkeley finds it good enough. I hear he lives like a king at a plantation called Green Spring—quite royal, so Sir John Berkeley informs me." He addressed General Massey. "Pray where is Sir John Berkeley? I thought he was to join use with his brave men of Somerset, his Presbyterians of Gloucester. Why does he not come? Lauderdale, you told me that the Severn Valley and the Marches and Wales would yield men at the beating of our drums. We have beaten our drums loudly from Scotland to Worcester, but no one hears. Where is Sir John Berkeley? Has he too deserted us?"

"He is on the way, Sire," General Massey said in some confusion.

The King stuck out his lower lip. "Always on the way, on the way. By God, I am tired of these military gentlemen who promise much and do little!"

"Sir John Berkeley is one of Your Majesty's most loyal supporters," Lauderdale rumbled, his voice over-loud in the small room. "He is the very essence of devotion, as devoted as Lord Wilmot."

"No doubt, no doubt. But Monington here has given us better service. You are loyal, are you not, young Monington?"

Richard dropped to one knee. "To the death, Sire!"

"There. You see? He is as loyal as his father was to my martyred father—to the death. At Naseby, was it not?"

"He died at Naseby, Sire, and my brother also."

"I did not know about your brother. Rise to your feet, sir. General Massey, we want young Monington near us, on our staff. We must make good use of a man who has shown undivided loyalty to our house, who is resourceful and who knows the country. We may need him if we have to flee again. Let us have him near our person."

The King walked across the room, held out his hand to the lovely girl. "Come, sweet Dierdre. I venture you will entertain us in ways more pleasing than maps and heavy talk of battles to be fought."

Silence followed the King's lightly spoken words. At the door he turned. "We do not share your melancholy thoughts, my brave gentlemen. We give you our royal oath that we shall be crowned King of the English in London town. We grow weary of running."

He lifted the girl's slender hand and tucked it under his arm. "Come, my lovely maid. You shall be my sweet companion for a pleasant hour."

The men watched the two walk down the long hall. Lauderdale spoke. "Would to God Prince Rupert were here to lead us through these dire and dangerous straits!"

"I give you amen to that!" the harassed general replied with deep fervour. "We move into Worcester to fortify the city and defend ourselves as well as may be."

"Into a trap!" Richard spoke impulsively.

"Aye, lad," said Lauderdale, "into a trap of Cromwell's choosing. I think we move near to the end. But we must not give up hope. Berkeley *may* have troops, or Lord Wilmot, though I doubt me if even they will rouse Somerset and Gloucester. General, pray be seated. While we have this lad who knows the land, let us map out a retreat from Worcester down the Severn to Bristol. There are ships at Bristol that will be under quick sail for France or Holland, or mayhap the far land of Virginia."

Outside, in the court-yard, the dancing became wilder. Lackeys passed about with flagons of Flemish wine. Faces reddened. Laughter was high and shrill. Couples broke off from the circle of the dance and slipped into the quiet darkness of the house. The King was making merry with a fair favourite—why not his Court?

But in the dark panelled room, dimly lighted by half a dozen candles, were a few men who knew that a desperate battle must be fought which might decide the fate of England. They bent over maps, planning, arguing, hoping.

"How many men have we, Massey?" the Duke asked, pushing his mop of red hair off his brow.

"At the utmost sixteen thousand weary, weary men, and if what this lad tells us is true, and Oliver is concentrating all his forces, he will have thirty thousand men against us at the lowest estimate."

"We may well wish for Rupert's cavalry. God's death, why did he go to sea?"

"Leslie will come up soon," Lauderdale said. "Show me the crossings of the rivers, Monington."

Richard pointed to the map. "The Severn here, at Upton, and the Teme at Powick. If Lambert and Fleetwood swing around from Banbury, they may make a crossing at either bridge."

"By God, they won't! We will defend the bridges to the last man."

They were interrupted by the arrival of a dispatch rider with a message from General Massey. The general held the paper to a candle. "Gentlemen, Harrison and Grey are already with Cromwell. Lambert will join the main army by tomorrow. We will march tonight. Once in Worcester we can fortify ourselves well and stand a siege in a strong position."

"Thank God!" Lauderdale said. "Let the King divert himself with a wench if he will. Eight months a king . . . but he will be no more than a king of the May, such as boys crown with flowers and rushes. Leave a guard for him, General Massey. We will push on to Worcester with all haste. Come, Monington. We need you to guide us."

"Sir, I will send dragoons with you who know every track through the hills."

General Massey was on his feet. "The main army will march by the Worcester Road, but we must make more speed." He addressed Richard. "Will you guide us the shortest way, sir?"

"The ancient track through the Malvern Hills is safe and swift, General Massey. The Romans used it once."

"Then let it be by the Roman way that we travel tonight. Will Your Lordship precede us?"

The Duke of Lauderdale nodded and walked slowly from the room. General Massey followed. The aides gathered up the maps. Richard went out with them. In the outer court the music grew loud and discordant.

> "Come merry men and lassies gay,
> Dance the laggard hours away.
> War and battles are far away.
> Come, merry men and lassies gay."

CHAPTER 7

Star-Crossed Lovers

THE waiting was almost unendurable. The country-folk about Coddington Manor went no longer to the field but gathered at cross-roads, small inns or coaching taverns, eager to hear the latest word of the armies.

Small skirmishes between scouting parties or foragers were daily occurrences along the Ledden, the Wye and the Teme. Rumours flew about like falling leaves.

The kitchen at Coddington Manor buzzed from morning until evening. The stable, the dairy, the gardener's cottage were other centres from which the stories widened and spread. Unrest dwelt over the house like an evil cloud blanketing the sky.

Sibyl ran from the kitchen to great hall, telling each tale she heard, unintentionally adding to the burden of anxiety that weighed on Dame Margaret. No word had come from her son. Every hour of the day she hoped someone would come who had seen Richard, or who carried a message that would tell of his safety. Her mother's heart was torn with anxiety.

The night brought intensified worry and unquiet dreams. The scratching of a bough against a window, the howling of a dog, the sharp bark of a fox became signals of deep meaning. She found herself sitting up in the great bed, listening, listening for a footstep, for the thud of a horse's hoofs in the court-yard, for the sound of a beloved voice.

In her mind she knew there would be no message from her son, but her heart yearned for the impossible. So many things had been left unsaid. It was always like that. Her very nature forbade the display of any strong emotion. All feeling lay buried within her. She thought it had died when her husband rode away for the last time, rode away to fight for another Charles of the Stuart clan. She had smiled when he turned to wave his last farewell, and she had waved gaily in answer, but her heart was heavy. When the great dogs roamed through the hall she knew he was to die, those ghostly dogs which showed themselves only to foretell disaster. She had seen them plainly the night before the great Battle of Naseby.

And now in the uncertain morning light from her window she saw them again. Cook came running to stand near her. She did not speak of what she and Graves had seen, but Dame Margaret knew. "I have seen them also, Ellie, the ghostly dogs."

"Death! Death!" Ellie whispered.

"Perhaps it is the blood of battle they snuff so eagerly, but I have no fear. It will not be Richard." Dame Margaret spoke strongly, without a tremor. "Say nothing to anyone and tell Graves to hold his peace."

"Madam, you are brave, and it ill becomes me to shiver along my spin. 'Tis not like seeing a Devon ghost, now is it? They're just prowling dogs lifting their noses to catch the wind. They can't be evil devils. I'll run and brew you a cup of tea and fetch your breakfast, and send the young ladies to you to keep you company."

"Thank you, Ellie."

The morning wore on. In the great room Dame Margaret took up her worsteds and swung the frame so that the light through the oriel window would fall on the tapestry. Let her hands be busy, so she would not think or let her too vivid imagination have its way . . . stitch the bright worsted in and out of the canvas—dark green for the trees in the background, lighter green for the shubbery, tender grass-green and the yellow of sunlight for a daffodil carpet beneath the feet of the riders in armour.

Sibyl burst into the room, her hair tumbled, her cheeks pink with excitement. "I've just come from the road. Soldiers are marching along. They asked Biggor the way to the Worcester Road. They were in haste, at the double. Biggor says they are Welshmen, on the way to battle. Indeed they must make haste or they won't reach the battle-ground in time to help the King."

"Sit down, Sibyl, and compose yourself. Take your kerchief and wipe the drops from your forehead. Your face is very red."

"I ran," the girl said. "I ran to tell you. Everyone says the battle will come tomorrow."

"Do not say 'everyone says.' That is an exaggeration. Who says the battle will be tomorrow? Biggor?"

"Yes, Dame Margaret. He had talked with men at the Feathers and the Talbot when he went to early market. Everyone says . . ." She paused. "Well, anyway some men have said there would be a battle."

"We've heard the same thing every day for a week, Sibyl. Do not be disturbed by rumours. When a battle is fought we will know about it soon enough—too soon. Sit down, fold your hands and compose yourself. How often must I tell you that a lady doesn't fidget!"

Sibyl sat on a stool and folded her hands demurely, her little soft shoes, side by side, peeping out from her full blue skirts of linsey-woolsey. "Dame Margaret, I'd rather be a boy. A boy doesn't have to sit thus, and he can run and climb trees and listen for the first cuckoo, and try to find which bird's nest it has taken this year, and . . ." She waved her arms about. "The whole world is a boy's. But a girl . . ." She sighed audibly.

A slow, reminiscent smile came over Dame Margaret's lips. "But you are a girl, so think of the pleasant things a girl can do."

"I can't think of a thing that's really fun, except to ride a pony. When I'm married, I'll have all boys—not a single girl."

"Boys to send to war?" Dame Margaret's voice was harsh.

Before she finished the door opened and Mathilda came in. "Guests have just ridden into the court-yard, Dame Margaret—Kathryn and Roland Audley and Mr. Bennett. Shall I bring them in here, or into the morning room?"

"Ask Graves to fetch them in here. I can't think what Kathryn is doing, roaming about the countryside with every road swarming with soldiers."

Kathryn Audley crossed the room, the two men behind her. She wore a Lincoln green habit of velvet, and her lovely pale gold hair was braided and wrapped around her small proud head. She made a little curtsy to Dame Margaret and waved her escorts away. "Why don't you walk in the garden with Mathilda and Sibyl? I wish to have a talk with Dame Margaret, a little secret talk." She gave Stephen Bennett a swift, brilliant smile.

Mathilda's face clouded. She resented Kathryn's airy dismissal. She looked at Dame Margaret, who nodded slightly. "Yes, do walk in the garden and show these young gentlemen our blooming roses."

Stephen Bennett did not disguise his pleasure at the arrangement. He bowed before Mathilda. "If you will be so gracious."

Sibyl caught Roland's hand. "Come with me, do. I want to show you a marsh-hen's nest down by the lily pond. Don't you think birds' nests much more fascinating than a rose tree with one red rose?"

"Why one red rose? Why not a dozen? Or perhaps Coddington Manor is obliged to offer one red rose to the Sovereign as a tribute." Roland followed her through the French window to the terrace.

Sibyl laughed. "I don't know all the customs of this manor. You know, we—Mathilda and I—live in Gloucestershire when we are not with our father in London. Do you like Gloucestershire, sir?"

"Very much. I go to Bristol quite often. We raise wool, and Bristol is our market."

"How very nice! Perhaps you will visit us at the Abbey. It is not ten miles from your market city. Come, let us walk very, very quietly. Perhaps we will see the hen on its nest."

There was a laugh in the brown-haired youth's voice. "Isn't it late in the season for a marsh-hen to sit on her eggs? Or perhaps you have late hatchings, as you have late blooming."

"Now you are laughing at me. Come, you will see."

In the great room Kathryn sat on a stool at Dame Margaret's feet. She was not unaware of the picture she made. Her pale blond hair was a contrast to the older woman's silver head. She assumed a serious expression as she gazed up at Dame Margaret, her blue eyes childlike and innocent. She was troubled a little, but not too much—certainly not enough to cause even a tiny wrinkle on her smooth white forehead. "If I could only be as calm as you are, dear Dame Margaret, calm and detached, and so full of wisdom!"

Margaret allowed a smile to come to her lips, but her thought was, *She wants something of me.* "Age helps, my dear. One should acquire some poise with the years."

"I am so troubled, so very troubled. What does one do when three men speak of marriage?"

"One chooses the best man, surely."

"But how can one be sure which one will be the best chance in the end? A girl has so little to guide her . . . a girl without a mother."

"Lady Harley has been like a mother to you, Kathryn."

The girl shrugged her shoulders. "Yes, I know. But I do not feel her wisdom as I feel yours. She is very positive and forthright, but that is not everything. One must have worldly experience to know the best thing to do. Marriage is a very serious matter, isn't it?"

"Very. How old are you, Kathryn?"

"Twenty, Dame Margaret." Her red lips smiled. "Old enough to know my own mind, I suppose."

"It is not a question of knowing your mind, Kathryn. Young people have little judgment in such things. I should think a marriage for you should be in the hands of Sir Robert."

"Sir Robert is much too interested in affairs in London to think of his ward. Besides, we—Roland and I—are quite independent. Although our fortunes are not large, I have, as you know, Audley House and the land that joins Coddington Manor on the north."

"Yes, I know." Margaret spoke dryly. She thought, This is what she came for, to know what Richard's inheritance will be.

"Not such broad lands as yours, dear Dame Margaret, but not too small in acres and meadows. Then there is the Virginia land."

"Virginia land? Do you hold land in Virginia?"

"My father had a grant from King James on the north side of the James River. They say it is very fertile. There are tobacco and orchards. My brother Roland talks of nothing but Virginia. Virginia is in the blood of all these young men."

Dame Margaret said slowly, "I was not aware of this trend. I am far away from the world, here at the manor."

"But you are always of the world—the great world of London, I mean."

"There is no great world, Kathryn. That died when the martyred King died. There is no elegance, no distinction, no beauty. . . ." She paused, watching the changing expression on Kathryn's face.

The younger woman's voice vibrated. "But there will be

when Oliver is king. That is why I can't make up my mind whether to marry Nicholas Holder or Stephen Bennett and go to Virginia, or to wait. Maybe at Oliver's Court there will be others." She settled back, her long fair hands clasped about her knees. "I do not want to be a spinster. Nicholas is rather nice, you know. He is to have an appointment in Virginia, at Jamestown the capital, perhaps. Jamestown will not have a fabulous Court, even with Sir William Berkeley the governor. Sir William may not be governor of Virginia for any great time."

She got to her feet and moved idly about the room. Margaret thought, Whatever she came here to say has not been said. She was silent, waiting.

After a time Kathryn said, "Do you think a man and a maid can truly love if one be for the King and the other for Parliament?"

Margaret smiled. "I would recommend you to Mr. Shakespeare. He has written a story of crossed lovers."

"You mean *Romeo and Juliet*? But they died!"

"They loved also, a love that transcended conditions and the enmity of their houses. If one really loves . . ." Margaret did not finish the sentence.

Kathryn was not listening. She pleated and unpleated the hem of her riding skirt with her white fingers, thinking of her own problems. "Richard would never give up his King." Her voice was low.

Margaret sat very still. This was what Kathryn came for— to ask me to intercede for her. That I will not do, now or ever. Richard is his own man, quite strong enough to know his own mind.

Kathryn pressed close to her knee, looking up at Margaret with the limpid eyes of a child. "I asked him to. I told him that the King was only a May king, with no crown. Cromwell has the power, and the people of England are with him. Why not give up the Frenchman and cling to the man who is England?"

"What did Richard reply, Kathryn?"

Her cheeks had a slight flush. The blue of her eyes changed. Margaret thought, She seems soft and pliable, but she has a hard core within her. She would not yield. She must have her way. And Richard will not yield.

Kathryn pouted a little, her lips drawn close. "Richard said it was not I who spoke, but my guardian Sir Robert. I was very angry. I said things I should not have said. Tell me what to do, Dame Margaret. He is so stubborn." There was a silence. Margaret pondered what to say. Kathryn did not notice her companion's hesitation. "I want to make him see that Oliver Cromwell is the ruler of England. It is most dangerous to cling to King Charles. It puts one in jeopardy, and one's property, dearest Dame Margaret. Advise me how to carry conviction in my words, so that Richard may see Cromwell as he is, a great soldier, so bold, yet in all cautious, having first care for the welfare of his men. The King's army cannot defeat him. He is a master of strategy, although he is a country gentleman. He understands the people. He is a statesman as well as a general. Some say he is like William the Silent, or perhaps another Gustavus. He will be King of England."

The girl leaned forward, her face alive with almost fanatical fire. Her eyes lost their look of round innocence. They shone with fervour. Margaret was astounded at such zeal. For the moment she was almost convinced that there was truth behind what the girl said, but her face did not show her inner thoughts.

She said, "Is this you speaking, or is it your guardian Sir Robert Harley?"

A slow flush rose to the girl's clear blond skin. "Why do you say that, Dame Margaret? Do you think it unbecoming that a young maid should turn her thoughts to the welfare of her country? The Stuarts have twice brought civil war to us and now an invasion. They do not know our people. Oliver knows us as he knows himself. Richard will not think of him as he is, Oliver Cromwell, a man whose heart is pure and unselfish, who walks close to God, without ambition for himself, only for the good of our dear country. He takes up the sword because he must, because God has chosen him to lead England. He keeps his army disciplined, while the Royalist army is a disgrace."

"Kathryn, what are you saying?"

"Do you not know what your own man, Sir Philip Brooke, said about the Royalist army? He told my guardian that the sins of the men were drinking and wenching."

"Kathryn! How can you use such a word?" Dame Margaret spoke with unaccustomed sharpness.

"I am sorry, Dame Margaret. I do not mean to shock you. I tell you only what your own officers say. Please do not think me rude or unmaidenly. I only want you to understand what is happening to us."

"I know well enough what is happening. The old England is dying. When Briton fights Briton, it is the wrath of God. I cannot see Cromwell as you see him. I believe with Marvell, that to cast the Kingdom into a new mould is to ruin the great work of time. I do not want to see the lovelocks and long plumes of the Cavaliers, or the badges and round hats of the Parliament men, or the sea-green ribbands of the Levellers. Among them they have torn to shreds the land I love.

"If you think I sit here at Coddington Manor without knowledge of what goes on, you are mistaken. The old King is removed, and the old lords follow. What happens then? We will not have the republic which they talk about so glibly, modelled after Plato, or after a new pattern of Cromwell. Once he gets the power, Oliver Cromwell will rule more absolutely than any Tudor or Stuart King, my girl. All Europe, and the New World too, were horrified at the first Charles's death. Our enemies take advantage. Russia imprisons our merchants. Scandinavia and the other European countries preach from their pulpits against the ignoble regicides.

"Oliver is sunk to his ears in his ambitions. He raises his voice to his Maker, calls on his God to stand by his side—for the good of England? No! For the good of Oliver and his family, his generals and all the relatives he has put in Parliament. It is well known in London that he has said, 'Break them, or they will break you.' I tell you, my child, that the guilt of blood lies on the head of this man Cromwell. His crimes in Ireland show that."

Margaret leaned forward and put her hand on Kathryn's shoulder. "My dear, I have underrated you, but you must listen to both sides before you form your opinions. In Sir Robert's house you will hear only praise of Cromwell. But bear this in mind, Kathryn: Oliver Cromwell, and no one else, keeps the long peace of Elizabeth broken."

Kathryn's shoulders dropped. Her eyes, fixed on Dame Margaret, showed despair and misery. "Richard will

never give up, either," she whispered. "Never." She got to
her feet slowly as the young people came into the room.

Mathilda's hair was flying, her cheeks glowing. Stephen
Bennett was at her elbow. Sibyl and Roland followed. Sibyl
ran to her hostess and laid a red rose in her lap. "The gardener
said it was the last one, Dame Margaret. Isn't it beautiful!"

Dame Margaret lifted it to her face. The delicate fragrance
brought to her, with overwhelming poignancy, the picture of
her husband bending over her, a red rose in his hand. She
heard his dear voice as his lips brushed her cheek. "It is the
last rose, beloved. . . ."

Kathryn was on her feet. To Roland she said, "We must be
riding on, dear brother. I am afraid I have wearied Dame
Margaret."

The men made their adieux to Dame Margaret. Stephen
lingered over the simple act of kissing Mathilda's hand. Her
downward glance was shy, a little pleased as he whispered
something to her. Dame Margaret noted it and smiled to
herself. She doubted if Stephen had spoken to Kathryn of
marriage.

Kathryn stood beside Dame Margaret as the others walked
into the hall. Her face was pale. "I cannot ask you where
Richard is, but when you see him, please say to him that I
must do what Sir Robert thinks best. One cannot always see
the way clearly."

"My dear child, do not struggle against Fate. Sometimes
there are forces that move us beyond our will, and in the
end we serve our destiny. I am glad you have talked with
me, Kathryn. I hold it dear that you have spoken from your
heart today."

Kathryn bent and kissed Dame Margaret's hand. "If only
I could know! If only I had courage!" She turned away and
hurried after the others, but not before Margaret had seen
the tears in her eyes.

She loves Richard, Margaret thought as she watched them
walk across the court-yard to where the groom stood beside
the waiting horses.

She left the room and walked slowly up the curved stairs,
her long black skirts sweeping behind her. She must go to
her room and close the door against the bright chatter of
Sibyl and Mathilda. She sat down on the window-seat and
thought of Kathryn, a Kathryn she had not known before.

She wished Richard might have seen her as she was today. Dame Margaret was not concerned with her words about Oliver or her belief in his destiny. What concerned her was the depth of emotion Kathryn revealed. It troubled her. Somehow she had the feeling that the decision Kathryn was about to make would hurt her son deeply.

She thought of Bradshaw, that vile, cruel man. It was not fair to fasten his treachery upon the girl, yet . . .

Near midnight a loud knocking at the door roused Coddington Manor. Graves wrapped himself in a worn robe and made his way along the dark hall and down the back stairway to the door that opened on the court-yard. He peered out the window and saw through the downpour of rain the black shadow of a coach. A man's face was dimly visible at the coach window, but he recognized Mr. Hugh Jordan, father of the two young guests, Mathilda and Sibyl. The butler unbolted the great door.

Mr. Jordan, muffled in a travelling coat, stepped out of the coach and hurried across the intervening space, ducking his head to avoid the driving rain. "Take the coach to the stables and give the horses a good rub down," he said to the coachman. Graves he greeted with a friendly smile. "Devil of a night! Thought I wouldn't make it. Can you put me up, Graves? I don't want to disturb Dame Margaret or my daughters at this late hour."

"Sir, I think Madam is already awake, and the young ladies . . ." He did not finish the sentence. Sibyl was already half-way down the stairs; Mathilda close behind. Sibyl threw herself into her father's arms.

"My child, wait until I divest myself of this wet cloak." Jordan tossed it to Graves.

"Oh, Father, Father, where did you come from? How wonderful to see you! Father, did you ride through the army?" She clung to his arm, lifting her face to his kiss.

Mathilda curtsied. "How delightful to see you again, Father!" She was no less pleased than her more impetuous sister.

Graves led them to the great room. With the bellows he blew a flame and built up the fire. "Be seated, sir. I will make you a hot posset at once, sir." He lighted the candles.

"Thank you, Graves. It would be welcome. I've had a

devilish drive from Hereford. Raining all the way. Twice we lost the road and slid into a ditch. Both times some Scottish soldiers pulled us out."

"Soldiers?" The two girls spoke at once.

"Yes, the roads were filled with soldiers."

Graves came in, carrying a tankard of hot spiced wine. Hugh Jordan took a huge draught. He moved closer to the blazing logs. His tall spare frame bent to the warmth of the fire. "Now to bed, my girls!" he said. "Get your sleep. We are leaving in the morning, early, very early."

"Leaving? Leaving Coddington Manor and Dame Margaret?" Sibyl wailed.

"I hope to persuade Dame Margaret to go with us. It is not safe for her to stay on here. If the Parliament troops win the battle, they will overrun this country clear to the Marches."

"Where are we going, Father?" Mathilda asked the question.

"Home. Home to Gloucestershire."

"Will you stay with us?" Sibyl took his hand, snuggling close to him.

Hugh Jordan looked down at the maid, who was growing every day closer to the image of his dead wife. His thin, scholarly face was worn. His near-sighted eyes showed strain. "I saw John Berkeley two days ago. He told me it was better to have you at home than in the disputed country. My cousin Cecily will be at the Abbey when we arrive home. She is to stay with us until June."

Mathilda's face brightened. "Our aunt who lives in Virginia at Jordan's Journey?"

Sibyl broke in. "Father, the nicest young man from Virginia has been to call on us. His name is Stephen Bennett. He lives at a plantation called Bennett's Choice. Isn't that a delightful name? He told us about other plantations—Flowerdew Hundred, Pace's Paine, Lawnes' Choice, Bennett's Welcome. They have the strangest names!"

Hugh Jordan patted Sibyl's shoulder. "You are the same little chatterbox. Didn't I tell you to scamper off to bed?"

Mathilda lingered. "Stephen Bennett is going out to Virginia with his uncle, Richard Bennett, who is Commissioner for Maryland and Virginia. They hope he will be the new governor, if Cromwell . . ."

"Ah! A Cromwell man."

"Yes, but he is just as nice as though he were a King's man, Father," Sibyl said. "He makes sheep's eyes at Mathilda. I think he is in love."

"Sibyl!" Mathilda's cheeks grew as red as roses.

Hugh Jordan looked thoughtfully at his elder daughter. "You are growing up, Mathilda." He started to say something, then changed his mind. After a moment's silence he said, "To bed, my girls!" He kissed each of them lightly on the forehead and gave Sibyl a little push toward the door. "Run. Sleep well, and in the morning we will make arrangements."

After they had disappeared up the stairs, each carrying her bed-candle, he turned to the butler. "Things are in a bad way, Graves. There seems little hope for a Royalist victory. I will try to persuade Dame Margaret to leave with us. Have you heard any news?"

"The stable-boy says there's much marching along the Ledbury Road. I have put all the plate in a safe spot. I hope you will persuade our mistress to leave, but I doubt if you can."

Hugh covered his mouth with a thin hand to hide a yawn. "I'll try, Graves. I don't think it is safe for her to stay here. Where is your master?"

"He's with the King's army, sir."

Jordan nodded. "Always for the Stuarts. Loyalty is good, but there are times . . ." He didn't finish.

Graves took up the damp, steaming coat and spread it on a chair back so that the heat of the fire would reach it. He took up a candle. "I'll light you to your room, Mr. Jordan."

Dame Margaret sat in the morning room. The French door was open to the terrace. The day was warm, the sun shone brightly. The air was heavy with the pleasant, acrid smoke of smouldering leaves from the garden, where Biggor worked clearing away the brush and old plants from the summer garden. The feel of autumn was in the air, with the copper beeches turning to a golden blaze of glory.

Margaret sat quietly, her slim blue-veined hands clasped in her lap, idle for once. A little colour on her cheek-bones made the ivory skin look clearer. Her mouth was set firmly and her eyes, focussed on her visitor, were veiled. Hugh Jordan stood by the door, his shoulders stooped, his long body thinner, his face deeper-lined than the last time she had seen him, a few months before.

She thought, Hugh will not live much longer. He does not take proper care of himself, and there is no experienced person to look after him, except this Cecily he speaks of. I must ask him more about her. He is a man who has lost his hold on life. When young, he sat for a little while in Parliament. Now he is staying alive only to finish his continuation of the great work Mr. Richard Hakluyt of our own county compiled to give to the world—a history of the English Voyages, the stories of the great Elizabethans adventuring into unknown worlds, Drake and Grenville and Humphrey Gilbert and the others. Hugh undertook the work with a scholar's enthusiasm and the admiration of a physically sick man for men of strength, courage and heroic endeavour. It is too much for him.

He turned toward her. There was so much regret in his face that her heart sank. She was almost inclined to reverse herself, to say she would go with them, leave the manor behind her and flee to some safe place, far away from Cromwell and his Roundhead army. But how could she flee? Flight was against her nature. She must stay. If Richard came home, she must be there to welcome him. What would her son say to a woman who had no courage, who turned and fled at the first sign of danger? Hugh had argued for half an hour. But Hugh was a scholar, not a soldier, and she was bred by soldiers. No, she would stay. She would not let him persuade her. She was aroused from her thoughts by his words.

"I worry about my daughters, Margaret. I observed Mathilda last night. She is a woman, almost. I must think about marriage for her." He paused and made a futile gesture with his hands. "I'm afraid I have buried myself in books and failed to watch over them as I should." He looked at Margaret with his pale, short-sighted eyes. "Once or twice the thought has come to me that Mathilda and Richard would make a suitable marriage, if you . . ." He did not finish.

Margaret shook her head. "Richard must choose for himself. He and Mathilda are like brother and sister. I want him to have the woman he loves for his wife, not a 'suitable' arrangement."

"I suppose you are right, Margaret. You are always wise.

But how can a young person know? The old way seems better. A suitable marriage, arranged by parents, has many advantages. Mathilda has her mother's little fortune, you know—not great, but also not inconsiderable."

Margaret said nothing. It was difficult to talk with a man who knew so little of the world. "Mathilda is still very young, only eighteen. There is time."

"Time? Yes, yes, there is time for her, but for me—not too much, Margaret." She uttered a sharp protest. Hugh shook his head. "I know. My physician has warned me to put my affairs in order." He changed the subject abruptly. "Where is young Holder? Mathilda's letters mention him frequently."

"Nicholas has recently gone over to Cromwell, I've been told. He did not see fit to tell me himself."

Hugh raised his eyebrows. "A Holder goes over to the enemy?"

"Nicholas is politic," Margaret said briefly.

Hugh walked about the little room, his hands clasped behind his back, his shoulders bent. Margaret did not break into his thoughts. He looked up to find her eyes on him. "I was considering what is best for my daughters. I am a man of books with little knowledge of the world of politics. Perhaps it is the part of wisdom to stop thinking of the King and think only of Oliver's Parliament. Perhaps the road runs too fast and sure in the other direction, Margaret. Perhaps we are on a hopeless road. . . . We have fought the battles of the Stuarts for a long time, my friend."

Margaret said nothing.

"I am not thinking of you, or of me, my dear friend, but of the young ones. We have our loyalties which are ingrained in us. But these young people—are we to encourage them to cling to a lost cause?"

"You think it is a lost cause, Hugh?" Margaret's unspoken fear touched her voice.

He ran his hands through his long, greying hair. "I don't know. I don't know. I hear so much from both sides. Everything is confused. The world about us is changing."

They were both silent. Sounds from without entered the quiet room—a horse neighing, a hen clucking to announce that her morning task was over, voices and laughter from the kitchen.

"Who is this young Stephen Bennett whom Sibyl was telling me about?"

"He is a nephew of Edward Bennett, the merchant prince."

"Ah, yes, a strong shareholder in the Virginia Company. He made a fortune with his ships and his tobacco. You know, Margaret, I was foolish not to hold my shares in the Virginia Company. Sir George Yeardley advised me not to sell, but the assessments kept coming in, so finally I let Sir John Berkeley persuade me to sell to him. His brother William is the governor, you know. I let John have my shares, but I still hold a grant of land on the south shore of the James. I have forgotten the acreage—around a thousand, I think."

"I did not know you were interested in the Virginia Colony."

"But certainly. Have I not been reading about that glorious country ever since I undertook to edit the new edition of Hakluyt? I have read everything that has ever been written about the New World, from Amadas' and Barlowe's wonderful story of Roanoke Island, Grenville's expedition and the colony he left under the care of Ralph Lane, and I've studied John White's drawings. You must see those drawings, Margaret. They are magnificent."

He sat down on the window-seat and picked up a hank of green wool. After looking at a new book a moment with his near-sighted eyes, he laid it back on the table. Then he resumed. "I've been steeped in Virginia ever since John Smith's first ship went up the James to found the new colony. If only I had strength in this poor body of mine, I would take my daughters and sail across the sea to that glorious New World of great rivers and endless forests. But I am old, Margaret, old, old, old. . . ."

She leaned forward. "But your life has been good, Hugh. You were happy in your marriage. You have written your books. You have two lovely daughters. Enough for a life-span, dear friend."

"I suppose so, and I am content, but one has dreams. Virginia is the great pleasant land . . . the end of the voyage. It is a return of the great days of Elizabeth for a quarter of the young adventurous souls of this country. Tell me something about young Bennett. Is he personable? A man of parts?"

Margaret saw the way Hugh's mind was working. "He

seems pleasant enough, of good address and manner, but he is a Parliament man."

"I know. I know." He eased his neck-band nervously. He rose and stood before her. "I wish you would make up your mind to come with us, Margaret. I cannot leave you behind with an easy mind."

She set her lips, her chin firm. "We have gone all over that, Hugh. I will stay here."

"But if the Roundheads sequester Coddington Manor? What will you do then?"

"I will meet the situation when it arises, Hugh. But you have not told me your plans for Mathilda and Sibyl. You cannot take them to the Abbey unless you have some suitable companion for them. They are no longer children. They must have more training to take their place in the world. Mathilda has outgrown governesses, you know."

"I have thought of that. My Cousin Cecily, Mistress Peter Montague, is here from Virginia. She will stay with us until June."

"Mistress Peter Montague? I don't believe I know her, do I? Your cousin?"

"She isn't a blood cousin, really. She was born Cecily Reynolds. She first married a man named Bailey, who died young, and then Samuel Jordan, my relative. They live in Virginia, at Jordan's Journey. I understand it is one of the great plantations on the James River, above Jamestown."

"I seem to remember Cecily Jordan, but I don't remember the name Montague. . . . Ferris . . . no, Farrar. Wasn't that her name at one time?"

Hugh smiled wryly. "She has had several husbands, I believe, but she is a fine woman, full of wisdom and very lively. My daughters will enjoy her company."

"I dare say, Hugh. But is a woman who has been married so many times a good influence for your young daughters?"

Hugh set his jaw. "I think so. She is already established at the Abbey, she and her husband—a good fellow indeed." Margaret rose from her chair.

Hugh said, "My coach is in the court-yard. I will see what is keeping the girls."

"I am sad to lose them, Hugh. They are dears. They have been a comfort to me."

"You are good to have bothered with them. Daughters are

a great care to a lonely man. I will take pleasure when Mathilda is well established. Sibyl I shall not worry about. She will live with her sister, once Mathilda has a home of her own. Now this young Bennett . . ." He paused as the door opened and Mathilda entered.

"Stephen Bennett is here, Dame Margaret. He says there are soldiers everywhere on the roads. He asks permission to escort us as far as Hereford. It will not be out of his way, for he is going to Bristol."

Dame Margaret, glancing at Hugh Jordan, smiled. She said, "An excellent idea, Mathilda! I see you are wearing your riding habit. I will give orders to have the groom saddle the bay mare, so you may ride part of the journey."

"Oh, Dame Margaret, the bay is your favourite mount. Surely . . ."

Margaret interrupted. "I want you to have Star, Mathilda. Better you than one of Cromwell's brutal soldiers."

Mathilda threw her arms about Dame Margaret's neck. "Oh, madam, I do not want to leave you. Come with us, please. Please come."

Margaret gently loosed the girl's arms. "I must stay here, dear. What if Richard were to return and find me not here? When this trouble is over, you will come back to the manor."

Sibyl ran in. Her little bonnet was crooked, her long fur pelisse open. She carried two pairs of doves in a wicker basket. "I will send you a message by my doves, dearest. Every night I will say a prayer for you and Richard." She kissed Dame Margaret's hand. "Now may I run to the kitchen? I have some things to tell Cook Ellie and Patsy. I've left several dresses for Patsy."

"But Patsy can't possibly wear your gowns!"

"I know, but she can make quilts or something. She likes the prints." With a rush and a flutter of skirts Sibyl ran out of the door.

The coach stood waiting. Four impatient horses arched their necks, rattled buckles and chains, scuffed iron shoes against cobbles. Mathilda, mounted on Star, was behind the coach. She had put the little dogs, Fifi and Prince Charley, on a seat inside. The coachman was in his high seat, the reins held high in his hand. Dame Margaret, with the few faithful servants who remained at the manor, stood near the ancient doorway, ready to wave farewell to the travellers.

Hugh Jordan, wearing a broad hat and wrapped in his heavy cloak, strode up and down. "Where's the child? Blow the hunting horn, Graves. Perhaps she has run to the stables."

At the sound of the horn, hounds began to bay and the barn-yard fowls set to cackling and crowing. Sibyl ran around the corner of the house, her arms piled with fruits. "I am sorry, Father. But I had to run to the lily pond to say farewell to the old drake and his wives. Then Biggor asked me to wait while he selected the pears and grapes. Where are my doves?" She rushed about the terrace for a last word with all the servants.

Cook Ellie said, "Mind you eat the Devon splits today, Miss Sibyl, lest they become soggy."

"Yes, Cook. Thank you for the jug of milk, Patsy. And, Graves, be sure to see that the boy gives the doves their grain every day."

"Yes, miss, I'll mind that, else he'll get a beltin' from me."

With a last kiss for Dame Margaret, Sibyl lifted her flying skirts and scrambled up the high steps into the coach. Her father followed, quite out of sorts at the child's dilatory tactics. Stephen Bennett, who had been talking with Jordan, mounted his horse and took his place beside Mathilda. His groom followed them.

Dame Margaret waved as the coach rumbled down the avenue of tall poplar trees to the road. The sun still shone brightly, but the day suddenly became dull and empty.

Graves said, "I have hidden all the plate, madam. Should I take down the portraits out of the great room?"

Dame Margaret considered a moment. "No, Graves. Leave them as they are. I do not care to stare at empty walls as long as I stay in the manor."

"Madam is considering . . ."

"No. I shall not flee from Cromwell's troops. Instead, let us make ready to welcome the King's men, when they return triumphantly from battle. Take the plate out of hiding, Graves. If His Majesty comes to Coddington Manor, we will receive him as we received his martyred father." She walked into the house, her long black gown trailing after her.

Her servants stood in the lower hall, watching her slow ascent up the curving stairs. Graves shook his head. "She will never give up, not until Cromwell's men are here, quartered in our manor, bivouacked in our meadows."

Cook Ellie said, "Patsy, you and I will pack Madam's clothes, ready to leave at a moment's notice. I will tell Smolkins to have the coach ready to be hooked up, in case it is Cromwell's men that come this way, not the King's."

CHAPTER 8

The Crowning Mercy

In Worcester Richard sat on his camp-bed, writing by the faint light of a candle shielded by his casque.

Loving Mother:

My humble duty to you, desiring your daily prayers for me. I shall try to tell you of events since we parted, but so much has happened, and in such confusion, it is difficult to set them down in order.

Late in the night on Friday August the twenty-second we rode into the loyal city of Worcester. Charles had an entry of triumph.

On the next day he was proclaimed King of Great Britain, France and Ireland by the Mayor and the Sheriff with due ceremonies. He issued a manifesto summoning all the nobility, gentry and commonalty of the county, from sixteen to sixty. It seemed from the shouts and cheers that all Worcester were loyal. There was refreshment for the foot-sore army, Scotch Covenanters for the most part. I'm not sure that I am in accord with their religious zeal, as on Sunday they straightway began to quarrel about a sermon preached by a Worcester divine, because, they contended, he gave too much authority to the King as spiritual head of the Church.

The grand muster was held on Tuesday in a large meadow west of the city. I say "grand" because that was the term used, but rather it was pitiful. A number of Cavaliers of good family came in, but with meagre levies of Horse. Among them were the Earl of Shrewsbury and three gentlemen of the excellent and chivalrous name of Blount—Sir Walter, Peter, and Robert of Kenswick.

These slight accretions show that the King did wisely to abandon an early attempt toward London. In all our army I doubt if we have more than two thousand English, and they

are poorly armed, with little ammunition. On the very day
of his proclamation here, so it is reported, a counter-proclama-
tion was read in London, and shortly the King's manifesto
was burned by the hangman. If this be the true temper of
London, it is no place for our Charles as yet!

Worcester, as you recall, lies on the east bank of the
Severn. There is a strong work, the Fort Royal, at the south-
eastern angle of the city walls. From the day of the manifesto
Charles had the Scots, despite their weariness, doing their
utmost to repair the fortifications which Lambert's small
garrison had abandoned on our approach. The Scots gave vent
to windy grumbling as shrill as their bagpipes. Then, after
leaving enough to man the walls, he marched the rest of the
army back across the Severn bridge. A little south of the
city they maintain themselves in such lodgements as they
have been able to throw up. The Roundheads, our generals
said, must at all costs be prevented from crossing the Severn,
from the east or south.

But, alack, before we expected them, a party of Roundhead
Horse appeared at Upton six miles below Worcester. We
thought the bridge there had been demolished. And so it
had, but some careless fool had left a plank across the piers.
A handful of Lambert's bold dragoons dashed across it and
into the old church. We had sore trouble prying them out of
the nest and while we were about it their comrades forded the
river. There was sharp and bitter fighting. My gallant General
Massey was wounded in the hand. In no time at all Fleetwood,
our nosey guest at Coddington—I do not like that man—had
repaired the bridge and passed a strong body of Foot over it.
The Scots drew back nearer the city, north of the Teme.

Now the passage of the Teme at Powick *must* be stopped.
This Great rebellion started at Powick a decade ago. We
have come full circle. The Teme, you know, flows eastward
into the Severn at right angles, about a mile and a half south
of the city. I trust we have *that* bridge *entirely* destroyed.
We have good men at Powick Town—Robert Montgomery
and George Keyth. They will fight to the death.

The night of the bloody encounter at the Upton bridge
Cromwell was reported to be quartered at Mr. Simon's house
at White Lady-Aston. The next day we could see him with
our own eyes not a mile away on Red Hill. He made a
bonnemine, but attempted nothing.

My dragoons laugh and call him "Sultan" Oliver. But, dear Mother, since I saw him at our manor I can not make light of this astounding man, Energy personified.

That same night—night before last—Lieutenant-General Middleton with fifteen hundred Horse and Foot crept up on Cromwell's headquarters at Speachly to give the grand rebel a comisado. They wore shirts over their armour to distinguish themselves from the enemy in the darkness. A fanatic tailor of Worcester named Guyse betrayed them to Cromwell and they were repulsed with loss. The traitor was discovered by our men and executed forthwith.

So not all Worcester is loyal. I have heard through an officer from Ledbury that Nicholas Holder was seen in Cromwell's camp. Rats, they say, desert a sinking ship—but are we sinking?

Yesterday at the King's quarters I saw the Earl of Derby who had come in wounded. Near Wigan a week ago he had attacked a Parliament detachment under Colonel Lilburne, only half as large as his own. Fierce fighting ensued in the lanes. Such was the discipline of the Roundheads that our Royalists were routed with slaughter. In his desperate flight the earl, he told me, had found hiding-place for two days at Boscobel House, which lies in a wilderness between Tong Castle and Brewood on the border of Shropshire. He was cared for by a most excellent woodman named Penderel, a retainer of the Giffard family, until he could proceed on his way to Worcester. I mention the incident because I'm sure I've heard of you speak of the Giffards, dear Mother.

We are being gradually hemmed in by superior numbers. Shall we bear ourselves to better fortune than the earl at Wigan?

It is midnight. I have no wish to sleep. It is better by far to spend the long hours with you, talking with quill and ink.

We await only the trumpet's call to arouse the army to victory or defeat. A merry party supped with the King tonight. He was gay and filled with hope, and his sureness of our success was contagious. He says we will ride to London and enter his city with all pomp. He spent an hour making a list of those who would ride with him, and another hour listing those on whom he would bestow special honours.

He jested with me. First, he said again he would make me

Governor of Virginia. I suggested Sir William and Sir John
Berkeley would not like that.

He laughed. He has the most infectious laugh, Mother.
"Perhaps we will make you Commissioner for Maryland and
Virginia." But there was Lord Baltimore to consider. It ended
by his giving me a grant of land of great size on the south
side of the James River, opposite to our city of Jamestown.

My Lord of Lauderdale said, "You have already promised
empires of land to a few great gentlemen of your realm."

The King had an answer. "So I have, but that is land farther
south, my good Lauderdale, land near the great Sound of
Roanoke and reaching from the Atlantic Sea to the South
Seas. I shall make good the promise to my ministers and my
chief advisers."

"Who hide in London, or on their estates, Your Majesty.
I do not see one of them here, where the battle is to be won."

" 'Tis true. But they are sedentary men. They are of value
in only one place. They are not like my Lauderdale, who
fights with equal skill on the field of battle and in the arena
of political strife."

My lord bowed his great head, vastly pleased. I deem it
all a game to keep thoughts away from a worrisome subject.
But the King loves a fight. I think he is always bored by
inaction.

Virginia is often spoken of among men high in his councils
as a land of promise, a fertile land that yields vast crops of
tobacco, corn and many other useful products. Perhaps I shall
one day see Virginia. I would like to see a land of virgin soil.
Think of planting a field without manuring it—just cutting
the land in a long furrow, seeding it and waiting for the
harvest.

But these are idle thoughts. What concerns me most is your
plight if we lose tomorrow. You and Cook Ellie *must go at
once to Devon*. I have arranged for your escort. John Prideaux
will come for you. If we lose, our homes may be sequestered.
Oliver will have more power than any man in our time. He
will want the estates of the Royalists for his own followers.
That is natural, is it not? We hold Coddington Manor because
Henry the Eighth took the land from the Catholic Church—
and so it goes. We are indeed in a great revolution, one that
has gone deeper than you can possibly imagine.

Do not fear for me. I have a place of honour near the

King, a good horse and my sword. So, Lady Mother, my salutations. May you walk with God!

Richard

My respects to the young maids, Mathilda and the dauntless little Sibyl, and to the household. John Prideaux has just stepped in. As he is going with dispatches to Hereford, he can carry this letter to you and then convey you south. He will explain matters that I cannot write. Put yourself in his care. Take the Jordan maidens with you. Go to Bristol or to Bath and then down to your own Devon. Wait for me there.

I forgot to mention that half the time Cromwell has his men on their knees praying, they say, and the other waking hours all spent looking to their weapons and at drill. Our men sleep, eat and dice since the fortifications were repaired. A contrast, is it not?

The anxiety that besets us will soon be settled one way or the other. Any outcome is preferable to the long waiting of the past weeks from Scotland to Worcester! Will it be failure or glory? Who knows?

Richard

In camp at Worcester
Second September, 1651
Sealed with my ring

After a few hours' fitful sleep Richard was awakened by an orderly who said that the King desired his presence. He dressed hurriedly. There was not a cloud in the sky. The sun was already blazing. The King climbed the ancient stone steps to the Cathedral tower. With him were half a dozen officers, including David Leslie, the commander-in-chief of the Scots. Charles had sent for Richard Monington so that he might point out the disposition of the enemy forces from his knowledge of the countryside.

From this height on so clear a day the terrain was like a map. The Severn and the Teme were silver ribbons in the still green land. Men and horses were pigmy in the fort and city streets.

Richard pointed west to the Red Hill and the woods where Cromwell's quarters lay.

"They are inactive," the King remarked to Lauderdale, who had just come up, out of breath from the climb.

"Yes," said Richard, "but look down the Severn, down toward Upton." He had turned half around and his long arm was stretched to the south. Excitement gave edge to his voice. "It looks like a long string of boats pushing up-river."

"There's no bridge over the Severn below Worcester," the King remarked.

"The boats may be meant for pontoons. And from the number of them Cromwell must have commandeered every boatman, carpenter and artificer from all the towns around."

"But they're just crawling," said Lauderdale. "They make no hazard, Sire."

Leslie said, "There's fighting near the broken bridge at Powick—about where the Teme can be forded. Fleetwood is attacking."

"That point is protected by General Montgomery. I have no worries over it." The King's eyes looked eastward again. There lay his arch-foe Cromwell, the man who had beheaded his father and taken away his throne—the praying hypocrite, he thought, whose lips give service to a personal God but whose heart and soul are on the growth of his own greatness. "Captain, show me the spot of sorest danger."

Unhesitatingly Richard pointed to the boats undulating in the distance like some river serpent. "There, Sire. If the enemy cross the Teme they will pour in and encircle us. It is not our Royal Fort but the rivers we must guard. I fear those boats."

"I fear them not," said the King. Stubbornly he turned to regard the Red Hill again. "My danger lies there," he said slowly. His young face was no longer carefree. He did not smile. He seemed to grow in stature, as he stood silent, his gaze fixed on Cromwell's camp. "Come," he said. "I will descend to the ground. I will place myself on equal footing with my men."

The first cannon shots started while they were descending the tower, but it was only desultory firing.

Mounted on a black charger, the King rode from post to post in the ambit of the walls, observing, advising his comrades and officers, calling many of his Highlanders by name. At headquarters in the city he conferred with the Duke of Hamilton and Sir John Douglas, at Town Hall with Major Corlies and Lord Cleveland, at Castle Hill with Lord Rathes and Sir William Hamilton.

Repeatedly Richard, who rode with the life-guard, tried to interest some superior officer in the boats, but he was laughed at. "It will take all day and all night to tow them up against the swift current," Sir John Douglas told him. "Don't worry about those silly boats, lad. We'll smash the foe before they ever arrive."

"Where is Buckingham?" the King asked one after another. No one knew.

Charles, impetuous, completely without thought of his person, often outstripped his guard.

But even when the afternoon began there had been as yet no hot strife except near the broken Powick Bridge. The King and his aides galloped there.

Montgomery saluted. "Sire, I have not enough ammunition to last me twenty minutes."

"Hold firm against a crossing, General," Charles commanded. "Use the pikes. I'll ride for help."

They spurred their horses east till they came on a Scotch sergeant bent over by the roadside nursing a wounded leg. "Where is your command?" the King cried. "Help is needed at Powick Bridge."

The trooper struggled to his feet and saluted. "Sire, help is needed *here*. I'll show you." Haltingly he led them to a knoll where through the trees the confluence of the rivers lay right before them, as though no more than a pistol-shot away. The boats *had* come, and, more, the two boat-bridges were nearly completed, close together, from east across the Severn, from south across the winding Teme.

"See, the crop-head devils are battening down the last planks. And see, on our side in the angle are Major Piscotty with three hundred men. Three hundred!" The wounded sergeant shuddered.

Piscotty's men were dismounted and fighting with pistols and claymores a "forlorn" party of dripping Roundheads who had evidently swum the last gap of the Severn to cover this end of the approaching bridge.

The sergeant went on: "Our Foot is coming up. But look at the great hosts waiting on yonder banks." Columns stretched toward the bridgeheads from as far as eyes could see. "Three hundred puir Scots against two mighty armies! Sire, it is a madness to think we can stay them for a moment, once the bridges are finished. Ride and urge the main relief,

I beg you. I'd give this right arm for Rab Montgomery, but is his need as great as ours?"

The King whispered one word, "God!" half prayer, half imprecation. The appalling picture was all too clear. "I thank you, Sergeant." He turned to his guard. "We will ride for the rescue."

In one last look at the Severn Richard thought he could detect the stalwart figure of Cromwell himself laying a plank on the pontoon, the busiest man among frantic workers. His eyes might deceive him, but he could not be deceived about Cromwell. He'd be the first across, leading the van in person and shouting his battle cry, "The Lord of hosts is with us!"

So the Royal party rowelled their spent chargers up the Worcester Road and met soon the long lines of Scottish Foot on the run and deploying as they found open ground.

The King shouted to Colonel Downing. "Make all haste! Hold the rivers! Send aid to Montgomery at Powick Bridge if you can. Be of good hope. The day will yet be ours."

As they dashed past the soldiers waved to him, crying, "For King and Covenant!"

Charles smiled for the first time, a grim smile. "You were almost right, Monington, but not quite." A plan was forming in his wily and resourceful mind.

They rode on.

Cromwell had divided his forces, some on the east, some on the west side of the Severn. Charles, versed in the lore of battle, knew that this was often the fatal error. In spite of his vastly superior strength, Cromwell might be defeated in detail.

Some wounded had been brought in and were stretched on the floor of the Cathedral. Richard was sickened by the sight. The King paused only for a moment to give them a word of encouragement and blessing; then he climbed the tower again for a quick survey of the hills. It seemed indeed that Cromwell had drawn most of his men across his precious boat-bridges. Now was the golden chance. The Royal Horse had hardly been engaged as yet. It was peerless.

The King came down the thousand steps quicker than any man had descended them before. He sent Richard and his other aides flying to collect whatever Foot might be found and all the Horse.

With all possible speed a sally corps gathered near the

Sudbury Gate at the south end of the Royal Fort. The Duke of Buckingham, at last blasted out of his languor, and Lord Grandison's cavalry had ridden there pell-mell. The Duke of Hamilton brought his own Highlanders. Sir Alexander Forbus, the commander of the Foot, presented his regiment of Foot. There were divers English lords and gentleman volunteers.

But the main body of Scottish Horse did not come. Some said they had got wedged up in the town; others that they would not obey Leslie's orders; others said Leslie would give no orders. The King waited for them anxiously; at last could wait no longer. He gave the command to advance. Under the protection of the fort out they darted through the gate and formed into line of attack. The King, a slim and elegant figure, rode up and down on his great black charger, shouting encouragement. One of the Roundhead great shots was laid down almost at his horse's hoofs. The horse reared and bolted, and Charles brought him to rein only after a determined struggle.

The Cavaliers fell like a flash from the blue on the breastwork Cromwell had raised at the cockshoot of Perry Wood. The fire from it was heavy, but the unwavering assault made the Roundhead regiments reel. The Highlanders especially caught fire from Charles's valour, flailing with the butt-ends of their muskets when their shot gave out. For the moment the King was master of the hostile guns and might be master of England.

But then the Roundhead Horse came charging and the balance of the battle was restored. The desperate fighting continued for three hours, as sharp a contest as ever man saw, maintained with noble gallantry. The Duke of Hamilton had his horse killed under him and received a wound that proved mortal. Sir John Douglas got his death-stroke in the advance. Forbus was shot through the calves of both legs. Richard found him lying among the trees. He begged leave to put him on a horse, but the knight refused.

"Fight! Go forward! Give them no quarter!" he gasped. Richard left him in the care of a wounded trooper and galloped to his place beside the King.

The horsemanship he had learned at Coddington stood him in good stead. He must keep close to the Royal Person and interpose his body—not easy in this tangle of full career—

not easy at all when they were among the guns. Once a pistol-shot grazed his cheek, and once a pike grazed his thigh. Escape seemed miraculous.

With everything to absorb him, with his loyal devotion ever demanded, he was still conscious of the heat of the declining sun. The casque and corselet were damnably hot.

To Cromwell messengers had galloped with news of the critical mêlée. His affairs were going well on the west side of the Severn. He had regiments to spare there. He brought them with him to relieve his battle-weary men. He threw himself in the fray—"a stiff business" he called it. "O Lord," he prayed aloud, "Thou knowest how busy I am to-day. If I forget Thee, do not Thou forget me."

At last some of the main Royal cavalry had ridden out, but not enough. For a little while Middleton and his Gordons struggled manfully against both Horse and Foot. Charles looked at them despairingly. He cried, "Oh, for one hour of Montrose at the head of my three thousand centaurs!"

But Montrose whom he had so greatly wronged was dead, and there was none now able to withstand the Roundhead onslaught. Middleton, wounded, ordered the retreat. An irresistible flood of fugitives swept in confusion toward the Sudbury Gate. In vain the King, with Richard by his side, sought to stay it. But there was no rallying this rout. Instead they were borne along by it.

At the gate, by accident or design, an ammunition cart had been overturned and one of its ox-team lay sprawled beside it. The passage was blocked. Richard cried, "We must dismount, Sire!" They leaped from their horses, leaped over the dead ox and were carried down Friars Street in the press of the flight.

Guns from the Royal Fort began to plunge shot into the street. The clamorous Roundheads had burst into the fort, put to the sword the few Scots left there and turned the guns on the fugitives, adding to their panic.

Across the city, at the north-west corner, what was left of the Scottish infantry was pouring over Worcester bridge and thronging past the Water House and the Key. All that hot afternoon on the west of the Severn they had contested every inch of the way in fiery pulses, fighting, from hedgerow to hedgerow, a battle in which the thickets and thick high fences favoured a defence against Horse, but not enough against the outnumbering regiments of Cromwell and Fleet-wood. It was not in Scottish nature to shun a bitter contest, to scant the full measure of courage. If they must fight on foreign soil in this Englishmen's quarrel, what did life amount to anyhow? The bleak towns they loved were far, far away and it would be a long day at best before they'd see them again. The carnage was awful. The remnants streamed toward Worcester bridge.

At Powick Montgomery had been dangerously wounded, and his men, breaking before Fleetwood's left column, brought a new and disorderly current converging on the same bridge and the suburb of St. John's.

The King finally freed himself from the press of the fleeing mob of darting into a looted bake-shop in Friars Street. Richard was behind him. Several others of the life-guard straggled in. They divested themselves of their hot armour.

Sweat streamed down Charles's face, stained with dirt. His dress was all awry. But there was nothing awry about his spirit. All the courage of the Stuarts flamed in his black and sunken eyes. Courage in the face of defeat and danger had made a man of a restless lad, a King of a play king. For a moment only he stood before that little group, a far more regal figure, Richard thought, than the debonair leader of the sally from Sudbury Gate.

Then Charles called for a fresh horse. Richard ran out of the shop and straightway found one in a side street, abandoned by its rider. The King mounted at once and resumed his efforts to rally the foot soldiers. Everywhere men were throwing down their arms, swearing they would fight no longer. He rode up and down among them with his hat in his hand, entreating them to stand to their arms and fight like men.

"Arms!" one of them shouted. "What can a man do against an enemy who has balls for his muskets?"

"Use your claymore, my man. Cromwell's men will flee from Scots armed with claymores. Fight for King and Covenant. Lift high St. Andrew's Cross! Fight for your country."

" 'Tis nae *my* country. 'Tis bloody English land. . . ."

The King said, "Then I had rather you would shoot me than let me live to see the sad consequences of this fatal day."

Abashed, they rushed on. He rode slowly back and forth, still seeing only soldiers that marched the wrong way—not into battle but away from battle. His face was lined and care-worn, an old man's face. Hatless, he sat his horse, erect in body.

Lord Wilmot galloped up. Runnels of sweat poured down his face. "Thank God!" he cried. "I find you at last, Sire."

The King stretched out his hand. "My friend! And are you my only friend—you and these few gentlemen?" He indicated the remnant of his life-guard.

"Not so, Your Majesty. At every strong point in the town men are dying to give you time to escape—charging in Sudbury Street and High Street, at Castle Hill, at the Town Hall."

"I see no sign of this resistance."

"Listen and you can hear it. You must flee, Sire. Ride with me at all speed to St. Martin's Gate to the north of town. Some of your gentlemen are there already, waiting for you. Not the Fore Gate. It is mured up and we can't get through. Everywhere else our people are being slain or taken. The rebels are plundering the lower town. You must flee before you are discovered."

"I will not flee." The King's lower lip was thrust forward. "I will *not* flee again."

"But, Sire, you must. We cannot allow you to be Cromwell's prisoner. For the sake of those who are dying for you!"

"I should die with them," Charles said. "But if you say truth, I must not let their sacrifice be vain. Come, my people, rally round me at St. Martin's Gate, where we may plan the next move."

With Lord Wilmot he rode down the street. Richard and his few comrades followed on foot. The great bell in the Cathedral steeple tolled the hour. Six o'clock.

At the gate a company was gathered who welcomed him— the Dukes of Buckingham and Lauderdale, the Earls of Derby and Shrewsbury, Edward Roscarrock, Thomas Blague, Charles Giffard—some forty in all. David Leslie was there too with a considerable body of Horse. The King looked darkly at Leslie.

A hasty consultation was held. Derby and Wilmot suggested an hour's march at least away from the city, to which all agreed.

At Barbon's Bridge about half a mile north of Worcester Richard Monington came upon John Prideaux and Digby. John had a rough bandage about his head. Digby had had his horse shot from under him. His platoon had been wiped out.

Digby spat. " 'Tis all over, Captain. And there sit Leslie and his Horse on their backsides fresh as the night they rode in. Why weren't they with us in Perry Wood? God blast them to hell!"

Richard gave John Prideaux the letter he had written to his mother. "I release you from your duties. Ride direct to Ledbury, then to Coddington. Deliver this to my mother. Stay at the manor for a week at least. The King may after all decide to retreat to the coast. If so, we must be prepared. My mother will understand."

John's dark eyes were deep in his head. His brown hair streamed over the bandage and down to his shoulders. "Sir, shall I go at once?"

"At once. You must have a horse. So must I—and you too, Digby. What can you do about horses?"

"Shall I unhorse three of these goddam cowards of Leslie's?"

Richard agreed with the dragoon's words of scorn, but he said, "Leslie's Horse is to cover a retreat."

However he managed it, the resourceful Digby got the horses. Richard waved farewell to John.

The Royal trumpet sounded. The King conferred with General Leslie. Richard could not hear the conversation, but Charles's face was black with rage. Looking under glowering brows at Leslie's unbroken ranks, the King was determined to turn back and charge the enemy again. At the moment when he was about to give the command, Buckingham and Lauderdale protested.

Richard heard Lauderdale say, "Your Majesty, the infantry is annihilated. Three thousand men at least are killed, twice as many are prisoners. Half the nobility of Scotland are taken. What could these platoons do to gain victory? Nothing! Nothing at all! We must fly if we are to save our skins."

He glanced at David Leslie, who sat his horse at the head

of his troopers, looking straight before him, with no expression on his face.

Buckingham raised his voice. "What help would a few Horse be, Sire, under a leader who does not command the loyalty of his men? No, my King. Let us admit defeat. London we cannot reach. But if you escape now, your hour of triumph is sure to come on a happier day."

The King turned to Shrewsbury. The earl's eyes were weary. He sagged in his saddle. "Do you agree with these gentlemen?"

"Sire, the road north is open. At the end of the road is Scotland, where Charles the Second is King."

The King lifted his head and gave a sharp order. A little column of forty men rode into the autumn darkness, away from Worcester and a lost battle.

The Horse decided not to go with them. Without the handicap of a broken King they thought they might better force a way to Scotland. It was a wild hope, and a fruitless way they took. All in the end were to die or be taken in the English lanes.

A proclamation, hastily composed, was posted on walls, offering reward in golden coin for the capture of "a dark-haired young man, above two yard high." The people would know that tall Charles Stuart was the man.

Cromwell's soldiers knelt in prayer. Exampled by their leader, they lifted their voices in a hymn of praise to the Lord God who fought on the side of the righteous.

Oliver addressed his army. He stood in the light of a bonfire and thanked his men for their courage and their fighting arms and their mighty spirit. "But give the glory to Him who has wrought so great salvation. The dimensions of His mercy are above our thoughts. This was the Battle of the Crowning Mercy."

So ended the third of September—Oliver's fateful third.

It was destiny. But not all destiny. There had been great leadership. Oliver had kept the whole battle in mind, fluid and moving, never weighted down by a preconceived plan, yet never allowing his troops to go beyond an objective. He had always complete composure.

Where Charles was an adroit opportunist and showed per-

sonal valour, throwing himself into the heat of battle, Oliver
was sound and thorough. He watched the strength and weakness of his troops, never acting rashly or on impulse, applying
the decisive impact at the crucial point at the priceless
moment. He had taken no real risk in dividing his forces.
He knew what he was about. All his former battles were
refought this day at Worcester—Edgehill, Grantham and
Gainsborough, Marston Moor, Naseby, Langport, Preston,
Dunbar. All that he had learned in the long years came back
to Oliver this day. He had fought before with generals who
surpassed him, Waller and Monk for example. Now he had
moved ahead on his own, a leader of larger vision, a leader
on the grand scale.

This was the end of battles fought between brother and
brother on English soil. The Great Rebellion ended when the
Scots' invasion crumbled.

The power lay in Cromwell's hands. His was a new age.
The monarchy had vanished with young Charles. That night,
as he knelt alone on a silent hill to offer himself to his
Maker, Oliver's spirit soared above the world he had known.

A soldier said as he passed, "There walks the King of
England."

London, his city of London, lay to the south-east. He took
his time on the way there, enjoying his relief and the plaudits
of his people. Of September mornings he rode slowly down
the Avon vale, the populace proclaiming him at every village
and town. He spoke to them only of God's Crowning Mercy.

Again he was a countryman riding through the lovely
countryside. How happy he was when an old friend rode up
to greet him, carrying with him his falcons! The Lord General went off a-falconing. "Lord, keep me from vain glory,"
he prayed as he watched his falcon, unhooded, soar into the
bright vault of the heavens.

Richard Monington rode beside Lord Wilmot throughout
the long night, Digby close behind them. They were the rear
guard of the two score men who rode with the King. They
dared not linger to sleep, for fear the daylight would show
Oliver's men the road they had taken.

At daybreak Digby made a fire under a tree at the edge of
a wood and prepared a scanty breakfast. Here, as they rested,
a consultation took place. Buckingham and Lauderdale wanted

the King to make all haste to Scotland, supposing the northern road lay open before them.

Lord Wilmot, a loyal adherent to the Stuarts, argued
against it. He was a sturdy, broad-shouldered man of ruddy
complexion, outspoken and very frank.

"The open road to the north is a trap," he said. "Oliver's
men may fall upon us at any time and capture His Majesty.
What then? I cast my lot for cross-country, over old roads and
tracks to the Welsh Marshes; from there south to Bristol and
the sea. The King's hope lies not in the land but on the sea."

The King spoke for the first time. "I do not desire to flee
to France again. There is something unkingly in crying
'Sanctuary' at every turn. I am weary of running."

"Ships from Bristol sail to Spain and Portugal, and even
to Virginia," remarked Buckingham. His long elegant body
was stretched full length on the grass under a great oak tree.
His arm under his head, he lay looking through the branches
to the sky, now faintly coloured with the red of early morning.

"Not Virginia, surely!" the King exclaimed. In his look
was no trace of the exultation he had worn in the heat of
battle. Now he was a weary and disheartened lad, who had
no home, no place to hide in safety.

"Virginia is not too bad. In truth if one relies on the ad-
vertisements of the London Company, it is the land of
promise, perhaps even Sir Thomas More's Utopia. Will
Shakespeare has set his *Tempest* in an island of the Indies.
It is the fashion now to be a planter and hold land in
Virginia."

"I won't have Virginia. I'd as soon go back to the Isle of
Scilly. I want to remain in England. When Cromwell comes
to the end of his luck, I must be near by." The King spoke
querulously in his weariness.

Lauderdale, who had been walking through the woods,
came up. He bowed and bent his knee to the King. His face
was grave, his voice not quite steady. "Sire, I have been giving
some thought to the plight in which we find ourselves. I
think I must leave your side. I must run like a frightened
hare. It seems my big red head cannot be disguised. If I stay
at your side I am a dread menace to my sovereign, to whom
I have given my faith and my seal of loyalty."

"Well spoken, Lauderdale," Buckingham's lazy voice broke

in. He did not change his position, but his handsome aristocratic face was as serious as Lauderdale's ugly phiz. "I've been
thinking also. We are too many to ride through the countryside. We draw attention to the King—we, in our Cavalier
habits. Something must be planned to insure His Majesty's
safety, which does not rest in the numbers that surround
him, but the skill in which a few evade pursuit. What think
you, Wilmot?"

"I, too, agree. I have talked with Giffard here. He knows
all the nooks and crannies of this country."

Derby said, "I can vouch for that. You've all heard the
story of how his retainer Penderel hid me at Boscobel House,
with those damned Roundheads passing daily."

Wilmot turned to the King, who was leaning against the
trunk of a tree, despondent and melancholy. "What does the
King wish? On to Scotland in a body, or break into small
parties and endeavour to make a later rendezvous?"

"Monk holds Scotland," Charles reminded him. "I won't
hide in the islands again. Lauderdale, you are right when
you say your great red head, which I swear holds much
wisdom, calls attention to us. Everyone knows Lauderdale
rides close beside the King. My good Lauderdale, I would
not have your head rolling from your body like a hoop."
Spirit was returning to his voice. "Instead, I beg of you to
keep it on your broad shoulders, against the time I am King
of England in truth."

"God send the day be soon!" Lauderdale answered fervent-
ly.

Buckingham rose easily. One lithe movement and he was
standing before the King. "I, too, menace the sovereign I
adore. I would ride with Lauderdale. Country-folk seeing us
will say, 'There rides the King and his courtiers, the Duke
of Lauderdale and the Duke of Buckingham, while you, Sire,
will be travelling another road. For my part, I would vote
Bristol as a rendezvous. Your Majesty has loyal friends in
Gloucestershire and Somerset, at whose homes you will be
both safe and welcome. Your Catholic subjects have many
a secret room where their priests and bishops were hidden
in the old days."

Shrewsbury did not speak when the King looked at him.

The Earl of Derby said, "Every hour I am near you, I
bring danger closer to you, Sire. I beg permission to ride

away alone, so that I will not call attention to your presence."

The King rose to his feet. "It is a sorry day when the King must part from his faithful gentlemen, but since your presence brings danger, it is wisdom that we separate now. While you have been contemplating our miserable situation, it has also been in my mind. I have had some conversation with Lord Derby and Mr. Giffard. We have made a plan. It is perhaps as well that none of you know the decision we have reached. This is the parting of the ways. You ride off on your own venture, I on mine. 'Tis like the stripping of an onion—skin layers peeling off one at a time until only the thin centre core remains. My centre core will be Mr. Giffard, Lord Wilmot, Captain Monington and his faithful dragoon Digby, who cooks such excellent breakfasts."

The horses were brought up then. At the last the King's gentlemen stood about him, unable to say farewell. Tears were in some eyes.

The King smiled, the first time he had smiled since Worcester. "Gentlemen, gentlemen, do not show such dampened spirits. We have fought hard, we have lost much, but we will win again with God's good help. Fare you well, my faithful gentlemen! You go your ways and I, your King, will disappear into the greenwood."

Courtier and soldier came to the King, bent the knee and kissed his hand. No words were spoken. Only the King smiled, as one by one they mounted and rode away.

When the last man was lost in the shadow of the forest, he turned to Giffard. "Lead the way, good sir. Your King's person and the future of the Royal Crown of England lie in your hands."

Giffard's grey locks fell over his face as he bent the knee to the King. "In God's hands, Sire, and the loyalty of your faithful subjects."

Richard and Digby fetched the horses, and five men out of forty disappeared into the greenwood. The King had recovered his gaiety. He hummed a song as he rode, one made on Will Shakespeare's lines:

> "Under the greenwood tree
> Who loves to lie with me . . ."

They rode without incident until the sun was low, shining in slanting rays through the forest. They dismounted. The

King, wrapped in his cloak, lay down beside a fallen tree, well sheltered from the narrow forest track. Giffard rode alone to make arrangements for the King's arrival at his house White Ladies.

Richard and Digby kept guard, while the King and Lord Wilmot slept. The horses they had concealed deeper in the forest, in case some stray countryman ventured through the wood at eventide.

Digby said, "How sweetly he sleeps, with his hand beneath one cheek! It is the attitude of childhood, zur. He is not uneasy, with only strangers to guard him."

"He trusts us, Digby."

"Zur, he does. Yet he should not give his trust so readily."

"What else can he do than trust us? Lord Wilmot lies with his drawn sword by his side. He too must trust us, for he sleeps with his mouth open, making strange noises."

Digby turned on his elbow to watch the track. "Captain, do you know where we be, in Staffordshire or Shropshire?"

"Near the borders, I think, beyond Kidderminster. I will be happy when we turn and move toward Wales."

"Aye. They will not suspect us of travelling south. I venture Oliver's men have spread out like a fan over the whole district, seeking the King, and here he sleeps under the trees as peaceful as a child."

"'Tis strange indeed that you, Digby, and I should be His Majesty's guard, a Devon man and a Hereford man, while his loyal Scots ride north."

"Those that be left, zur. Never did I see such slaughter. It fair turned my stomach. I was afeared more than once."

Richard grinned. "I was afraid too, Digby. Once in Perry Wood I all but turned and fled. I think I would have, except that my horse was hemmed in close by other sweating, frightened horses. The din of artillery was terrific. Then suddenly we were out of ammunition, and General Middleton ordered the retreat. He was wounded, blood streaming down his face. Men were falling from their horses; if not dead from wounds, they were trampled to death."

"I was there. I know. Praise the Lord that left us scratchless this day."

Richard was silent. Digby got up, walked down the track and took up his position thirty or forty yards away.

Richard listened to the night sounds—the sharp bark of a

fox, the cooing of a wood pigeon, the faint rustle of small prowling animals. A hare ran along the narrow path. An owl's mournful hoot came from the trees overhead as it sought its evening meal of field mouse or rat or young hare. Richard thought, Hunters and the hunted! We become animals, fleeing from an unseen enemy.

Before light a nightjar's call came softly. It was the signal arranged with Mr. Giffard, but they must be cautious. Human shadows moved against the heavier shadows of the trees. Digby stood waiting, his pistol in hand. The King stirred and sat up. Wilmot was on his feet; Richard saw the light flash as he moved his sword. Richard was motionless, standing directly in front of the King. For a moment all the forest noises were suspended, waiting.

Then Giffard came forward, followed by two of his men, William and Richard Penderel. The woodsmen knelt before the King, attesting their loyalty and devotion.

The King bade them rise. "There must be no more of these signs of devotion. I must be one of you, not a man set apart. I would that my habit were different, not so conspicuous."

Giffard said, "Sire, we have countryman's garments ready for you. Richard Penderel will fetch them from his home, Hobbal Grange, hard by."

The King stood beside William Penderel, who towered above him. "Good yeomen, you must lend me your strength and your woodsman's sagacity, as well as your garments, else I am indeed lost."

"Sire, you are not lost. My four brothers and I have taken an oath to hide you and keep you safe from Oliver's men."

"Are Cromwell's men about?" Lord Wilmot asked.

"That they be, but on the Great Road. They search the northern way, hoping to overtake those who fled toward Scotland."

The King turned to Lord Wilmot. "You were right. We must turn now and seek a road to the south. Charles Stuart will not be caught in that snare."

Digby had prepared breakfast of the bread and cheese the Penderels had brought with them. The King sat down on a log to eat. "Sit down, all of you," he said. "We may as well begin now. We are no longer a king and his officers, but woodsmen and yeomen, tenants of Mr. Giffard. Monington, you still look a soldier. Best get yourself into rustic brown as soon as you can."

It was near to sun-up when they reached the entrance of White Ladies. Charles Giffard approached the King. "Sire, will you ride up the terrace, through the long door and into the hall? If any of Cromwell's soldiers venture here, they might recognize your horse."

Charles, laughing, rode up the terrace into the great hall before he dismounted. Two other Penderel brothers awaited them. They had news of import. David Leslie and some general officers were near at Tong Castle. There was talk about the advisability of the King joining them and going to Scotland.

For the first time since Worcester the King's temper flared. His dark eyes flashed. His ugly mouth curled. "That is absolutely impossible! The country would rise against us. As for David Leslie, a man who could not bring his troops to my rescue when they were in good order would never stand by me when they are in flight. Let us hear no more of this. I shall put myself into a disguise and endeavour to get away in a country fellow's habit."

"Sire, Richard Penderel's garments are waiting for you in the bed-chamber," Giffard said.

"Captain Monington, I now appoint you Gentleman of the Bed-chamber. Will you accompany me, to see that when I change I look like a woodsman, not a gentleman attired for a masque?"

CHAPTER 9

The Flight

MISTRESS GIFFARD sent up some biscuits and sack for the King by a faithful boy of the house, Bartholomew. Twenty-five miles of riding after the heat and struggle of the battle had wearied the King. Sleep in the forest had rested him some, but he showed signs of fatigue.

When they had come to an inner parlour off the bed-chamber, John, the eldest of the Penderel brothers, was brought in.

Mr. Giffard said, "John, this is the King. Have care of him. Preserve him as your brother William did the Earl of Derby."

John knelt at the King's feet. "Majesty, my brothers and I will guard you with our lives. But you must make haste and depart from here. A troop of rebels under command of Colonel Ashenhurst be quartered at Cotsal, no more than three miles distance. They scour the country seeking 'a dark young man two yards high.'" John stopped abruptly, embarrassed at the long speech he had made before his sovereign.

"Rise, John. It shall be as you say. Call your brothers William and Richard to take me to the hiding place you have designed for me."

To Lord Wilmot, who was pacing up and down the bed-chamber, he said, "John Penderel will guide you to some safe house where you may rest for the moment. It is not good for anyone to be found in the company of Charles Stuart, lest you be brought before the Black Tribunal, charged with high treason and lose both your life and your estates." A slight smile twisted the King's lips. . . . "The friendship of a king is danger indeed."

He turned back to John Penderel. "Do you have in mind a place of safety for Lord Wilmot and Captain Monington?"

"Sire, there is Father Huddleston who ministers to us

hereabouts. He lives now at the home of Mr. Whitgreave. I believe, Sire, that he will undertake to secure them for a day or two, until we . . ."

"Excellent, my trusty man! Now for my masquerade."

Mr. Giffard went to the door of an adjoining room. William Penderel entered, followed by the boy, who carried an armful of clothes. Bartholomew's eyes were round. He stumbled and lost half the clothes from the pile. Tongue-tied, he bowed so low that he was almost bent double.

The King said, "What have we here? Come, Captain, relieve the lad of his burdens before they all fall to the floor."

Richard Monington took the rustic garments from the lad's arms and laid them out on the wide bed.

"Sire, perhaps hair-cutting should come first," William Penderel said.

A gasp went up from the gentlemen. Cut the long black curls that were so much a part of the King's majestic mien!

Charles lifted the heavy hair that fell below his shoulders. Strong curls slipped through his fingers. No one moved or spoke for a moment until he said, "Come, come, gentlemen. 'Tis better far to be bereft of my locks than my head. The shears, good Giffard, and Master William here will be my barber. A good cut, my man, a good countryman cut."

He sat down on a stool near a window. William, shears in hand, approached the King. He hesitated, growing red in the face, his fingers white on the shears.

The King said, "Now, Penderel, no hesitating. Have you never sheared a sheep?"

"Many a one, Sire, many, but . . ."

"On with it, and off with this mane, and burn the mop when you have finished the task."

William grasped the shears. All his brothers were now there to watch. They stood by, gaping. " 'Tis not a sheep trimming, Sire," John said. "My brother lacks firmness. I will take the shears and in a short space the King will have a cut like a true countryman."

The King talked to Wilmot as he turned his head this way and that. "You must think of yourself from now on, my good Wilmot. You will set out on the journey about which we have already spoken. Be prepared to rendezvous at the place already selected."

Wilmot moved his hands nervously. "Sire, I think I shall stay near by. If you should need me . . ."

"No. I will not have it. What could one man do? Or three? Or four? If I had a troop of Horse, all imbued with the loyalty which you and these five brothers own, I might ride straight after Oliver and cut him off from London. Alas, there is no Horse! But I have for my protection five noble brothers." His flashing smile transfigured his sallow face. "Who would want more than five faithful friends?"

The brothers looked from one to another, then toward their sovereign. Charles rose. His beautiful hair lay on the floor about him. William and John had sheared off ten years. It was a young boy with a Roundhead cut who stood before them, but he did not lack an appropriate majesty as he held his hand to each of the brothers to kiss.

"This must be the end of bowing and kissing hands, my lads. When I divest myself of these trappings, I shall stand before you naked, a man like unto yourselves. Let us hope I conduct myself like a good yeoman. Come, Captain Monington, my Gentleman of the Bedchamber, what have you ready for me?"

The King took off his Garter blue ribband, the George of diamonds, his buff coat and his princely ornaments. He set aside his ring for Lord Wilmot. With Monington's help he put on a country fellow's habit—a noggen coarse shirt, ordinary green cloth breeches, a leathern doublet, a green jump-coat and a steeple-crowned hat. There was some talk of how to dispose of the clothes the King had taken off. They could not be burned because of the odour, and no place in the house was safe if Oliver's men searched. Nor would the garden do. Any burying in the earth might be readily dug up. The King himself suggested throwing them into the privy-house.

When Charles stood in front of the reflecting glass, the distorted image bore little resemblance to his former look. Still John Penderel was not satisfied. The hands and face were too smooth and clean. Charles laughed. "A little chimney soot may help until you procure some walnut stain that will be most lasting."

While the King was dressing, Mr. Giffard entered with the news that Colonel Blague and Colonel Roscarrock, who had been with them when they first fled Worcester, had come to

White Ladies to urge the King to ride to Tong Castle, two miles away. They were prepared to march to Scotland, protected by Leslie's Horse. Charles shook his head. "I have said my say on that subject. I have no faith in David Leslie, nor will I ever trust my person to a man who failed his sovereign at a most critical moment."

When the two officers entered the bedchamber, they paused at the threshold and looked from one occupant to the other. Charles was in the act of lifting some garments from the bed, and they did not recognize him.

He laughed aloud at their discomfiture. "It augers well for my disguise," he said. When they had finished their plea for him to ride with them and Leslie's Horse, he repeated what he had already said to Giffard.

He took up the George and other ornaments from a dressing table and gave them to Colonel Blague. "Where I am going I shall have no need for them. Good day, gentlemen. I will not discuss my future with you, nor my present. My plans remain secret from you and from all else save these loyal men. God with you!"

So he dismissed his officers and put himself under the protection of the yeomen.

Monington and Digby slipped out the back door while the officers, Wilmot and Charles Giffard argued and discussed the King's business. He might yet be persuaded, the officers thought.

Lord Wilmot said, "Gentlemen, ride with all haste to Scotland, or wherever you are going. The King has made his decision. Let it rest at that. He has showed bravery and courage in battle. I think he shows wisdom now. A king's crown rests not with us, gentlemen, but in the hands of his loyal people."

They rode away. Lord Wilmot mounted his horse, with John Penderel behind him, and took a path through the forest. After a half-hour the King went down the secret stairs and out through a court-yard that led to the woods. Monington and Digby watched him go. William and Richard Penderel were beside him. They had put a woodsman's bill in his hand such as they themselves carried. They walked away, three woodsmen bent on their task of gathering wood in the forest. The King had rubbed his hands on the back of the

chimney and put them to his face. His gait was slowed down
by the heavy rustic boots he wore.

"No one will recognize Majesty now," Digby said to Richard Monington. "Clothes make a man—or at any rate a
gentleman, leastways his outsides."

Richard nodded. He felt curiously empty and weary. The
danger that had ever threatened the King during the trying
days had moved away, to hover like a dark cloud of thunder
over Boscobel, where William Penderel was housekeeper.
Now that he was stripped of all his gentlemen, the onion was
indeed down to the hard core.

With Digby beside him, Richard presented himself at the
home of Mr. Whitgreave, an honest gentleman, with whom
the priest Father Huddleston lived. Both of these gentlemen
had served in the army of Charles the First and therefore
could be counted on as friendly. They were met here by
Lord Wilmot, already domiciled at Moseley Hall. They sat
down with the priest and Mr. Whitgreave to a simple supper
of cheese and bread, washed down by milk. Lord Wilmot was
disturbed by the turn events had taken. He must be repeatedly assured by Mr. Whitgreave and Father Huddleston
that in all England there was no more loyal family than the
Penderels.

The priest said, "We Catholics know what it is to go into
hiding, and not one of us would betray any refugee, let
alone the King. Let us not fear, my lord. God will protect
Charles Stuart, and he will be God's instrument. When we
have finished our meal, let us go to my study. I will draw a
little map to show you various gentlemen's houses where His
Majesty will find welcome." The priest smiled sadly, his
thin, lined face showing his tender compassion.

"These houses have 'priest's holes,' as we call them, hiding
places in chimneys, secret rooms, and stairways giving on
stable or garden or river-bank. It is best that he should stay
in the forest for the time being. Cromwell's men do not
know this countryside. They will turn to the greater houses,
searching right and left, but the forests are strange to them
and spirit-haunted. The Roundheads have no liking for
ghosties or devil's disciples." He crossed himself as he spoke.

In the little study the priest took quill and paper. With
certain skill he drew a small map showing the Severn from
Salop to Worcester, then to Bristol.

"Oliver has gone down from Worcester to Gloucester, then turned toward London. The King had best go from here to Stratford, Long Marston, Cirencester, Abbots Leigh, Bristol."

The men examined the map. From Boscobel to Abbots Leigh there were six houses that were possible refuges. Lord Wilmot nodded approvingly.

"Yes. Yes. Now if we can only get a ship at Bristol!"

Father Huddleston said, "If you do not have good fortune at Bristol, cross quickly to the south." He drew a line direct from Bristol to the Channel. "Along the way are Castle-Cary, Trent and Lyme. Or from Trent to Lyme, Salisbury, Hambledon, Brighthelmstone, as destiny directs."

Lord Wilmot passed the paper to Richard. Richard studied it for a time. "Get it in your minds, sirs. There must be no written evidence," the priest said.

Lord Wilmot looked at the map once more. "You have it, Monington?"

"Sir, I have it firm in my mind."

The priest took the paper, tossed it into the fire and watched it burn to a thin grey ash.

"And so, gentlemen, I suggest that you retire to the priest hole, which is here, beyond the chimney-breast, and sleep. Tomorrow is another day." Their host moved to a painting, pressed a piece of moulding in the panel, and a door swung open.

Carrying a lighted candle shielded by his hand, Whitgreave led them up dusty carved stairs, so narrow a man must move along sidewise. At the head another door swung open and they stepped into a small, mean room, without windows, save a small opening near the chimney. Blankets were spread on pallets.

Lord Wilmot and Richard Monington bade Thomas Whitgreave good night, and he left them a jug of water and a tallow dip. Lord Wilmot snuffed out the candle. They could hear the rain beating on the roof beneath the little tower where they lodged.

"I would rest easier if only I knew where our poor master has laid his head this night," Wilmot said as he stretched his broad shoulders on the husk-filled pallet.

Richard was too weary to talk. Worcester battle was two days past, with only a short rest in the forest. He was asleep almost before he pulled his blanket over him.

Tomorrow was another day.

Charles Stuart's case was more parlous. He had followed
William and Richard Penderel, whom he chose to trust, into
the great wood. Dressed as he was in rustic habit, he made
his way with the brothers to Spring Coppice, about half a
mile from Giffard's home. There William left them and
returned to Boscobel for a horse. It was sunrise on Thursday
morning when the King and Richard Penderel came to the
densest part of the wood. The heavens had opened up and
the rain poured down with melancholy monotony.

The woodsman could find nothing for the King to sit on
that was not soaking wet. He left the King alone and went
to his brother-in-law's house near by. Here he begged a
blanket and food. He told them, "He has had no food for
a full day, walking all the time in heavy boots which have
blistered his feet sorely, but he does not complain. Now
he stands under a tree like a lost sheep."

The good wife said, "The poor lad! Take the blanket and
go on with you, Dick. I'll come anon with victuals."

After a short time she followed him through the wet woods,
her skirts pinned back, a big cape covering her ample form
and the food which she had fixed and kept hot in earthen
dishes: scalded milk, eggs cooked with a rasher of bacon, and
bread hot from the oven. The King saw her coming. He
leaped to his feet and stood in the shadow of a tree.

Trusty Dick said, "No fear, Bill Jones, no fear. 'Tis but my
sister Joanie bringing you victuals and milk."

Charles sat down again. When she came up to him, he
said, "Good woman, can ye be faithful to a distressed
Cavalier?"

"Yes, sir. I will die rather than betray you." The King was
satisfied. Goodwife Yates had the same honest, open countenance that made her brothers men to be trusted.

"Sir, no one shall know from me, but have a care. The
Olivers are riding along the main road. Before God, it is
raining here as though the heavens were weeping! On the
main road it is dry. So Oliver's men will stay on the road."
She crossed herself. "It is the Holy Virgin herself who pro-
tects you, sir."

"Thank you, my good woman." And the King set to eating in a manner as lusty as any woodsman. With every bite

he swallowed he thought, In case we go hungry on the morrow! He smiled and waved as she trudged homeward through the forest.

That night they moved on. They came to a mill where Penderel thought there might be shelter, but the miller shouted to them to move on—rogues and vagabonds were not wanted. So they fled in the dark to the river, tired and wet as they were.

They had no way of knowing that the miller had hidden some Royalist fugitives and dared not let strangers in for fear they might prove Roundheads.

The King and Penderel came to the house of a loyal gentleman. They had gone seven miles from White Ladies. The old man was reluctant to let anyone stop under his roof. His son, he told Penderel, was a prisoner at Shrewsbury, and he could not jeopardize his own safety, and perhaps his son's life, to take a refugee within. "No one at all will I shelter, good man, save only the King himself."

"In that case, sir, you will succour my master, for before God it *is* the King who throws himself on your mercy."

So there were a few hours in a secure hiding place, a barn with clean straw to sleep in. Hot wine and warm food the King had to drink and eat.

In the morning the man of the house, Mr. Francis Woolf, came to the King and told him that his son had come home in the night. It was therefore most dangerous for His Majesty to remain, as the Roundheads were busying about, up and down the highways. The King told him that he would move on, but that his feet were very sore and blistered from walking in heavy boots. Woolf consented to his staying with great reluctance. He and Penderel would scout about and see if it would be safe to move on. He thought the King should have different clothes, but they had nothing to offer.

The habit of the King was indeed rough throughout. The old steeple-crowned hat was greasy from sweat for two inches above the band. It had no lining. The brim turned up. His green cloth jump-coat was threadbare, worn down to the white threads in places. His breeches, belonging to one of the tallest Penderels, had long knees down to the garter. He had wrapped boot stockings of white flannel about his legs. Richard Penderel had cut them away at the top so that they would not be seen above the green yarn stockings, darned at the knees, with no feet. The boots were so old that gravel sifted in through the soles, but he had little rolls of paper between his toes to keep them from galling. He carried a long thorn stick, crooked in three places, which he refused to give up for a better one, because this stick he had cut himself and rubbed down with ashes from a camp-fire, until it had a nice glow.

While Woolf was talking with the King, Richard Monington and Digby came in. They had been seeking the King when they met Richard Penderel, who led them to him. They brought with them a linen shirt which Father Huddleston had given them for the King, to replace the coarse noggen shirt that scratched his delicate skin.

Monington's rustic brown suit was a match for the King's, and he had cut his hair round fashion. His skin needed no walnut stain. Indeed as the two stood together, there was not an inch difference in their height or the slimness of their bodies. Each had large, deep-set eyes, of equal darkness.

The King looked at Richard, measuring his height with his eyes. Smiling, he said, "One might say that a drop or two of Stuart blood runs in your veins, my good captain."

Richard bowed. "That would indeed be an honour, Sire."

"Tut, tut! No Sire. One must remember that at all times. Bill Jones is my name, christened by Penderel here. Now, my men, let us be off."

"My brother William is come with a horse," Richard Penderel said. "A ride for a time will ease your aching feet."

Mr. Woolf said, "Sire, my son says there are two companies of militia at Madeley. They have outposts. They are seizing bridges and boats on the Severn, so there is no chance for you to cross the river in secret."

The men held a consultation, out of earshot of their host. Monington told the King that Lord Wilmot had gone to Bentley Hall near Madeley, the home of a Colonel Lane who was a staunch adherent to the Stuart cause. But at the moment, on account of the activities of the Roundheads at Madeley, it would be best for the King to repair to Boscobel, the most retired place for concealment in all the country.

The King asked the date. "All days in the greenwood are alike. I have lost count," he said.

" 'Tis the seventh of September, Sire," Richard Monington said, "four days from the Battle of Worcester."

For Charles's guidance he reproduced from memory the priest's map.

The King scrambled to the back of the fat old farm horse, mounting from a log. "I do swear this is the heaviest, broadest horse a king ever mounted."

William, the spokesman brother, said, "Must be a solid animal, sir, to bear the weight of three kingdoms."

The King laughed aloud at this, and swore he would reward him well when he became King in truth. "I will make up what you lose on my account. You might get one thousand pounds, because that sum is on my head. If they discover that you have aided me, you'll all have hanging for your pains."

William shook his head. "We be King's men, not Cromwell's." And that was his final word.

They separated then. Digby was sent to Bentley to apprise Lord Wilmot that the King would put himself under the care of Colonel Lane as soon as it was prudent.

Richard Monington went ahead with William Penderel to his home at Boscobel in order to clear the way and prepare for the King's safety. They took a short cut through the wood's bypaths. When they came there late in the afternoon, they found that a Colonel Carlos, who had seen the last man fall at Worcester, had taken retreat in Boscobel Wood, since his own home, eight or nine miles distant, was unsafe.

When the King arrived, he was delighted to see his loyal officer, but William Penderel was disturbed—Colonel Carlos was too well known to the country-folk. Charles would not hear to Carlos leaving him. "Let him stay just a day." Even though scouts were everywhere about, the Stuart luck must hold another day. But the house would be unsafe for both. It was Joan, William's wife, who suggested the tree—a great pollard oak, large and bushy, where the children played. The tree stood less than a furlong from Boscobel House. Since it commanded a broad view from the edge of the wood, it would be a safe hiding place.

The idea tickled the King's fancy. He complimented Joan on her sagacity. He vowed she should have a fine new gown for the yearly fair, and betook himself, a cushion under his arm, to the oak.

It was indeed an ideal place of concealment. In due course Digby, who had now returned from Bentley, and Richard

Monington helped the King to the retreat. Colonel Carlos climbed up after him. Richard walked around the tree, viewing it from every angle. Not a trace of the men could he see. While the Penderels stayed at Boscobel House, he and Digby set about the task of piling wood and picking up faggots, lest Cromwellians should wander down the road seeking refuge—Digby close by the tree, Monington deeper in the wood. It was deemed that Digby would more readily play the countryman than Richard.

Near sunset a small body of Roundhead militia stopped to speak to Digby. "Have you seen any rogues and scamps running this way, yokel?"

"Aye, aplenty of they. Two times the fingers of this hand, countin' yon soldiers."

The soldier laughed, but the leader scowled. "Rogues, I said, not soldiers."

"There be rogues aplenty livin' roundabouts, but I've seen nay foreign rogue on this road."

"Well, keep an eye. The officer at Madeley pays a shilling for information about refugees from Charles Stuart's Scots."

"Does he that? Well, I'll be on the lookout. Have ye yerself captured a few?"

"Nay, not one, but 'tis said many have been took yonder —the Earl of Derby and the red-headed Scottish duke. They'll be taking the earl before the Black Tribunal, 'tis said."

"And the duke?"

"He's bound for London and the Tower. We have no use for Scots amongst us, that we ha'n't, nor King nor soldier."

The soldiers moved on down the road. Digby went back to his work. After a time Monington joined him and together they moved up to the oak.

"Sire, did you hear what they said?" Richard asked of the green leaves.

"Yes, 'tis bad, very bad news indeed." The King's voice sounded very near. "My good, loyal Derby! My staunch Lauderdale! It is as the ancient seer said, 'Those who follow the Stuarts stand in the shadow of doom.'"

A premonition came upon Richard Monington at the King's words. Spoken as they were out of the air, they were disembodied, like the words of an ancient oracle, or of a prophet speaking from the sky.

"I release you all, now, at this moment—you, my faithful

Carlos; you, Captain Monington; you, Digby, best of cooks. Stay no longer with me. Go seek out your own fortunes. Near me, you stand in constant, ever-present danger. Away from me, you are your own men. I repeat, I release you from any oath of loyalty."

Richard said, "Sire, if doom overtake the Stuart, it will be but for the moment. Your star will rise again. On that I pin my faith. . . . Here's our William. He comes smiling, beckoning you to descend. I bend my back for Your Majesty to use as a mounting-block."

The King stepped onto Richard's shoulder and let himself stiffly to the ground. Carlos followed. The King said, "I could eat a saddle of good mutton, I'm so hungry. I hope you have one in your fold, good William."

William scratched his head. "Sir, it is not the mutton that is lacking in the sheepfold. But, sir, we poor folk do not kill sheep, save on high days and holidays. If the neighbours smelled mutton roasting . . ."

Charles laughed. "You think of everything, good William. No doubt clever Joan has a proper supper suitable for men who have sat all day among the leaves of a pollard oak. What a King am I!" he exclaimed.

But he ate good Joan's food in silence. Only by the appetite he displayed did she know that the meal was pleasing.

Once he spoke aloud. "Where will I find another servant like Derby? What will that devil's son do to Lauderdale in the Tower?"

No one spoke again, save to give good-night greetings. William led the King to the little hiding room, built in the time of King Harry. He told the King that it had been the refuge of the Earl of Derby before Worcester.

The king lay down on the pallet in the little dark room, no more than five feet square. There was not space enough for him to stretch his tired limbs.

Carlos and Richard went out to the stables. Digby had made them a bed in the hay-mow, where Carlos slept peacefully, as though he were without a care.

Richard lay awake for a while, thinking of the day's adventures. He was amused by the number of Royalist colonels that kept cropping up. If each represented a regiment, how could the Stuarts ever have been defeated? . . . He had seen greatness in the face of Oliver Cromwell. The young King was slight beside it—there was no gainsaying that. And yet Richard knew his loyalty was no whit diminished. He tried to account for this to himself. Was it family tradition, born and bred in him? Was it the romance of a lost cause—lost at least for the present? Was it companionship in strife, disaster and danger? Was it the Stuart charm?

When Richard awoke, Carlos was no longer in his bed of hay. Richard repaired the damage to his rustic clothes, washed his face in the horse trough. He was combing out his hair when Carlos and Digby came along the wood path. Digby had a dead lamb on his shoulder, skinned and ready for the spit.

"The King's breakfast," Carlos said. "William would not slaughter, but I went a-hunting at Newburgh fold. My long knife was sharp and swift. The King must be served as long as may be."

The two men talked as Carlos washed the blood from his hands. Digby had already gone to the kitchen.

Carlos said, "Today I must find a new place. Too many country-folk know my phiz. Things seem to be quieting down at Madeley for the moment. Tonight, we think, you can safely escort the King to Bentley Hall. Colonel Lane will devise some way to pass him on to Bristol. Every day he stays here is a day lost and a day's danger gained."

Richard agreed. "I have hope of Bristol. Sir John Berkeley is not too far away."

Carlos shook his head. "No. Do not go to Berkeley. He will be watched. Cromwell well knows his loyalty to the King. You must think of other men not so prominent. I myself may make my way to France." He extended his hand. "Good fortune, my lad! Good fortune!"

Richard grasped the hand. It was icy-cold from the trough water. "If you go through Ledbury, remember Coddington Manor is only three miles distant. My mother will greet you with open arms, first for your loyalty to the Stuarts, second for news of me. She will be hungry for news."

"Tell me the way. Perhaps that is a safer route than the one I contemplated."

"I'll do better. Digby shall go with you. He can meet me at Bristol and bring me news of my mother. God with you, Colonel!"

"And with you!"

"Keep close to him, Digby. Get him safe to Bristol and on a ship for France or Ireland. In Bristol go to the house of Gabriel Spencer in King Street. He's an old friend. Till lately he was a tailor in Ledbury. Now he has a shop in Bristol. I'll endeavour to join you at Gabriel's. If you haven't come I'll leave word for you with him. You do the same for me. He is a Loyalist and beholden to my family."

On Sunday the King was up betimes. Richard and Colonel Carlos went to his hiding place where he had passed the night. They did not disturb him, but backed quietly down the secret stairs, for they had come upon the King at his devotions. After a time he descended the stairs to the kitchen, his handkerchief to his nose, for it had begun to bleed. Goodwife Joan had a cure, she said, and placed the blade of a common knife on the back of his neck. After a time the bleeding passed, and the King, grateful to her, repeated his promise that she should have a new gown for the fair, shoes, hosen and a gay bonnet. He laid a gold piece on the table.

Dame Joan curtsied, but would not touch the coin. "I would make confession, Sire. When your beautiful curls fell from your head, while they were being so roughly cut the other day, you bade us burn them. But, Sire, we did not burn all. William and I kept one long lock, so that our children's children will know that our King honoured this house with his presence."

Tears came to Charles Stuart's eyes. "My good woman! My good, good woman! You and your husband and his brothers give me strong courage. You are the very heart of England. I pray God that, when I am King in truth, I may always reach the heart of England."

He wiped away a tear with the back of his hand, for Joan had gathered up the handkerchief, damp with the King's blood.

At that moment Colonel Carlos came in carrying a leg of mutton which had been roasted and was already cold. The King cried out with pleasure. He asked for a trencher and with a sharp knife cut collops from the leg.

"To the kitchen!" he said. "Let us all go to the kitchen, and I will show you how Bill Jones can cook a proper breakfast. Goodwife Joan, a frying-pan and butter! Carlos, stoke the fire. You shall be the under-cook, but I will be the master. Digby, for once you must yield your place."

They all sat down at the King's request and had a right merry breakfast.

As they ate, the other Penderel brothers entered, one after the other, to report on their scouting. The highway was free of Cromwell's men for the moment. Mr. Whitgreave and Father Huddleston would meet the King at midnight in a little grove close to Mr. Whitgreave's, and from there he would go on to Colonel Lane's, where Lord Wilmot already rested.

The King was well pleased with this plan. "I run like a hare this way and that, back over the same track," he told William Penderel.

William said, "Sire the animals of the greenwood know well how to protect themselves."

"And I am learning, I am learning," the King replied.

So that Lord's Day the King spent quietly in the garden at Boscobel, most of the time sitting in the little arbour built on a rise of ground. The arbour contained a stone table and stone benches. The King and his gentlemen read and conversed. More than once the King walked the garden path between Goodwife Joan's rose bushes.

So they set out, late that night. Colonel Carlos took leave of His Majesty and he and Digby departed. Then the Penderels mounted the King on the fat horse. John, William, Trusty Dick, Humphrey and George each took a pike or a bill over his shoulder. Some had pistols. They were ready to defend the King.

The by-way journey through the forest was without incident. When they came near their destination, the King dismounted. A moment later Father Huddleston and Mr. Whitgreave came to the grove. The priest went over with the King the points on his map, which was again burned.

The time had arrived for the King to say farewell to the five brothers. A sad farewell it was, and he was as deeply moved as he had been when Joan showed her devotion.

Richard Monington thought he had never felt more loyalty to Charles than when the five stalwart brothers, each in turn, knelt to kiss the hand of their sovereign. No one spoke. At last the King said to William, smiling a little to ease the emotion, "I am thankful for that dull jade of yours, and I shall always remember what you said to me: 'My liege, can you blame the horse to go heavily, when he has the weight of three kingdoms on his back.' "

William answered, "Aye, that I said, and being a plain countryman I speak what my heart says. God keep you, Sire, for three kingdoms will wait for your return."

The brothers went away and in a moment the deep shadow of the forest held them as its own.

Father Huddleston watched them. "There go Courage, Honesty, Faithfulness, Honour and Wisdom, five heavenly jewels, set in the hearts of earthly men."

Lord Wilmot was waiting for the King in the orchard of Bentley Hall. It was there that Whitgreave and Father Huddleston knelt to take leave of their King. Father Huddleston was sad. "My prayers go with you, my liege."

Charles, too, was saddened. "I am leaving all my faithful friends behind me. What am I to do?"

"Have faith, Sire, that other friends will rise up to help you. Look forward, not back, for the bright future lies before you."

"I pray God your words prove true, Father."

At Bentley they were greeted warmly. Colonel Lane imparted good news. His young sister, Mistress Jane Lane, planned a trip to Bristol. She had obtained a pass for herself and her servant, to go to visit a friend who was about to have a child. The King should ride as Jane Lane's servant, a country boy, son of a near-by tenant.

So the King became Will Jackson, and left the old Bill Jones behind when he discarded the clothes he had been wearing in the forest.

Colonel Lane brought out new garments suitable to a household servant—a suit of sober grey as near like the holiday suit of a yeoman's son as could be. The colonel, who was a good sturdy man, red-faced and rotund, a soldier turned country squire, tutored the King in the behaviour of a serving-man. In spite of instructions the King offered the wrong hand to help Jane Lane to mount, much to her amusement.

The party set off led by a cousin of the Lanes, Mr. Henry Lassells, cornet to the colonel in the late wars, who had been taken into the secret. He rode single. In the company were another sister of Colonel Lane, Mrs. John Petre of Buckinghamshire, and her husband, on their way home from a visit. They rode double. The Petres were quite unaware that the King rode with them. Charles, mounted behind Jane as her attendant, slumped and made himself look shorter. Jane was a pretty blonde, and Charles, who never could resist a pretty face or buxom figure, thought it a delightful way to travel. Jane could hardly control her excitement.

Lord Wilmot, Colonel Lane and Richard Monington carried a hawk and spaniels with them as though to go a-hawking in the next county. In order to avoid attracting attention they took a parallel road, planning to sleep that night in Warwickshire, at the home of Sir Clement Fisher.

All went well until somewhere along the road Jane's horse cast a shoe. They stopped at a little forge in a small village. Charles led the horse to be reshod. He sat down on a bench at the door of the forgehouse and chatted with the smith, who was a gossip, full of talk of war and battles.

"That rogue, Charles Stuart, is about to be captured," the blacksmith told his customer.

Will Jackson said, "That he is. No doubt he'll be hanging for leading in the Scots."

"You speak like an honest man." The smith did not glance at the countryman. His eyes were on the iron heating in the forge.

After the horse was shod and ready, they went on their way. Near Stratford they saw a troop of Cromwell's dragoons riding along the road ahead. Timid Mr. Petre was afraid they might seize his horse. Mr. Lassells said to the King and Jane privately that he thought they would have the best chance of escaping notice if they rode the short remaining distance alone. The King agreed. So Lassells and the Petres turned back to enter Stratford by another route.

The King and Jane jogged along through the soldiers, who very politely opened for them to right and left, and into the streets of Stratford. Jane kept her bright eyes on her horse's neck, and Charles kept his on her much prettier one. No one observed them as they made their way through the town. They met a very worried Mr. Lassells at Long Marston, three miles west of Stratford, and relieved his anxiety. Here they met also Lord Wilmot, Colonel Lane, Richard Monington and the Petres, and all took up quarters at the home of Mr. John Tomes.

Charles's wits had been sharpened by the experiences of the past ten days. He was alert, and his watchfulness and ingenuity saved him in an awkward adventure. The cook at the Tomes house was cross because Charles could not manage to wind up the jack properly. He gave a quick answer.

"I'm the son of a poor tenant of Colonel Lane in Staffordshire, ma'am. We ha'n't roast meat often, and we don't make use of a jack. Is it wonder that I'm clumsy?"

The cook, busy as she was getting food ready for her master's guests, did not answer him or ask further help.

Lord Wilmot and Colonel Lane left them the next morning for Sir Clement Fisher's, and Mrs. Petre and her husband departed for Buckinghamshire without once suspecting that the farm boy was His Majesty the King.

The party was small again. Richard rode not far behind Mistress Lane and Charles. Lassells followed, overtaking them at an inn in Cirencester, where he secured a good room with a trundle bed. He took the servant, Will Jackson, into the room with him, and the seeming master lay on the trundle bed while the servant slept soundly in the large one.

They were now not far from the end of the Bristol journey. Richard took leave of the King, to ride ahead and make inquiry about ship sailings, while Mr. Lassells, Jane Lane and Will Jackson rode on to the Nortons' at Abbots Leigh.

They were all in good spirits. A long, dangerous journey had been accomplished. They had passed Cromwell's men from time to time, had heard talk that the King was dead . . . was in the Tower, waiting to lay his head on the block . . . was safe in France. They had smiled to themselves momentarily, but they knew they were not yet out of the woods.

Once a Scot, hiding in an old house, saw Charles and recognized him, but the King had no fear that the soldier would report him to the Parliamentary officers.

They rode into the court-yard at Abbots Leigh. Mr. George Norton, who did not know that the King was in the party, welcomed Jane Lane and Mr. Lassells. He explained that his wife was in a delicate way and unable to greet them. He sent Jane's servant around to the stables. As the King was leading the horse away, he saw the butler turning to stare at him.

This was ill luck, for Charles recognized John Pope, who

had been in his father's service when he was a boy at Richmond. Whether the man knew him or was only troubled by
an obscure resemblance, he could not tell. He was quite alone.

The King groomed the horse, not wanting to present himself in the kitchen until he had formed some plan to escape
the butler's eyes. He was sure the man would recognize him
in time, especially if he got close, for he remembered Pope
clearly. At Richmond he had served Tom Jermyn, a groom of
the bedchamber.

He did not know that, at this very moment, Jane Lane was
talking to the butler, asking him to find a room in the house
for her servant Will Jackson, because he had been very ill
with the ague and had not yet recovered. It was a plausible
story, for the King's worry, his want of the meat and food
to which he was accustomed, had made him pale.

The butler replied that he could do as she wished, that
there was a very good room, close to the chamber occupied
by Mr. Lassells, which happened to be unoccupied. It was
far from the other bedroom wings. This he repeated. He
would conduct the servant to the room at once and see that
he had proper food for one with the ague.

Pope laid such emphasis on the location of the room that
Mistress Lane was worried. She mentioned it to Lassells. "I
think you should speak to Will Jackson immediately, sir. He
should be on his guard, in case the man recognizes him." She
did not know what good reason there was to fear this.

Lassells agreed. Professing that he wanted to look at his
horse which had shown signs of colic, he made his way to
the stable. There he found Charles Stuart leaning against a
stall, watching the horses feed. His hair was roughed up,
and without pretence he looked wan and ill.

Lassells, usually verbose, for once was brief. He disclosed
the situation quickly. He was more than disturbed when the
King told him that he had seen the butler before. "I am trying to think of a believable story," Charles said, "but none
comes to my mind. I believe the only thing to do is to talk
frankly to Pope and throw myself on his mercy."

Lassells begged him not to be hasty. "Wait until I have
time to make some inquiry. Meanwhile Mistress Lane has
arranged with the butler to put you into a chamber next to
mine. Let it stand at that until tomorrow, when I will talk
to Mr. Norton."

"Norton has no idea whom he entertains?"

"None whatever. Will Jackson you are, as far as our host knows. That is well. Leave this matter to me. There will be a way out."

As they talked, the restive horse moved about the stall, kicking and biting at the horse in the next compartment. He flayed about with his heels, sending a shower of fresh manure over Charles's stockings and breeches. The sight and the smell upset the King's stomach and with noisy retching he rid himself of his last meal. This was happening just as Pope put his head into the stable.

The King staggered to the door on the way to the horse trough to cleanse his garments with water applied with a stable broom.

Lassells stood by. He dared not offer assistance. The butler did not hesitate. He took up a currying brush and set to work on the King's breeches. In a short time they were presentable. The King clung to the door, unable to stand erect.

"I had better show the lad his room, sir. . . . Come this way, boy," John Pope said to the King. "I'll get you a drink of ale to settle your queasy stomach."

As Lassells watched them go through the kitchen door, apprehension assailed him. When he came to the great hall, he found Mr. Norton and John Lane standing near the fire, talking with Monington, who had left off his rustic clothes and was dressed as a merchant in grey wool with green knitted hosen. Mr. Norton was saying, "Of course you will stay the night here, Captain Monington, though I regret that Mrs. Norton may not offer you proper entertainment. You cannot ride back to Bristol in the dark of the moon. This is Mr. Lassells, who also is my guest." The two men acknowledged the introduction.

Lassells said, "Perhaps Captain Monington would like to share my bedchamber. It is large and comfortable, with two beds. The fire is already burning brightly."

"That's kind of you," Richard said. He sensed instantly that something was on Lassells' mind. "If our host will permit——"

"Of course; a very satisfactory arrangement. Perhaps you'd like to go up at once. I'll have my man Pope bring up your saddle-bags."

"Please do not trouble," Lassells interposed quickly. "I'll help him up with them." He lifted the bags from a chair.

"Supper in an hour, gentlemen." Norton saw his guests to the stairway, then hurriedly followed Jane Lane to the east wing. He was a worried man, for the midwife had told him that his wife was very near her time.

Lassells and Richard walked quickly along the gloomy halls.

"Is all well with you? Where is he?" Richard asked.

"In the chamber next to ours. That is why I asked Norton to put you with me. I am glad you're here. I may need your help. I'll tell you when we're safe in our chamber."

Lassells closed the door, after looking to see that they were not followed. He told Richard about the King's suspicion of the butler. "He wants to disclose himself to the man, and trust Pope to keep the secret. I am not sure it is a safe solution." Lassells walked about the room. He was a short man with bright blond hair and deep blue eyes that met one squarely.

Richard said, "The King has a sort of Scotch wisdom. He trusts to instinct about people. Perhaps his way is right. Can we go to him without danger of being seen?"

"I think so. I saw Pope go in some time ago carrying a tray. He must have left by now. I swear I never saw a sorrier figure than the King was there in the stable. Surely he was a sick man, if I ever saw one, with his face livid and his nose pinched in." Lassells went on and on telling about it, picking up details.

"Let us go now," Richard said, impatient of the other's lengthy description. If there was danger, it should be met at once, without delay.

The King called "Enter," in response to Lassells' gentle tap on the door. Charles was sitting up in bed, with a tray of food on his lap. A small tin bath, full of water, was standing near the fire-place. Damp towels were piled on the floor.

Charles smiled at Lassells' astonishment. "Feed a fever, the butler tells me. A good warm sponge, he says, then into bed, made very comfortable by warming pans."

Lassells looked more worried than ever. Surely the butler would not take so much care of a sick groom.

Charles, well bathed, well fed, had lost his fears. "Who knows? The gods provide us with what we most need—rest and comfort and a degree of safety. Tomorrow I will interrogate the man Pope. Until then, let us drink this good sack he has so thoughtfully provided, and let me hear the news of Bristol, Captain Monington."

Richard had no good news to report. There was no ship for France or Spain or Portugal, or even for Virginia, for at least thirty days. The earlier story about the capture of the Earl of Derby was true. He would be condemned and no doubt beheaded. Lauderdale was in the Tower. Buckingham was still at large, but being hunted. "Mr. Giffard was taken, Sire, but made his escape."

"Thank God for that!"

"Bristol is filled with Cromwell's men. Every road throngs with them. I myself have been questioned more than once, but, like a chameleon, I take on other colouration. Now I am a London merchant, with interest in the Virginia tobacco, waiting for a shipment that is slow in arriving. Gabriel Spencer, an old friend in Bristol, loyal to our cause, helped me to dress the part. I walk down the quay each morning and meet with other merchants at the tavern—a good device for hearing about the movement of ships."

"Excellent! And now what of your own affairs? Is there any news of your home?"

A dark look came over Richard's face. "Sire, Digby has not come to our rendezvous, but yesterday I saw, at a distance, my neighbour Nicholas Holder. I turned aside so that I would not accost him."

"You cannot trust your neighbour?"

"Sire, no. He was a King's man for a time, but when Cromwell seemed likely to win, he proved a turncoat. I have an itch to accost him with my sword, but if I got into a brawl, I might in some way lead the wolves to you. Private quarrels must wait."

The King pushed the tray on his knees. Lassells quickly took it up and set it on a long Spanish chest. Richard stood by the fire. He could not shake off his moodiness.

The King asked, "What do you say now, Monington? Linger in hiding for a month, or try my luck moving southward to a Channel port?"

"Sire, Bristol is the most dangerous of your ports now. They watch closely, thinking you've come this way. Half the people I saw or talked with thought you were dead, or captured and in the Tower. A few hoped you were safe in Scotland. I would cast my vote for you to move on. I have talked with Lord Wilmot. He is safe, staying at a house a mile or two from here. He thinks as I do, that you should move on to Castle-Cary. Francis Wyndham will guard you well."

Lassells exclaimed, "But how?"

Richard held up a warning finger. He had heard a step in the hall. He moved cautiously toward the heavy oak door and stood so that he would be out of sight when it opened. Lassells stepped behind a screen.

When Pope came in for the tray, the King was lying on his side, resting. The butler took up the tray and went out of the room quietly, without glancing to left or right.

The King said, "You had best depart, gentlemen. If I need you, I will beat on the wall. Good night. I shall sleep quietly and well between sheets this night."

If the King slept quietly, Richard Monington did not. He moved from side to side of the great bed, unable to lose himself in sleep.

Before his eyes was the picture he had seen near Tetbury on the way to Bristol—a coach driving rapidly down the road, a horseman beside it. A woman's bright, eager face was at the open window. She was looking at the horseman as he bent to hear her words. The woman was Kathryn Audley, the horseman Nicholas Holder. They had not seen the countryman who turned his horse into a path by the road. It was that glimpse of Kathryn Audley, and not the King's danger, which kept Richard Monington from sleep.

A strange, muffled cry broke the stillness of night . . . another and another . . . then silence. Richard leaped to his feet and ran into the hall, holding his dagger unsheathed.

There was no sound. The hallway was in deep shadow. He could discern no movement from either direction. The moon through the oriel window gave a dim light that fell directly on the door of the King's chamber. He moved slowly along the wall and turned the knob. The door was unlocked. He entered quietly.

The King spoke softly. "Who?"

"Monington. Did you hear cries?"

"Yes. Weird sounds, like a soul in torment."

"What are they? I did not dare walk the halls to find out."

They both listened quietly but there was no repetition of the curious wailing.

"I shall sleep at your feet, my naked knife in my hand, Sire."

"As you will, Captain. I vow I shall sleep indeed, with you on guard."

Once more, later by an hour, the sounds came through the night, but the King was not aroused. Richard went into the hall, to the far end of the corridor. He saw a white figure moving toward him. The moon behind it made a sort of nimbus about its head. He flattened himself against the wall. When the figure came nearer he saw it was a young woman carrying a candle . . . Jane Lane. She was weeping.

He spoke softly, not to frighten her. "Is there trouble?" he asked.

"Trouble enough, Captain Monington. Mrs. Norton has been delivered of a son, still-born." She moved on down the hall. Richard went back to the King's chamber. Charles still slept, quietly as a child.

CHAPTER 10

The Royal Miracle

THE following morning the King rose early. He swore to Richard and Lassells that he had a good stomach and would breakfast in the buttery hatch. The men tried to dissuade him. Richard said, "From here to Bristol, every little knot of men gathered together talking have but one subject of conversation."

"I know, I know. But we must not slink away like criminals. Let us be bold. Did you not see how we rode through Cromwell's dragoons at Stratford?"

"I wish Digby were here to go to the buttery with you, but he has not returned. I am uneasy about him." Richard was uneasy about Coddington Manor and his lady mother, but he did not speak of that. When one serves a sovereign, one does not speak of private matters.

The King left them and went down the back stairs to the kitchen. There he found Pope, the butler, and several house servants eating bread and butter and drinking ale with a fat country fellow and two companions.

Pope indicated a seat beside the fat man, who at once began to talk about the Battle of Worcester. He was in the fight, he said, when the King's men sallied from the Sudbury Gate. "A hot fight it was. Many a man lay down for good that day." He helped himself to another slice of bread. He eyed the King for a moment.

Charles noticed Pope hovered near, polishing a silver tankard with a cloth. He asked the countryman questions, not knowing yet whether he was friend or foe. "What regiment did you fight with?"

"The King's Regiment of Guards, Major Broughton's company." He eyed the King again. The others had left off eating. Pope moved a step or two, until he was directly behind Charles.

176

Charles spoke quickly. He grasped the opportunity boldly. "What manner of man is the King?" he asked. "Tall or short, lean or fat? We hain't seen him in Herefordshire."

The man swigged down his ale. "Tall—three inches higher than you be. He wore kingly clothes, with medals and orders on him, and he galloped hatless up and down the line, swinging his sword. Gar! 'Twas a fine brave sight to see him with his long black hair flying out, and his eyes lighted by fire— a fair, brave sight."

"He's a Scot," one of the men said shortly.

"Aye, a Scot he is, and we be beholden to his father and to the bonny Queen Mary Stuart, though it's worth a man's head to speak so." Charles glanced at the house servants. They nodded. He settled back a little, lifted his pewter mug of ale, drank deep, set it down again and wiped his lips with the back of his hand.

"Yes, three inches taller than you be, my lad." The fat man held his hand up sideways. Charles stiffened. He glanced at Pope, who had moved to the other side of the table, facing him.

The King rose slowly, his hand on the table. He looked at Pope. "Thank you, sir, for the good food. A good breakfast in the belly gives strength. Yesterday was my ague day. It leaves me with knees as weak as a suckling pig. Good morning."

He walked slowly from the room, his hand against his side as though he had pains. The men's eyes followed him. He heard Pope say, "He was a sick pup when he rode in with Mistress Lane, yesternight. The stable lads had to lift him off his nag."

"He looks like . . ." The countryman choked on a piece of crust. Pope gave him a resounding slap on the back, and he did not finish what he started to say.

The King climbed the stairs toward his chamber. Pope was close behind. Jane Lane was walking down the upper hall. Charles stood aside, his hat in his hand. She paused a moment, inquired about his ague and went on toward the wing where Mrs. Norton lay, very ill indeed. Pope watched the King enter his chamber and then followed Mistress Lane down the hall.

Lassells and Richard Monington had been waiting in the upper hall. They talked together and joined the King a few minutes later. Lassells was much perturbed. "I am sure Pope recognized you. I saw him watching you closely when you encountered Mistress Lane. What are we to do?" he cried, greatly agitated. "We have no way of knowing whether we have loyal adherents in this house or not. Mr. Norton has no idea of your identity. All we know about the Nortons is that Jane Lane says they are loyal. This butler is always hanging about. I don't like it."

The King broke in. "I am determined to talk to Pope and discover myself to him. I think he is an honest fellow. What think you, Captain?"

Richard answered promptly, "A bold course is best, Sire."

"Good! Then send him in. I will talk to the man *alone*."

The butler was in the hall when Richard opened the door. He said, "Will you go inside for a moment, Pope?"

The man gave him a piercing look, went in and closed the door.

Lassells walked nervously up and down their chamber. "I don't like it! I don't like it!" he repeated endlessly. "I wish Lord Wilmot were here to advise us. What do you think, Monington? You are too damned calm to suit me."

Richard grinned. "Perhaps I believe in the Stuart luck or destiny or whatever you may call it. Or perhaps I believe the King has good judgement."

They were interrupted by a light tap. Lassells opened the door. Pope, grave and unperturbed, said, "The King will receive you now, gentlemen."

Lassells gave him a swift glance and left the room. Richard waited a moment. "Is this house safe, Pope?"

Pope answered, "The master and mistress and most of the household are loyal, but there are some rogues. I have told His—" he glanced quickly over his shoulder—"told him that Lord Wilmot must not be seen coming here. He is too well known. I have suggested that I go to Lord Wilmot's hiding place tonight and fetch him here in the darkness."

Richard nodded. "That is wisdom, Pope. The King does well to trust you."

The butler drew himself up. "Sir, we have always served the Stuarts."

Richard laid his hand on the man's shoulder for a moment. "And my people have also. Yes, after nightfall. We stand together, making our endeavour to get him safely out of the country."

Richard was pleased that Pope made no further protestations. He had affirmed his loyalty once.

That night the butler brought Lord Wilmot to Richard's bedchamber. "Better he is here than in the chamber of a groom," he remarked. "Will Jackson can assist me to serve three gentlemen their wine without comment of the house servants should they happen to come this way. I think everything is quite safe, sir."

Pope stirred the great logs into a blaze. The firelight flickered on the polished floor and lighted the deep shadows of the walnut panels. The King lay on one of the great beds, his face shadowed by the red velvet curtains of the canopy.

Lord Wilmot sat on a velvet-covered stool near the bed talking to the King in a low tone. The others stood by the fire while Pope filled the wine cups.

Richard thought the strain was showing on Lord Wilmot. The lines of his dark face were deeply etched; his eyes moved restlessly. He gave the appearance of a man constantly looking over his shoulder for an unseen enemy. Of the four the King showed the least strain.

He has faith in his star, Richard thought. He knows he will survive. He feels it in his heart, therefore he is at peace with himself. Richard wished he had the same composure. He was beginning to worry again about Digby. He should have been in Bristol before now. Two weeks were time enough. Had he run into trouble at Coddington Manor, or had he been taken by soldiers along the way? Where was Carlos? Had he got ship to France? Alone, Digby could get through—he was almost certain of that. Digby was a countryman, wise in the ways of the forest and the countryside. He was of too small importance for Cromwell's men to bother with. But the company of William Carlos added danger. He was an officer on whose head was a price. Still, the Roundheads' chief concern was for the one big game, Charles Stuart, whose capture would mean large rewards in money and rank. Perhaps smaller fry would be overlooked. Richard settled himself in a tall-backed chair and watched the moonrise through the oriel window.

There was something almost uncanny in Charles's luck.

Richard thought of the number of people who knew his secret, who had passed him along. It was like some old fabulous tale of mediaeval times and the Crusades, when minstrels had moved from castle to castle seeking prisoners and releasing them. Now the people and the nobles were united to serve Charles. Escapes had been narrow, accomplished by the King seizing the poker by the hot end and moving on unscathed. One thing was certain: Lord Wilmot, his father's faithful Harry Wilmot, must never travel with him, for his presence at any time was more and more a menace, especially as he had refused to wear a disguise.

"As Monington's already told you, I understand, there's no ship at Bristol for a month," Richard heard Wilmot say.

"And what then?" the King asked.

Pope ventured to speak. "If you will allow me, Sire, I will go into Bristol. I may be able to find some small fishing craft that would take you to the Lizard or some Cornish or South Devon port. If you will trust me, Sire . . ."

"My good Pope, have I not said I put my life in your hands? By God, I believe them capable hands! Here's my faith on it to seal the bargain, if you like."

"Sire, Sire!" The man sank on his knees by the bedside and kissed the hand the King extended. "I will go at once—tonight. I know taverns that keep revel all night.

"I wish I might go with you. A little revelling would be good for me. I've been a monk too long." He sighed and clasped his arms behind his head and lay looking at the dark folds of the canopy. "A nice sweet maid, and the curtains pulled close—ah!"

The room was silent. Richard had seen the King's eyes rest on Jane Lane, but he knew he would not trespass there. Pope opened his mouth, then shut it firmly.

Wilmot said, "Many a man has betrayed himself in the bedchamber. His guard is down, and the wrong woman . . ."

"Yes, I know, I know. I'll stay a monk until I reach France, and then, by my Knight's Oath, I'll toss the maids with the vigour of another Borgia!" He sat up, his eyes bright. "They tell that Caesar Borgia had a virgin every night. Those were glorious days."

"Before John Knox came to Scotland, Wilmot said dryly.

"Ah, the dream breaks and fades away," the King said.

"Presbyterianism is a dour belief, no religion for a gentleman." He laughed softly at his conceit.

Pope left the room. The King looked after him. "I believe, if I had talked a little more, the man would have fetched a plump dairymaid to the bed of William Jackson. But, as you say, Wilmot, there is danger in these pleasurable moments."

"Grave danger, Sire. . . . Perhaps we should plan the next move now. I have no hope that there will be a ship available in Bristol for weeks. Cromwell is using ships for prisoners. All the prisoners that he doesn't behead or put in the Tower, he plans to send to the West Indies, Antigua, Barbados and the Somers Islands. There will be thousands of prisoners. Sire, do you know it is said Oliver lost only two hundred men at Worcester, while we lost twelve thousand, mostly prisoners?"

Charles groaned and rolled over so that his face was hidden in the bolster. "I don't want to think of it. Why do you remind me, Wilmot?" He sat up and swung his feet over the bed. Lassells hastened to place the steps for the King to descend.

"I'm going to my chamber and my bed. Make any plan that you think best. Remember that if we can't go by sea, Cary-Castle is a safe place. Francis Wyndham, brother of the Lord Marshal, who is our good friend, lives at Trent not far from the castle." He yawned and went to the door. "We had better arrange to have Mistress Lane informed of our plan, so she may leave with me. It is safer travelling as her escort."

Lassells said, "Mrs. Norton is very ill. How can Mistress Lane leave without arousing suspicion?"

The King thought a moment. "We will write a letter which we will deliver to her in the morning. We will say that her father is very ill indeed, and that she must return home at once. That will leave her free. Then she and William Jackson can set off for Trent and Castle-Cary. We may discover some place in Dorset or Devonshire from which a ship is sailing for France. Don't despair gentlemen. Our way is still open before us."

He closed the door behind him. My Lord Wilmot's eyes turned from Richard to Lassells. "His faith is beyond all conception. I would like to tell those desperate wretches who harbour in their thoughts wicked designs against the sacred person of the King, that God Almighty would not have led him through so many wildernesses of affliction, snatched him so from the midst of his enemies, unless there were ahead of him a great design of kingship."

Lassells agreed with him with a more loquacious enthusiasm than he had shown of late.

Richard said, "Pope told me the prisoners are being sent in numbers to Bristol. Dungeons and prisons are filled with the wretched men. He told me that a soldier wearing a buff coat talked to a press of people at the docks. He boasted that it was the King's coat he wore, and he himself had stabbed the King as he fled from Worcester."

"What manner of man was this?"

"Pope said he was a thin, dark man, with grizzled hair and dragoon boots and breeches. I wondered somehow if it might be Digby. It would be like him to think up some such thing, in order to make the people less mindful of the King. But Digby has not appeared at the rendezvous I gave him, so it must have been some other friend. The longer we succeed in concealing our Charles's movements, the less the people will be looking for him. Let us hope the Bristol people believe the dragoon's tales."

Wilmot nodded. Lassells said, "He bears a charmed life." Richard laid his hand against the bed-post. It was not good to boast of one's blessings, lest they be taken away.

Lord Wilmot said, "No matter what, I shall get into this bed and sleep. Four days and nights with so little rest have made me dizzy and my brain dull." He stripped himself of his garments and got in between the sheets. Lassells climbed into the other bed.

Richard smiled. They had forgotten him. "I'll keep watch until Pope returns," he said. He took up his cloak and went into the hall. Opposite the King's door and their own was a great bow-window that went from the floor to the high-pitched ceiling. Richard stretched himself on the cushioned window-seat where he could watch both doors.

His very bones were weary. He lay without moving, his dark cloak as one with the shadows. A fear of what had transpired at home gnawed at his vitals. He thought of his mother sitting as proudly as a queen, answering with un-ruffled calm the questions of Cromwell and his generals. His mind turned to the Lady's Bower. His blood tingled at

the remembrance of that brief moment when Kathryn lay
in his arms, the ecstasy of her lips against his. For a moment
it seemed that his passion had met a response in her, her lips
were hot and she had clung to him—only a moment, and
then her lips had gone cold, her body without life.

What an actress she was! he thought bitterly, remembering
her bright face upturned in the coach window. Nicholas
Holder! His anger rose. He should have pulled the swine
from his horse and run him through with his sword. He
wondered what expression would have come across Kathryn's
face if he had yielded to that impulse. Horror? Scorn? Or
would there have been tenderness and a little pride? Some
women wanted a master. Some loved best when the man
was ruthless.

A slight sound, a floor-board creaking, caught his ear. His
eyes turned to the deep shadows at the end of the hall that
led to the stairway to the kitchen. He made out a figure
moving cautiously. As it neared a window, the twin of the
one where he rested, the moonshine caught the gleam of
metal. Richard moved his feet slightly to be sure they were
free of the cloak. He made no other move. It might be Pope
returning. When the figure came closer into the full light
cast by the window behind, Richard saw the man in profile.
It was not Pope, but a stranger.

The figure moved with infinite caution, his hand on the
dark-panelled wall. He had an unsheathed dagger in one hand,
with the other he felt for the door-latch. As he bent forward
to peer within, Richard sprang. The man fell, half in and
half out of the doorway. The dagger turned in his upflung
hand, piercing his gullet. A strange gurgling sound and he
was quite still.

The King called, "Who's there?" He sat up in the moonlight, looking toward the door.

Richard replied briefly. He pulled the man's stout body
within the room and closed the door. The King leaped from
his warm bed and darted across the room. Silent he stood
looking down on the sprawling inert body. Richard lighted a
candle. To his astonishment his hand was steady. He carried
the candle across the room to light the dead man's face. He
had never seen him before.

The King made a slight exclamation. "It is the countryman
I told you about. He was at breakfast—the one that talked

of Worcester battle and said the King was three inches higher
than I. He deceived me. I thought he didn't know me, but he
did."

"He kept quiet for the reward," Richard muttered.

"But the dagger—he meant it for me!"

"The reward says, 'dead or alive,' Sire. No matter. His
treachery has overtaken him. 'Hoist on his own petard.' "

"We must dispose of this carrion. If someone comes
in . . ."

Richard looked around. The long Spanish chest would do
for the moment. He opened the lid. The chest was quite
empty. It gave off a strong musty odor. He lifted the man
into the chest, closed it and turned the key.

Sitting in the tall chair by the fire, the King watched him,
with bare feet on the stretcher.

Richard took up the candle and examined the floor. "He
had as much blood in him as a stuck pig," he muttered and
looked around for a cloth to clean the blood from the floor.
A pair of towels hung on the rack near the stand that held
the copper ewer and basin. He rubbed the towels over the
sticky mess with his foot. Then he started toward the fire.
He paused—no burning to make a stench in the night.

The King sat with his elbows on the chair arm, his chin
in his hand. In an even voice he said, "The chest."

Richard took up the towels with the tips of his fingers.
With face averted he opened the chest and tossed the blood-
covered rags within.

"We will have to tell Pope," the King said. Richard nodded.
The body would certainly have to be taken away.

The King looked thoughtfully at the fire which Richard
was feeding with dry sticks and a round log. When he spoke
it was not about the body in the Spanish chest. That matter
was closed. He said, "We must write the letter to Mistress
Lane, that her father is extremely ill and she must come home
to Bentley at once."

Richard assented and went to his chamber for writing
materials.

The King wrote the letter. He took pains to have it very
neat and in good order. Richard held the candle near the
table. "It would have been better if the table had not been
shaky," the King complained. "Now someone must advise

good Jane Lane of the plan, so that she may act her part in the morning."

"I will tell Mistress Lane, Sire, in privacy. Her room is along the south hall."

The King shook his finger. "No playfulness, my fine captain!"

Richard grinned. How like Charles! "Perhaps you would swear me into your monkdom until Your Majesty is in France."

The King laughed aloud. "Not that, Captain! Not that! It would stretch loyalty to too fine a thread."

Pope scratched at the door at daybreak. His mission to Bristol had been fruitless. The King was asleep. Richard Monington had drowsed in a chair drawn up by the fire. He leaped to his feet, his dagger drawn, as the door opened. Pope, startled, drew back, his arm bent to protect himself. Richard slid the dagger into the sheath. He smiled at the expression of alarm on Pope's face. "One does not know who comes," he said, his voice low, not to disturb the sleeping King.

He beckoned Pope to the window and opened the lid of the carved Spanish chest. The first light of the sun slanted through the leaded window and touched the ghastly face of the dead man.

Pope uttered an exclamation. "The fat soldier!" he muttered. "He sat beside the King at breakfast. I was uneasy about him. I did not know whether he was King's man or Oliver's, friend or foe."

"I don't know which army he fought with. It was the gold that tempted him, or maybe he was sent to assassinate." Briefly he told the story of the night. "We must get rid of this carcass. How?"

Pope thought a moment. "It is early. No one will be astir. Let us carry him to the stable-yard." He lifted the corpse from the chest to his shoulders, a fat man and heavy, but Pope was broad of beam and strong of arm and limb. "Please to go ahead and see that the way is clear."

Richard moved cautiously along the passage-way, down dark stairs, through the pantry. Outside the crisp morning air felt clean and good against his cheeks. It was not quite light, a grey, dismal dawn that foretold rain.

Pope was breathing hard behind him. He let the body slide to the ground. "Sir, when I get my breath, I think I had best go through the orchard to the wall that gives on the highway. The body will be found by the patrol, and no questions asked. Too many stragglers wandering about to cause comment."

"Let me help you."

"Sir, no. The blood will soil your clothes."

"Blood has already soiled my hands, but I had no time for care when I saw him lifting the latch to the King's chamber."

Pope raised the body again and moved into the shadows of the stable-yard. A horse neighed; a hen ran out from the hay; a rooster in the fowl-yard mounted a dung heap and lifted his daily warning.

They went through the orchard, down toward the high brick wall that shut it off from the Bristol highway. Richard climbed the rough wall and sat astride the top.

" 'Ware of broken glass on top of the wall!" the butler exclaimed.

"I've already found it!" Richard laughed.

"He weighs too much," Pope grunted as he pushed the body upward so that Richard might grasp the dangling arms. "He was never a foot soldier."

"If he was ever in the wars, I'd wager he drove a sutler's waggon," Richard said, pulling the man athwart the wall. Pope scrambled up. Together they heaved the body into the ditch outside the wall.

"The bushes will hide him from the road. A man gets his deserts, I'm a-thinking," Pope remarked as they walked toward the house. "What troubles me, Captain, the wretch had two companions. They left him and went on to Bristol. Do you think they might return? Did he tell them about the King? Have they gone to get the soldiers?"

Richard paused, looking at Pope. "God's wounds," he said, "we'd best get the King away from here at once!"

They had come to the court-yard. There were sounds of activity, clattering of pots and pans. The butler indicated a walk that led to the rose garden. "Go that way to the front door. I'll let you in, sir."

Pope disappeared as Richard mounted the stairs. At the cross-hall he met Jane Lane coming from the master wing. She was walking slowly, looking down. Richard caught sight of her white face. It was drawn and weary. She looked up quickly and stepped back, starting to curtsy. Then she said in wonder, "I thought you were the King."

Richard, without replying to her words, plunged into the happenings of the night. "We must get the King away at once." He explained the plan. "I'll send Pope with the letter. As soon as we've had breakfast, we must leave."

She nodded. "I wish it were night instead of daylight. There are so many seeking him now, so many men with hatred or avarice in their hearts." She went on her way.

Richard stood for a moment, watching her. The good loyal girl! he thought. Again she must take up the heavy burden.

Richard woke Lassells and explained the urgency of a swift departure. Lassells was gloomy. "Every day increases danger, every hour. Since Bristol has no ships, we must move on southward."

When they entered the King's chamber, they found Lord Wilmot and the butler assisting the King with his dressing. Wilmot was disturbed, but the King was in good spirits. When Richard entered he said, "Ah, I was about to tell my Lord Wilmot how you killed my assailant last night and threw him into the chest there."

Wilmot looked bewildered. Lassells uttered an exclamation and opened the lid of the chest. It was empty. The King crossed the room and bent over it. "It's empty, but the bloodstains remain." He looked from Pope to Richard. "You removed it while I slept!"

"Sire, yes. The wretch will do no more harm in this world with his wicked dirk."

Charles laid his hand on Richard's arm. "My friend guarded my door last night to good purpose. Let us speak of it no more."

Lord Wilmot's anxiety deepened. "You must go from here at once, Sire. I'll leave immediately and make my way to Wyndham's home at Trent to advise him and make all arrangements. It will be wise for you to follow in an hour or two."

The King turned to Richard. "Has Mistress Jane been informed of our plan?"

"Sire, yes. She will be ready at once." He said to Lassells, "Perhaps it would be wise for you to ride double with Mistress Lane, and the King ride single. The portmanteau can be strapped to his saddle. It will be natural then for him to ride behind you. In case of any trouble along the road he can have a chance to get away."

The King nodded. He moved over to the fire and stood beside Richard. "Yes, you are right. No one will pay any attention to a country boy jogging along on his nag behind his master and mistress."

Pope was leaning over to pick up towels from the floor. Suddenly he dropped them and stood erect. "My Lord Wilmot, look to the fire-place and what do you see?"

Wilmot and Lassells looked. "By the Eternal God," Lord Wilmot exclaimed, "I never noticed the resemblance before! Let Monington don the habit of a countryman such as His Majesty wears and he would pass . . ."

The King looked at Richard. "Do not listen to them. Wilmot is a designing person. Already you have served your King handsomely."

Lord Wilmot said to Pope, "Can you obtain such a habit?"

"Readily, my lord. My son's clothes, which he left when he went to London, are in my armoire. I'll fetch them."

Lassells said, "What are you talking about?"

"Don't you understand? The same clothes on two men," Lord Wilmot said, "give you two Kings. One rides west and one rides south."

The King spoke angrily. "No, I won't permit it. Monington saved me once last night. That is enough. We will be taking no greater chance than we have taken all the days since Worcester."

They overruled the King after a brisk argument. It was Richard who decided things in the end. "I shall ride to Bristol. That would be the port you would be most likely to seek. I shall be sly and devious, while you ride boldly down the highway, an honest man, bent on an honest journey."

The King nodded. "Yes, that I will do. But you, my captain, have a care. I want you alive when I am King once more."

Pope returned. His placid, imperturbable face was disturbed. He took Richard aside. "It is as I said, sir. The two companions have come back. They were seated in the kitchen when I went down. They asked about our visitors. No doubt they have a pack of soldiers hiding outside the wall."

Richard said, "I'll be dressed in a moment. You bring breakfast, and bread and cheese for my saddle-bags. By the time you return, we shall have plans all laid. Where are these men now?"

"I think they went into the court-yard. They asked me about their friend, whom they called Sylvester. I said I had not seen him, but I told them to remain and I would have Cook make breakfast. They are waiting."

"You're a fair honest fellow, Pope, and you serve the King well."

Within the hour horses were at the front door. Mistress Lane and Lassells mounted double. The King assisted the young lady. Then he looked to the portmanteau, made it secure with straps, vaulted into the saddle, and the party trotted down the drive. Wilmot left to go his own way.

Shortly before they departed, Richard went down the back stairs, his grey hat securely on his head, his suit of sober grey, though badly worn, a fair match for the King's dress as a yeoman's son. He paused at the door of the buttery for a moment, making sure that the two men saw him. He crossed the court-yard, mounted his horse, which was already saddled, and cantered down the drive. At the gate he met the party and fell in behind the King.

The two rogues jumped up from the table and ran toward the stables. Their horses had been moved from the court-yard rack and were now tied to a rail on the far side of the stable-yard. By the time they got to the gateway, the little party had almost reached the crossroad.

The King glanced over his shoulder. "Here they come, Monington. I still think it is not the thing to expose you."

Richard grinned. *"Au revoir,* Your Majesty. A safe journey and sanctuary in fair France!"

Richard turned his head, saw the riders as though discovering them for the first time, lifted the reins and galloped off down the Bristol Road in frenzied flight.

The two renegades, shouting, rode after him, almost crowding the King's horse to the ditch as they passed.

Lassells wheeled his horse with such haste that Jane was almost unseated. "Have care! Have care!" she cried, her arms tightening about his waist.

The King turned his horse, and they took the cross-road that led to the south. A mile below they turned off the main highway into a by-track through the forest which Pope had described. The sun was up, the sky clearing. The clean smell of the woods came to them, and its dark shadows closed in upon them. Again the forest drew an enveloping curtain about the King. The second phase of the Royal Miracle had begun . . . always a house for sanctuary . . . always a loyal friend to hide a King in flight.

But down the Bristol Road there were no protecting trees to stretch cool green arms about Richard Monington. For him there were only bright sunlight and the open road. An hour he travelled, passing country carts and horsemen. A bend, where two roads crossed, gave him his chance. Suddenly he took the turn through a little wood. From a safe spot behind trees he saw the riders gallop on. If he could keep them from discovering the ruse for half a day, the King would be safe.

Richard had no illusions. Between where he lay and Bristol were hundreds of Oliver's men. He dismounted and walked his horse in and out under the trees. The fallen leaves would hide hoof-prints, if the two rogues came back to look for him. He went on until he came to a hedgerow along a meadow where cattle grazed. Beyond it was a river. He had come to the Avon.

Here he made a decision. He unsaddled his horse and hid the saddle in the thorn hedgerow. He thought of turning the horse loose in the wood, but at that moment four or five horses galloped into sight in the meadow, their manes and tails blowing. He would put his horse in with them, a secure hiding place for it.

He found the gate by walking along the hedge. He found also a path leading from the gate to the river, a lovely sheltered path under the beeches. He opened the gate, led his horse inside and loosed it. After making the wicket secure, he turned toward the river. At the foot of the path he came on what he was seeking, a small boat moored to a rickety wooden landing. He untied the line and got in. The sculls were in the bottom, and four or five small casks of cider. Without doubt the farmer was going to Bristol market, though no farmhouse could be seen from the landing.

He drifted down the river, lying low in the boat, keeping close to the bank and overhanging bushes. The sun was warm. He took off the woollen cloak, looked to see that the gold Wilmot had given him was safe in the roll about his waist.

The quiet of the river and the trees and the cloudless sky entered into him.

Richard's boat drifted slowly down the gentle stream. The countryside was quiet. He saw no one. Birds and farm animals and the fish that broke the surface of the water were the only living creatures, except the insects and water-flies that darted about him.

He had no idea where he was, but the position of the sun showed that it was past four o'clock. If he reached Bristol by nightfall it would be easier to slip into the city. He had no pass—that was a difficulty he would meet when it arose. He was drowsy. He turned the boat to the bank and tied up under a screen of willows. For a moment he thought of sleeping in the bottom of the boat, but decided to find a secluded place ashore. It was more open country now, a meadow and a field where hay had been stacked. A hay-rick could be an excellent hiding place. It was colder, now that the sun was low. Although he saw no signs of life, he was cautious in approaching the rick. Once there, he burrowed in, feet first, and fell asleep.

It was quite dark when he woke. He heard voices and looked down near the river, where he had tied the boat. Lanthorns were bobbing up and down. He heard a rough voice say, "It's the boat all right, but the bastard has got clean away."

"He can't have got far," another voice said. "We'll beat the bushes."

"You can't see at night. I say, let's plug one of these cider kegs. I feel a great thirst." They argued for a time, but the zealous one was overruled.

"We'll get him at Bristol. All patrols are on the outlook."

"He'll never go to Bristol. Dunster Castle, more like, where Milord will harbour him in some dungeon and he'll never be found."

"Damn those houses with priest's holes, so cunningly hid!"

"Here, take a swig of this cider. You'll forget today's hard riding. Let the patrols capture King Charles."

"But the reward! We want the reward."

"You fool! Do you think we'd get a smell of the gold? The officer'd take it to hisself. Have another."

"Don't mind if I do. Give me the keg in my own hands."

Richard lay still. Let them drink the well-aged cider. When

they had taken enough, they'd sleep, no doubt, or go roaring back to the highway. He wondered where they had tied their horses, but he dared not search.

The talking at the boat grew louder, and drunken laughter filled the air. Richard pulled himself out of the hay-rick. He saw that the rogues had made a little fire and were seated by it. He crawled on hands and knees over the stubble until he could no longer hear the voices. He made his way toward the highway. First, he took off his coat and brushed the hay out of the cloth. His breeches were slick from wear and had gathered no grass. His boots were heavy and difficult.

The road toward Bristol was clear of vehicles and riders, but there were a number of carts and a few coaches coming from the city. Once he was stopped by a patrol, but they only wanted to inquire if he had seen a party of horsemen— a woman and a servant riding double and a man riding single. Richard said he had seen no such party. He was just on his way home after visiting a neighbour at a farm on the river. They let him go without further question.

Richard's heart was light. The King had evaded them. They did not suspect him of going south. By now he and Jane and Lassells must be safe at Castle-Cary or some Loyalist house near by.

He walked along until he saw the swinging sign of the Turk's Head, a roadside inn. He went inside and sat down at a table in a corner. There were a few farmer lads and a party of travellers. He ordered bread and cheese and a small beer. While he was eating he heard a commotion in the inn yard. A coach rattled over the cobbles. The stable-boys were called for to change horses. There was a clank of chains and buckles as the horses were unhooked and the relief horses led out.

He got up and looked into the yard. He saw several horsemen and grooms. Two women were being helped from the coach, an older woman and a young one. Both were wrapped in dark cloaks with the hoods up, half covering their faces.

Richard stepped back and returned to the obscure corner. He was glad his table was in the shadows, for the younger woman was Kathryn Audley. He heard her asking for the ladies' parlour, the innkeeper replying that there was only the common room, but he could show Milady to a suite on the first floor.

Richard watched the innkeeper take up a candle and lead the way down a narrow panelled hall. He sat back, his heart beating painfully. The sight of her undid all the fine reasoning he had brought to bear since he had spied her on the road near Tetbury. He forgot how she had repelled him at Coddington Manor, forgot her cold still face and her cruel words. Tonight she filled his heart, a woman to be desired. He must see her, talk with her.

Richard made inquiry of the barmaid, a plump, red-cheeked country lass. The coach usually rested at the inn an hour or two. The passengers would eat supper and the hostlers feed the horses. It was a coach from London to Bristol. The other diners had gone out of the room, drawn by the arrival of the coach. The girl was communicative. Last week a coach had been attacked by highwaymen, not far down the road. The footman had been wounded when he resisted and tried to run away. The highway was dangerous from here in.

She leaned closer, her hair brushing his cheek. " 'Tis said they are looking for the King. It would be a bigger reward than the travellers' gold."

Richard asked, "Is the King in this neighbourhood?"

"No one knows, sir, but soldiers say that he was seen on the road with a man and a woman, all on horseback."

"Is there a rich reward?" Richard asked after taking a deep swallow of beer.

"Big, very big. But there's people about here that wouldn't turn the King over to the soldiers, no matter how much gold they'd get." She looked into Richard's eyes. "What's your name?" she asked abruptly.

"Dick . . . Dick Richards. I'm from down Somerset way, walking to Bristol to get ship to Virginia."

"Have you got the coin to pay?"

"No. But I've heard the company will pay the passage for young yeomen. 'Tis farm boys they need."

The girl sat down on the bench. "You'll have to indenture yourself for seven years. Would you like that?"

"No, that I would not. But I don't like being pressed for the army, either. I'd no' mind fightin', but I don't want to be sent out to the Low Countries or them other foreign parts."

The girl nodded. She seemed no longer to be suspicious. "Suppose it's well enough if you get a good master. My brother, now, he went to Barbados. He got a bad master, and he up and killed him." She arose for a customer had come into the room and was making for the bar. "They hanged him," she said in a flat voice, "hanged him by the neck until he was dead." She walked to the bar and drew the ale the customer had ordered.

The man, a hard-faced, dark-eyed individual, took the pewter mug and came over to the table where Richard was sitting. "You mind?" he asked after he had seated himself on the bench.

Richard said "No." Had the man come on the coach? He'd like to ride from here to Bristol, if a seat didn't cost too much. He had walked all day and he was dead-tired. He babbled along, country-fashion. He was quite aware he was under scrutiny. The suspicion in the man's eyes died out after he had asked a few questions about farm work and cattle. Richard's ready answers satisfied him. Richard told the same tale about wanting to go to Bristol that he had invented for the barmaid. Virginia was his object, if he could get passage there.

"Got a pass?"

"Pass? Why should I have a pass? Oh, I know what you mean, sir, a pass to go on a ship."

His companion's thin lips drew into a humourless smile. "I mean a pass to go into Bristol."

"Why, no, sir. I did not know about passes. I thought . . . I've been to Bristol before, on market days, without a pass."

"Not now, my good lad. We're looking for a renegade King and his followers, and no one enters Bristol without a pass."

Richard looked downcast. He scratched his head and his eyes dropped to the table. He appeared in deep thought. "Now that be very bad luck," he said slowly.

The man pounded his mug on the table. "Two ales," he cried to the barmaid.

"Yes, Mister Colby, right away." She came over to the table and set the mugs down. She wiped off the well-worn table with a cloth, where the ale had slopped over. "The lad's set on Virginia," she said to Colby, "but he's not got passage money."

"Too bad. They say you can get fifty acres free, if you've got passage, but . . ." He shrugged his shoulders.

"A poor man's got little chance," Richard ventured.

"That's God's truth, but it will be better, now that Oliver's in control. The people went wild when he got to London. I saw the procession myself. Never did I hear such screaming and hollowing from the people. They'd put a crown on his head, they would. But Oliver's too smart for that. He's got his Parliament and he's got his army."

"Has he got the King?" the girl inquired.

The man's face darkened. "No. But, by God, he will get him and chop off his head, just as he did the father's!" He got up and stretched his arms above his head. "Well, I'm going to catch me a nap before I drive on to Bristol." He nodded to Richard. The girl followed him to the door and they had a word together before he went down the hall.

The barmaid came back to the table. "Colby drives the coach. Some say he's in with the highwaymen and lets them know when he's got passengers of wealth." Richard said nothing. The girl looked at him. She dropped her voice. "Colby thought you looked like the King, but he changed his mind."

Richard put back his head and laughed. "Now if that isn't a good one. Me, look like Charles Stuart!"

"Well, you do, at a distance." The girl was a little miffed at Richard's laughter. "Of course, close up you don't at all. The King is handsome." She went back to serve half a dozen fresh customers.

A boy came in carrying some logs and built up the fire. The newcomers took their mugs and sat down on the high-backed settles that angled from the fire-place.

When they threw back their cloaks, Richard saw they were in the scarlet uniform of Cromwell's army. He debated what to do. Retreat now would certainly attract attention. He made a sign to the girl. When she came to his table, he ordered a supper. She hesitated a moment. "You'll first have to pay the reckoning for the ale and for the supper before you get it. That's the way the innkeeper is. He's not a trusting man."

Richard put his hand in the leathern purse which hung from his belt and took out the coins in small bits, a shilling for the supper and tuppence for each mug of ale. Satisfied, the girl went away and returned after a time with a slice of cold meat, cheese, bread and hot mulled wine.

Colby came back into the room. One of the men at the fire called to him, "The hostler says you've broken an axle and won't go on until you get another."

Colby uttered an oath and muttered something about bad

luck all the way from London. To the barmaid he said, "When that damned innkeeper comes home, tell him to inform the ladies that we'll not start until daylight." He stamped out. The barmaid lighted a candle and disappeared down the hall. A few men wandered in, countrymen by their habits. Richard lighted his earthenware pipe when he saw the soldiers had lighted theirs. Soon the low-ceilinged room was heavy with smoke from pipes and the fire.

When the barmaid returned, he crossed the room to the bar. The men at the fire-place stopped talking. He could feel their eyes when he leaned over the bar to ask for a room.

"There's none save a cubby down the hall," the girl said. She dropped her voice. "I'd ask you into my bed, but my husband's sleeping there." She laughed. She lighted a bed-candle from one burning on the bar. "Money in advance," she said. Richard counted out three shillings in the small coins Wilmot had provided him with before he left. He felt a hand on his shoulder.

"What say you have a drink with me and my companions?"

"He's just going to bed," the barmaid said, handing him his candle. "He ain't the King, if that's what you're thinking. He comes from down Somerset or thereabouts, a farm lad named Dick Richards."

The man looked at him closely. His hand dropped to his side. "I see now. If you're not close to . . ."

Richard said. "I'd be proud to have a drink, sir."

The soldier said quickly, "No matter, if you're off for bed. Another time perhaps."

The girl went to the door and showed him the way. "Second door to the left," she said. "Don't take the first. There's a fine lady resting there."

Richard's cubby was on an angle from the hall. It was not more than ten feet long and six wide and contained nothing but a bed and a wash-stand. He put the wooden latch across the lock. There was a narrow window high in the wall. He stood on a stool to look out. He saw there was a light in the room the maid had said was Kathryn's. He sat down on the side of the narrow bed, his head in his hands. He should get out of this place, but he was too weary, too sleepy to think. He heard men's voices. They seemed to come from the court-yard or stable, because he heard horses moving about, stamping, champing their feed. One voice was louder than the rest.

"I'm not satisfied. What if his skin *is* darker than the King's—didn't you ever hear of walnut juice? I say, let's take him into Bristol. Let the captain see him. If he *is* the King, and we let him get away, then what? How do we know his name is Dick Richards? How do we know he's a farm boy?"

Richard did not hear the reply, for the men moved off.

He got to his feet. He must get away. But one thing was certain: he had no intention of going without speaking with Kathryn Audley. He washed his hands and face, smoothed his hair with his two hands.

He snuffed the candle and went out into the hall. He stood at Kathryn's door listening. She was talking; her voice raised as though to speak to a person in another room. Her words came clearly. "The soldiers have seen someone they think looks like the King. They are going to take him to Bristol. I wonder if it *could* be the King himself." There was a waiting as though the other woman spoke.

"I know, Lucy, but even though he is the King and we are for Cromwell, I hope he gets away."

Richard knocked gently. The voice on the other side of the door said, "Who is there?"

"A stable-boy, with a message from Mr. Colby." He heard the bar withdrawn. The door was opened a crack. He pushed it wide and stepped inside. "Don't cry out. It is I, Richard."

She moved backward into the room without speaking. Her blue eyes were frightened; her face paled. "Richard!" she whispered.

He shook his head, pointing to the door of the other room. "Tell her the coach won't go out until morning."

She went to the door of the bedchamber. "The boy says the coach will not go out until morning. So we will be here the night." She went into the room. Richard heard her say, "You may as well stay in bed. I'll come in later, after I have written a letter." Returning, she closed the door and came slowly toward him. Richard watched her. His heart pounded so violently that he thought she must hear its beating.

"What is it? Why are you here?" she whispered.

"The soldiers are for grilling me. They think I am the King."

She stopped him. "I heard them talking in the court. You are in danger. Even though they find out you are not the King, they will put you in gaol. You must flee." She was frightened.

"How can I flee when you are here beside me? Oh, Kathryn, Kathryn!" He put his arms about her. He kissed her throat, the little pulsating veins in her forehead. Her mouth against his was hard and possessive.

Presently she pushed him from her. "Richard, you must go at once. It is not safe. Oh, I can't bear to think of you in a dungeon! They do terrible things to the King's men. The army has gone wild. They loot and kill. Hundreds of prisoners are in the Tower. Lauderdale and they say Buckingham and others have been hanged. Bristol gaols, I'm told, are crowded with Scots and Loyalists who are to be transported to the Indies and Virginia. Oh, the sights I've seen on the road here!"

"One sight I saw on the road—your face in the coach window, and Nicholas Holder riding beside you."

"What! You saw me? It must have been before he left to ride ahead to Bristol. My maid Lucy and I stayed awhile at Tetbury. . . . Oh, Richard, what am I to do?"

"Kiss me," he said, his arms close about her shoulders. "Kiss me. Let us forget the whole mad world and think only of ourselves. You are so beautiful, so desirable." He drew her to him. She took his kiss as though she would draw his soul away, yet yielding nothing. Then she broke from his arms.

"You must go, Richard. I am wrong not to have told you before. I am going to Bristol to wed Nicholas Holder. He has been appointed to allot prisoners. I have an aunt there. In the new year we are sailing for Virginia."

Rage, ungovernable rage, came over him. He stood, back to the door, his hands clenched.

She put her hands to her breast. Her long, pale gold hair fell across her white shoulders. She held out her hands; tears lay in her eyes.

"Don't look at me with your eyes on fire, Richard. Oh, Richard, I cannot bear it!"

He wrenched the door open and strode out into the hall. What did it matter? The King was safe. He was no longer a decoy. Let them take him to Bristol.

He entered the low-ceilinged, panelled room. He walked to the bar, gave his order and sat down at a table in the middle of the room. The barmaid had gone. A fat man with a leathern apron drew the beer and brought the tankard to the table. Richard threw down a coin. The door opened and three soldiers entered. They paused, looking at Richard stupidly, surprise on their red faces.

Richard watched them cross the room, listened without moving to the spokesman's words. "Charles Stuart" they called him. He was under arrest as traitor to Cromwell and the Commonwealth.

He got up without objection, after he had said, "You make a mistake, sirs. I am not the King of England."

It was some time before this that Dame Margaret wrote a letter.

My dearest son:

My prayers have been answered. You are safe after the great tragedy of Worcester. Your message has reached me at last and those days of intolerable waiting are past.

I have not asked our Lord to let me see you, only to know that you walk on this earth, my dear son.

John Prideaux came and stayed with me. He was followed some time later by your dragoon Digby and Colonel Carlos. They managed to get horses and we started for Devon, leaving our belongings behind. Now I am safely arrived at Portledge with my old friends.

In a few weeks I shall go to Buckland Brewer. You remember I have a farm and a good house there. It is not Coddington Manor, but it is well built and staunch and has stood since the reign of Elizabeth. My tenants are of the best.

Cook Ellie and Old Graves are happy to be back in Devon, so I will set up my household goods in my early home for the present.

It is to me a deep sadness to write to you a letter that contains only dismal news.

Coddington Manor is no longer the seat of the Monington family. It had been your father's home, and the site of his fathers' home back to the years before Henry the Eighth, of blessed memory, ruled England.

Now, by this strange turn of the wheel, it goes into ownership of the Holder family, who have always coveted the orchards, the vineyards and the green fertile meadows of Coddington Manor.

This will shock you, Richard, but it did not come as a shock to me. After you went away and the great disaster of

Worcester bore in on us, there were straws that showed the way the wind was blowing.

Nicholas turned to Cromwell. I understand he did not fight, but was sent to London during that tragic time. He demonstrated to Cromwell's ministers how great was his interest in the Parliamentary cause by betraying his neighbours, giving lists of Royalists and designating their properties, their flocks and herds—a sort of private Domesday list of our county. He is playing up to the Harleys and has, I have heard, asked for the hand of Kathryn Audley, their ward.

One other betrothal may come soon, that of Mathilda and young Stephen Bennett, a relation of the London merchant. Hugh Jordan, Mathilda's and Sibyl's father, came to Coddington Manor for the purpose of taking his daughters home. At that time he met young Bennett, who was visiting the Holders. Stephen was much interested in Mathilda. He lives in Virginia and has land there. This is all little more than rumour or conjecture.

I pray for you each day, and for your charge. May the good God give you wisdom, so that you may be successful in all your undertakings!

Digby will take this letter. He leaves today to search for you. Colonel Carlos, well disguised, will start with him, and at Bideford Digby will find a fishing boat to take the colonel to Cork, where he will be safe. They do not love Cromwell in Ireland. This may delay Digby somewhat in meeting you at Bristol.

John has gone away—I know not *where*.

May God protect you, my dear son!

Your devoted Mother

At Portledge,
Fairy Cross,
North Devon

Oliver returned to his City of London. He went to his house at the Cockpit, but he might, if he said the word, have gone to Whitehall as King of England. Indeed, Parliament granted him Hampton Court as a residence, and £4,000 a year.

Everyone praised him. Ambassadors from foreign lands crowded about him to make humble obeisance and beg friendship for their countries. From a soldier and a great general, he became curiously gentle, remembering again that people of Protestant faith were battling all over Christendom for peace. He had his generals and his army, and with them he could do as he willed in matters of State. The glamour of Victory was wrapped about him. All was his. The Stuart King was gone, and with him the Crown. The old Church had lost its place. Parliament he would dissolve. A republic or a commonwealth—it did not matter.

All of fair England, all of Scotland and Ireland and those new lands beyond the seas, Virginia and the Indies, lay in his hands. The surge of power was upward. No one stood so tall as the Puritan county squire turned general.

Mr. Milton wrote a sonnet to Cromwell, "Our chief of men," but it carried a warning, for it contained significant words, "Yet much remains to conquer still."

In the dungeon of Bristol gaol Richard Monington lay, wearied beyond all endurance by questioning and torture. But not a word was got from him, whether by small tortures or great. At last his torturers gave way and pushed him into a dark cold cell below the water level.

He lost count of days. Fever came; ague shook him—gaol fever they called it. His hair and beard grew rank and foul, his body covered with vermin. One day they took him to the sunlight and walked him on the quay with half a hundred others. He was so weak he could scarcely lift one foot after the other. As he staggered along the rough, slick stones he noticed a beggar sitting on one of the sleds the labourers used to carry tobacco from the ships, a beggar singing for pennies. He had a small musical instrument. Richard passed him. Then he paused. The man was singing an old song Richard had often heard in his own county:

> "I'll buy a cottage near his manor;
> Which done, I'll make my men break down his fences,
> Ride on his standing corn, or in the night
> Set fire to his barns, or break his cattle's legs."

Richard moved closer and looked into the man's eyes. His heart gave a great leap, but he made no sign as he passed on with the other prisoners. The beggar who sang the old song was Digby.

BOOK TWO

The Voyage

CHAPTER 11

The Ship

THE ship pitched unmercifully. There would be a long rolling swell, then a short wave that seemed to rack the oaken beams until they moaned and creaked in protest. Prisoners and indentured men were packed into the hold as close as Newfoundland dried fish. In truth the vessel *St. George* sailed every third voyage to Newfoundland for a cargo of wet and dry fish and returned up the Channel to Bristol or rounded the Lizard to Plymouth. The smell of codfish—Poor Jack the sailors called it—added to the stale odours of bilge, turned their queasy stomachs, and their retching and belching added to their misery.

Richard Monington moaned and tried to raise himself, but the canvas hammock swayed so that he fell back again. His head was bursting. He put his hands up to find a great bandage wrapped one side of his head and down about his throat. The air was fetid with human bodies. He tried to bring his mind to focus. Where was he? And how had he got on a ship? There was a flash of memory—a fight, the wet round stones of the quay, the sleds filled with sweet-smelling tobacco as the bales were lifted out of a ship's hold. He seemed to see himself struggling with a great press of men that shoved him this way and that.

He did not see the men vertically, but obliquely. He was not walking, but being carried on a rough litter; the canvas scratched his wounded cheek. Someone was talking. "Shove through, shove through! Make way! God damn the rascals! They crowd like rats leaving a sinking ship. They're in a great hurry to leave Old England."

Another voice: "They won't find Virginia God's Heaven, what with the Indians cutting throats and lifting the hair off their heads with a scalping knife . . . and, for food, down to the bottom of a barrel of corn."

Someone laughed. "Better Bristol gaol in good old England for the likes of me. Leastways, a man gets bread and water...."

The voices faded, not because his litter-bearers had stopped talking, but because he, Richard Monington, found the effort to remember now too great. He lay, white and motionless, in his hammock, his mind wandering, half in the world, half out, in a sort of continued dream.

It was day. He could see light through a high port, cut in half by the horizontal deck.

Once a seaman came and fed him an ill-tasting liquid through a pewter blow spoon. He could not open his jaw except with the greatest effort. It might be broken, or perhaps the bandage clamped it too close. After the heat of the liquid reached his stomach, he felt warm. He sank into unconsciousness.

Deep in the night he woke. The hammock in which he lay jerked and pulled and rolled. The sea was tossing. He heard a voice say, "We are running into high wind. The air is thick. The bowsprit broke and a brass gun loosened and rolled about the deck. Now I've got another injured man on my hands. That makes a baker's dozen." Richard judged he was the ship's doctor.

"What about this one, Frake? Is he alive, or do we heave it overboard?"

Richard felt a man's head against his chest. "His heart's beating, slow, but he's alive. Gaol fever for months, a sword wound, then this crack on the head with a stave."

The other voice, harsh and grating. "Why give him space? We're overcrowded a hundred head as it is. And we've got three decks where there used to be one. Let him lie on a deck and give the hammock to a working seaman."

The doctor dropped his voice. "Remember, Mate, there's gold coin for each of us at the end of the voyage, if we get him there whole and of a piece. The lady is generous. She said ..."

"Hush," the harsh voice broke in. "Here comes the master on inspection. He wouldn't want to see us speaking and talking together. I'll leave you."

Richard made an effort to move his fingers. He did not want to be heaved overboard as dead. He felt the doctor's fingers on his wrist, heard him say, "Good morning, Captain West."

"If you can call it a good morning, Doctor." The captain's voice was clear and authoritative. "How is this man here? I understand he's been unconscious ever since we left Bristol. What happened? A blow on the head?"

"Sir, yes. The litter-bearers dropped him on the quay when the riot began. It looks as though he got bashed about by both sides."

"If it were an ordinary case, I'd say let him die and drop him into the sea, but it seems he has friends, friends with influence in London."

"He'll need them. He's indentured, isn't he?"

"Yes. You think he'll live?"

The doctor pondered. "I think so. He is young. He has a strong muscular body. His bones will knit. It's the shoulder and collar bone."

"Would broken bones cause this prolonged unconsciousness?"

"No, sir. A blow on the back of the head—probably a stave when the yeomen tore into the guards."

"I've never found out why," the captain said. "I wasn't aboard ship that night."

The doctor answered, "Countrymen trying to rescue some of the Royalist prisoners that have been indentured to Bennett."

"Bennett?"

"Yes, Bennett, owner of this ship, Edward Bennett, of London, who has made a fortune in the tobacco trade—aye, and in trade in white slaves."

"Shush, Doctor. That we don't speak about. Why not get this fellow on deck? We'll be bearing down on the Azores in a day or two. Nothing like the sea air for curing."

The ship lurched again. Both men fell against the hammock, which began to swing violently.

"Good that he's lashed in," the doctor said, steadying the ropes.

The captain did not heed him. He ran up the ladder, cupping his hands and shouting to the mate, "Get your watch aloft and take in topsail. Helmsman, bring her up into the wind. Look sharp now, hard over."

As the ship swung, a great blast of wind bellied the sails

and laid her over on her beam ends. She staggered and lost way. A mountainous wave breached her.

The captain roared aloft, "No time to furl sail. Cut 'em away."

Richard heard running footsteps. He opened his eyes slowly. He heard men cursing, women praying, crying to the Lord to save them for their children's sake.

"She's laying like a log in the sea," a seaman's voice cried out. "She can't bear up. The mountains of water will press her down."

On the deck the captain shouted, "Pay off and let her run before the wind. Trim the jib." There followed the loud noise of canvas ripping.

"The foresail's blowing off piece by piece into the sea."

A great crash followed. Voices loud and excited floated down. The captain's voice rose high and desperate. "The mainmast's down. Take axes and cut her free. Get that mast clear of the ship quick!"

Men hacked at the splintered stump. Others cut away the tangle of ropes and shrouds.

"Man the pumps. Mr. Webb, chalk-line the sides, so we can tell if we are getting ahead of the water."

Voices were stilled. The roar of the wind and the pounding of waves against the sides filled the air, together with the groaning and protesting of the ship's ribs and timbers.

Once more the captain's roaring voice broke over waves and the mighty splash of water running across decks. "Unshackle the prisoners, Mr. Webb. Send every man who can stand on his feet to the pumps. By God's footstool, let them strip their guts to keep this ship afloat!"

The moans and groans of men about him bore into Richard Monington's consciousness. He made an effort to move, but found he was lashed into the hammock. The storm was rising, the wind increasing in fury. Women shrieked and called to God Almighty to protect them and their children.

Richard worked feebly at the lashings, without success. Presently someone came and loosened the cording.

A Scottish voice said, "Now, laddie, ye're free. Can ye stand on your feet, now?" Richard made an effort, but his bones were as water, and he sank down. "Ye can't, so ye must lie there while I go and work the pumps." The man leaned over and whispered, "A fellow who calls hisself Digby is searching for you, if your name's Richards."

Richard nodded. His lips were dry, his tongue was thick. He whispered, "Where?"

"On deck. When I see him, I'll tell him." He leaned his face against Richard's ear. "King's man?"

"Yes."

"Worcester?"

"Yes."

"There'll be ten of us now."

"Where are we going?"

"Virginia—to the plantations."

Richard sat on the floor, his back against a bulkhead. It felt good to change positions. He began moving his fingers and toes. He was pleased to find that he hadn't a broken arm or leg. Only his shoulder and head bothered him now. After a time he closed his eyes and slept—a fairly peaceful sleep.

It was light when he wakened. The sea was gentle. The ship moved easily. A cabin-boy came with a bowl of thin gruel. Richard took it in his hands and drank until the bowl was empty.

The boy said, "Christ! I thought you was dead yesterday."

Richard said, "Not quite. I'm hungry now."

The boy looked over his shoulder. "I'll bring you something stronger at noontime, if I can get to the locker."

By noon the ship's doctor had Richard lying on the weather deck, flat on the boards. Richard didn't feel their hardness. The sky was blue; the sea was blue, with little rippling white crests of waves. A gentle warm wind was blowing. Land birds followed the wake of the ship. To the south dark peaks of the Azores cut the horizon. The ship had come into quiet water in the lee of high headlands.

When it was brought to anchor, a boat was swung over the side and seamen rowed into the sand bay. Fishermen were hauling in nets as the sun was sinking. Richard thought lazily that it was the wrong time of day to fish, but he was too sleepy to reflect. After he had drunk another bowl of gruel, he felt a little stronger.

For three days the ship lay at anchor off the little outer island of the Azores, three days to repair the damage the storm had wrought to sail and mast. Richard lay on the deck by day, and by night with the aid of the cabin-boy crept down the ladder between decks. No one bothered him. The doctor came once and felt his pulse. He put his two hands against Richard's shoulders, pressing deeply. Richard winced, but the pain was not too bad. The doctor, a quiet man of some skill, muttered words about rest, sun and sea air and went away.

It was not until the ship had been under sail for twenty-four hours that Digby came. He sat down on the deck beside Richard, looked at him for a few moments before he spoke. "You're surely disguised, zur. I don't doubt but that Dame Margaret would recognize you, but no one else."

Richard laughed. He was feeling somewhat better. He could move his jaw without unhinging it, and his knees were getting stronger. He could manage the ladder without the help of the cabin-boy. Only his arm and shoulder remained stiff. It was good to see Digby's weather-beaten face. He noticed a fresh scar on its side, a long red welt like a saber cut.

Digby said. "That's a little token I got in the big storm. It explains why I wasn't with you sooner."

Richard said, "Digby, you must be my memory. Tell me how I got on this ship, and why." He glanced down at his clothes. He was dressed in grey wool. The suit was rumpled and creased and the hosen torn. "I don't remember these clothes. . . ." He paused, silent under the worried expression in Digby's eyes.

The dragoon said, "I heard you disguised yourself like the King."

"God!" It came back to him then. "What day is this?"

" 'Tis of a Wednesday, the third day of January, zur."

Richard sat very still, his eyes fixed on the blue ocean. After a time he said, "Worcester was the third day of September."

"You came into Bristol two weeks later, zur. That I know, although I was not there. I had to go out to Lundy Isle to find a fishing boat to take Colonel Carlos to Cork and then wait for one to take me up the Channel to Bristol. It was a long, wearisome business, zur. I guessed you might have been captured and I hung around the gaol dressed like a beggar. Your lady mother is safe at Portledge. I have a letter for you hidden in my pallet. She stood the journey well and so did Cook. Dame Margaret has courage enough for six. Now she is safe in her own Devon."

"Thank God, Digby! And Charles Stuart?"

"Escaped to France the middle of October. He had a lively jig time before he made it. At Trent that sweet girl Jane Lane left him. She's a true heroine, zur. The King should make her rich if he ever comes into his own."

"A wonderful girl," Richard said. "Her courage never faltered. Tell on."

"Other friends took over the King's safety. At Lyme they thought to get their boat. The skipper was willing, but the grey mare was the better horse. His wife, fearing Old Noll, locked the King up for the night and in the morning the boat was gone without him. Then they went on to Salisbury, finding friends everywhere. That was a good map the priest made for Mr. Charles at Boscobel. What was his name, zur? Father Hurlston, was it?"

"Huddleston," said Richard.

"Well, at Hambledon a Royalist nearly beat up the King for a Roundhead because of his cropped poll. He and Lord Wilmot must have danced all about the southern shires, till at last they found at Brighthelmstone the boat that had been chartered. Nick Tattersell, the skipper, was loyal, but they took no chances this time. They kept Nick up all night smoking tobacco and drinking beer in the inn so he couldn't tell his grey mare nor nary body else. Charles is in Paris, under the protection of the French king, and there he's likely to stay for many a year, zur. Oliver's in the saddle now, as firm as any king ever sat on his throne."

Richard said, "I doubt if it will be so long."

Digby insisted. "But, zur, Oliver rules England firmly. The people acclaim him. He makes proclamations. After Worcester he made a big one. He prayed that 'this crowning mercy should provoke those that are concerned in it to thankfulness, and the Parliament to do the will of Him who hath done His will for it and for the nation . . . and that justice and righteousness, mercy and truth may flow from you, as a thankful return to our gracious God.' I learned the words for you, zur—fine words, but what he means is for the people to give thanks to Oliver, not to the Lord. He's got an army of fifty thousand. Some say they be sucking away the blood of England, zur, with all the taxes it takes to support them."

Digby turned over on his stomach and placed his chin on his folded arms. "The prisons be crowded with debtors. The people don't have trust in Parliament. Some ha' been arrested for taking bribes to let King's men out of prisons. They say Cromwell will send Parliament home, so he can rule to suit hisself."

"Tell me, Digby," Richard said, "how did you find out so much about the King's adventures after we went our separate ways from Abbots Leigh?"

"Why, at Gabriel Spencer's to be sure—where you appointed for me to meet you in Bristol. Many Royalists came there by night in secret, among them one Thomas Blount—I think you know him, zur—who seemed to have followed every step Charles took. He counted that forty souls, by and large, had known who the King was and where he was during the month and ten days of his escaping, and not one of them betrayed him, though they would have had a pot of gold if they had."

Richard felt pride in that display of loyalty. Digby was proud also, but his pride came from their ability to outwit Old Ironside's men.

"'Tis said one man told the King himself that his father had called five sons to his bedside and said to them, 'Always be loyal to the Crown. No matter if the Royal Crown is hanging on a bush, it is still the Crown.' "

"Well said indeed, Digby. It sounds like our five Penderels. I don't believe Oliver will be able to arouse any such loyalty. It was a miracle, a Royal Miracle. We are defeated now, but the King will come home to his kingdom. Mind what I tell you."

"Yes, zur, that's what *he* said, and that's what I believe. A man must learn to wait in patience, that he must. There's more to be told, zur. But I see an officer looking down at us. We be prisoners of war, zur, along with ten Scots and others that you be acquainted with. We be sold out to the plantations in Virginia, zur, for seven years."

Richard felt no emotion. He was dead to feeling. "I heard the master and the doctor talking," he said after a silence.

"When they asked your name I said Richards, zur—Dick Richards or Richard or Richards, as they say in the Marches. I heard at Gabe's that was the name you'd given the soldiers." He laughed slyly. "No need of them knowing too much. They might take into their silly heads to want ransom money from your lady mother."

Richard nodded. " 'Tis better, thank you, Digby. Are we both sold to Edward Bennett?"

"Zur, I gave myself up to be with you, but I couldn't manage it. I'm to go up-river to Jordan's Journey. I'm bought by a spritely woman whose name they said was Mistress Cecily Jordan, and by her new husband named Montague. She's some kin to the young ladies who often stay at the manor, zur."

"Oh, *that* Jordan. I'm sorry, Digby. You've proved yourself my devoted friend and I'd feel better if you were near by. But there are still some months unaccounted for, between mid-September and January."

"Yes, zur. That's a fact. Well, your gaol fever will cover months, zur. I'll recount it to you later. There will be plenty of time. It will be two long months before we sail up the James River in Virginia, zur."

Richard did not sleep that night. He spent the deep hours trying to fit in the known facts Digby had told him with the dream-like picture that came to his mind. Digby had said nothing yet about Kathryn Audley. But that need not mean he hadn't seen her. Gabe Spencer would have known all about her being in Bristol. She would likely have been at Gabe's shop. Anyone from near Ledbury was bound to go there.

Vague pictures formed themselves in his mind. . . . Being brought before the governor of the prison . . . "On request of Mr.—" what was the name now? Barrett? Oh, Bennett of course . . . "you are given the freedom of the city, but must report here each day." . . . Stumbling out into the sunlight— the gaol fever had been on him for weeks—stumbling toward Gabe's shop. . . . A familiar figure at the garden gate of a noble house on Queen Street—Kathryn Audley . . . Kathryn and Nicholas Holder . . . Kathryn standing beside a garden wall, weeping, crying out . . . Nicholas Holder handing him a sword, shouting, "Fight, damn you, fight!" . . . Nicholas Holder with a sword in his hand . . . a sword, and a sharp paralyzing sting in his own cheek.

That was it. They had fought in the garden of some house in Bristol. He could see the old garden and a glimpse of the Cathedral tower over the ivied wall.

They must have fought. The scene was too vivid to be the figment of a dream. . . . Nicholas' face, the sneering smile, the arrogant air . . . he was strutting as a cock struts before his hens, the silly ass. Richard felt how weak his own arm was. He must have gone very slack from illness if that jackanapes got under his guard with an upward thrust. A pain came over him, a dull pain that cramped his vitals. A strange emptiness. He wished he had not remembered so clearly what Kathryn had told him, when they stood alone in the moonlit garden, "Richard, Richard, my dear, it is too late, much too late. I married Nicholas last month. I could not do otherwise. My guardian..."

He took her in his arms and kissed her mouth hard, until she broke from him. What did it matter? It was the last time.

Nicholas came then—Nicholas and his swords. The very sight of Nick had unleashed all the bitterness in his heart, but what he had said, if he had said aught, he could not remember. . . . Nicholas Holder could win against a man who had gaol fever and a weak arm. . . .

The guard coming for him . . . who had called the guard while they fought? . . . Back to the gaol, his liberty revoked, and the fevered oblivion of illness. . . .

He turned on the deck and pillowed his head in his arms.

A chill wind blew up toward morning and Richard, weakened as he was, took a heavy cold. This and his mental anguish, added to all the physical hurt he had endured, all the lingering of the gaol plague, brought him close to death. For days he was out of his head, moving in a world of fantastic and terrible dreams. Only Digby's tireless nursing, by day and by night, brought him through. Only the dragoon's watchful tenderness at last banished the Spectre who, almost as tirelessly, had stood by Richard's side.

You and the salt sea air, now balmy, and, above all, Digby fought down the rancorous poison in the blood. And though he was still weak, and though it would still take a little time for his wounded jaw to be quite healed and his broken shoulder quite strongly knit, Richard was now definitely in the way of full recovery.

Three men sat in the owner's cabin of the *St. George.* The long table was piled with papers and packets. In September Richard Bennett had been appointed one of the four Commissioners for Virginia and Maryland by Cromwell's Council of State. On the recommendation of his fellow commissioners,

It was expected that he would become governor but he had not yet taken the office formally. That would come about at a session of the House of Burgesses which would be held in Jamestown in April.

Richard Bennett and William Claiborne had boarded the *St. George* when she put in at the Somers Islands, where some little time before they had come from Virginia to consult Sir John Danvers, the governor, on matters concerning trade between the colonies and the ever-increasing problems of white indentured servants. With them, acting as his cousin's secretary, was young Stephen Bennett, who had boarded the ship at Bristol.

Richard Bennett was an impressive figure. He sat taller than the other men, his shoulders were broader, but his waist was as narrow as young Stephen's. His face was oval, his nose high-bridged, his blue eyes were clear and frank, his mouth was firm and wide. His brown hair had a grey streak, almost an inch wide, that began at the hair line above the left temple and reached clear back. His distinction rested not in his features, but in the quiet serenity of his strong, purposeful face.

William Claiborne was a grey-haired, deep-bodied man, with dark, penetrating eyes. He was slated for election to the post of Secretary of State by the General Assembly of Virginia.

The talk with Sir John Danvers had brought up grave issues, problems that belonged to all the Western Islands as well as to the Virginia Colony.

Bennett broke the silence. "It is unfortunate, Claiborne, that I am coming back to Jamestown with ill news of two varieties. First, the Navigation Act has been passed, but news of that may have already arrived, since it happened in October. They say it was intended as a deterrent to Dutch monopoly of trade. I say that such an act, making it mandatory that *all* goods entering England or English territory be brought either in English bottoms or in ships of the country where they were grown or manufactured, will kill our trade with the continent."

"Perhaps that is what they want," Claiborne said bitterly. "My agents in London write that there is little interest there in the affairs of Virginia. They are too concerned with the affairs of the new government. What does it matter if the colonies sink or swim?"

Bennett drummed on the table with his fingers. "I agree with Sir John Danvers. This Act of Navigation will be the destruction of our trade. We can't exist if we are to ship only in English bottoms to English ports. We have as many Dutch ships calling at our plantations now as English."

"There is talk of war with Holland," Claiborne remarked, looking up from the papers he was reading.

Bennett shook his head. "War, war, war. How can the people bear up under another war? The Navigation Act will be hard on us, I grant you, but the immediate trouble to our people is the plan of the Board of Trade to limit and restrict the production of our money crop, tobacco. It will keep the price up—overproduction always sends prices plunging—but can our planters be made to understand this? Did ever a man take over a colony in more adverse circumstances?"

He turned to Stephen who had taken up his pen. "Don't write that, Stephen. I'm not dictating a speech to the Assembly. I am thinking of what to do with Sir William Berkeley. He has made no move to leave his plantation, Green Spring. I do not think he would go so far as to stir up rebellion. He has not been too bad as a governor, excepting for his narrow religious views."

Claiborne answered sharply, "How can you say that, Richard, when he banished you for no reason at all, except that you were an elder of the Ancient Church? I hold that he has been a bad governor, not reprehensible as Sir John Harvey perhaps, but he *has* persecuted the Puritans. He has lavished his venom upon the Unitarians. He has taken land and given to his favourites. Surely you don't hold with religious intolerance."

Richard Bennett did not answer for a time. He sat quietly, looking down at the papers strewn over the long table.

Claiborne, roused by his quietude, rushed on. "You must banish Berkeley by Act of Assembly."

Bennett said mildly, "I think you exaggerate Sir William's power, Claiborne."

"Exaggerate his power! I can't understand what you are thinking about, not to know that he will undermine you if he can. You know as well as I that half the planters, particularly those from the Northern Neck, are Stuart sympathizers. Of course he will work against you, if he still has the power."

Stephen Bennett spoke for the first time. Looking at his cousin, he said, "Sir, Cromwell has power now, not Charles Stuart. And you, as Cromwell's representative, have the power, not Sir William Berkeley."

Richard Bennett looked thoughtful. "There is no one in all of Virginia Colony who wants power less than I." He took up a paper from the table. The Great Seal of Cromwell's Council of State was uppermost. "Do not fear that I will be weak, William. This is the power I mean to invoke, and once invoked, I shall maintain it. Divine power rests in God Almighty, but earthly power lies here." He laid his strong lean finger on the seal.

He turned to Stephen and broke a long silence that had followed his declaration. "How many Royalist prisoners have we aboard?"

"Twenty or more, Your Excellency. The ship's manifest will be in my hands, with full details, before we reach Jamestown. It will have the name of every man, his age, home, where captured and terms of indenture."

Claiborne yawned and took up a bundle of papers. "I think I'll go to my cabin, Richard. I will look over these tobacco lists at my leisure."

Bennett's eyes met his. He said, "William, don't worry about Berkeley. The monarchists have had time to reflect on the news that came by the *Swan* of Charles Stuart's defeat and flight, and get used to the idea that England is no longer a monarchy. What they think in their hearts we cannot control. Loyalty to a cause, even a lost one, is every man's privilege."

Claiborne paused at the door. "Sir William is very well entrenched, you know. He's been here since '42. He knows the people and they know him. He is a strong adversary, impulsive, courageous, narrowminded, ruthless. I wish you had more troops."

"You know I am not a soldier, Claiborne. I'm a Puritan, a man of peace. I always hope that political differences may be settled by council, instead of arms."

Claiborne shook his head doubtfully. "I hope you are right, but Sir William will not give in readily. What is your plan, in case he resists and refuses to abdicate—if that is the word one uses in speaking of a governor stepping out of office?"

"I have a plan to arbitrate and compose our differences without force. The man who works for peace walks with God."

"You talk as the Quakers talk, Bennett."

"Why not? They surely are a godly people who have right on their side."

"Sir William Berkeley wouldn't think so."

Bennett pushed his chair back from the table. His ordinarily mild countenance changed. His voice was harsh when he spoke. "There will be no persecution of any man for his religious belief if I am governor of Virginia. But do not worry. Whatever happens, I think I shall be able to handle William Berkeley."

After Claiborne had departed, Richard Bennett sat for some time looking out the port at the racing waters. Stephen waited for him to speak. His cousin was deeply moved. This was a subject that had not been mentioned between them in the days of preparation for the new undertaking. Stephen knew Richard did not seek to be governor. He preferred, when the period of his commission was over, to go back to his plantation, Bennett's Welcome, on the lower James. But their uncle, Edward Bennett, that great merchant, wanted strong representation in Virginia to protect his own interests and, as he said, the interest of the planters in all the colony.

Stephen knew that politics did not interest Richard Bennett. Growing tobacco did. He had yielded to the force of Edward Bennett's arguments and allowed himself to be appointed commissioner last September.

Stephen, having been a year in Edward Bennett's counting-house in London, knew how great was Edward Bennett's power in the new government of England. Titular head of the Puritan Bennett family, the notable merchant, from his counting-room in St. Bartholomew's House, ruled the clan with a hand encased in a velvet glove, but the strength of iron was there also. Edward Bennett's ships, Edward Bennett's cargoes, Edward Bennett's wealth had played a great part in the story of the plantations from the early days of the Virginia Company. Now, in the second generation, the name was still potent.

After a time the tenseness in Richard Bennett's face relaxed. He turned to Stephen. "There is a prisoner in this ship by the name of Richards. I wish you would see that he is put on the list of indentured men for Bennett's Welcome. There is a Blount I want also, and a certain man by the name of Skynner. You will recall that Mistress Holder in the note she sent with her husband's report commended these three as likely to prove good workmen. I have bought five Scots, all prisoners after Worcester. Write the indentures, check with the master of the ship and get the signatures. They are to be transferred at Jamestown and sent across the river in one of my shallops to Bennett's Welcome. Assuming that I shall be chosen governor, I shall work on my proclamation after I get to my plantation, but certainly not today. I find myself weary and not interested in political affairs. The days go slowly on shipboard. I long to put my feet on good Virginia earth."

Stephen said, "I wonder if we are having an early spring, whether the tobacco beds have been seeded."

"Are you planting tobacco at your plantation this year?" his cousin asked. "If you are, remember to keep down to your allotment."

"Sir, I've written instructions to my overlooker every month. I hope he has followed them. I'm afraid we're going to have a struggle to make the Virginia planters understand the wisdom of cutting down their acreage of tobacco. I'm not sure I fully understand myself, although Uncle Edward thinks it an excellent idea."

The commissioner sighed. "Edward Bennett is a London merchant, and we are Virginia planters, Stephen. As I've said, the new plan has to do with keeping up the price. That is the merchants' philosophy which we are obliged to accept. We must make our people grasp that we are competing with Spanish tobacco, and their tobacco is first-grade. Quality, not quantity. Tell our people that, when they harass you with questions."

Stephen looked startled. "Sir, do you mean that I have to explain to all the planters about cutting their acreage?"

"On the south side of the river at least. But don't look so disconsolate. You can convince them that it is for their own protection, if you try."

"But what if I'm not convinced myself? If the price goes down, we sell more tobacco and make more customers."

The governor laughed. "That's your first task. Convince yourself that we seek quality, not quantity, in our tobacco. I'll leave you to fix up the indenture papers. I'm going to walk a hundred times around the deck to get rid of the doldrums."

Stephen took down the black japanned box that held the commissioner's important papers and searched for the indenture form. It came to him that he did not like the idea of indenture of white men as practised in the colonies. Seven years was a long time out of a man's life—seven years, and at the end what? Fifty acres of land and some tools. No, the old way was better—tenancy for three generations.

He found the paper and began to make out a set of articles from the copy.

> *This Indenture . . . Sixth Day of March, in the Year of our Lord Jesus Christ 1652. Whereas I _____ _____, of _____ _____, will put myself apprentice to Richard Bennett, Esqre., Planter, of Bennett's Welcome Plantation, on south side of James River, in Isle of Wight County, Colony of Virginia, to dwell with him from above date for seven years, as a faithful servant, to serve in the best manner I can. Shall receive training or cause to be taught a competent apprentice, and be given for said faithful service, meat, drink, competent lodging, apparel and all things fitting to my condition.*
>
> *At end of period of servitude shall be granted fifty (50) acres of land, according to custom of the country.*
>
> > *Name*   *Name*

The quill scratched across the page. When he came to the end Stephen read it through carefully, then sanded the paper. He shook his head slowly. His red-brown eyes were somewhat saddened, as he thought of the condition of these men, whose only crime was that they had fought on the losing side. Seven years' servitude! That would not set well with a free-born Englishman or a Scot.

But even servitude was better than hanging. . . . He took the paper and went on deck. The sun was an hour over the horizon by the yardarm. He walked swiftly to the master's quarters. The captain of a vessel had power to arrange indentures, if the paper had not been signed before leaving port.

The master, West, was drinking rakee, a liquor quite as strong as brandy. His face was red and he was in a jolly mood.

Stephen asked to have the prisoner Richards brought up so he might sign the papers.

"Surely, sir. Glad to accommodate His Excellency in any way." The Master clapped his fat hands together. When the cabin-boy appeared, he gave an order to bring up a prisoner named Richards. "Do you think you can find him, boy?"

"That I can, sir—him that's had his head all swathed in bandages and his arm held up by a bit of canvas to save his shoulder."

The captain said, "Well, get along, fool. Why are you standing there staring?"

The skinny boy fidgeted and snapped his knuckles. "He's been sick unto death, sir, with gaol fever. Then he was wounded in a fight. And afterward he got beat up shameful —that was on the quay at Bristol when they had the riot. He might be still weak in his knees."

The captain said, "Well, give him a shoulder, if you've got the strength in that skinny frame of yours."

"Yes, sir. I'll be glad to help, sir."

The captain excused himself. He must go forward and take a look about. One never knew when a pirate would sail up out of the horizon.

Stephen Bennett sat down on a sea-chest and waited. He wondered idly why the commissioner had spoken of these prisoners by name. Usually they were numbered. Some preferred to remain without a surname and be called Tom, Dick or Harry. One never quite knew what the commissioner was thinking. He was the quiet kind, who had little to say that was not pertinent to the subject at hand.

Stephen's mind turned from his cousin to Mathilda Jordan. There was a girl who could make a man lose his head. He wished he had had the courage to speak to her father when he rode with them to Hereford on their journey to Bristol. He could not screw his courage up to the point. All he could do was to look a lovesick calf. Mathilda had been sweet, quite different from her manner when he first met her. He had thought she was attracted to Nicholas Holder, but Nick had married the lovely Kathryn Audley. Ah, well, he hadn't been altogether a fool. Before he left Bristol he had written to his Uncle Edward in London suggesting that he get in touch with Mr. Hugh Jordan. If Jordan agreed, then a marriage settlement could be arranged. That seemed the wisest course.

Uncle Edward had power and wealth. Stephen himself was in a firm state, ready for marriage. He had his plantation, Bennett's Choice, of five hundred acres along Pagan's Creek; also a dozen black slaves, five white men at indenture for four years, tobacco and maize and a nice herd of cattle. He wished he had plucked up courage to approach Mathilda herself, but while she was sweet she was reserved, not gay and friendly like little Sibyl. Yes, he should be married. Perhaps one day he would be appointed to the Governor's Council or win a seat in the House of Burgesses.

Stephen's thoughts were interrupted. The prisoner stood in the door, a tall man, very thin, one arm in a canvas hammock. His head was wrapped in a cloth bandage so that only one side of his face was free. But that side showed a proud, bridged nose, a wide mouth and a long line of firm jaw. The one eye that was visible was dark and unfriendly.

The cabin-boy walked beside him, the prisoner's arm over his shoulder. The prisoner was breathing heavily, as though the exertion of coming up the ladder was almost too much for his strength.

After a moment's scrutiny Stephen motioned him to a seat. "Sit down, Richards. I see you haven't recovered from your illness." He crossed the room and poured a stiff measure of Canary from a decanter the captain had left on the table. "Here, drink this. It will warm your innards at least."

The prisoner took the cup and drank. A little colour came into his pale face. "Thank you, zur," he muttered.

Stephen went back to the desk and took up the indenture articles. He read them through in a dead level voice. "Are you ready to sign this indenture?"

The prisoner nodded.

"What is your full name?" Stephen thought he hesitated too long, trying to think up a name.

"Richards, as you said, zur."

"Your Christian name?"

A quite perceptible hesitation followed. "Richard."

Stephen raised his brows. "Richard Richards?"

"Nae, Richard ap Richards."

"Ah, a Welshman." Stephen leaned over the desk and took up a quill. "Richard ap Richards" he wrote in the first blank space. "Village?"

"The Marches, zur. No village."

Stephen filled in the second blank. He pushed the paper toward Richard. "Make your cross here, and here. The second copy is for you. Can you manage with your left hand?"

"Well enough." The voice was sullen and ungracious.

Stephen sanded the paper. He leaned back in his chair. "So you are from the Marches near Herefordshire?" He did not wait for the prisoner to speak. "Lovely country, Herefordshire. I've been there recently myself."

The prisoner said nothing. Stephen leaned forward. His smile was friendly. "My cousin, Commissioner Bennett, has bought your indenture. You will be taken to his plantation, Bennett's Welcome, on the south side of the James River below Jamestown. If you are a good man, one who knows the land and will serve him faithfully, all will be well. He is a good master. You can help yourself if you show willingness. That is all. You may go. I'll see that you have extra drink allowance and extra food."

"Meat without worms would be agreeable."

Stephen watched the prisoner and the cabin-boy walk slowly down the deck. He was not pleased with the interview. The man was gruff and unresponsive.

Richard lay flat on the deck until Digby came to him with his pannikin of supper. Digby said, "Orders have gone out that you are to have extra wine and double food." He raised an eyebrow. "The doctor? Or did you bribe someone?"

"Neither. A young fellow, who said he was the commissioner's cousin, sent for me to sign indenture papers. I'm to go to Commissioner Bennett's plantation. If I'm friendly and loyal for seven years, I may get to be an overlooker."

Digby grinned. " 'Tis not likely to be seven years. I've been talking about, here and there, and listening. There's ways of running off or buying off. Some, they say, that go to the islands manage to return to England on the same ship that brought them over."

"That is, if you have gold—which I haven't. They stripped me flat in Bristol gaol."

Digby started to tell him about the purse that a masked lady had brought to the ship. He had seen Kathryn Audley— Kathryn Holder as she now was—at Gabe Spencer's. He knew she had given him the purse for Richards—she used that name—because he was Richard's friend. He was to give

the mate and the doctor each five twenty-shilling broads if
Richards came safely to the voyage end. She did not know
he had recognized her through the mask. But this wasn't the
time to tell about the purse. Later, when they arrived at
their destination. He had the gold carefully hidden under a
board in the hold.

Instead, Digby said, "Here at last is the letter from your
lady mother."

Richard took the badly crumpled piece of paper and read
it as he ate and downed a cup of Canary. In his weakened
state tears sprang to his eyes as he thought of his mother and
her love for him. He cursed to himself when he read that
Nicholas Holder had robbed them of their home. The score
against that villain lengthened.

"I'm a Welshman from the Marches now," he said. "My
name is Richard ap Richards."

Digby nodded. " 'Tis well, zur. If the great un found out
that you helped with the escape of 'you know who,' he'd bring
you back to England and clap you into the Tower."

"You may as well stop saying 'sir' to me, Digby. Dick it is
from now on."

"Do you think, zur, that this young Bennett knew you?"

"How could he?" Richard was genuinely surprised.

Digby said, "I learned about him when I went with Mr.
Prideaux to your mother's. Bennett had been a-visiting a
feller named Holder—Nicholas Holder, a King's man turned
over to Cromwell."

Richard thought of what his mother had written. "Yes,
he's been at the manor, but not, I think, when I was there."

"Yes, zur. That is, I mean you'd know. He's looking very
close at the young lady Mistress Mathilda, Cook told me."

For Mathilda's sake Richard hoped he was a different
breed from his friend. He had borne himself decently enough
in the interview over the articles. He looked like a man.

Digby went on: " 'Twas said in Bristol that Mr. Holder was
coming over to America—Virginia or Maryland, I cannot
venture which place—he and his new wife."

Richard Monington was silent. Digby's words bore down on
him, opened a wound. He could not think of Kathryn as
married to Nick Holder. He had not believed her when she
told him at the inn that she was going to marry Nick. Before
the duel in the Bristol garden she had said it was an ac-

complished fact, but everything about that duel was like a dream, without substance. Well, it was bitter fact.

Digby took up the empty pannikin and cup and went away. Richard lay back on the deck, one arm beneath his head, looking up at the heavens. The stars came out, as brilliant and as hard as diamonds, against the dark velvet of the sky.

A thought came to him out of the dullness of his despair. He was not done with Kathryn Audley. Nor was he done with that thief Nicholas Holder. They were woven into his destiny. He had thought of Virginia as the end, a clean cut from the old life of the old world. Perhaps he had been wrong. Perhaps it was only a continuation.

BOOK THREE

Virginia

CHAPTER 12

The River and the Village

THE *St. George* passed the Point of Comfort shortly after the sun had crossed the meridian. The captain ordered the sail doused to do his duties to the fort according to custom. A shot from the fort replied, and the ship, under the majesty of full sail, moved slowly toward its anchorage. A boat put out from shore, and a customs officer came on board to examine the ship's list of passengers. Here customs duties were paid, and the powder allowance for the fort measured out, before the ship could proceed up-river to Jamestown, under the hand of Captain Chichester, James River pilot.

A few small boats rowed over from the shore, and one or two canoe-loads of Indians paddled about the ship to satisfy their curiosity and perhaps sell a few articles like buckskin pouches, beaded and fringed, or clay pipes or baskets woven of reeds.

The ship had taken on unusual activity ever since land had been sighted off the Capes. Passengers and prisoners were on deck, watching with eager eyes the gradual enlargement of objects on the beach and along the shore.

The dark blur on the shoreline soon became trees, tall pines rising skyward, sentinels that guarded the wide river. There were high banks on one side, with the forest clinging to the land's verge. On the opposite shore were low land, swampy stretches and sand beaches. The great river was an estuary, an inland sea, tidewater for many miles up-stream.

The March day was mild. The sun shone. The air, fragrant with the clean scent of pine and fir, was soft against the face. The weather, ever since the ship had left the Somers Isles, had been unpleasant. A series of storms, gusty winds from mild to cyclone force, had beset them.

From the Cape of Fear to Hatorask the ship had tossed about in the edge of a hurricane which blew out to sea. As they approached the Virginia Capes a welcome quiet followed the storm.

After two months and more the food was deteriorating and getting low. A few cases of scurvy appeared, but lemons and other fresh fruit, taken on at the Southern Isles, had rectified that condition.

They had had the good fortune not to come in sight of Turks or Algerians between England and the Somers Isles, nor had they seen a Spanish ship, although several had been reported cruising about the islands. For one thing the majority of ships sailed from England in September. During that season the pirates lay in wait behind the Canaries or the Azores or the Westerly Islands. The voyage had taken nine weeks in all, excusing the two weeks they lay in a dead calm near the Somers.

The New World lay before them, Virginia, the strange land of beauty and of terror. It took courage to leave known things behind and fare forth into the unknown, but the Elizabethan venturers had had that courage. It was they who charted the unknown sea and gave life to a New World. It had not been the task of weak men. It took courage and strength to fight and overcome the perils of the sea and the savagery of the land. Great men had done it, great in their own day and great in their influence on the days to follow.

Three men of one family had led: Sir Humphrey Gilbert on the sea, Sir Walter Raleigh at Court, and Sir Richard Grenville, the man who achieved the impossible, on land and sea. Then came Ralph Lane and John White, governors, one of an expedition that failed, the other of a Lost Colony.

The candle had been lighted, a feeble thing, but other men came who had vision and courage. The Roanoke Island failures led in time to a new settlement. This time the James River was chosen to bear the ships of the adventurers, a new settlement on James City Island. The candle burned more brightly. Stronger men took up the burden of adventure.

John Smith came, and Captain Newport and John Rolfe and Sir George Yeardley. The Virginia Company of London began sending out their governors and their settlers. Nearly half a century had passed.

The ancient colonists had fought a strange untamed land. Men planted and harvested. Sometimes they won a little, sometimes they lost, but always they achieved some margin of gain against famine, against storms, against the dark mystery of the forest with its host of savage Indians, against a loneliness that mounted until it drove men to madness.

The Elizabethan giants gave way to lesser rulers and lesser men, but the dream of the New World lived on from those original venturers who first seated Roanoke Island in the days of Sir Walter Raleigh.

From father to son the venture carried through the generations. Nor was courage lacking in some to seek the New World their fathers had glimpsed, endeavoured and lost. "The long continuation" they called it, from the first voyagers to the settlements that struggled to hold along the mighty James. Each bold spirit added his strength and courage to build a force that would one day conquer. . . .

Such thoughts as these ran through Richard Monington's head as he stood by the rail on the lower deck. Perhaps the same thoughts were in the minds of other men and women on the *St. George.*

The customs boat rowed ashore. The sail hoisted, the *St. George* began its journey up the great river, tawny as the coat of a lion from the spring floods. The breeze was slight. The ship moved slowly on the quiet stream under full sail. Toward sunset they approached Newport-Neuse. Here they would take water from a sweet spring that gushed from the earth. Ships going up-river or coming down stopped here to replenish water casks and to allow south-shore planters to come aboard and purchase.

Hhere where the two Neuse brothers from Ireland had made a plantation, a small settlement had grown up with a few defending guns and a few soldiers. Besides the constant danger from the forest, the threat was ever present that Spaniards would sail up the James or a pirate ship enter and devastate the little forts.

When the ship anchored at Newport-Neuse, Commissioner Bennett's shallop came alongside. The whole ship's company turned out and stood at attention when he and Mr. Claiborne went over the side.

Richard Monington stood at the side of the ship and watched his new owner disembark and step on the deck of his shallop. He studied him with some interest—a strong face, rather kindly. He noticed that white men sailed the little boat, but there were six oarsmen, all black Negroes, ready to row if the wind died down. William Claiborne went with his brother commissioner, and two servants who looked to the personal luggage of the travellers.

Digby edged through the crowd that lined the rail until he stood beside Richard. He was full of news he had picked up from passengers and crew.

'Twas the man who would be governor, himself. He had boarded the ship very quietly when the *St. George* put in for water at the Somers Isles. He had stayed in the owner's cabin, walking about only at night. He was a nephew of Edward Bennett, the owner of the five-hundred-ton *St. George* and a dozen other like vessels. One of the great merchant princes was Edward Bennett.

He had also been an owner of many shares in the Virginia Company of London before it dissolved. The younger Bennett, Stephen by name, was a cousin of the commissioner, and his secretary.

"Young Stephen Bennett," Digby said, "has a large plantation called Bennett's Choice above the governor's holding, near Pagan's Creek. . . . The commissioner is a Puritan elder, as is his Uncle Edward. They have power with Parliament."

All this Richard listened to with awakening interest. "At least you are owned by the highest in the land," Digby said with a sidewise grin, "while I, devil take it, belong to a scatter-brained woman who lives some miles up the James in the wild Indian country."

"I wish Bennett had bought you, Digby. If he only knew, you're worth five ordinary men."

"But how is the commissioner to know that?" Digby said querulously. "I can't tell him, nor can you, zur. Who then?"

"Perhaps I can speak to the commissioner." Richard turned quickly. He recognized the voice of young Stephen Bennett. "If this man Digby is such an excellent worker, perhaps it can be arranged."

Digby took off his greasy cap. "Zur, what about the lady who bought me? Will she give me up so willingly?"

"Your papers won't be signed until we reach Jamestown. I will look at the records. If you are not designated by name or number, we can send another servant. Who is the lady?"

"Zur, they say 'er name be Mistress Cecily—something that I disremember. She lives at a place called Jordan's Journey."

The young chap whistled. "Ah, that changes the situation! Madam Montague is a determined character."

Digby's face grew gloomy. "My luck fell into the ocean," he said. "Women, they cause trouble enough." He turned back to the rail, his shoulders drooping.

Stephen glanced at Richard and thought he detected a glimmer of amusement in his eye. Stephen said, "It may be that Madam Montague has not asked for Digby. If she hasn't, a transfer may be arranged, so that he may go either to the commissioner, at Bennett's Welcome, or to my plantation."

Richard said, "Thank you, zur. 'E was close to me in the wars, zur, and has been close since. 'Twas him that saved me."

Stephen nodded. "I'll see what can be done." He walked away through the crowd, stopping to speak to a man or a woman or a child as he went. His smile comes readily; his voice is cheerful, Richard thought. Perhaps these Puritans may not be so bad, once one knows them. Then he laughed harshly. He had forgotten that Richard Monington, Lord of the Manor of Coddington, was no more. In his place stood a prisoner, a bondsman, named Richard ap Richards. A Welshman—would be his new name soon be Welsh Dick, or would he be Taffy the Welshman?

Richard looked about at the press of people, men and women who lined the ship's rail. It was as though he saw them for the first time. Indeed it was, since through so much of the voyage he had lain demented. From the Azores to the Somers Isles he was not conscious of people, only of his dreams.

As he looked at them now, his heart sank. The poor wretches—half of them were sick, scarcely able to stand erect by grasping the rail. They had hollow-eyed, cadaverous faces, bent shoulders and backs. The children were incredibly thin. There were a few neat, fresh-looking women, but for the most part they were a frowzy, sickly, unhealthy lot, with untidy hair and dresses.

A curious grin crossed his lips. He, with his bandage, his wretched clothes, his one eye showing, fitted in well with the other rogues and rascals from the Clink or Newgate or Bridewell.

The sun was dropping behind the pines. The river, tawny by day, was red gold at eventide. A man in worn clericals came on deck. He lifted a book and began to read the Evensong.

Evidently it was no crime to read from the Book of Common Prayer in Virginia, as it was in England.

The man's voice had power and a certain quality of enveloping kindliness. People turned to him. When he began to pray, they knelt down on the bare deck. "O wondrous land, O fertile land of wealth and beauty, take us poor, frightened, homeless wanderers to your broad bosom. Protect us. Feed us. Let us multiply and grow strong so that once again, in God's sight, we may walk as strong free men."

People about him turned eyes filled with tears toward the minister, tears that overflowed and rolled down their thin cheeks, not easy tears of childhood, but the hard, torturing tears of a betrayed and outraged people.

"Let us stand as free men in a New World. Let us be proud and upright and faithful to a new land, and by our pride and our wisdom give strength to the land, so that we may rise together, the land out of pagan savagery, the people from oppression, toward freedom." The voice died out.

Above them wild geese wedged their way across the darkling sky. Fish, leaping, broke the water of the golden stream. It seemed for the moment that the trees and the land itself had turned to molten gold.

A child's voice broke the stillness. "Mother, Mother, breathe of the sweet, clean air. May I say a prayer to God for so much beautiful clean air?"

In the morning Jamestown lay before them. The faces of the passengers showed their discouragement only too plainly. A woman of thirty or so, with unkempt hair and ragged frock, spat over the rail. "I'd as leave be in gaol as this stinking, scurvy place. Call it a town? I calls it a putrid slum. That's what I calls it. Count for yourself—a dozen houses of brick, all in all. The rest are tumbling down, the thatches falling off. Merciful God, is this the New World of opportunity?"

"Shut your wide mouth," a man's gruff voice broke in. "Whatever it is, 'tis better than you're accustomed to, my girl. Didst hear the little laddie last night? Behave, and do as he said—breathe the good sweet air—and push the fool stench of gaol from your lungs."

Richard moved away and found a place by the rail where he stood alone. The ship was moving slowly to her anchorage in midstream off the island of Jamestown. The village was indeed meagre, situated on low land. There were two rows of houses on the right, set out in grass plots and gardens with some regard to order.

Some of the larger houses were of brick, but for the most part they were built after the manner of the old country, of wattles plastered over with clay, with the dark beams showing through. Some were thatched with reeds, others with bark of trees put on like tiles. The chimneys were large and wide, some brick, some plastered over. On the left, beyond the church, were larger and more commodious houses. The frowzy woman had not noted them. A group set side by side, twenty or so, were of brick, at least forty feet long. Some were two-storied, with chimneys at each end. Some were roofed with slate or tile.

The church, not yet completed, was fair and large, with a Norman tower, and seemed almost the centre of the town. The streets that ran parallel to the river were wide, thirty or forty feet, Richard estimated. The huts or smaller houses were set out in rows, which formed a triangle of about half an acre. In this triangle were a market-place and the guard-house.

In all, not a bad plan, Richard decided. The stockade was high, at least fourteen feet, made of trees eight to ten inches in diameter, set upright with ends pointed sharply. The fort was a separate stockade with several entrances.

Richard could not see what ordnance was within the triangular fort, which appeared to be about a hundred and forty yards long on each side. Near by was the munition house. Beyond the fort on the waterside were warehouses and animal shelters. Beyond the little town the forest loomed dark and formidable.

A crowd of a hundred or more was gathered in the market-place, and another at the long wharf which extended well out into the water. The people waved and shouted. Women's and children's clothes made bright spots amid the greenery.

Digby came up and stood beside Richard. " 'Tis better than I thought, zur. See, along beyond the island—it's an island at high tide—is a bridge or causeway, and an open space with a great house; and farther beyond are other farm places and beaches, where doubtless there be farm-houses. Look, zur, across the river. Small streams empty into the James, and by each stream is a field fair-ploughed, zur, getting ready for seeding. 'Tis a grand sight, this great river."

Richard said, "The people are pointing down-stream, shout-ing and waving. Ah, a puff of smoke from a cannon! We will hear the sound in a second." He turned to look down-river. Two ships were sailing up the river with canvas spread.

Digby said, "Without a doubt 'tis the rest of our convoy which we have not set eyes on since we ran into the big blow after we sailed past Land's End."

"This is the first I've heard about a convoy." Richard shaded his eyes with his hand to watch the ships sailing majestically up the stream.

Small boats began to move away from the shore, some under sail, some rowed.

"Here we get our feet onto the earth," Digby remarked. "I've a mind to fall on my knees and kiss the ground. But I won't. I'll get myself a bit of tobacco leaf and a clay pipe the first thing."

Richard said, "We are to march over to the warehouse, where we will be checked in, examined for illness, catching-sores and diseases. So the doctor told me when he changed my head-piece this morning."

Digby looked at Richard anxiously. "Will there be a scar, zur?"

"There will be a scar. It's not quite healed, so I must wear this bandage for a week or two longer."

"What kind of a scar? Will it show much?"

"It will show—a red streak right across the temple to remind me that I have still a score to settle with Master Nicholas Holder. Your own cut—the one you got in the storm—seems to have healed over."

Digby did not reply at once. His deeply lined, weathered face was grave. His wide mouth worked a little. Anxiety shone in his deep-set eyes. "Master Richard, excuse me for my boldness, zur. 'Tis a new country and a new life. 'Twere better to live the new and forget the old."

Richard's voice was harsh. "I'll not forget Holder."

"Then I may as well tell you now, Mr. Holder and his lady are aboard one of the convoy. They sailed from Bristol the day we sailed."

Richard turned from the rail. His fingers dug into Digby's shoulder. His face was as white as a bit of parchment, and the visible eye gleamed with anger. "What did you say?"

Digby slid out from under Richard's hand. "I said Mr.

Nicholas Holder and his lady wife sailed from Bristol the day we sailed, nearly three months ago."

"Do you know that to be the truth, or is it some tale?"

" 'Tis true enough. I saw with my own eyes. I heard with my own ears, when the lady gave me a gold purse for you. I've kept it hidden under a board in the hold, safe for you till the end of the voyage. First, I've taken from it five coins each for the doctor and the mate since you've lived through the crossing. She told me I was to do that, zur."

"What's this? The lady? Mistress Holder? How did you know her?"

"I'd seen her at Gabe Spencer's, zur, and she knew me for your friend. But she didn't think I'd recognize her through the mask she was wearing when she came to the ship. She stood a-looking at you lying there white as a dead fish. And her a-crying and kissing your hand. 'Twas no way to act, and her not a month married. . . ." His voice trailed off.

Richard endeavoured to keep the tremor out of his voice. "When was this, Digby? Why have you not told me before?"

"Well enough is well enough. How could I talk, with you either lying still and white as death, or glittering your eyes and thrashing your arm and legs about, talking and muttering like unto a wild man from early in the morning until twelve of the clock in the night, muttering like a man bereft of his senses? And then when you came to, I thought I'd not fash you about this Mistress Holder till we got to Jamestown. Just to mention her seemed to put you out of your mind."

Richard said nothing for a time. He would use no money brought by Kathryn Holder. Let Digby buy his freedom with the gold. Not he. When he spoke, his voice was steady. "Did you sit beside me all the hours of my illness, Digby?"

"Did what they would let me. 'Twas hard to get things at first, until I bribed the cabin-boy. He was your friend from the start but a broad from Mistress Holder's purse was a great encouragement. After that it was better. Soup and a little wine."

Richard held out his hand. "Thank you, Digby. In my life I've never had a better friend."

The dragoon looked at his rough, gnarled hand for a moment, then a smile illumined his stern visage. " 'Tis a New World, zur. A man may clasp the hand of his betters without fear."

"You have no betters, Digby. No man stands superior to you in honesty and faithful friendship. I thank you from my heart."

Digby turned away. He could meet adversity with a laugh, he could parry curses with something stronger, but praise defeated him utterly.

The cabin rattled as the anchor was lowered over the side and came to rest in the tawny river.

The mate bellowed out, "Passengers will be put ashore, proceeding in alphabetical order. Please step to the foredeck. Indentured servants and prisoners will go below, to be ticketed and registered. All ashore! All ashore! All ashore!"

They were at the end of the long voyage. This was Virginia. These were the people who would make a New World. These few, these feeble few, must grow in strength, in wisdom, to meet the dangers of a primeval forest, the promise of a fair virgin land.

Richard went below to gather up his few belongings and push them into a canvas bag. He thought he should be melancholy and discouraged. Here am I, Richard Monington, a man without property, penniless, weak in body, a prisoner, without king or country, yet my heart is strangely light. I look on the past without bitterness, for my heart and soul are inflamed with desire to meet the challenge of the future.

O Strange New World, what have you to give to the despairing children of the Old?

With Digby's aid he hoisted the canvas bag to his back. They were among the last to leave the *St. George*. A few minutes later he stepped into a boat rowed by four bronzed watermen. In a short time he had joined the press of men who walked toward a long warehouse.

People from the village crowded against the ropes that made an aisle from the ship's passengers. Shouts of welcome greeted them as they moved forward. Drums were sounding, pipes playing. He looked at the faces of his companions of the voyage. Their eyes were shining with excitement.

They entered the long warehouse under a cluster of mighty oaks. Inside, near the wide doors, were long tables of food, jugs of milk and ale. Small children carried bunches of field flowers, which they thrust into the hands of the visitors.

Every voice spoke welcome, even to the indentured prisoners who stood apart from the passengers.

A man, a heavy man with a strong ringing voice, mounted a stool. "Welcome to Jamestown! Welcome to Virginia! Welcome, every man and woman, every chick and child, to Thompson's Tavern, where you will be served a free dinner!"

"Welcome! Welcome! Welcome!" The word rang through the great cavern of the warehouse until it became a chant, rising to the brilliant blue of the skies. "Welcome, friends and neighbours! Welcome, friends and neighbours! Welcome to our New World of Virginia!"

CHAPTER 13

Jamestown

RICHARD stood near a broad door in the warehouse that opened toward the south. The air was soft and warm, the sky without a cloud. The fruit trees were blooming in the little gardens and small shrubs were covered with white blossoms. The oak leaves were unfolding, tender green, soft as velvet, pink mingled with the green. Wavelets lapped the water's edge, where children were chasing small crabs along the narrow strip of sand. Back of the two rows of houses was the dark rich green of the forest, starred by the glistening white of dogwood blossoms. The cottage doors and windows were open, without life. The Jamestown folk were in the village triangle or in groups along the shore and wharf.

Three ships in one day! The excitement mounted as more and more people came ashore.

Richard turned his eyes to contemplate the scene in the warehouse. Here all was excitement and confusion. On one side were the passengers returning home, greeting family and friends. On the other the indentured prisoners in long files moved up to the table where the sheriff sat together with customs men and clerks. At another table were two medical officers who felt pulses, laid their heads against chests and looked at tongues.

On the west side of the room a group of small farmers dressed in leathern breeches of Osnaburg or dowlas, some in smocks of blue linen. They had come from the York River or the lower James to pick up an indentured servant or two.

The planters from the upper James and the Northern Neck were a different breed. They sat on comfortable benches on a raised platform, so they might examine the indentured men as they walked across the platform when their numbers were called by the ship's purser.

The planters were well, even elegantly, dressed. They resembled squires from any English county. Their breeches were of doeskin, their coats and waistcoats of good cloth in pleasant shades of puce and buff. The waistcoats were more ornate, brocaded, with silver buttons. Some wore riding clothes with high boots, well varnished. No one wore armour or carried a sword, but some of the riders who had dismounted and left their horses at the hitching post, with Negro grooms in attendance, had holsters for pistols or muskets on their saddles. They had dispensed with the Cavalier insignia, but they still wore plumes on their broad beaver hats. Others wore the grey of the Puritans, the grey stockings and plain buckled shoes, with a stiff, high-crowned hat. Puritans and Cavaliers mingled, talking amiably or bidding heatedly for the body of a white man. Muscular strength was what they looked for. Points important to them were good teeth, good health and a willing disposition. For this they offered small pay, clothes, food and housing.

Richard watched the procedure dully. He was tired of standing, tired of the press of people, nauseated with the thought that one man could buy another in the promised land.

A man edged up to the open door behind him. His ankle was heavily bandaged. He was old and walked with a cane. He leaned against the door-jamb and looked Richard over with sharp bright eyes, deep set under heavy brows.

"Who are those men on the platform?" Richard asked.

The man craned his neck, so that he might look into the room. "Those be the planters from the upper James, Mr. Cary and Mr. Fitzhugh sitting in front, and Major Beverley—that's him examining the servant. He is going to build a house of brick on his three-acre plot beyond the Vale. That's Mr. William Stafford there, down at the end of the bench. He's a knowledgeable man about slaves, he is. He don't have many white men, he don't. He's got land and tobacco and cattle in York. That's Colonel Thomas Ludwell, just stepping in, the tall man with dark eyes that are sharp enough to see right here to the door. He's got the largest estate in York, on the Eastern Shore, maybe twenty thousand pounds of tobacco and three brick houses yonder beyond the church. You see the two women just entering, talking to Colonel Ludwell? One's Mrs. Bushrod. She has a likely plantation. And the other's Mistress Cecily Jordan, she that married Peter Montague. I didn't know she'd come back from England."

Richard straightened himself, so he might look over the heads of the crowd. He could not discern the features of Mrs. Bushrod. She had sat down beside a man whom his informant had pointed out as Nathaniel Bacon the elder.

Mistress Cecily moved across the platform and stood beside Major Beverley. Her eyes ran over an indentured man as though she were judging a horse or a Highland bull.

"She must have just come on one of the ships," the old man said, edging his way in. "She's been gone, she has, for a year or more. 'Twould be well enough if she stayed a year longer. I wondered what brings her back so soon."

He pushed himself into the room, looking over Richard's shoulder. He watched Mistress Cecily closely. "She'll be buying another man," he muttered. "I hope she don't put him into my quarters. The last one she got right out of the Clink, a thieving rascal who pilfered the littlest thing just to be thieving, and as for whoring, he was after the women black and white."

The old man stepped back to the ground as Madam Montague came from the platform and walked slowly down the queue of indentured men and women. There must have been a hundred or more in the line.

Mistress Cecily, followed by two clerks carrying lists, took her time, stopping to look closely at the men with an air of complete detachment—chattels, to be valued according to ability to labour.

Richard watched her approach. A woman of middle years, she must have been beautiful in her youth. She was trim in figure, with brown hair that showed no grey. She was dressed in a blue taffeta silk, full skirted, with a modesty of thin white and small flower filling the top of the bodice.

Her step was firm and vigorous. Richard took an instant dislike to her. Who was she, a colonial, to judge white men as she judged cattle? He turned away and looked out the window. He heard her say, "No, I don't want a sick man. It would cost too much to fatten him up to where he would be of any use at Jordan's Journey."

A familiar voice broke in. "Good day, Madame Montague. I did not know you were expected so soon. When I last saw you in England, you said you would not be home in Virginia for some months."

"I grew home-sick, Stephen. I grew tired of England and

English ways, so I came on the *Goodspeed*, which arrived this morning a few hours after your ship, I understand. Pray, how is your cousin the commissioner, who is soon to be our governor, I hear?"

"Quite well, thank you. He left the ship at Newport-Neuse and went directly to Bennett's Welcome."

"Please extend my humble duties. Say that we will all be in Jamestown when the Great Assembly opens next month."

"I'm sure he will be pleased, Madam Montague."

She said, "I suppose it will be puritanical and dull, not the gaiety and ceremony Sir William insisted on. Not that I stand for the Stuarts, but you must admit that Sir William Berkeley has had a very pleasant Court here at Jamestown for the past ten years."

Stephen said, "I understand he still holds Court at Green Spring."

"Tut-tut. Don't be envious, Stephen." She started to move on down the line. "By the way, do come up to us next week end. My young cousins came over with me, Sibyl and Mathilda Jordan. I believe you have met them in England."

Richard, astonished, turned quickly. He saw Stephen Bennett staring open-mouthed in his surprise. Mistress Cecily had a mischievous look in her large red-brown eyes. "Do come," she repeated as she moved away.

Stephen followed Madam Montague. They stopped close to Richard. Stephen stammered in his excitement. "Where . . . where is she? Where are they? I mean, are the Misses Jordan here in Jamestown? May I see them?" Stephen was plainly flustered.

Mistress Cecily smiled. The mischievous twinkle in her eyes deepened. "I am sorry that I did not see you earlier. They sailed up the river with my husband not an hour ago—immediately after we landed, to be exact. I stayed on to arrange about the indentured men. Why, Stephen, I believe you are blushing! It can't be that you are interested in my young guests."

Stephen dropped his voice. Richard caught a word or two. "I am . . . Mathilda . . . my Uncle Edward Bennett has written to her . . . father . . ."

"So! Then you *will* come to Jordan's Journey."

"Indeed I shall, with your permission, Madam Montague, as soon as I can make arrangements with the commissioner."

"Will he approve?"

"I am of age and I own my own plantation, as you know," Stephen answered a little stiffly. "And another matter—if I have your permission to bring up business at this time. There is an indentured man here I had planned to buy, but they tell me that you have bespoke him. His name is Digby, one of the prisoners taken after Worcester."

Cecily Montague looked at a paper she held in her hand. "Digby . . . Digby . . . yes, his name is on the list my Bristol agent gave me. However, I have just purchased two Negroes from Governor Berkeley's overlooker. I might let you have him." She looked at Stephen shrewdly. "Why do you want him? Is he a strong worker? Young?"

"No, he is in the middle years, but he seems to be a companion of a man I bought. I thought the two together would be a team."

"Point out Digby to me."

Stephen glanced about the warehouse. "There he is, ma'am —the thin one with grey hair and the big nose over by the door."

Madam Montague's shrewd eyes took in the lean frame, the drooping head, the thin, lined face. She pursed her lips, tapping the paper against her palm. "He looks whipped down, fifty at least, too thin . . . but sometimes those meagre fellows are tough and wiry. I've been fooled on some of the big lunks. They've more fat than sinew. Oh, no matter, you may have him. I'll tell my overlooker to select another. Is he a *bona fide* prisoner or is he one of the spirited fellows? The spirited ones are never satisfied and they aren't willing workers. I don't hold with kidnapping or spiriting. What are you prepared to offer for the fellow?"

Stephen glanced at Digby. He didn't look worth much as he sat back to the wall, his lean face grey with fatigue. Perhaps he was soft. But Stephan had taken a fancy to Richard, and the two seemed close and friendly. He had not figured out the relationship—comrades in war no doubt, or perhaps neighbours, men of the same country. As for that he hadn't quite placed Richards, a cold and reserved fellow, but he felt drawn to him. Perhaps that was because of his uncomplaining attitude. In spite of the gaol fever, he felt the man had strength in his wasted frame. A few weeks in Virginia would set him right.

Cecily Montague was looking at him curiously. "Of course you'll pay me something for my bargain. If he is worth anything to you, I should have a token for my trouble. I've laid out six pounds in passage money. Then there are the papers."

"Certainly I will guarantee the fees, passage money, and something in tobacco when the harvest comes, to compensate you."

Mistress Cecily was a shrewd bargainer. "How much tobacco, Stephan? You are vague. How much for my rights in the fellow? I don't want you to think me a soul-seller, but I want to know what you are prepared to pay. I may tell you I don't want him, but I can put him up on the block. I don't want any sick, weak or lame men, I admit, but he may be stronger than he looks. You know the rule—no servant sold off a ship for ten days after arrival—but in this case I won't wait until the gun is fired."

"I am willing to go by the custom of the country and pay a bonus for a contract made in England. Suppose you set your price, ma'am. If it is not too high to pay for a mature man, I'll meet it. What is the term of servitude?"

Mistress Cecily spoke indifferently. "The usual, I suppose—four years for a man of his age. Perhaps it is five. I haven't looked at the paper."

Listening to the conversation, Richard Monington was glad that his bandaged face did not betray his rage. To be herded into this great warehouse was bad enough, but to see men and women, free-born and white, standing on the block to be examined like cattle, with lips pulled back to show the condition of teeth—to see hands run over their bodies to ascertain their strength, hands lingering on thighs and breasts of women, thumping chests and backs of honest men—God, what an outrage! It was mediaeval, like the sale of serfs in old times. Surely this Virginia, this New World, was not a land for free men. . . .

Stephen Bennett's voice broke into his thoughts. "I'll agree. Twenty pounds in sterling. That's the amount Peter Folger paid for Mary Morrils and considered it a fair bargain. I'll pay you the amount you laid out for clothes."

Madam Montague signalled to her overlooker, a stocky, ill-favoured fellow in rustic clothes who was standing near a group of men and women across the room near the block.

He had a paper in his hand, checking the names against the human beings.

At the signal he came over. She said, "Hayes, what has the agent laid out in clothes for a man named Digby?"

The man ruffled through a sheaf of papers until he found what he was seeking. "Three pairs shoes, three shirts, three pairs drawers, two jackets, one hat, a promise of twenty-five shillings per annum in wages, a good kersey coat."

"Total it. I don't need the items." Mistress Cecily reached impatiently for the papers. "Here it is—six pounds, ten shillings, eight pence—and that makes, in all, getting the man over and clothing, around twelve pounds, plus the tobacco, for the bargain."

"Done!" said Stephen with a laugh. He turned to the overlooker. "Get Digby's papers transferred to—" he started to say Commissioner Bennett, then changed his mind—"to me," he concluded. He would work out with the commissioner an arrangement for the men to be together.

The overlooker glanced at Madam Montague. "I haven't seen the man Digby. Is it wise to sell him sight unseen?"

She laughed. "Look at him—over on the floor by the door —the sleeping one."

The overlooker's eyes followed her extended arm. He grinned. "I can replace him readily, Madam Montague. There's a good strong wench that will do fine, a broad-beamed country lass, not afeared of field work."

"Buy her, and see that you don't go wenching with her. I don't want my white women dropping brats every spring like the mares." They moved off toward the long table, where the clerks were stamping and transferring the indentures. Richard watched them go—the woman walking lightly with firm even steps, a woman beautiful in her middle years, with an air of authority that a man of property might envy. He wondered why Mathilda and Sibyl Jordan had come to visit her in Virginia. It was evident from the conversation between her and Stephen Bennett that the young man was in love with Mathilda and wanted to marry her. In the back of Richard's mind there was something his mother had told him, or perhaps it was Digby or John Prideaux; he could not remember. He was too weary. He was bone-tired from standing, too weary to be resentful as he should be about the thing that was going on about him.

Here was a warehouse in which the sweet odour of tobacco filled the nostrils. On one side the black men wheeled great hogsheads of tobacco to be shipped to Bristol or Bideford. On the other stood tired, tragic folk who had left the Old World behind them to venture the New. Not all of these people of indenture were prisoners who had fought a losing fight for a Stuart king. Some had come of their own will to better their condition in the new Virginia. Others had been kidnapped or were vagabonds, whores or prisoners. There were gentlemen also, if he were any judge, come to make wealth from tobacco—tobacco, fabulous word which spelled not only wealth but independence, a coveted place when they returned home to England! Some must be furriers or skilled workmen or artisans who would build houses, set up shops; some, men and women of a religious faith that was not in favour at home, Dissenters and the like. Had he not heard in earlier times that the authorities had caused the drums to be beaten and warning given to all those folk who were disposed to go as servants to Virginia, that they should repair to the county village to hear the conditions on which they might indenture themselves or pay passage; or that they should go to St. Katherine's docks near the Tower of London in order to gain information from a Virginia agent?

These things Richard had heard and to them paid no heed—yes, and grim stories of kidnapping and spiriting, those terrible practices, enticing and inveigling boys and girls onto a ship about to sail.

He remembered, too, having heard on a visit to London that the Marshals of the Admiralty and the Cinque Ports were ordered to search all vessels in the Thames and at the Downs for kidnapped children.

These rumours had made little impression. Richard Monington, Lord of the Manor of Coddington, had little interest in such violations of law, other than to deplore the infringements of human rights. Now he recalled with sharpened memory how lightly he had considered such crimes.

He had heard about the registration of ten thousand servants at Bristol. He knew about the Act of Parliament, passed a few years before, cautioning officers of the law "to be very diligent in apprehending all persons as are faulty of this kind, either in stealing or selling, buying, inveigling, purloining, conveying or receiving children so stolen, and keep them in safe imprisonment until they can be brought to severe and exemplary punishment." Still the crimes made no impression on him. Now he was to know to his cost what such inhuman behaviour meant.

Let the men who had raped a woman in the fields or entered and stolen in a home or knifed a fellow in a quarrel on the highway be sent out, but not children, defenceless children, such as he saw now with his own eyes—that group near the open door, huddled close together for security, some of them no more than twelve, with thin white faces; those little girls, with pipestem legs and scrawny bodies, underfed, tear-stained. He forgot his own condition as he watched them being taken away by their owners in parties of two and three or singly.

He knew now what "taken by the spirits" meant—a barbarous custom not worthy of a strong people. "Kidnabbing," he had heard it called also, a horrid word. Let them indeed fine and imprison the wretches who had done such evil tricks. The gibbet was too good for them. . . .

A servant came to offer him a cup of hot broth and a plate of some sort of stew he called loblolly, with a chunk of bread for dipping. Richard ate hungrily.

After a time Digby got up and came over. The queue was moving up. Many had dropped out of the long lines, taken away by their owners. Digby said, "Let me come close. I will hand you my coat. Wrapped in it is the purse with gold. Hide it. Ask to go to the little house behind this building. Secrete the purse on your person."

"Where?" Richard asked, sarcasm deep in his voice. "Where shall I hide it?"

Digby scratched his head. "I don't know. They may take your bundle. Why not in the leather bag at your waist? Slip it under your tunic."

A guard walked along the line. Digby stepped back to his place. Richard, with permission, stepped out to the privy. He feared that he might be stripped and searched there. The purse would then inevitably be discovered. But this usual procedure was not exacted in his case. On his return he heard his named called, and Digby's. Stephen Bennett crossed the room. "I had not intended to have you in the line, Richards," he said. "Come along, Digby, we must make haste. The tide is turning. The wind is just right to carry us down-river to Bennett's Welcome."

Richard picked up his blankets and followed Stephen. Digby took the bundle from him and followed. They went out a door opposite the one where he had been standing, weaving in and out of the crowds that jammed the buildings. They reminded Richard of throngs of emigrants he had once seen at Tilbury dock embarking for Holland, Puritans and Separatists who found England too dangerous a place to live in under Charles the First, weary people, bewildered for the most part.

Here were children sitting on bundles on the floor or leaning against the wall. With the natural curiosity of youth they wanted to run out through the open doors into the dusty streets, but their mothers admonished them. One woman sat with her back against the rough board planking of the wall, suckling a thin pale infant at her breast. Two small children lay across her lap and her legs, which were stretched out on the floor. They were asleep. The man who stood beside her was weary, his hollow eyes sunken. He seemed almost too tired to turn his eyes on the kaleidoscopic movement of the crowd.

White men, Indians and Negroes moved in and out the door. Indians dressed in buckskins, red-bronzed and imperturbable, stood against the wall, watching with unreadable faces, but their black obsidian eyes darted this way and that— snakes' eyes, Richard thought as he passed. The Negro slaves were engaged in wheeling luggage, boxes and bundles from the warehouse to carts or sleds. These were pulled through the dust to the river-bank, to be loaded on shallops and small boats belonging to planters of the upper James, or to be sailed across to the southern shore, Isle of Wight County and Nansemond County.

The Negroes were laughing. They called cheerily to their comrades. Snatches of song drifted in from the wharves along the river, where they were busy loading and unloading cargo.

The three left the warehouse. The noise and confusion died away. It was a short walk through a lane, along Water Street to Orchard Run and the old wharf. They passed John White's property and Jaxon's before they reached the fort. The way led along Captain John Harvey's old place, almost in ruins.

"The Holder tract is there by the old wharf," Bennett explained. Seeing a look of interest in Richard's face, he added, "It was abandoned some years ago, but my friend Nicholas Holder has come out from England to reclaim it."

Richard said nothing. He felt depressed.

They stood now waiting for Bennett's sloop, which was anchored in the stream, to send a rowboat ashore. Stephen looked about.

"Governor Wyatt had the house there on Back Street, the large one. Sir William Berkeley used it while his town residence was being built, over yonder beyond the Vale. You can see the church tower through the sycamores. On the other side is a good house. I hear Major Robert Beverley is negotiating for it, to build himself a town house for use when the Assembly is in season. Where the river turns are the county houses and Colonel Ludwell's residence. John Baldwin's is a step farther north, and abutting his property. Thomas Hampton has a fine large plot on Backwater Marsh. The great piece to the north-east belongs to Richard James. He has a brick house under construction."

Richard asked, "Has Sir William Berkeley been banished?"

Bennett looked glum. "Not yet. He has retired to his country place, across there on the main. A beautiful spot it is, and well protected by rivers and wide creeks, an ideal retreat."

They stepped into the small boat. Two Negro slaves were at the oars. Richard sat on the thwart facing the island. As they rowed out the view of the town widened. The island was small and low, with swamp-land and marsh to the north against a narrow river.

"Pitch-and-tar swamp," Bennett pointed out. "It runs across the island. Sir George Yeardley held an acreage between the Backwater and the swamp in '24, as well as a great plantation on the Eastern Shore beyond the York River. They say he was a good governor, a man interested in protecting the planters. Some of the others have not had that idea. Like Spanish governors to the south, they took what they could. They taxed the people beyond endurance."

They reached the shallop and clambered over the side. Digby threw the packs aboard before they stepped in. The view from the shallop was even better. A number of small black and white houses stood out with thatched roofs. The rays of the dying sun picked them out from the dark green of the swamp and the forest. The houses nestled close together, with gardens at the side and rear. Along the swamp the grounds were more extensive.

The Reverend Thomas Hampton holds the large site, touching Baldwin's land. You remember I mentioned it. Some of the houses have washed away in the floods of spring. Wattle and earth are not lasting in this climate; that is why we are building of brick now. Brick for permanence," he added, a certain pride in his voice.

"Who lives in the large house, there by the water?" Digby asked.

"That is the old State House. It is said that Sir John Harvey lived there when he was governor. That was back in '35. Governor Berkeley owns it now, but my cousin is negotiating for it."

Richard said, "I thought the commissioner lived on the plantation called Bennett's Welcome."

"So he does, but most of the planters own town houses, especially the men who come to the Assemblies. The inns can't hold them all, and only a few county houses are completed."

The men were hoisting sail. The wind came up as the sun dropped below the horizon. The mammoth pines along the river-bank were silhouetted darkly against the golden sky. A great heron flew low along the reeds that grew heavy and thick at the mouth of a narrow creek. A fish leaped and splashed into the water, making an ever-widening circle. The quiet of evening was upon them as they sailed slowly downstream. When they passed Hog Island, they came about and tacked toward the Isle of Wright and Nansemond shores.

It was dark when the boat found the entrance of the creek which curved its gentle way through marsh reeds to the wharf.

Half a dozen servants were at the Bennett's Welcome landing to take the lines and make fast the boat. By the time the shallop was unloaded it was quite dark. The men took up the loads and walked in single file between the reeds up a narrow track. Richard and Digby stumbled along the unfamiliar path, following a Negro carrying a lanthorn, until they came to a low mud cottage, thatched with tule reeds from the marsh.

Stephen Bennett, who had gone on ahead, met them at the door. "You will sleep here tonight. Tomorrow we will give you other quarters. The boy will bring you a change of clothes which will do until you get your regular allotment. Food will be brought over from the kitchen. I hope you will sleep well your first night on Virginia soil."

They went into the house. A small Negro boy was lying on his stomach, blowing the embers of an almost dead fire. There was a light made of rushes stuck into a stone crock at the side of the fire-place.

Richard looked about him. It was a large room, twenty-five or thirty feet in length, with a rudely built stretcher table, a few chairs made of barrels, cut so that some staves were left to make backs. A seat was made of braided rushes. On either end of the room were four pallets of rough canvas filled with corn-husks. A small table with a heavy pottery wash-bowl, a ewer, and a bowl for slops, made up the furniture.

Digby turned one of the pallets over and shook it violently. "Who sleeps here?" he said to the boy, indicating the extra pallets.

The boy stopped blowing and waited to catch his breath. "No one sleeps here now. Him died yester morn. Him had the pox and him died." He puffed out his cheek and blew a heavy puff into the embers. A piece of lightwood caught fire. A moment later there was a good blaze, which reached the fat pine-wood. The odor of resin filled the room.

"Pox huh! We don't want to catch the pox." Digby took up the pallet by the corner and threw it out the door.

The fire was roaring, a grateful warmth permeated the room. Richard sat down on a bench near the fire and began to unwind the bandage from his head. It came clear without sticking. Digby watched him, leaning forward as he threw the rags into the fire. "The wound's fully healed," Digby said with satisfaction, "but there is a red line from your eye to the top of your ear."

Richard nodded. He was too weary to reply. What if there was a scar? It didn't matter. It would be a constant reminder that there was still a score to be settled with Nicholas Holder.

The boy got up from the earthern floor and dusted off his ragged cotton breeches. "Angela will send supper," he volunteered, his eyes on Richard's face.

"Who is Angela?" Digby asked.

"Angela's my ma. She came here on a ship from Guinea."

Richard stretched his legs. "Boy, bring me a pail of hot water and some soap. I want to bathe."

"Soap, sar? Ah don't think she'll give me none. We uses sand to scrub. Want that I bring you some nice white sand?"

Digby moved over to him. "He said soap. If you want to save yourself a licking, you bring soap."

The lad rolled his eyes, the whites glistened in the dancing light from the fire. "Yes, sar. I tell she." He leaped toward the door as Digby took a step toward him, and disappeared into the dark.

Richard laughed. "Maybe a good sanding is what we need, Digby. I think it will take a dozen baths to cleanse the foul ship's filth off my body." He got up and stretched his arms above his head; his finger tips touched the king beam. "Pox or no pox, I'll sleep tonight." He drew out the bag of gold. "It's your turn. Conceal this till we get new clothes," he said to Digby. Then he stripped his tunic over his head and threw it into the fire. "It will smell," he remarked, "but I don't mind. A good wool smell will ward off flying midges. I noticed they were thick in the marsh."

In a short time the boy came back with the change of clothes which Stephen Bennett had promised. Then he made another trip and brought a pail of steaming water which he placed on a trivet by the fire. "Angela she's comin' soon carryin' your hot supper—" he smacked his lips—"loblolly with mutton, and good bread made of Indian meal."

Richard had hardly bathed and put on the fresh shirt when a tall, broad-shouldered Negress walked into the room, a tin tray balanced on her head. She wore bright red calico wrapped around her body, the ends wound like a halter over her firm throat and tied at the back. The other end of the calico was twisted and tucked into the waist to hold the garment in place.

Richard thought she had the look of a Greek statue, only her ebony skin was wrong. The copper rings about her arms and ankles clattered as she walked, and they reflected the firelight, gleaming faintly. A pagan, if he ever saw one!

She placed the tray on the table and made a curtsy, bowing her head slightly. Then she went about setting up the table with two heavy wooden plates with curved sides, and spoons of wood. The stew was in a wooden bowl. She ladled the steaming food into the plates. She glanced swiftly from one man to the other, a keen, appraising glance. She took a step toward Richard, crossed her bare arms over her chest, inclined her head. *"Moni, moni."* she murmured. Her voice was low and musical.

The boy went to her side and took her hand. "Her gives greeting. Her says, 'I see you.' "

Richard smiled. "And what do I say?"

A flash of white teeth. The boy said, "*Moni, moni.*"

"I see. I repeat the greeting, 'I see you.' "

"Sar, yes."

"*Kudi,*" the woman said, pointing to the table.

"Her says, 'Food, sar.' "

Digby pulled up a chair and Richard walked to the table.

The woman smiled, bowed again, and the two Negroes walked out the door.

Digby stood watching her disappear into the night. He turned to Richard. "She's fair bright, that black creature. Did you notice how she picked out the master from the man? Yes, she's fair bright." He took up his wooden bowl and started for the fire-place.

Richard spoke sharply. "Sit down at the table, Digby. This is the New World we are in. No master and man here, remember."

Hesitatingly Digby pulled up the barrel chair opposite Richard.

" 'Taint the thing, zur. I don't rightly think I should table with my betters."

"We are equal now, Digby. We're servants of His Excellency Commissioner Bennett, or rather I'm his servant and you're the servant of his cousin Mr. Stephen Bennett. Get that into your head, my man, or we will both be in trouble. One thing is sure: we must keep them from knowing who I am, or where I came from. No one must know. Those things must be secret."

Digby grinned. "Secret? Well, maybe, if you can keep the James River between you and Mistress Audley."

Sleep did not come readily in spite of the weariness of his body. Richard turned restlessly on his pallet. The corn-shucks crackled with each restless move. He was conscious of the night noises, a hound's bay . . . the screech of an owl in the forest . . . frogs sounding their bellows . . . the peep of birds in their nests. The soft air that came in through the open door was fragrant with the perfume of some unknown shrub or flower and the pungent smell of pine and cedar. The stars shone in the dark sky; a crescent moon was falling behind the spires of the pine trees. All was tranquil without; only his thoughts were muddied and roiled like an unhealthy stream. Peace was a phantom, something one pursued but never reached. Cruel thoughts burned deep and consumed peace. The forest was primitive beauty, but savages lurked under the trees—savagery and killing among the wild things as well as the human, savage lust and savage murder in animals and in men. . . . And where was Nicholas Holder?

Digby had fallen asleep the moment his body touched the pallet, but Digby's thoughts were not complicated. He was a simple man, with no cares but the business of feeding the body in order to survive. Life was something to be lived and enjoyed. A few friends, work, a little play were enough to satisfy a simple man. He, Richard Monington, should be sleeping, his body scrubbed clean, lying on a clean pallet, with clean air drawn into his lungs with each deep breath. . . . He must crush out envy and despair. Would work help put savagery behind him? Would the work in field and forest, the heavy driving labour that would be his, give him peace? Would Kathryn Holder yield him peace? Where were Kathryn and her wretched husband? If they had been on one of the convoy ships, as Digby said and as Stephen Bennett had confirmed, he had not seen them in Jamestown.

His eyes closed, blotting out the bright stars and the young moon. His ears no longer heard the stealthy footpads of forest denizens or the flutter of the night-bird's wings. Sleep came softly into the room, quiet, restful, welcomed sleep, sleep without dreams.

CHAPTER 14

Bennett's Welcome

THE plantation bell rang when the first streak of dawn touched the eastern horizon. The cock on the dunghill raised his head to crow, his bright red comb quivering with the effort to greet the sun. Other birds and animals gave their exertions. Cows in their stalls stopped chewing their cuds and lowed for their food. Sheep in the fold, chickens in their run, ducks, drakes, geese, lifted their voices. Horses neighed, stamping for their morning ration of grain. A guinea-fowl shrilled, a peacock screamed. It was the beginning of a new day.

Digby was awake at the first tap of the bell. He sat up on his pallet and glanced across the room. Richard was sleeping quietly, his cheek pillowed in his hand. Digby threw off the covers. He crossed to the wash-stand, splashed water over his torso and face, dried himself with a rough crash towel. He put on the clean shirt which the Negro boy had fetched and was ready for whatever the day brought forth. He laid out the fresh clothes for Richard. He tidied up, smiling as he worked.

Next he took up the bucket, went outside and walked to a small brook near the rear of the cabin, where he got fresh water for Richard's bath. That task being done, he sat down on one of the two benches which flanked the door. The cottage where they were domiciled was at the verge of a deep pine forest. The smell of pines was in the air. It was good to see the blue sky with an eagle soaring overhead. A small bird was building a nest in a poplar tree, scolding its mate for not bringing sticks and moss fast enough. In the meadow the cows grazed, some standing knee-deep in the waters of the creek. Near by the shallop lay at the wooden wharf.

He saw men moving off in a procession toward the open fields beyond the meadow, carrying axes and bills on their shoulders. It stirred him deeply to see them at the task of cutting wood in the forest or tilling the soil. Too long he had been fighting wars. Now he would feel the earth under his feet after the long months at sea. He hoped they would set him to the plough. He wanted to turn the earth in a long straight furrow, see the good black earth of swamp-land brought to cultivation. No rocks were here, the bane of Devon yeomen. Birds were singing a song he did not know, only it was sweet as the nightingale's song, sweet and clear. He turned his head to watch the songster in a bush that was covered with white bloom, as white and glistening as fresh-fallen snow. It was a large bird, all mouselike in color, until it flirted its tail to a fan, when white stripes showed.

In the sheepfold he could see a shepherd with a long crook moving among the flock. He opened a gate, forcing the sheep to go through one at a time. They took the path that led to the thickets and disappeared in the woods.

Presently Digby noticed the small black boy coming toward him along the narrow path, carrying a basket. Every now and then he paused, looking up into the trees, mocking a bird's song. When he saw Digby he hastened, smiling, his strong white teeth gleaming. *"Moni, sar."* He repeated his mother's African salutation.

Digby fell into the game. *"Moni.* I see you. What is your name, boy?"

"Puti, sar. It is a foolish name. I would be pleasured if *you* called me Hen-ne-ry."

"I think Puti is a better name. I know many Hennerys, but only one Puti. I shall call you Puti," Digby paid no heed to the disappointment in the child's face. "What have you in your basket?"

"Breakfast, sar. Angela sends it to you. She says the bacon is for the master, the loblolly for you."

Digby took the basket and carried it into the house. He found Richard on his feet, stretching his arms sleepily. He was rested. The grey ship pallor had gone, leaving his face a more healthy colour, save only the thin red line that marked a sword cut.

"Breakfast already? The night has passed as a moment instead of hours. What have we to eat, Digby? I feel my stomach flat against my spine." He dashed water on his face and sat down at the table. "Sit down, Digby. How often must I tell you? Boy, what have you in that pot which is steaming so mightily and sends off such a pleasant odour?"

"Sas'fras tea, sar. Angela she say it gives a sick man strength."

Richard laughed. "I'm no sick man. I can vouch for that by my appetite. Pour a cup of the ambrosia."

"I don't rightly understand the words you speak, sar."

"Very well, sas'fras tea, if you will." He reached across the table, took two boiled eggs from the basket, broke them into a cup and sprinkled them plentifully with salt. "Ah, three rashers of good crisp bacon and hot scones! What more can a man want on a fine March morning?"

"What indeed, zur?" Digby replied, his mouth full. "The eggs are fresh. It's been a long time since I had the taste of a fresh egg on my tongue."

The light faded from Richard's face. A picture of Codding-ton Manor rose before his eyes: little Sibyl hastening from the fowl-run with a basket of eggs in her hand; Cook, in her clean shining kitchen, watching the sands run in the hour-glass as the water bubbled around the white shells. He glanced up. Digby was watching him with anxious eyes. The good faithful fellow! He must put these sad thoughts of his home behind him. That old life was past. It would take patience to meet the new. He smiled at Digby, whose look of worry faded instantly.

"My friend, we're in luck. We live on a great plantation where they have bacon and eggs for breakfast. It's better than the Britsol gaol, is it not?"

"You speak truth, zur, God Almighty's truth. I've been looking at the lay of the land while you slept, zur. There's sheep and kine running in the woods, fat cattle in the meadows. I've seen nary a human, save hands going toward the wood lot with bills and axes, and Puti here, who is Angela's little errand boy."

Puti grinned. "Master Stephen he say, when you fill your belly, I, myself, I to bring you to the master's office."

"Good. I'll jump into the creek for a bathe, and come with you."

Richard and Digby stood in the outer office waiting to be called. Half a dozen men of rustic type also were waiting. They eyed the new-comers curiously but did not speak.

The office was a small building, set aside from the house which was a long structure of clapboards with brick ends on the two wings and dormer windows set in the high-pitched roof. Other buildings were clustered about the dwellings: a smoke-house, a dairy, a wash-house where women were bending over tubs. Through an open doorway he saw a great loom. An elderly woman was threading the warp from a shank of wool, dyed butternut colour, while a young girl stood by ready to help. The girl was rosy-cheeked, with flaxen hair. She was smiling as she set about her tasks. She wore a dark cotton gown and rough shoes, but she had a bright-coloured kerchief around her neck with the ends tucked into her bodice. The older woman wore a drab, dun dress, and her mouse-coloured hair was pulled into a tight knot at the base of her neck.

There was activity in the barn-yard. Carts were being hooked up to fat oxen; a riding horse of good breeding was being saddled by a groom. Richard saw the Negress Angela at the door of the kitchen, a separate house with a great chimney at one side. The ends of the building were of narrow brick.

There was a garden behind the green hedge. The thin narrow rows of earth were broken by lines of fresh, tender green garden plants poking their heads through the soil. Cabbages and onions were large enough for eating. Beyond the garden was an orchard with peach-trees in leaf and apple-trees in a shower of pink bloom.

Richard thought, It is all orderly and neat and well cared for. There's even a herb garden by the kitchen door. Cats sleep in the sun, unafraid of the hounds. The dogs lie in that neat gravelled path, bordered with small boxwood plants, which leads from the kitchen to the house. A home of peace.

One at a time the waiting men stepped into the office and came out by another door which gave on a walk leading to the stables. The men who remained, tired of staring, talked among themselves. He heard snatches of their conversation, which seemed to be about Governor Berkeley.

"He'll not leave Jamestown. He'll fight a new governor. He'll not recognize him when he's chosen by the Assembly on April thirtieth."

"Berkeley's a fighting man," said one who was dressed in

grey with a wide white collar and a broad black hat on his head. "He knows our commissioner is no man to stir a fight."

" 'Tis against Commissioner Bennett's principles to make brawls or stand for gun frenzy. He's like a Quaker, he is."

The man with a hat smiled a little. "Christ was a man of peace, and our commissioner is a Christlike man."

A third man, who had not spoken, a blacksmith by the look of his arm muscles and his broad back, said, "Berkeley would ha' wiped you Christlike men from the earth. Look how he strung up a Puritan preacher by the thumbs and set many an one in the stocks in the broiling sun. I'd be thinking you should fight back at him now. He's your enemy, he is. I'd think you'd hate his entrails."

The Quaker shook his head. "That is not the Friends' way. Our leader, Mr. Fox, is for peace and quietude, not wrangling and quarrelling. We do not hate our fellow men. We give love, even to our enemies."

"And let them drive the few of you out of Jamestown down to the backwoods of Chuckatuck—aye, even farther south if I've heard the truth, down to that country they call South Virginia."

"The soil is rich at Chuckatuck and farther south. Along the Chowan River and the Great Sound the earth is deep and strong with fertility."

"Just the same, I say the answer to Berkeley is guns and cannon and a ship of war." The blacksmith squared his shoulders and clenched his strong fist. "Strength against oppression is what I say. I shall fight to seat our commissioner firmly in his governor's chair, I will."

The conversation was interrupted. A man opened the door of the inner office and beckoned the three men.

Digby glanced at Richard. "It looks as though the old governor is going to hang on and make trouble for your master. Heigho, there may be fighting for us to do, instead of ploughing! Seems as though I'll never feel the pull of the leather around my neck—with a good ox ahead of me and the plough running smooth in the earth."

Richard looked at Digby as he thought, A true Devon man he is, with his feet on the earth and his roots deep.

The door opened, and a stocky man entered. He had a long nose, thin lips and a bush of red hair hanging low over his narrow forehead. He beckoned Richard. "The master will see you now. Step lively." As he looked at Richard and Digby his eyes narrowed. He's a fox, thought Richard.

Commissioner Bennett sat at the long stretcher table, young Stephen beside him. A mass of papers spread along the wooden board, polished smooth by long usage. Richard realized that the commissioner was not so old a man as he had thought from the brief glimpse he had had of him on the ship. He had been fooled by the streak of grey in his dark hair. He could not be older than the late forties.

His expression was one of serenity. Whatever troublesome thoughts passed through his mind, they were not allowed to disturb his inner calm. He glanced at the paper before him. "Richard ap Richards," he read aloud. "John Digby. You were both in Charles Stuart's army?"

"Yes, sir," Digby replied. Richard bowed his head in assent.

"Taken after the Battle of Worcester, I see. A sad thing— men of one nation fighting against each other. I deplore the necessity of a civil war." He said to Stephen, "You are sure you want both of these men? Have you thought it over carefully?"

Stephen said, "Yes, sir. If you are willing, I will pay the costs of Richards here. I have already settled with Madam Peter Montague for the man Digby."

"Very well. I will sign the transfer papers. I suppose you are sending them on to Bennett's Choice?"

"Well, no. Since I am to stay here as superintendent, I will keep them here."

"As field hands? Richards doesn't look husky enough for field work."

"I have other plans, sir. I thought I would take them with me when I visit the planters along the upper James and the Northern Neck, to acquaint them about the Parliament's plans for cutting the tobacco planting."

The commissioner drummed on the table, the habit he had when thinking. He had large capable hands. Richard thought, He has a large capable body and the appearance of strength and determination. "They are soldiers," Richard Bennett said. "They can handle muskets, but they do not know our Indians or the intricate Indian paths through the woods, if you go inland."

"I plan to take my shallop up the Chesapeake to the Northern Neck, follow the Potomac, then send the shallop back to meet me at Curl's Wharf. I will arrange with one of the planters for horses to make the trip across. It is not too far to walk, if need be."

The commissioner nodded. Stephen got up and went to the large map that was nailed to the whitewashed plaster.

Richard watched him trace out the journey with his finger. It was a skillfully drawn map of the James River and the waterways that flowed into the great bay called the Chesapeake. There was a vast territory below the James, with rivers running south-west into a large body marked Roanoke Sound. The intervening space was marked *"Heath Patent,"* and the wide river growing out of two smaller streams was named Chowan River. He was too far away to make out the small lettering, but he read "Thomas Woodward's Map" across the verge of the parchment.

The commissioner did not speak at once. After a time he said, "I thought you needed yeomen. You've been talking of free men as tenants on your plantation."

"So I have, sir. But tobacco seems to be the immediate thing. I should be able to reach the majority of the larger planters before they set their tobacco."

Bennett nodded. "Perhaps you are right, Stephen, but I want you here before the time for the Assembly to open. The ships ———" He bethought himself of the indentured men and did not finish the sentence. Then he resumed: "Yes, you are right. Take your men. Better let them live in the cottage next to that of the Ancient Planter. He will indoctrinate them into the ways of the plantation." The commissioner nodded to the two men. "Good day. I hope you adjust yourselves to our Virginia way of living. If you do, you will have no trouble. I, myself, do not hold with whipping, but that is a matter I leave to my overlookers." He left the room, walking with the easy movement of a well-co-ordinated body.

Stephen Bennett rose when the commissioner rose. He addressed Richard. "You will need a few days to gain strength. A sick man will be of no use to me." He took up the paper that the commissioner had left on the table. "I see you made your mark on the covenant. That does not fool me. You are a gentleman and have no doubt been an officer in the Royal army. But that is your secret. I have no wish to pry, but it would be a great service to me if you would assist me with these papers, help me figure allotments of tobacco to the acre. A great service."

Richard said, "How did you discern?"

Stephen smiled broadly. "A ring with a crest on it, for one thing."

"I might have stolen it on the battle-field, stripped it from a dead man's finger."

Stephen shook his head. "There are others things that a man does not disguise, or, if he tries to disguise them, that do not fool a careful observer."

"I once fooled the great Oliver—" Richard grinned at the remembrance—"fooled him well, and two of his generals, though one of them was suspicious."

"Mayhap you did, but you did not fool me, nor the commissioner either. But that is your affair. My affair is that you make a willing servant, and we will have no trouble. For the present you will report direct to me, not to Higgins, the commissioner's overlooker. Master and man, I take it." He looked at Digby.

Richard answered, "Nay. Two soldiers, comrades who fought a losing fight. Let it stand at that, sir."

Puti was waiting by the door to guide them to their new billet.

Digby said. "We'll go back for our gear."

" 'Tis all moved. This way, sars." He led them to a small cottage in a grove of oak trees, a more substantial house than the one they had slept in the night before. It had two entrance doors with a small garden, carefully tended, on one side; on the other, the earth was turned over as though it had been seeded. An old man sat in a chair on a bricked terrace under the trees. His beard was white and pointed, his hair carefully brushed. He leaned forward on his thin hands clasped over the rounded knob of a blackthorn stick. A large deerhound lay at his side. The dog raised his head, but at a word from the boy rested his head on his crossed paws and closed his eyes.

"Who is the man?" Digby asked, his voice lowered.

"He is an Ancient Planter. We calls him St. Crispin, sars. He live there in the part of the house on the far side, where he sit now. He sightless."

The old man raised his head, his face as wrinkled as a bit of old parchment, and of parchment colour, but his brow was broad, his features were strong and well defined, his nose was straight. His eyes gave no indication that he was blind. The peaceful look on his face showed that he bore no grudge against the fate that deprived him of his vision in his declining years.

"Name yourselves, sirs. I am Thomas Chapman, an Ancient Planter, at your service."

Richard stepped forward. "I am . . . er . . . Richard ap Richards, sir, indentured. We arrived on the latest ship from England."

"No need to stumble over your name, good sir. It's probably not your own, nor do you speak like a Welshman, save to the uninitiated."

Richard laughed. "You are discerning, ancient one. I am a Herefordshire man, born and bred."

"Aye, that is better. And your companion?"

"Digby, sir, John Digby, from——"

The Ancient Planter interrupted. "Let me tell his origin. Speak a few words, please."

" 'Tis a fair, fine day, and the apple orchards are heavy with bloom."

"Devon, my lad. A Devon man always has an eye to apples."

"Aye, sir, and a tongue for cider." Digby was grinning broadly.

"Devon-born am I. Buckland Brewer, near . . ."

Digby interrupted, "Near Monkton. Well I know the spot, and the fine church by the roadside."

"Do you now? That is splendid. I am thinking you are the two Royalist prisoners that Stephen has brought across the river. He told me this morning that he was going to fetch me some house guests today. Step closer, Richards, if you please. Since my eyes have failed me, I must use my fingers so that I may see my friends."

Richard stopped. The Ancient Planter ran his long sensitive fingers over his face. "Good! A high brow and a strong, straight nose, a firm mouth and a lean jaw, with a cleft chin. What complexion—fair, sanguine or dark? That my fingers do not tell me."

"Dark, sir—dark all the way, eyes, hair and complexion."

"Ah, dark. 'Tis strange. The oval face, the long jaw bespeak Norman blood, but you said Herefordshire, did you not?"

"Sir, my mother was Devon-born, near Bideford."

The old man's face lighted. "Splendid! Splendid! Already we are friends by ties of Devon birth. But pardon an old man. Digby, let me see you. Ah, hard-bitten, a soldier, lean and brown and sinewy."

"My eyes are blue," Digby said, "and my hair on the red side, and I grant you the leanness. 'Tis some months since I've eaten what my stomach cried for."

"You'll eat here. The plantation provides well for its people. Not like the old days. I went through the Starvation Time, with only a spoonful of meal a day for porridge. That was real starvation, with the climate sickness and the ague fever to burn a man to a cinder. Yes, and the savages dancing their wild hellish dances in the forest, and preparing poisoned arrows for any man who ventured without the stockade. . . ." His sightless eyes turned away, as though he had withdrawn into the past.

Puti beckoned, and the two men followed him into their side of the cottage.

"He's like that, the Old One. He forgets sometimes. The master say, when you are ready, I should to take you to Higgins, the overlooker, to get clothes issue."

"What's that?" Digby cried, a comical look on his lean face. "Issue! It sounds like the army all over again."

Puti was eager to give information. "You get new boots and shirts and underdrawers and a Sunday shirt and a cloak of kersey and a wide hat and——" He paused. "I wish I could draw a wide hat."

"You'd be lost under the brim and we couldn't see you. Come on, Puti, we'll draw the clothing."

"But him? Can't he go too?"

"No. He can't go. He's been sick on the bed and his knees ain't so strong."

Puti lingered. "The overlooker say he don't want no more sick ones around here."

Digby gave him a paddle on his little rump. "Get on with it."

Richard, left alone, sat down. The room was larger than the one they had had, and it had puncheons instead of an earth floor. Two bedsteads, home-made, were in either end of the room. The washing arrangements were behind a rustic screen. The table was the same, and the chairs, but the brick hearth before the fire-place was larger. One window looked out on the

stream, the other on a vegetable garden. There was a cover
over the wide porch. No, it was not too bad. The old man
would be a companion. Since he had lived so long in Virginia,
he would tell them about the times when the first settlers came.
Richard felt a desire to know something of this New World
where destiny had placed him.

The morning had proved of interest. What matter if Stephen
Bennett was shrewd enough to place him in his former station?
Bennett did not know who he was, or whence he came; only
that he was born a gentleman and had followed the Stuarts.
Gentleman-born! What good did it do to be born a gentleman
if he were to be sold like cattle on a market day? The thought
made him indignant. How easily in this new country they
talked of buying and selling human beings! Had they forgotten
the freedom won at Runnymede? The rights a man had under
the Great Charter? The new should go on from where the
old left off, not drop back to the days before King John and
the barons.

There was something wrong here, something that did not
belong to a New World where men sought freedom they
had not had in the Old. Cromwell was to bring that freedom
by his New Model. Well, let his sworn representative, Richard
Bennett, prove that the Lord General's words were worth
more than the paper they were writ on. Richard did not know
whether to believe that the commissioner's expression was one
of kindliness and benignity or of a smug complacency.

Young Stephen was inclined toward friendliness, but he
wanted a body-guard for a difficult and perhaps dangerous
journey. Let them prove themselves, these Bennetts! He wondered when the opportunity would come to seek out Sir
William Berkeley.

His thoughts went back to something the men had discussed
while they were waiting in the outer office. Sir William
Berkeley did not intend to give up readily. He would make a
fight against seating a new governor. He would not recognize
the right of Cromwell's men to govern Virginia. Puritans and
Dissenters would make up the new government if Bennett
was seated, good men perhaps, but unacquainted with the
art of governing. From what little he had picked up on the
ship, the only office Richard Bennett had held was this brief
time he had been one of the Council of State's Commissioners
to Maryland and Virginia. Under Berkeley's administration

he had resided mostly in Maryland, where Sir William had held him in banishment. Now he returned to be chosen governor. How was he to maintain his rights? What constabulary or soldiers there were on Jamestown Island must be Berkeley's men.

Another thought flashed across Richard Monington's mind: What was it the commissioner started to say about ships, then checked himself so suddenly? Was he expecting ships? Was Cromwell sending him support?

Digby returned. His arms were filled with clothing. Puti trailed him carrying six pairs of heavy shoes. He had tied the shoes together with strings made of vines or raffia. On his woolly head he had two wide-brimmed felt hats. The crowns fell down to his ears. He was grinning widely. His comical appearance brought a smile to Richard's face and drove away his heavy thoughts.

Digby said, "The overlooker was not going to give me your issue. He's that red-head who looked sly as a fox. We saw him in the office. I don't trust Mr. Higgins farther than a man can throw an ox by the hind leg."

"Nor I," Richard agreed.

"Mr. Stephen came in and settled things. He said you had had a severe illness on shipboard and must have a few days to recover. Higgins muttered something about having enough of sick men, but he counted out the clothes and here they are." He lifted up breeches and shirts. "Not too bad," he remarked, examining the texture of a shirt, "a little rough for your skin, Captain, but easy on my tough hide."

Richard said, "No rougher than the garments His Majesty donned at Boscobel."

Digby turned from the table, the blue Osnaburg shirt crushed against his body. "That's a fact, zur, purely a fact. Do you know, the thought of those days had gone clear from my mind? I haven't thought of King Charles for weeks on end." There was an expression of astonishment on his face. "Think of that—forgetting our King!"

Richard said, "Hush! That word must not be spoken here. Forgetting is the best plan, but I wonder if all goes well with him at the French Court."

"Not in Virginia, as some said in Bristol." Digby smiled.

Richard, too, grinned. "That was *my* doing. I told that little tale when I was up before the Cromwellian board after the soldiers took me in. I said that, as far as I knew, the King was bound for America—the Somers Islands or Virginia, I didn't know which. It took their stupid minds off France or Holland for the moment. Pray God he prospers!"

"Amen," said Digby devoutly.

The work in the office was not too difficult. It consisted in going through a list of the tobacco areas and the names of large property owners. The regions to visit were along the upper James and the Northern Neck. The lower James and the York River, to the Chesapeake, had been listed. It gave Richard a knowledge of the country, for they—he and Stephen Bennett—were working with maps. When they came to the Northern Neck, Stephen said, with a wide grin on his pleasant face, "I'll have to watch you when we get to this district. It's the stronghold of the Cavaliers."

Richard raised his straight brows. "How could an indentured man, with no funds, escape in this vast country?"

"He couldn't. That's why I mentioned it. None of the planters could afford to harbour a criminal now, with the Commonwealth in power."

Richard did not reply, but the thought took hold. Digby had the purse of gold pieces. They must hide it. At the moment it burned heavily against his side. He found it made a bulge that might be noticed. They must hoard it, hide it in some safe spot until a chance opened for them to get onto some outgoing ship. A Dutch ship would be safer than an English, unless the two countries went to war. A French or Spanish . . . No use wasting thoughts on escape now. They would have to learn more of the country, seek out men who could be trusted to take them out to a ship lying off Point of Comfort or the Capes. . . . He realized Stephen Bennett's eyes were on him, a sharp, penetrating look which made Richard aware that under the easy manner was a shrewd, observing man.

He turned back to the map and went on copying. He would familiarize himself with the names of the great landholders who would likely be Stuart sympathizers. This would come when they visited the plantations. Digby was a master at ferreting out facts.

Commissioner Bennett came into the office, passing Richard with a cheery "Good morning." He went into the inner office followed by Stephen, who closed the door. The rumble of their voices penetrated the partition but their words were not discernible.

Presently the door opened. He heard the commissioner say, "You must be here a week before the Assembly on April thirtieth. I won't be away more than a week. My wife wishes to go to Chuckatuck to visit her friend Madam Phillips. She will take the children. If you finish your preparatory work before I return, leave a note for me, giving me your itinerary. I suppose you'll go up the Northern Neck first."

Stephen hesitated. "Well, no, sir. I have about decided to leave on Wednesday and go first to the upper James."

Richard Monington looked up in time to catch a brief smile on the commissioner's face. "I understand there are some charming English visitors at Jordan's Journey."

Stephen's face was as red as a beet-root. "Yes, sir. So . . . so I've heard sir." He stammered a little. "A lo-lovely girl, Mathilda Jordan. I'd like . . . I'd like to marry her."

"So your uncle wrote me." Richard Bennett laid his hand on the younger man's shoulder. "I wish you well, my boy, but don't allow courting to interfere with your investigation. Time glides along swiftly. I want the influential men in the colony to be notified about the plans for tobacco planting before the Assembly meets on April thirtieth."

Stephen said, "Mr. Claiborne thinks you should not announce the cut in acreage until you are seated firmly."

The commissioner's face hardened. "I know that. We have discussed the matter. I do not think it would be fair to the planters not to let them know before they set their crops. It's been a cold winter, so we are in time. Claiborne has departed for Maryland. I shall take up my duties as I see fit."

Stephen started to speak.

"No, Stephen. I know what you are going to say. Berkeley will not give up readily. I've offered him peace. If he doesn't take peace, we shall be obliged to use force. I've told you many times that I am always for peace, but this does not mean that I will be a timid governor." He walked out of the room, leaving Stephen standing at the door.

Richard bent over his papers as though he had heard nothing. Jordan's Journey was their objective this week. He would not have chosen to discover himself to Mathilda or Sibyl. He would avoid contact with them if possible; but if it could not be avoided . . . well, fate always took a hand in his affairs. . . . Let come what may come! Never turn away from one's destiny. That was what his mother had often told him. He had respect for her wisdom. One thing he devotedly hoped was that he would not meet Kathryn Audley.

The day before they were to sail up-river, Richard was working alone in the office. He had almost finished his lists when he ran across a paper tucked into an envelope. He glanced through it hastily, then read it more carefully. It was dated Mar. 12/1651-2. It was evidently an article of agreement among the commissioners.

No person was to be prosecuted in Virginia because of his former adherence to the King. The former governor and his councillors were to be exempted from any oath of allegiance to the Commonwealth for a year, during which they were assured of their property rights. They were privileged to depart the colony, and they were permitted, individually and among themselves, to pray for and speak well of the King, but not on public occasions. They might enjoy the rights of free-born Englishmen, the right to worship according to the Book of Common Prayer, and pay the clergy their accustomed dues, provided these things which relate to kingship or a king's government were deleted.

The item that engaged Richard's closest attention was a line "No person will be penalized for a former service to the King, either here or in England."

This gave him pause. When the time was ripe, he could claim immunity and false indenture under that clause. Richard thought, These are extraordinary terms. Is Claiborne to treat Maryland, Lord Baltimore's colony, under the same terms? He's there now, looking into things.

A second paper fell from the envelope. "Reduce all plantations within the Bay of Chesapeake. Compel their due obedience to the Parliament and Commonwealth of England."

These were stronger words. Perhaps Lord Baltimore's Maryland was more set to rebellion than Virginia. . . .

He laid the papers in their place, closed the box that held the lists, locked it and put it on the shelf behind the table. He walked slowly to the cottage. He now had plenty to think about beside his own unhappy condition.

CHAPTER 15

Jordan's Journey

EVERY sail, every canoe, every pontoon on the James was the object of anxious scrutiny by the planters. Lookouts lay on the banks at Jordan's Journey sheltered by bushes, watching carefully. Until the craft was identified as a friend, the watch was not relaxed. Although it had been some years since an Indian invasion from the north or west, each plantation kept the lookout with the fidelity of a sentry in a watch-tower of a fortification.

The mid-April day was fair. A blue sky with a few cumulus clouds floated lazily across the eastern horizon. The air was warm and bumble-bees droned over the garden.

Madam Montague sat on the piazza, her capable hands folded in her lap, taking her afternoon relaxation. She scorned a "nap," the custom of the country, but she was not above drowsing in her high-backed chair. Near her, seated on the steps, Sibyl was rolling a seam on a ruffle of silky mull. If it passed inspection, the flounce would be sewed on a shift for Mathilda's hope chest. Sibyl's strong brown fingers, so sensitive in handling the bridle reins, were awkward with the needle. When Mistress Cecily's eyes closed, she wrapped the offensive sewing material in a fair white towel and tiptoed down the steps. Avoiding the oyster-shell path, she ran across the lawn to the lookout under the great tulip poplar tree.

Here she found Jacob baking appones in the ashes of a small fire. Jacob was one of the first Negroes brought over from Africa in a ship of Thomas Jordan. He was gnarled and bent like an old wind-blown tree, and his woolly head was white, but his eyes were as keen as a forest animal's. He greeted "little miss" with the eagerness of a lonely man who has the garrulousness of old age. He stirred the fire, built around a small platform of bricks, and put a pannikin of sassafras tea to heat on two hot bricks.

Sibyl ran into the little summer-house on the brow of the bank and came back with a white china cup. This was a daily event, drinking her tea, then taking over the watch for half an hour while Jacob—whose African name was Lenzi— "caught himself a nap." Sometimes the nap lasted the best part of an hour, about the same period that Mistress Cecily could be counted on to sleep.

Jacob said, "Today is a day for 'coming,' so Lenzi will sleep as light as a kingfisher sleeps in the reeds."

"Why is it a day for 'coming,' Lenzi?" Sibyl enjoyed using the Negro's African name.

"This morning when I walked across the road a green snake rested hisself on a limb of a mulberry and made no move to run away. I myself, I will see strangers before the sun sets yonder."

Sibyl laughed. "You're a fraud. You heard the mistress say that her cousins, the Jordans, the Parkers and the Reynoldses, were expected before sunset."

"No, little miss, they be familiars. The green grass snake with the brittle tail tells of strangers not familiars. Presently you will see a sail. Then you will please to call Lenzi, ifn he still sleeps?"

"Yes, I will call you. Sleep deeply, Lenzi, and dream of that country where the leopards stretch along the limbs of trees, and the great water beasts with huge jaws lie in wait in the rivers."

"No, little miss. To dream of killers is evil. Rather will the dream be of wild birds in the forest, the song of fishermen hauling in their nets, or the women's song as they tend the gardens outside the villages along the river."

"The villages you have told me about where you were chief?"

"Yes, little mistress, where Lenzi sat in council, dressed in his white robe, under a mwavi tree, and gave out judgements." The old eyes looked toward the river. For a time he was silent. "Before the Arab traders came, long ago; as far away as the sun or the moon." He moved off and lay down in the shade of a mulberry tree.

Sibyl was saddened. She thought, He longs for his village and his wives and his children. It was foolish of me to say words which brought up dreams of his far-off home. She drank her tea and sat down on a bench in the little latticed summer-house. There was no boat in sight on the river. It was curious that she believed Lenzi. Some stranger *would* come before sunset.

In the short time that she had been in Virginia she had become familiar with the quiet, gentle land. She had listened by the hour to tales of the old days when the Ancient Planters first came. Then the wild savages lurked in the forests, ready to leap out with knife and tomahawk and fire-brand, to kill and scalp and burn. A dozen times had she begged Mistress Cecily to repeat the story of Captain John Smith, that brave, gallant gentleman who had come to Virginia to settle the new land. A dozen times had she heard the story of the lovely Pocahontas, daughter of the wily Chief Powhatan, who rescued the brave captain when her father had his head on the block. Sibyl could see the young girl laying her head beside the Englishman's. "If you strike off his head, strike my neck also!"

Men were brave and women beautiful in those days, not dull as they were now, each person thinking of his own little corn-patch or his tobacco rows. Men no longer wore stout armour when they went through the forests, or carried banners before them to the sound of bugles. How courageous they were, those Ancient Planters! Defiantly they turned their faces straight toward danger, against thousands of savages that hid in the forests; a small company of heroes surrounded by thousands of naked enemies.

They were wonderful men. They were as valorous as men in the olden days, as the Crusaders who ventured all for the cause of Christ and love of Him. They were heroes, like Richard the Lion-hearted. Richard . . . The name brought Sibyl back to the present. Her heart felt pain and emptiness. Where was her dear Richard? Not one word from him since the cruel Battle of Worcester when he vanished with his King. *Her* Richard was lion-hearted. He had fought bravely, John Prideaux had told Dame Margaret and Dame Margaret had written the Jordans. John did not know where Richard was. He did not know then where his King lay hidden. Sibyl had heard later that Charles had escaped to France. Those days of flight were full of pain and uncertainty, but not tragic like the terrible day when she had discovered her dear father, his head on his arms, leaning over the long table that held his books and the papers on which he had been writing. She had thought he was sleeping there in the old library, the room in which he had spent so many hours. But when she touched his cheek, it was quite cold.

She had never seen a dead person before. She had thought of death as something horrible, but it was not. It made one sad, but not terrified. His face was so peaceful. He had gone to sleep so easily.

There was a half-finished letter on the table, addressed to Edward Bennett, Esqre., of London. Sibyl had glanced at it. She could not read it because her father's hand lay on the paper, obscuring some of the words. But she could see one paragraph toward the end of the page. "My daughter and your nephew would make a suitable marriage. Mathilda's dower is not so large as I would wish, but it is ample if they are to live in Virginia.

"I will speak to my daughter . . ."

Sibyl had not moved for a moment. Her dear father! He was thinking about Mathilda when life left him. Sibyl had kissed his hand and walked slowly from the room. In the hall she had met Mistress Cecily. Sibyl could not speak. She had pointed silently toward the library. Something in her face caused Mistress Cecily to run down the hall and open the door.

Things had moved swiftly after that . . . people—doctors and barristers, sempstresses fashioning black garments . . . the ring of the bells in the village church, a solemn mournful sound as the family stood at the verge of the grave . . . the rector speaking slowly, in hushed tones . . . ashes to ashes . . . the tears in the sexton's eyes as the first earth fell . . . dust to dust . . . it was so hopeless, so finished . . . as though everything was ended.

But suddenly now she remembered other words the rector had spoken as he walked down to the path to where the coffin rested under the lich-gate, "I am the resurrection, and the life: whosoever believeth in Me . . ." triumphant words, as though He said to her, "This is *not* the end."

Sibyl thought she would never feel young again. She was no longer a child. She had seen Death close. Mathilda wept for her father, but Sibyl could not weep. She thought how tired her father had been those past weeks. How often he had turned white and put his hand against his heart!

There was no pain in his face as he lay in the narrow coffin that last night, with the tall lighted tapers placed at his head and feet. When she went in to kneel beside him and say the last good-bye, a childish rhyme had come to her: "Matthew, Mark, Luke and John, bless the bed that I lie on."

Then came the voyage with Uncle Peter and Aunt Cecily. She had told them to call her "aunt." It was better, she said, than coz, when they were really only second or third cousins. Aunt Cecily had been so kind. She knew what to do and what to say. . . . "Let her alone, Peter. She does not have to cry to prove she feels sad for her father. It isn't her temperament. Mathilda cries, you say? Well, that is Mathilda's temperament. Sibyl is growing up, my dear."

Uncle Peter had replied to this, but Sibyl had not been able to hear what he said. He was of fine presence. He looked no younger than his wife, but she was frank to say he was two years her junior. A quiet man, with a quiet smile and a twinkle in the depths of his eyes. Sibyl could see him through the open door, looking up from the book he was reading while his wife paced the floor, a habit she said, being always in motion.

Aunt Cecily's voice came to her clearly. "I think I have talked Mathilda out of wearing the willow for Nick Holder. Young Bennett is the man for her. He's nice, even though he *is* a Puritan."

Peter had got up and begun to pack his long clay pipe with crumpled leaf. He said, "My dear, you cannot refrain from attempting to make marriages. Young people might like to think that Heaven is responsible."

"That may be so, my sweet Peter, but a little nudging does no harm. Young girls do not know what is best for them. As for Stephen Bennett, he's a good match for any girl, with his plantation over the river from Jamestown, and his Puritan uncle bound to be governor."

"Since when have you flopped over to the Commonwealth, my dear?"

"I haven't flopped. I intend to hang in midair. But, at the moment, it is well not to talk in public about any allegiance to the Stuarts. 'God save the King!' may be said in one's quiet prayers. I feel a draught, Peter. I think I'll close the door."

Sibyl thought of this little incident as she sat watching the quiet river. A fishing canoe slipped out of a stream and moved slowly along the opposite shore. Aunt Cecily was wise. Sibyl hoped Mathilda had forgotten Nick. She had behaved very well when she saw Nick and Kathryn that day in Jamestown. Then there was her father's half-finished letter, which Mistress Cecily had given Mathilda to read. Surely that alone would make her think kindly of Stephen Bennett. . . . But a girl had no say in choosing a husband.

Uncle Peter was one of their guardians now, Uncle Peter and Dame Margaret, who was far away in Devon. She moved a little so that she might have a broader view of the river. The sun struck something bright. A sail was turning the bend, the canvas slack, for the wind had dropped. The shallop scarcely moved. The man at the helm was tacking, taking every advantage of the slightest breath of wind. The tide would turn presently, and this would help him. They were too far away for her to make out the number of men in the boat.

Lenzi was still sleeping, lying on his back, his wide mouth open showing his toothless gums. Let him sleep. It would be some time before the boat came opposite to them, unless a breeze rose when the tide turned—a small tide, so far from the mouth of the James, but perceptible.

She saw Mathilda crossing the greensward. She had on a soft mull dress of delicate green colour, and she was swinging a basket in her hand. The sun fell on her hair, turning it to gold. Her curls flowed over her white neck and shoulders to her waist. She had bound her hair back from her brow with a rose-coloured ribband.

Mathilda went through the little white paling gate into the garden. She was going to gather flowers for the table. Sibyl remembered that guests were coming, cousins of Aunt Cecily: Jordans and Reynoldses and the Parkers of Macclesfield in Isle of Wight County. They were all closely related and formed a clan. Her aunt would expect her to primp and make herself comely.

Well, there was little she could do with her dark skin and dark-brown hair. She noticed that men liked girls with golden hair and blue eyes. . . . She didn't like to waste time curling her hair with rags or making spit-curls about her forehead, held in place by applying quince juice. Mathilda was the beauty, not waxen-white as alabaster like Kathryn Audley, but with a nice warm skin, white as milk. She blushed a lovely damask-rose pink, which she loathed, but Sibyl thought it vastly attractive to blush so prettily. *She* never blushed. If she did her skin was too dark for the pink to show. Heigh-ho! She was glad she was not of marriageable age, even though Aunt Cecily had told her that she married at fourteen. That was to Bailey, who died. When she was nineteen she had been twice married, the second time to her mother's cousin, Samuel Jordan. He also died and left her Jordan's Journey, a goodly inheritance. Then there was another, before Uncle Peter came along.

Sibyl didn't want husbands. She would like to have a dozen nice brothers, but that wouldn't happen unless Mathilda married as many husbands as Aunt Cecily. . . . The canoe on the far side had disappeared.

The river Sibyl watched had carried Indian war canoes. Though the watch was set, there was really no danger from Indians now. Maryland and the Swedish settlements along the Delaware were a guard to the north. The Eastern Shore Indians were friendly. The Indians to the west were at peace with the settlers for the moment, but no one knew when some untoward incident between hunter and trapper might upset the uneasy balance between peace and war. The horrible massacre of '22 was never far from the minds of planters who dwelt at the edge of the great forest.

Canoes of warriors passed down the river from time to time, now happily on peaceful intent, such as their journey to the oyster-beds and summer fishing grounds, but who could tell when war paint would darken their faces into diabolic masks? Yet the colonists pressed their trade. They came up-river with cargoes of beads, hatchets, knives, coats and bells. Some of the trade goods were for the Indians, others for small planters living in outlying districts, too small to sail their own ships to their own wharves.

The traders returned after some months with hides, beaver fur, tobacco and corn. This had been the custom since 1607, when Captain Newport brought over the first colonists and seated them at Jamestown on the small island. A venturesome group they made—six councillors, a clergyman, a surgeon, twenty-nine gentlemen, six carpenters, a mason, two brick-layers, a blacksmith, a barber, a sailor, a tailor, twelve labourers, a drummer, four boys and twenty-eight divers, others—a hundred and five souls in all. The gentlemen, who made up the most numerous class in Captain Smith's colony, were not trained to the heavy work of clearing fields in the vast forest. The summer illness took many, the famine many more, but in spite of adversity, of massacre and of death from the climate, with the new-coming colonists to augment the seating, the Virginia Company of London had a report of twelve hundred people in 1620.

The rivers were many and deep-channelled, the natural highways for the people which they travelled diligently, apparently with no fear of the Indians until the great massacre of '22.

The very day when the blow fell the Indians had moved freely in and out of the village and the plantations, bringing presents of deer meat, wild turkey, fish and fruit—in perpetual good will and love, in freedom and friendship, they had said, but they spared not man, woman or child. When the count was made, three hundred and fifty-seven were dead, killed by the muskets the English had traded them.

Sibyl thought it strange she had not seen an Indian yet. She wondered if their skins were very red. . . .

She noticed that the shallop was tacking again. There were four men to be seen now and they had set a course that would fetch up at the Jordan's Journey landing. She got up to call Lenzi, but he was already awake. He sat on the ground, his hand shielding his eyes.

" 'Tis a fine shallop coming to see us. Strangers—didn' I tell you, little miss, there would be strangers? Keep looking whilst I run tell the mistress she got guesties on the way. Then I run to the landing."

Sibyl wished Lenzi would hurry, for the shallop was nearing the dock. The bank was high, almost forty feet above the little sandy beach where the wooden wharf ran into the water. She ventured farther out on the bank. Catching a small sapling for support, she peered over the bushes that grew thickly down it. Lenzi was at the dock now, waiting to catch the line which a black slave on the boat held coiled in his hand.

A voice rose. "Stand by for a line!"

"Aye, aye, sar. Cast. Easy, sar. Easy, lessen she grate against the piles."

A man leaped to the wharf. He said to someone on the ship, "I'll be back presently. Just finish up the papers, will you,

Richards? I may want them tonight. Thank you, Lenzi. Is everyone on the plantation in good health?"

"Yes, sar, we is all tol'able. 'Tain't time for the seasoning ever till August, sar. They's all up yonder. Mistress, she's sitting in she's rocking-chair. Just make yourself at home, Mr. Stephen."

Sibyl leaned forward until she almost fell. Her foot slipped and started loose earth down the bank. She began to slide downward. Stephen Bennett looked up, startled when a shower of earth fell into the path ahead of him. He saw Sibyl half-way down, clinging to a bush.

"Hold fast! Hold fast! I'm coming to you."

Sibyl clung desperately to a small cedar. Resin stuck to her hands, giving off a pungent odour. She had scratched her arms and her legs, and there was a rent in her skirt. Stephen Bennett would think she was nothing but a hoyden. Perhaps he wouldn't marry Mathilda because she had a tomboy sister.

Stephen climbed up. He was laughing when he reached down a strong arm. He dragged her up the bank and set her firmly on her feet. He was laughing when he tilted her chin with his hand and kissed her cheek. "My dear child, what were you trying to do? Jump off Lovers' Leap?"

Sibyl fought back her tears. "There isn't any Lovers' Leap here. It's at Flowerdew Hundred, and I wouldn't jump into the river for any gentleman."

"Good! Stick to that idea, my dear." He looked about. "Where is ... where is ..."

"Mathilda?" It was Sibyl's turn to laugh. "She's in the garden, cutting flowers for the table. I saw her going through the gate not half an hour ago."

Stephen hesitated. "I suppose I should make my manners to Mistress Cecily. ..."

"She's busy, I'm sure. Heaps of cousins and nephews and nieces are coming.... Ah, there's Mathilda now."

Mathilda came through the gate and across the green. Her arms were filled with branches of dogwood. The blossoms glistened white as snow. In her softly floating green gown she was like a flower. Stephen looked at her as though he could never get his fill.

When Mathilda saw Stephen, she paused for a moment. The flowers dropped from her arms and she moved swiftly across the grass toward him, her hands extended. There was an expression of wonder, of joy, on her sister's face that Sibyl had never seen before. Stephen was moving swiftly too, almost running.

Sibyl turned away. They had forgotten her. She would walk down to see the shallop. She liked boats. Anything to get away! She felt a wonderment that two people should show so much feeling in their faces. It embarrassed her. "I suppose this is the love people talk about," she muttered as she went down the path to the landing. Tears came to her eyes.

In the little cabin of the shallop Richard was writing a letter to his mother, the second one he had written since he came to Virginia. The first he had sent out by the returning vessel, but he had no way of knowing whether it would ever reach Devon. So he recounted his adventures again, and how he had come to Virginia as an indentured servant. He said nothing of his wound and little of his illness. He wanted his tone to be light, as though he held no bitter thoughts. He continued:

Let me describe Jamestown. I wish I might write with a better heart about this village, that I could say it is like Ledbury or Hereford or Leominster, but I cannot. True, there is a market-place, and a market-house set like that of Ledbury on high timbers, the auction block below with an enclosed room of some size above, reached by an outside stairway. Here the clerks and their assistants sit, checking records and sales. It is plastered outside, with the oaken beams showing.

The fort is located on a low level. 'Tis said by the historians that it covers "as much land as Queen Dido had from the king for her city, as much ground as could be encompassed by the hyde of one ox, cut into thin strips." The north side is made into a triangle, palisaded. The south side is next to the river. The angles are bulwarked by watch-towers, with ordnance of a very old type, from what I glimpsed.

On either side of the fort is a street of houses enclosed in hedges or white paling fences. The market is in the middle ground, near the Parade. Storehouses, a *corps de garde* and a small chapel are near by. The chapel is being repaired. It has a chancel and pews of cedar and a communion table of walnut. The windows are fair and broad, devised to open and shut. The pulpit is of the same cedar, the front hollowed from a log. The church has two bells at the west end. They have

ermons twice every Sunday. There is a Thursday sermon,
with two preachers who take their weekly turns.

The church bell rings every morning at ten, and all men
stop their labours to address themselves in prayer. It rings
again at four o'clock, before supper, for the same purpose.
These were the rules of Sir William Berkeley's time. Our
Governor Bennett will change to more preaching and more
prayers no doubt. Everyone calls him governor now, for
while he has not been formally chosen by the Burgesses, his
election is certain.

I write you at length about the church lest you think this
place too heathenish. You will want to know if there is
a place suitable to worship. I tell you there are hundreds of
places suitable to reach God. The forest trees are cathedrals,
reaching the sky. One can lift up one's face to see the shafts
of sunlight falling in straight slanting rays through the green
roof of the trees to the flower-strewed earth at one's feet.
The birds are a choir of surpassing sweetness. So do not grieve
that I cannot worship in some vast cathedral like Wells or
Bristol or Exeter.

The houses are small by our standards. A few of them are of
brick, one-story for the most part, but with windows pierced
into the roofs for extra space and light. Some are made of
upright poles covered with a fabric of clay and ground oyster-
shells, something like ours in the days of Elizabeth. They are
comfortable within, with great roaring fires if the nights be
cool.

Now that it is coming summer the housekeepers carry away
the shag rugs and lay nicely woven mats of reeds made by
the Indians. These mats, which are put direct on the wide-
planked floor, give a cool summery look and have the
fragrance of freshly cut hay.

The better houses, instead of being roofed with tiles or
thatched, are roofed with tree bark, shaped like tile. These are
weather-proof and warm in winter and keep out the heat of
the piercing sunbeams in the warmer days.

One misses arras, hangings of tapestry or the gilded Cor-
dovan on the white walls of the rooms. One man told me:

> "We dwell not here to build us bowers and halls
>   for pleasure and good cheer,
> But halls we build for us and ours, to dwell in
>   them whilst we live here."

Those last words—"whilst we live here"—bespeak the attitude of many Jamestown and other Virginia people. Most
planters, I am told, think only to stay until they have amassed
a fortune. Then they will return "home" to England, to live
like princes, above their station. Sons are sent home to the
universities to prepare them for life in England.

This seems wrong to me. Virginia should be the *homeland*,
and so considered. If I were wed and the good God gave me
sons, I would want them to think of making this New World
strong. Colonies that develop well must be home. The other
idea is too much like the Spanish plan, to rob the colony of
its wealth for the glorification of the mother country. I say,
let the mother country find glory in that her sons and daughters give life and strength to the colony. The colonies should
be like Cornelia's sons, the jewels in her crown. But enough
of this. With so many words you will think me growing senile.

I had been told by Digby that Kathryn Audley and her
husband, Nicholas Holder, were on one of the ships in our
convoy, but I did not see them till we made trips into Jamestown from Bennett's Welcome to gather stores. Then I saw
them several times, without their recognizing me. I dislike
Nick with all my might. When I have seen him in passing
I must walk in the woods to cleanse myself of evil thoughts.

Kathryn is still of extreme beauty. People gape as she makes
her dainty way in the dusty streets of Jamestown. A small
black boy in livery follows her everywhere, even to church,
carrying her wrap, her nosegay, her prayer-book or her fan.
The like of this is strange to the village. Kathryn's husband
will be secretary to Mr. Claiborne when he comes down from
Maryland as secretary to the colony.

I wish I could think that Kathryn looked sad, unhappily
married, perhaps pining for me, but I cannot in truth. Her
face is beautiful, cold without expression, but I believe she
enjoys the adulation of the villagers.

What has become of Roland Audley? It was said he wanted
to come to America. I suppose Sir Robert has kept him at
home.

"I am told that Nick will encourage the planters to organize
fox-hunts and deer drives in the autumn—to carry on traditional living, I presume.

But I must not be sarcastic, dear mother. I am quite strong
again and in the best of health. There is talk that I will be

going on a long journey, with Mr. Bennett and some officers, a voyage of discovery, although we go part way by land. We will go to the south. It is said that there is the most fertile land yet seen in Virginia, along the shores of the Great Sound of Roanoke, and along two mighty rivers, the Chowan and the Moratuck.

I may even take up land myself—in Mr. Bennett's name of course. A plantation of thousands of acres is better than the fifty allotted a redemptioner when he becomes a free man here in Virginia. One good crop of tobacco would give a man enough wealth to build a fine new home and buy a few slaves.

Fancy a white slave talking in this manner! But it won't be long, my dear mother. Time goes swiftly here in the New World, where work begins with the dawn—"from can-see to can't-see" the black men say.

Digby is a treasure. When we return home, I want him to have a niche in the church dedicated to "A Faithful Man."

If circumstances were different, you might come out with Cook Ellie. The sea voyage is healthful. But until I have worked out my indenture, I must remain as I am.

Now, Mother, let me warn you: there is no good trying to devise ways to send money in sterling to me. It would never be delivered. No matter how honest the captain of a ship is, there are men with greedy fingers who would get it. The only way you might help would be to arrange a small account with an agent in London—possibly Edward Bennett. Then I could draw on it, to buy some of my most pressing needs for clothes and shoes. My master provides clothes of a sort, but you would not approve of their texture.

Say your prayers for me, but do not spend any hours in worry. I am strong in health—I am very much alive, not dead on the battlefield of Worcester.

> With love and devotion,
> Richard

I have been writing this letter for some days. I carried it with me when we sailed on a shallop with Stephen Bennett on some tobacco business. Everything in Virginia is tobacco. They buy slaves and white men with tobacco. They pay the clergymen with tobacco. They sell tobacco on the Bristol and Bideford markets and keep their accounts in London. Their agents buy household goods and clothes and send them back

in ships that land at their own wharves. It is a closely tied-
together plan, which reminds me of mediaeval times when
each man raised all the food he needed on his own land. Not a
bad existence, if one has his own land.

We are tied up now at the wharf at Jordan's Journey on
the James, near the mouth of the Appomattox River. Bennett went off to the plantation house in great haste. He did
not confide in me, but Digby says he has gone courting
Mistress Mathilda—your dear Mathilda Jordan, who is here
with her cousin, Madam Peter Montague. I wish——

At that moment in his letter Richard heard a girl's voice
hallooing from the dock. "I'm coming aboard." The voice
was clear, but there was a little sob in it. It sounded familiar.
He heard Digby stammering a protest. Digby was an accomplished liar when occasion demanded, but he would be no
match for Sibyl. If Sibyl wanted to see the shallop it would
take more than an old dragoon to stop her from seeing all of
it. No use trying to hide now. Sensing Digby's anxiety lest he
betray his master—who had given strict orders on that point
—Richard went out on deck at once, crying, "Sibyl! Oh,
Sibyl!" He saw that she had been crying.

She gave him one astounded look. She could not believe
her eyes. "Richard, it's you. It's you!" She flew into his arms,
kissed him a dozen times, wept over him, kissed the thin scar
on his face.

"Why had you been crying when you came aboard the
ship, my sweet Sibyl?" he asked her when she quieted.

She looked puzzled. "Oh, I remember. It was Mathilda.
She . . ."

"Mathilda?"

"Yes. She was running toward Stephen Bennett, holding
out both her hands. I think she is in love."

Richard was obliged to laugh. "And you cried because she
is in love with a very nice young gentleman?"

Her big dark eyes grew round in puzzlement. "No, I don't
think that made me cry. All at once I was very lonely. I didn't
seem to have a sister."

"Well, you'll have a brother, my child. Think of that idea
for a while and there'll be no need of tears."

They sat talking. Richard introduced Digby to her and it
was evident that each took an immediate liking for the other.

They got along famously. Sibyl must know everything from the moment of the battle. Richard and Digby rehearsed all the long story of the King's flight and escape, and their own condition and indenture.

When they had finished, she was very sad for a moment; then she leaned over and impulsively kissed Richard's hand. "But you are alive, dear Richard. Nothing else matters."

He explained why they must not talk of old days and told her his new name of Richard ap Richards.

She clapped her hands. "I shall call you Taffy." She began to sing, "Taffy was a Welshman, Taffy was a thief."

He thought it time for her to go to the house, as the sun was getting low. "Again, we have a secret, Sibyl. You kept the other. Mind you keep this one."

She asked, "From Mathilda? Or only from Kathryn Holder?"

"Not from Mathilda, if you think she can do as well with a secret as you."

She puckered up her lips. "If she marries Stephen, she will be obliged to tell him."

He had not thought of that contingency. How wise was this charming child! He remembered her cleverness at Coddington Manor when he was in danger from the Roundheads.

"We will keep the secret from everyone for the present." She caught his hand, reached out for Digby's gnarled paw. "Just we three. Ah, Richard, what a wonderful world this is!"

Now he had a fresh postscript to add to the letter to his mother. He must find a good honest West Country captain, sailing direct to Bideford Bay, to carry it.

The moon was high, but the guests still sat at table, laughing, telling anecdotes with the zest that comes only with a close family association.

Stephen sat beside Mathilda. He joined in the laughter at the correct moment, but could not disguise his joyful abstraction. Mathilda dissembled with greater readiness. She listened to a gentleman on her right, one of the Isle of Wight Parkers, as though she were deeply concerned with what he said.

The slaves came and went, bringing food, passing the strong heavy wine made from native grapes.

Mistress Cecily was gay. Her eyes sparkled and laughter came easily. "Peter doesn't understand why I didn't weep for my husbands when they died. How could I? I was too young. Besides, I didn't love them as I love Peter. In Virginia, when one is a widow, one marries quickly. It is not good to be without a man to run the plantation. Slaves must have a strong master, and too, if the Indians came . . ."

Laughter suddenly died. There was a significant silence. The elder Jordan, Thomas said, "There is peace now, for which God be praised."

A young Reynolds leaned forward, pushing his wine-glass aside. "Peace because of Sir William's firm hand. What will happen now that Cromwell is in?"

Peter Montague said, "I fancy everything will continue in the same way. Governments change, but people go on about the business of living."

The younger man was persistent. "I've been told that the western Indians are uneasy. Maryland is on the verge of a war. When white folks quarrel and war, that is the time for the red man to slip in."

"You credit them with too much intelligence, Christopher."

Thomas Jordan said, "I say, don't underrate the redskin. He may not be intelligent by our standards, but he has cunning and shrewdness. He doesn't fight fair. Look at Powhatan in the old days, pretending friendship. Think of '22." He turned to the older Reynolds. "You surely, sir, should remember the hellish massacre across the river at Bennett's and at your own place."

Reynolds' knuckles were white when he grasped the table board. "I don't need to be reminded."

Peter Montague eased the tension. "Let us not be unduly apprehensive, but we need not be unwatchful. Christopher has been in the western mountains. He has been among the red tribes. We see little of the Indians here, but we must not relax our vigilance, especially now that there is a change of government." He glanced at his wife.

Cecily rose at once. "We will leave the men to their Madeira." The women and the young girls got up quickly, with a rustle of silken skirts and scraping of chairs. The men stood. Peter Montague escorted his wife to the door of the drawing-room before he returned to the table.

Cecily said, "You young people may go out on the piazza, while the elders sit in the great room. Mathilda, why don't you get your zither? Music is so romantic in the moonlight."

When Mathilda returned from her room with her zither, the three young girl visitors were sitting on the steps, talking animatedly.

"Christopher shouldn't have talked like that. It makes Uncle Thomas feel so depressed."

"Why?" Sibyl asked.

The pretty little redhead, Debby, said, "You'd be depressed if the Indians had carried off your wife!"

"Oh, I didn't know. Has he never found her?"

"Never. And that was thirty years ago. Why, she could be an old woman by now—a squaw maybe, with Indian children."

"Debby! How dreadful!"

"I know it's dreadful, Louise, but that's what may have happened. And think of what we know happened at Bennett's Welcome! All those people killed, fifty or more, the Sheppards, the Ferrises, Madam Harrison, Richard Woodward, Mr. Thomas Bacon, Lieutenant Pierce and his men, Mrs. John Wilkins . . ."

"How can you remember all the names?" Louise asked.

"I can't remember all. I wish I could. They were heroes, and we forget them too soon."

Sibyl said, "I think you're right, Debby. They were heroes."

Debby went on with a rush, her voice rising. "Mr. Thomas Batts told me how he got away. He's gone to stay in the south, where Nathaniel Batts lives as a kind of governor. The Indians there are gentle, the Chowanoke and the Tuscarora. Mr. Batts says there are lots of people going down there to live. Mr. Skinner and Henry Phillips and Peter Collins have got a big grant of land. Sir William signed the papers before the new governor could take over. Mr. Woodward has been down twice. He says it is wonderful."

Mathilda sat down on a bench where she could look through the dining-room window. Presently Stephen got up and left the room. She heard Mistress Cecily say, "The young ladies are outside, Stephen."

A moment later he came through the door. Mathilda

touched the zither softly, a signal which spoke to Stephen. He moved across the piazza and sat down beside her. "I thought I could never get away," he said, dropping his voice. "I knew they didn't want me there. They wanted to talk about my cousin and the changes that the new government will bring."

"I am sorry Christopher Reynolds spoke out. He is so intense."

"I don't mind. He is worried, that is plain. He is afraid that Governor Bennett will not be strong enough to keep down uprisings. But he need not worry. I could have told him, but he wouldn't believe me. He must find out for himself that Richard Bennett will be a strong governor, not a weak one. A man may be gentle in manner but have the strength of iron in his soul."

Mathilda said, "They are uneasy . . ."

Stephen interrupted her. "Come, let us walk in the garden. It is a night like a play by Mr. Shakespeare."

Mathilda's voice was very low. " 'In such a night . . .' "

"Ah! You do understand. Come, the moon is beautiful. If we walk under the poplar trees, we can see its reflection in the water."

The young girls on the steps watched them move slowly across the grass. They laughed softly. "They are sweet, aren't they?" Debby said. "He is very gallant, the young Mr. Bennett. I was trembling for fear of what Chris might say. One never knows."

"Uncle Peter would not let him go on. He changed the subject," Sibyl said. "Anyway, Stephen is a man of parts. He knows that there must be differences of opinion."

"How worldly you are, Sibyl!" Louise exclaimed. "You are younger than I am, but I would never think such things. Yes, you are worldly. You've seen the King and been to London. Why, I've never been beyond the Capes, even to go up to Maryland."

Sibyl did not answer. She felt pleased. She *was* worldly. She shared a secret with Richard. She had walked with danger, there at Coddington Manor, and she had not been afraid.

A mocker tuned up in a gay, thrilling song of poignant sweetness.

Debby sighed. "I wonder if I will ever find a lover. There are so few men here in Virginia, and they talk only about

Indians and tobacco. Look at Chris and Edward. Instead of walking in the moonlight with us, or skipping a contra-dance on the green, they are sitting at table guzzling wine and talking about the price of pork."

But the men seated about the table were not talking about the price of pork, or even about the new plan for tobacco, which Stephen Bennett had explained to them a few hours ago.

They were talking about Sir William Berkeley, and whether or not he would accept a Puritan governor in a Virginia that had been his own borough up until now.

CHAPTER 16

A New Governor Lands at Jamestown

WORD had been given out that Richard Bennett would land at the south gate of the Palisado. On this day he would go before the General Assembly.

Jamestown had not seen such a crowd packed around the Parade or on the water-front since the Starving Time, those terrible days when necessity, like an armed man, drove them to seek ships that would take them back to England. In its crush it resembled the stampede on Roanoke Island when the settlers left by Sir Richard Grenville rushed to the shore at the arrival of Sir Francis Drake and his ships, fell on their knees and begged him to carry them from the accursed island home to England.

But in the Starving Time of the Jamestown colony they did not go back to England and leave the new fair land of Virginia to savagery. At the very moment of their departure Lord de la Warr's ships came sailing up the James, bearing new colonists and food.

At the sight of the rescue ships the disheartened, beaten folk took new courage; they sailed back to Jamestown, back to their plantations, to make a stronger, more lasting fight against homesickness and the terror of the country. More was saved that day, so many years ago, by Lord de la Warr's ships than the lives of a few hundred men.

It was a miracle, a sign from God, that they must hold what they had won. A homeland was saved and the seeds of a nation took deep root. A victory was won that had no parallel in history.

How many of the crowd who waited for Governor Bennett's ships had been on this spot at the Starving Time, when England all but lost a continent? And how many of these remembered it now? Not many—a few Ancient Planters to whom the long years meant more than a number of days or an endless chain of sunrises and sunsets. To those heroic men they meant the continuation of a great dream of exploration, which had had its seed in the fertile soil of Elizabethan times. The growth, so slow, so backward, meant sacrifice and suffering, weary hearts of men, agony of women's tears.

The growth from the first planting was as inevitable as the rising of the tide or the pull of the moon.

It was not a continuation of the purpose of a few great men. It was the continuation of the hope, the energy, the determination of many stubborn folk, who since Elizabeth's day would not bow to the will of savagery, to the green tide of the ever-invading forest or to the terror of lonely living and lonely dying. It was a great surge forward, which would gain a reward commensurate with the effort of the humble and the great.

On this clear bright April day they might forget the barbarity that lurked in the forest. But could they forget the man of envy and hatred who hid himself at Green Spring, the man who waited and bided his time, Berkeley, who had governed them for ten years and who, they were sure, would not give up without a struggle?

The new governor had scotched the enemy before he could strike a well-planned blow.

A blow had indeed been planned. The followers of the Stuarts had gathered quietly in the night. From the Northern Neck and the upper James they had come at Berkeley's call to his mansion a few miles from Jamestown. Muskets and powder were well hidden, ready for the day.

To capture Richard Bennett, hold him as hostage or hang him from a high gibbet would not have been difficult, except for one thing—the ships of war that had sailed up the river and anchored opposite Bennett's Welcome late the previous afternoon. Two ships, with soldiers in armour hidden below decks, had sailed between the Capes and passed the Point of Comfort without a pause, although they gave the usual one-gun salute to the fort. Half a dozen small sail-boats had put off at dusk to carry the news of Sir William and the Stuart followers waiting to strike for the young King to whom they still gave allegiance.

Now, on the morning of April thirtieth in the year 1652, the people waited—a quiet crowd whose stolid faces revealed nothing of the thoughts hidden in their hearts. Puritan and Stuart follower stood side by side. They had been ruled by good governors and bad since the first year when John Smith and Captain Newport had raised the flag of England over the new land.

A farrier, who had left his fires, said to a neighbouring shoemaker, " 'E can't be worse than Sir John Harvey, nor better than Sir George Yeardley. I've seen them all in the half century I've been on this little strip of land."

The shoemaker, who wore the leathern apron of his trade, said, "We can take the good with the bad. Since we beat off the Indians and old Opechancanough died in '44, we've lived fairly well, I'm a-thinkin'. Long as the folk pay their just debts, we'll get along."

"If he's good as Sir William, we'll not suffer." A blue-smocked yeoman joined in. "I'm not understanding this new tobacco plan. Cromwell's telling us to quit planting and raise more cattle. Cattle running in the forest is a trouble. We don't have enough corn to fatten the rangy beasts." He wandered off to find a more advantageous spot to view the procession. The other two watched him push his way toward the front.

"Country yokels always complain," the rugged farrier said. "Suggs, do you recall when a man had a bodkin punched through his tongue if he filched a pint of oatmeal for his flattened belly, and was chained to a tree until he starved?"

"That I do, John. Remember the tales of how the up-country men dug holes in the earth and hid themselves until they famished, when they were too sick to work? I never believed that tale, nor the one about eating toadstools, chewing horse-hides and swallowing fried snakes.

"Starving Time was bad enough."

A little crowd gathered where they were standing under a water oak. An old man, bent over a cane, shambled up. "Those tales are trifling. I recollect a man who was so hungry he killed his wife and ground her to powder. They burned him, they did, and good riddance! Aye, all those things Captain Smith brought on us by his discovery of Virginia. Some said it would be the greatest day of their lives when the Indians boiled a mare to eat; that they wished Cap'n Smith was on her back, boiling away in the kettle."

A young man, wearing good proper Sunday best and a

beaver with a plume, paused to listen. The old man had seated himself on a stump. It was not often he had an audience.

"Aye, and they writ a paper called 'The Unmasked Face of Virginia,' or some such name, telling the troubles of the people who had been lured to Virginia by a passel of fine words that made it out a 'eaven on earth and——"

"You remember a heap, Grandpap," the young man said. "Do you remember any bad times in the old country?"

"I remembers people a-fightin' their brothers, and I remembers hearing tell they cut the head off a king. Aye, I remembers a man's body quartered and sticking on a pike over the gates of London."

"Then it's no worse here than at home," the youth said. "We've got a civil government and an assembly, and a man can call himself free, can't he?"

"If he ain't indentured." A new voice broke in. "Seven years is long passing."

"Well, I say we're lucky we ha'n't got Sir John Harvey to be our governor. We've got a nice Puritan elder, and they be gentle and kind people."

The farrier, who had been silent, said, "Some say gentle people ain't fit to govern. . . . I'm going to Thompson's Ordinary for a pint." He walked away swinging his broad shoulders, swaggering through the crowd.

If one knew the people, it was plain to read that their temper was an attitude of waiting. Every country, every region had its representatives. There was no sign of tension. The throng was greater now. Small boys thrust their way to the beach. Women in wide silk dresses, hats with ribbands, carrying little sunshades; women in laced kirtles, bright cotton skirts; women in gay calicuts with mob-caps—all pressed forward and stood back of the lines of foot soldiers formed for the parade to the wharf. Hundreds of men were there—planters in fine coats, brocade waistcoats and plumed beavers; men in Puritan drab, with stiff high-crowned hats of black.

Every house was gay with banners and wreaths. People whose houses gave on the river asked friends to join them. Their little lawns blossomed as a garden in spring with the bright-coloured clothes of the women.

They had a cheerful welcome for a new governor, but he must show his mettle before the people of Virginia accepted him to their hearts. Their eyes and their thoughts turned from the direction of Green Spring across Powhatan Creek to the stately ships lying on the breast of the mighty James.

The taverns and ordinaries were emptying one by one as the gentlemen and countrymen, planters and free yeomen set tankard and mug on the tables and went out to join the concourse on the beach.

A whisper ran through the crowd that Berkeley's coach had crossed the Back River and was at Friggett Landing. With him were twenty young gentlemen on horseback, besides his grooms and men in livery.

He had only to cross Back River Marsh, take the road that crossed James Baldwin's land, the small lane between Major Beverley's and Richard Lawrence's, cross the Vale and he would be on Fort Hill close to the church. There he would be on higher ground in a strategic spot near the Old Fort. Perhaps he had men in boats sailing across Sandy Bay. He was a bold fellow, was Sir William Berkeley, who feared neither man nor devil. Certainly he would not be intimidated by a Puritan governor, even though he *was* Oliver's man. Oliver Cromwell was three months away across a great ocean.

The uncertainty which governor, the old or the new, would prove the stronger checked the people of Jamestown from demonstration.

Many a free man cared not who governed so long as he was allowed to fill his land, sell his crops in peace, with a guaranteed protection against Indian depredations.

With silent unreadable faces they watched the ships move slowly in toward shore until they lay by the first line of cypress trees which marched out into the water, well beyond the shore-line. There were twenty-five feet of water at the lone cypress that stood out beyond the rest. The ships could move no closer, but those on board knew that this was close enough for the range of their guns.

The people nearest the water's edge saw Governor Bennett come onto the deck. He was dressed in dun-coloured clothes with a simple collar of thin white linen. He did not wear arms, but two men in light armour with swords stood one on either side of him. He took position at the prow of the vessel, which they now saw was a ship of war. The guns in the portholes of both ships were trained on the shore. This was an unexpected development. They had no inkling of the arrival of warships. Glances were exchanged along the line of watchers, swift glances that held something more than surprise—was it apprehension?

A small, misshapen man wriggled his way from the front row and gained Back Street. From there he walked to Thompson's Tavern, mounted a horse and galloped across the Vale to Friggett Landing. The news he took to Sir William would not be welcome. The messengers of the night before had not spoken of a broadside of heavy ordnance that would be trained on the shore, but only of a signal gun.

He met Sir William and his men in the lane behind Major Beverley's land. He gave the message to the young lieutenant riding ahead. The lieutenant swore at the news about cannon. "Ride on, fellow! The governor's coach is around the turn."

The messenger shook his head violently. "Sir, no. I must return at once to watch Bennett and his staff step into the boats and come ashore." He wheeled his nag and was off in haste. He had no intention of incurring Berkeley's wrath as the bearer of ill news.

Richard Monington stood beside Digby near the ship's rail. It was young Stephen's idea that the two men, being each of a height beyond six feet, should be the body-guard. They would walk in the procession on either side of the governor, a step or two behind. They wore cuirass and helmet, each with drawn sword in his hand. It had all been rehearsed: Secretary Clairborne was to walk first with his escort; then the governor's staff; then the governor with his two guards.

Now they waited for the small boats to take them ashore.

A change in the character of the crowd might have been noted by an alert eye. Men in rustic, up-country dress, faded blue smocks or woodsmen's tunics were moving quietly into formation. They made two lines around the soldiers from the fort, beginning at the water's edge, apexing on Back Street, then going down to the water again. The lines enclosed the landing-place, with the fort as centre.

An observant person would have suspected small-arms under the covering smocks, suspected that muskets might stand in Berkeley's town house near the fort.

But no one was searching the crowd with practised eyes as

Berkeley's followers drifted in one by one and became a part of the throng about the landing-place.

Word ran through the crowd that Sir William's coach was now at the fourth ridge. There he would wait until Richard Bennett put his foot on the soil of Jamestown.

So they remained: the new governor on his ship, the old governor on high ground back of the town, a commanding position.

The first shore-boat was alongside the ship of war. A platoon carrying muskets came out of the fort. They wore the uniform of the Home Guard. They marched down the street, the crowd making way, and took their place behind the soldiers drawn up at the landing. They too were Berkeley's men.

The grounds of Berkeley's town house seemed suddenly to fill with groups of two or three. Far back of the crowds across the Vale other adherents surrounded the church where the ceremonies were to take place.

The farrier and the yeoman from Gloucester came out of Thompson's Ordinary, wiping their lips on the back of their hands. The farrier had the keen bright eyes that had been missing. They swept the crowd. "Almighty `Christ," he whispered to his companion, "Berkeley's going to act!"

The countryman said, "How do you know, John?"

"Look, man! Look about you. Don' ye see the bulge under the smock of the fellow by the tree? The one to the left of you? Arms—small-arms and a dirk as well. See how the Berkeley men are placed in the crowd."

"God ha' mercy, there'll be bloodshed!" the yeoman whispered.

The farrier shook his head warningly. "Hist! Wait. It won't come when he lands. Later."

"Why do you say that?"

"See yon Puritan parson in his robe, carrying the Holy Bible in his hands. He's waiting to speak from the Word as the new governor steps ashore. Berkeley's too wise to attack with the minister standing by, even though he's Puritan. The people would turn against him. He'll wait mayhap until they are ready for the ceremony, before the procession enters the church. Let's edge out of the crowd and cross the Vale to the church side. It's there the trouble will start."

The countryman said timidly, "Which side are you on, farrier?"

"The winning side, fool!" He grinned. Pushing through the crowd, they made their way to the Vale. They crossed the circle of Berkeley's men, who eyed them with suspicion.

"I want to see the governor step ashore," the countryman complained. "I came all the way just to see the new governor."

"You'll see him, right enough, and the old one thrown in. Follow me. We'll take our place among the tombstones, where we can see the procession as it marches from the landing."

On the ship everything was quiet. In the first boat the waterman sat at their stations, oars vertical, at the ready. Mr. Secretary Claiborne and his aides stepped into the flat-bottomed boat and were rowed ashore. The second boat carried the trumpeters, drummers and guards; the third, the men of the governor's household, Stephen Bennett among them. The fourth bore the women, sombrely dressed in grey woolsey, with plain white collars and dark hooded capes. Madam Bennett, quiet, sweet-faced, her young children at her side, looked over the massed heads with eyes expressionless and calm.

At last Governor Bennett with his two guards came down the ladder. A murmur ran through the crush on the shore, but there was no cheering when he took his place. Digby and Richard remained standing as the rowers stepped the oars into the locks. Bennett made a fine figure in his simple clothes, his plain hat. The people commented when he set foot on the island that he wore no armour.

He took a step beyond the lapping water and fell on his knees before the minister. The people about him knelt, but the company in arms bowed their heads without kneeling. Richard and Digby also remained standing, swords unsheathed. The colour-bearer held his standard high.

The prayer was short. Bennett rose to his feet. Digby, close to Richard Monington, said, "Glimpse the crowd. Yon jumpered men have the looks of soldiers to my eye. Watch them closing in. Shall I give the signal?"

After a swift survey of the soldiers behind the guard, the circle of russet-clothed men and men in blue smocks, Richard nodded.

The colour-guard advanced before the crowds could push foward. The trumpets sounded and the roll of drums. A flag was run up on each ship of war. Suddenly the decks of both ships were crowded with Parliamentary soldiers. They swarmed over the sides into waiting boats.

Captain Robert Denis and his staff came in the first boat. They took their places beside Governor Bennett before the crowd had recovered from its first breathless surprise.

Boatload after boatload came ashore. The numbers were so great that the people had to fall back from the beach to the first street of the village in order to make room for them to land.

Captain Denis gave a sharp order. The soldiers marched forward in two lines, enclosing the Home Guard within a square, the rustics and blue-smocked men in the centre.

Another sharp order and a platoon walked through the crowd, disarming every man who carried a weapon.

It was all so swift, so unexpected, that Berkeley's men had no time to escape, nor had they time to hide the muskets in Berkeley's house on the shore.

Something in the quiet thoroughness of the movement, its bold and rapid strategy, caught the fancy of the throng. A cheer broke out, followed by another, until the air was vibrating with huzzas for Governor Bennett.

Soldiers were still landing from the ships. At length seven hundred of Oliver's men had their feet on the soil of Jamestown. Four abreast, they marched smartly down the dusty, unpaved street toward the church where the Assembly was to meet.

Richard Bennett stepped into his place. Soldiers in front of him, soldiers following, he marched in stately triumph to the church.

The surprise had been complete. For the first time Berkeley had been outwitted. The dull Puritan had proved no dullard at all, but a shrewd and competent planner.

Richard watched the people through the visor of his headpiece. The stiff waiting looks had given way to general approval. Evidently they were thinking he would not be too bad, this Bennett, whom they had known as a quiet, peace-loving planter. Indeed he might prove stronger than Berkeley, and kinder to the commonalty.

Marching along, Richard caught a glimpse of Sibyl standing on the piazza of a long frame house, set in a large garden near the water. He turned his head slightly. Mathilda was

there, and Madam Montague and her husband, and a group
he did not recognize. They were waving, huzzaing. The men
stood at salute, as soldiers would, when the governor passed
by.

Mistress Cecily gave up riding to the church in her coach.
Peter persuaded her that the throng was too great to make
the attempt to pass along Water Street or Back Street. She
yielded reluctantly. "The dust is to the ankles," she complained. "I will be obliged to change my new satin shoes to
the heavy leather I wear on the plantation."

"No one will look at your boots," Peter suggested. "They
will be too occupied staring at the governor's party and the
soldiers."

"You may be right—if I walk. But if I arrived in my coach
and descended gracefully as a lady should, with my satin-clad
toes pointed properly and my skirts tilted in a provocative
manner, everyone would look at me." She turned her head.
"Mathilda and Sibyl, hasten! We may as well get on, so that
we will be in our seats before the governor arrives."

She joined Peter, who was waiting on the steps of the
piazza.

"My dear, you do have proper seats for us, do you not?
You, a Burgess, have some rights." There was a touch of
asperity in Cecily's voice. She didn't like the idea of heavy
black leather shoes under her lavender taffeta skirts. But
Madam was philosophical and she took the good with the
bad.

She lifted her voice. "Sibyl, bring your cape. It will be cold
in the church. You know the roof is not yet fully covered.
Hurry!"

They passed out of the gate and fell behind the crowd.
Sibyl was in a yellow sprigged calicut. Mathilda wore a pale
rose dress so long she must hold the skirt above the sandy
road with both hands. She had a little hat wreathed in roses,
with black velvet ribbands. Narrow velvet bands circled her
wrists and slim throat.

"You look sweet enough to eat, Sis. I hope you sit where
Stephen can see you." Sibyl skipped along beside Mathilda.
Her skirts were short, so she was not obliged to hold onto
them. Her broad hat of Italian straw hung down her back,
held in place by a yellow ribband.

"You must put your hat on properly when you go into the church, Sibyl," Madam Montague said over her shoulder.

"Yes, Aunt Cecily."

They took a short cut through the Vale and arrived at the church door. Richard Bennett had not come yet. The procession moved slowly to the beat of the drums. It crossed and recrossed the village, so that the people could see from their own stoops.

The church was reserved for the Assembly members, their women-folk and prominent planters. There would be no seats for the townfolk.

Madam Montague paused in the churchyard, where many of the Burgesses were talking together in small groups. She spoke to John West, Argoll Yeardley, Thomas Pettus, George Ludlow. Thomas Woodward came forward to kiss her extended hand. She waved her fan at young Benjamin Harrison. He left the company of a group of planters, Colonel West, Colonel Mathews and Nathaniel Littleton.

She unfurled her fan, put it before her face and whispered, "Tell me, where is Sir William! Did *he* know that Governor Bennett had all those soldiers down below decks, to spring out at a moment's notice?"

Harrison shook his head. "I don't know. I've just come down-river in my sloop. I was myself surprised. I cannot speak for Sir William."

"I wonder what he will do. Surely he can not contest now."

"One never knows." Young Harrison kept looking toward the companions he had left. "Pardon me, madam. My friends are going into the church." He bowed and walked rapidly away.

Peter Montague offered his arm to his wife. Sibyl and Mathilda fell in behind them. The church was already crowded. The usher escorted them to seats reserved for the Burgess of Peter Montague's district. These seats directly faced the choir, where the governor's chair was placed under a canopy of red velvet, edged with gold galloon. From this position of vantage they were able to see the door through which Richard Bennett would enter.

After she had seated herself in her pew, disposed of her fan and her reticule on the prayer-bench, Madam rose to her feet to survey the audience. She bowed to her divers friends: Members of the Assembly, who had already taken their seats;

Captain Francis Eppes, Colonel John Cheesman, Colonel Ludlow and William Barrett, who were Councillors. Colonel Yeardley and Thomas Pettus came in to take their places. They also were on the new Council.

She saw John Hawkins sitting near John Moore and Arthur Skimmer. John Knott, the Puritan from Nansemond, was close by Joseph Bridger of Isle of Wight. The Reverend James Bray of Jamestown was talking with James Benn, a good Puritan but not so strict as his father Christopher. There was a church on his plantation.

She did not see Ralph Wormeley, nor any member of the Virginia oligarchy—Beverley, Burwell, Byrd, Carter, Ludwell, Page, Randolph, Tayloe. They would probably be at the door to escort Richard Bennett to the governor's place. The King's men in this Assembly would be as numerous as Cromwell's Puritans, but many Royalists were not committed to Berkeley.

She saw the Godwins and Thomas Woodward standing near the door with Dudley Digges of Mulberry Island, and Henry Baker, who had a grant of twenty-five hundred acres on the Chowan River. William Boddie from Isle of Wight rose from his bench to return her bow.

"Where is Thomas Blount?" Cecily whispered to her husband. "I don't see him or Edward Chauncey or either of the Relphs. Are they in the South, taking up land on the Sound of Roanoke?"

Peter looked around. "Blount's over yonder, behind Scarborough, sitting beside Colonel Hill."

Cecily cramed her neck. "Oh, yes, I see them now. Blount is looking rather pale. I suppose he's been having the fits. I wonder if Ludlow has recovered from his attack." She nudged Peter. "Look! There's Elizabeth Outland from Chuckatuck, seated near the Gookin men; and Tooke of Lawnes Creek. I declare, almost all of Virginia is here today, Puritan and Royalist. I'm glad I came, Peter. I wouldn't have missed this. Who would have thought the King's men would turn out in such force for a Puritan governor?"

"They don't dare stay away," Peter said. "Hush, my dear. Remember how your voice carries."

Sibyl pulled at Mathilda's sleeve. "Quit popping your eyes out, searching for Stephen Bennett. He won't come until the governor appears. Over there, across the second pew on the left, do you see Kathryn Audley, looking like a queen, and

Nick, dressed so soberly—not as he used to dress, always as gay as a peacock? He's a Puritan now in sombre grey. He's play-acting, Nick is. He'll edge his way into the good graces of the new governor."

Mathilda lifted her head. Nicholas Holder was looking squarely at her. He touched his hand to his lips, a little furtive gesture. Mathilda looked straight at him, through him. Her eyes did not waver, nor her colour change.

She's through with him, Sibyl thought, watching her sister as she let her eyes wander over the crowd. She's out of love with him. Sibyl sat back with a contented sigh. She could now give all of her attention to the ceremonies which were about to take place.

At the fourth ridge Sir William Berkeley, seated in his carriage, waited impatiently for a report from his men. From time to time he looked at his round silver watch. If all went well, the little plan he had made would be now in motion. But why had no one come? He had heard the sound of trumpets, the roll of drums, but not the musket fire which should follow the first salute upon Bennett's landing on the island.

Sir William opened the door of his coach and stepped to the ground. The young men on horseback followed his example. Lee, Major Beverley and Tayloe were nearest to him. The master of Green Spring was in his Court dress, with a dark red tunic of striped silk and a broad collar of lace. He wore a full wig of curling brown hair, and his small-clothes were satin, his hosen silk. His shoes were buckled with Spanish paste, he wore his ribbands and decorations and carried a dress sword with a jewelled hilt.

He called Major Beverley to his side. "What do you think has happened to our men?" he asked, his heavy brows drawn together.

Major Beverley, deeply worried, said, "Your Excellency, I fear something untoward has befallen them. We should have had a report by now. Can Bennett have discovered . . . ?"

Berkeley answered scornfully, "Nonsense, man! Bennett's too stupid to see beyond that nose of his. Something has miscarried with our people. Signals have been misunderstood— but I do not see how that could be. Everything was carefully planned. Every officer repeated my program: 'Somewhere between the landing and the church, at a signal I shall arrive. I shall enter the church, proclaim Charles the Second King of Virginia. Then I shall prorogue the Assembly in my authority as governor, completely ignoring the advent of a Cromwellian official.' "

Beverley said, "A master plan, Your Excellency, if I may say so. You are within the law of the land, since Bennett, although the Council of State appointed the commissioners who have nominated him, cannot be made governor-in-fact without the vote of the Burgesses and the authority of the Grand Assembly in full session. The Burgesses alone can choose a governor."

"Exactly, Major Beverley, but what is this commotion? Is that a rider with a message?"

A young gentleman dismounted quickly from a sweating horse and approached Sir William.

"What news?" Berkeley asked, raising his voice. The gentlemen pressed forward.

The rider saluted. "Your Excellency, evil tidings! Seven hundred Parliamentary soldiers, who were secreted in the two ships of war, came ashore immediately after Richard Bennett landed. They surrounded our men, disarming every one of them."

"God's death, you lie, sir!"

"Your Excellency, I swear I saw them myself. They are marching toward the church at this moment. Listen. You can hear the marching drums."

One of the gentlemen said urgently, "Excellency, you must turn your coach. Ride with all haste to Green Spring. We will ride with you to protect your person."

A second gentleman added his plea. "Sir, you must ride north to Lee's house. From there we will escort you to Maryland, where you can be hidden at Richard Brooke's plantation until we can take ship for Holland."

A third had his word. "Sir, let us go to the western mountains. Byrd will show us the way to safe hiding."

Berkeley, his face like a heavy cloud that foretells a hurricane, stood with his feet broad apart, his hand on his sword. He did not answer his gentlemen. Thoughts as black as his looks rushed through his mind. After a moment he turned and strode to his coach. Ignoring his grooms and outriders, he stepped inside and slammed the door. He thrust his head out

the window. His voice was like the voice of Jove thundering
from Olympus.

"William Berkeley does not acknowledge defeat. Coachman,
drive with all haste to the church. I do not wish to keep
Oliver's governor waiting."

CHAPTER 17

The Grand Assembly

GOVERNOR BENNETT, the Councillors and the officers of the Assembly stood beside the church door waiting while the Ancient Planters, as part of the governor's company, filed inside to take their places. Captain Denis' guard of halberdiers were ranged to the number of fifty on either side of the door, wearing their fair red coats according to old custom.

The colour-bearer was about to step forward to dip the colours when Sir William Berkeley's coach drove up, escorted by a company of young men. Sir William descended and his company dismounted.

At the entrance they encountered Governor Bennett and his company. Roundhead grey and Royalist elegance and splendour stood surveying each other, humility and arrogance, simple country gentlemen and titled nobility. There was a moment of intense silence when time itself seemed suspended, as eye met eye across the lowered standard. A breathless stillness crossed the churchyard while the crowds were motionless. The people in the church near the open door were silent, not knowing what dire thing might follow.

The voice of the clerk of the Assembly broke through the heavy silence. "My lords and ladies, the Captain General Governor of the Commonwealth waits at the door. We, the members of the Assembly here present, bid him enter." A trumpet sounded and a roll of drums.

Sir William Berkeley inclined his head, the colour-bearer lifted the banner, and Bennett, after acknowledging Sir William's salute with a brief bow, walked slowly into the church and took his place in the chair under the velvet canopy. A page placed a velvet cushion on the kneeling bench in front of him.

As his staff were taking their places, Richard and Digby behind him, Berkeley and his gentry entered and walked to

the left side where space was reserved for Burgesses. Those
gentlemen, seeing that there was a scarcity of benches, left
their seats and ranged themselves along the wall, leaving room
for Sir William and the young men who accompanied him.

Berkeley continued to stand and with great deliberation
surveyed the crowded church. When he recognized a friend,
he bowed slightly. The person so honoured rose and returned
the bow. When Sir William sat down, a murmur went through
the church.

Cecily clutched her husband's hand. She whispered, "Oh,
Peter, he's never going to challenge the governor in church!
I'm frightened."

"Challenge Bennett? With seven hundred of Oliver's soldiers
outside! Nonsense! Look at his two guards in armour with
their hands on the hilts of their swords, ready to leap in front
of Bennett."

Cecily eyed the men. "They do look monstrous strong . . .
and the halberdiers at the door . . ." She smiled suddenly.
"The Puritan is a cautious man, is he not?"

"A man of peace, prepared for war." Peter's eyes twinkled.
"I think I'm going to approve of Bennett as governor."

The confusion of seating was over. The governor leaned
back in his fine elbow chair. Sir William, at a lower level, sat
in stately grandeur.

The Puritan minister, whom nobody knew, arrayed in black
gown with simple white linen falling-bands under his heavy
chin, moved toward the pulpit and bent his head in prayer.
"O Lord, bless this day and the people here assembled. Guide
this man who is our governor in the way of light, of truth and
Christlike humility, so that he may govern wisely and justly
for all the people of Virginia. God bless our noble Lord
General Oliver Cromwell and give him grace to rule with
wisdom and authority. In the name of our gracious God,
amen."

A long silence followed the short prayer. A tension trembled
in the air that converted simple silence into a noise like
thunder. "God bless Oliver Cromwell"—not "God Save Our
Noble King," but Cromwell, Cromwell the Lord General. For
the first time that name had been spoken within the walls of
the church at Jamestown.

The clerk of the Assembly, Mr. Croker, began to read in an
even, monotonous voice. That morning the Burgesses had sat

in secret session, according to the laws of the Grand Assembly, to choose a governor in the place of Sir William Berkeley. "After long and serious debate and advice taken for settling and governing Virginia, it was unanimously voted and concluded by commissioners appointed by the authority of Parliament, and all the Burgesses of the several counties, plantations and hundreds respectively, that Richard Bennett, Esquire, be governor for the ensuing two years."

There was a flutter, a swift turning of heads, lifted eyebrows. Many present did not know that a meeting had been held that morning.

Parchment rattled as the clerk took up a second page. "Likewise Colonel William Claiborne to be Secretary of State, and Colonel John West, Colonel Mathews, Colonel Littleton, Colonel Yeardley, Colonel Thomas Pettus, Colonel Humphrey Higginson, Colonel George Ludlow, Colonel William Barrett, Captain Bridger Freeman, Captain Thomas Harwood, Major William Taylor, Captains Francis Eppes and Levey and Colonel John Cheesman to be Council of State."

Again the crowd stirred; there were known Royalists among the members of the Council as well as Cromwell's followers. What did it mean? The clerk looked up. He waited until quiet was restored.

"The Council shall have the power to execute the laws and do right and equal justice to all people and inhabitants in the colony—" he paused here and raised his voice—"according to such instructions as they have received from the Parliament of England, and according to the known statutes of England." The clerk laid the paper on the reading desk. He motioned for the people to rise. "God save the Commonwealth of England and this country of Virginia!"

A cannon boomed, the first gun of the salute to the new governor.

Richard Bennett moved over to a table where an open Bible had been placed. The clerk administered the oath. It was no different from the swearing-in of the earlier governors.

When the governor was again in his chair, the Burgesses rose, and as the names of the counties were called by the clerk, they walked forward to take the oath.

"Raise your right hand," Mr. Croker said. "You and every one of you shall swear by the Holy Evangel . . ." His voice dwindled into a meaningless jumble of words, a sing-song rhythm, as the men of the counties filed past. The quiet of the church was broken by whispers and a rumble of low voices.

Richard Monington wished devoutly it would end. The armour weighed heavily. The casque made him feel hot and heady. No one could recognize him through it, but he dared not turn to feast his eyes on the fair vision of Kathryn Audley. He had glimpsed her as he marched down the aisle. Her loveliness, her beauty, the nearness of her swept over him like a torrent. His hand trembled on the hilt of his sword. He had thought all emotion spent, but that was mind trying to dictate to feeling. When he saw her, he knew that love was not dead. Love cannot be strangled by reason.

The clerk's dry voice broke in. "Isle of Wight—Mr. Robert Pitt, Mr. George Hardie, Mr. John George, Mr. John Moore. Raise your right hands."

Richard knew all the reasons why he should stamp out thought of this woman, but she was wrapped about his heart, clinging, smothering his clear vision. Women were like that. Perhaps she was evil, a thing of the devil to tempt him.

"Lower Norfolk—Messrs. Loyd, Lambert, Woodhouse and Barr . . ." Only "Holy Archangel" came out of the mumbled words. "Warwick River County—Colonel Mathews, Mr. William Whitby, Mr. Henry Lee . . ."

Would the thing never end? The governor was as still as though he were cut in stone. Sir William Berkeley was out of range of Richard's eyes. Richard wondered how Digby was enduring the inaction. He thought, How often I have ordered soldiers to stand at parade! I did not know it could cause a man such discomfort.

". . . Gloucester—Mr. Hugh Gwyn . . ."

The cannon sounded at steady rhythmic intervals. The clerk's voice stopped. People moved and squirmed; silk skirts rustled.

Sibyl whispered to Mathilda, "Doesn't the altar look sweet with those waxen dogwood blossoms? The old sexton told me that he always trimmed the altar himself."

"Hush, Sis. The governor is going to speak. You must be quiet."

"I'm tired of sitting so still. I wish I were outside, sitting on a tombstone. I could hear just as readily and I could move my limbs and feet and raise my arms."

"Hush, child!" Mistress Cecily tapped Sibyl's arm with her closed fan.

The governor had no papers before him. Instead, he stood silently, sweeping the company with his steady eyes. Presently, when the swishing of satin and silk skirts and the rattle of dress swords ceased, he spoke.

"I will not make an address or bother you with promises of what I shall do while I am Governor of Virginia. Let time take care of that. What I am going to say is contained within the Articles of Surrender, which were read at an early meeting of the Assembly.

"If there is anyone present who does not wish to hear what I have to say, let him leave at this time."

No one moved. Heads were turned slightly. Furtive glances were cast to the left of the church. Sir William looked straight ahead.

Governor Bennett spoke a word to Richard. "You and your companion may leave now." Richard and Digby saluted and walked out of the church.

Sibyl whispered, "Aunt Cecily, may I go?"

"Yes, but no farther than the churchyard, remember. Don't go wandering about the town."

Sibyl slipped from the pew and out the side door. A number of children left at the same time, glad to be released.

The governor raised his voice. "The Articles agreed on and concluded at the lawful meeting of the Assembly set forth the surrendering and settling of this plantation under the government of the Commonwealth of England and our duly chosen representatives.

"I shall not rehearse them all, sixteen in number, but I shall point out some of them in their turn. First, it is agreed that all the plantations of Virginia, and all inhabitants thereof, shall be and remain in due obedience and subjection to the Commonwealth of England.

"There will be a full and total remission and indemnity of all acts, words and writings done or spoken against the Parliament of England.

"Virginia may enjoy ancient bounds and limits granted by charters of the former Kings, and all land grants under colony seal by any precedent governors shall remain in force and strength."

There were noddings and glances of approbation, showing

that many were afraid the old lines and divisions would be
declared illegal. Bennett's word scotched the rumours that
had been flying about.

"The privilege of having fifty acres of land for every person transported shall continue.

"The people of Virginia shall have free trade as the people
of England enjoy, to all places and with all nations, according
to the laws of the Commonwealth.

"They shall be free of all taxes and customs whatsoever,
and none shall be imposed without the consent of the Grand
Assembly; nor shall forts or castles be erected, nor garrisons
maintained, without the consent of the people's Assembly;
nor shall there be any charge required from Virginia in respect
to the present fleet."

Bennett moved a step or two forward, his hands dropping
to his side. His eyes rested for a moment on Sir William, then
turned away. "Neither former governor nor Council shall be
obliged to take oath or engagement to the Commonwealth of
England for one whole year; nor in that time shall governor
or Council be censured for speaking well of the King in their
private houses or neighbourhood conferences.

"Three men of the present governor's choice shall be sent
home to give account of this surrender.

"The Royal Governor Sir William Berkeley and his Council
have leave to sell or dispose of estates and transport themselves where they please, and shall have equal and free
justice. They may hire a ship for England or Holland to
carry away their goods. Wherever they go, they will not be
troubled or arrested.

"I may add here that this is not an act of banishment such
as was formerly exercised in the Virginia government. It is
presumed that the aforementioned will desire of their own
will to leave.

The governor did not wait for the stirring and whispering
to subside. His tone was strong and firm as he continued,
"All persons now in this colony, of whatsoever quality or
condition, who have served the King here or in England,
shall be free from all danger of punishment here or else-
where."

"Very lenient," Cecily said to Peter. "I hope Sir William
sees the difference."

Bennett went on: "No person in a court of justice in Virginia shall be questioned about his loyalties.

"The Book of Common Prayer will be permitted for a year, provided those things which related to kingship be omitted when used publicly.

"Quit-rents granted unto us by the late King for seven years shall be confirmed. Any goods coming into port on order shall be free.

"The Act of Indemnity and Oblivion is in force so that the inhabitants of this colony shall live in peace, quietly and securely under this government.

"These Articles bear the seal of the Commonwealth and the signature of Richard Bennett, William Claiborne and Robert Denis.

"Ladies and gentlemen, that concludes my message to you."

The clerk gave a signal. A bugle sounded. The people stood while the governor and his Council walked in procession from the church. Those inside did not stir until Richard Bennett had entered a waiting carriage and been driven off, his guard and soldiers following him in orderly procession.

When the carriage turned, Sir William Berkeley, looking neither to right nor left, strode out and got into his carriage. Surrounded by his escort, he drove away to his manor-house of Green Spring. He was thinking about those Dutch vessels that were trading in the James River. They were beholden to him, they were armed, and they might be pressed into service. He would see.

Relieved of the presence of two governors, the audience gave voice to their thoughts. They streamed from the church and filled the churchyard in groups to release their feelings.

"A noble pronouncement . . . as fine a document as we have seen in our time . . . lenient . . . turn the other cheek . . . Don't you recall how Sir William banished him to Maryland because he was Puritan and believed in Cromwell? . . . A Christlike man . . . too weak . . . We shall come upon troublous times. . . . Did you note the Indian chiefs seated on the right and the Ancient Planters in front rows? . . . Someone planned this; it smacks of a play."

"Doubtless young Bennett. He's been in London. He must have attended the theatre in the old days."

"I've been told he was rather a gay blade in London. . . .

Nothing was said about cutting tobacco acreage. Are you cutting down?"

"Not I, but Cary is. He's going to raise more corn. He thinks we'll get a better price if we grade."

"Have you seen Nathaniel Batts since he came up from the south? He's having good luck with tobacco using Rolfe's methods."

And so the conversation went on in the churchyard. In the village the people moved to the Parade where the new troops were drilling, as smart and snappy as King's men.

Presently the watch went through the town ringing his bell. "Governor Bennett has ordered the release of all prisoners from gaols, stocks, pillories or ducking-stools, with the exception only of political prisoners, and those held for the crimes of rape, sodomy and murder."

The crowds surged toward the public stocks. Timothy Tiddler, sleeping peacefully on a bench, his legs stretched out before him, woke with a start, and with blows of his sturdy fists fought off the good-humoured gaoler, who came with his great jingling keys to release him.

The maid Tamar, one of the governor's servants, hung her head, allowing her long raven-black hair to fall over her tear-stained face when she was released from the gaol, where she had been for a fortnight because she had refused to tell the name of the father of her still-born child. The crowd cried, "Scarlet woman! Magdalen!" as she hurried away toward the Back Swamp.

Richard watched her. He thought he had never seen such agony in a human being as looked out of her tragic eyes under heavy brows that grew almost together.

Digby said, "Poor wench! They're hard on a transgressing woman in these parts."

Richard did not answer, but the lines in his forehead deepened. "God curse such hypocrites!" he muttered.

They were standing at the dock where the sloop was tied up. They went on board. A Negro waterman smiled his welcome. "They is makin' a big fuss about our massa, now ain't they?"

Digby grinned back at the Negro. "A big fuss. You are right, Enoch. Here, unbuckle this armour, my lad." He took the breast-plate the man unlaced and dropped it on a thwart. "Good riddance!" He addressed Richard: "This old dragoon soft as a stripling. I thought I'd have dropped to the floor when the clerk read out the names. I was squirming and trying to ease the pressure against my ribs. Yes, it's soft, I am. 'd not march from Scotland to Worcester like this."

Richard did not answer. He stood at the rail and gazed moodily across the water. Digby looked at him anxiously. He tepped to his side and unlaced the breast-plate. The head-iece he hung by a thong to a wooden peg behind the door. Ie fussed about, casting furtive, anxious glances at Richard. 'Fussin' like an old hen," he muttered to himself.

Enoch had retired to the little galley. He came up with a plate of loblolly and cold appones. He approached Richard. "Sar, better you eat here than there. So many people runnin' bout lookin' for food. Massa says, eat first . . . no come back to ship until middle of night."

Richard took the pewter plate and sat down at the table. "So the galley slaves have shore leave. How kind! How ex-ceedingly kind!"

The Negro did not observe the bitterness in the indentured man's voice. He said, "Yes, Massa kind. Always kind. Not ike massa at next plant'n. He whip and scourge and do evil every day. . . . You eat, sar, then go to town. . . . Women down that-a-way—" he waved his hand to a strip of beach at he east end of town—" 'way down, past cypress trees."

Digby said, "Well, whatever! So there are whores in this New World."

The Negro shook his head, not understanding the word. "Women, playful women, who make very merry with white men and soldiers."

Richard spat, disgusted, but Digby laughed. " 'Playful women.' Very apt. Very apt indeed."

Richard leaped to the dock and Digby followed. The cap-tain's mood is not good, Digby thought. I must watch over him, lest he say or do something untoward to injure himself. It must be hard for the captain to place himself in his mind as an indentured man, open to insult, neglect, even injustice. A man is what he thinks he is, and the captain certainly does not think himself the slave he has now become.

The sight that met their eyes as the gaol spewed forth its inhabitants! This man with his ears half cut away, that one branded on the forehead with T for Thief! An ill-bitten crew, as mean and uncouth as any denizens of the Clink in London!

A thief is a thief in any language, and the brand was there in shifty eyes and evil expression.

"Thompson's Ordinary is the place for small beer, sir," Digby said, breaking the long silence. "I've been told 'tis good beer and not watered. The labouring folk go there to drink and talk, and one picks up gossip."

"You learn quickly, my man."

"Aye. Eyes and ears open. 'Tis this way up to the fourth ridge. There's a pit barbecue, where an oxen is roasting, and little pigs. Free, sir, to show the generosity of the new governor."

They left the sloop, followed a lane to the Back Street and walked in the direction of the swamp. It was in this quiet lane that Richard saw Kathryn. She was on horseback with a group of riders. They were galloping along the road with such speed that the common folk had to jump to get out of the way of flying hoofs.

Richard stepped to the hedge, but Digby was obliged to leap to the opposite side and found himself caught in a brier patch. Richard's anger rose easily these days. He caught the bridle of the last horse. He jerked so violently that the horse stopped in its tracks and the rider, a woman, all but slipped from the saddle. She raised her whip and brought it down smartly on his knuckles. He looked up.

"Richard!" Kathryn cried, her face white. "Oh, Richard! I did not know. Oh, Richard, I am sorry, so sorry."

His voice was scathing. "So you did not recognize your equals. It was just a poor devil who got in your way."

"How can you be so cruel?" she whispered, fighting to keep the tears out of her eyes. "Why do you blame me? Oh, Richard, I had nothing to do . . ."

"Who then turned me over to the guard in Bristol after Nick wounded me in the garden?"

She stared at him, her blue eyes wide. "Not I, Richard, I swear. By my hope of heaven I swear."

"Swear not to me, my girl."

She leaned down. "Oh, why did you say such things to Nick that day? He will never forgive."

"Say things to Nick? I remember nothing of saying things— only of steel meeting steel to my sorrow." He tossed his head. The long black locks fell aside. The line of the scar stood out, angry red.

She put her hand to her heart. "I tried to prevent it. Truly I did. I pleaded with you to go away, but you must stay and insult him, calling him 'coward, betrayer' and other names I cannot speak."

Richard laughed grimly. "I have no recollection, but I am glad my fevered brain spoke the truth." He stood off, allowing the reins to drop from his hand. The quivering horse shied away.

Kathryn tugged at the reins. "I must talk with you, Richard. Nick is leaving tomorrow for Maryland with Mr. Claiborne. I must explain."

He looked at her steadily. "And you would make a cuckold of your husband? I did not think such evil of you."

Kathryn's face was white, her eyes blazing. "I wish I had laid my whip on your face instead of your hand."

He laughed shortly and took a step toward her, turning his cheek. "The other cheek," he said. "A scar from milady's whip would honour a poor servant."

The raised whip veered and fell on the horse's flank. The animal leaped forward and galloped down the lane.

And suddenly Richard's conscience smote him as he thought of the gold she had given Digby for him. "Where is that ordinary?" he said harshly to the gaping Digby. "I have a desire to drink to a lost lady." Digby looked at him curiously, for he knew the lady well, but he made no comment.

The tables were jammed with roistering, noisy men, drinking the health of the new governor. Free beer, free food, free prisoners—surely a day to celebrate! After a time Digby found a table that two men were leaving. He beckoned to Richard who seated himself while Digby made his way to the bar.

The barmaid looked at him sharply. "The colour of your money first, man. I do not know you."

"Nor I you, my wench, though I say it to my sorrow."

The buxom, rosy-cheeked barmaid laughed, showing two dimples and white even teeth. "You're a quick one. Where do you come from?"

Digby jerked his thumb over his shoulder. "Across the river," he said.

"Oh, one of the Puritans!" She tossed her head.

"I ain't sayin'." Digby laid a coin on the bar. "Two tankards. My friend has a thirst."

The girl looked at Richard who sat staring at the table. "Who's the handsome?" she asked. "He be stranger too."

"Same as me, over the water."

The girl looked at the innkeeper. He was at the far side of the room, his back to them. She pushed the coin toward Digby and nodded to a door back of the bar. "Bring your friend. There's a quiet room in the garden. We like men from over the water around here."

"You're quick too. What's your name?"

"Jennifer. They call me Jenny." She leaned over the bar, careful that none should hear. "Worcester?"

"Aye, Worcester."

She stepped from behind the bar and opened a door. "Bring your friend," she whispered. Aloud she called to a boy who was polishing glasses at the end of the bar. "Take my place, Bill. I'll be gone for a minute."

Digby beckoned to Richard, who joined them and the three went through the door. Following a long passage, they skirted the busy kitchen and found themselves in a neat little garden, at the end of which was a garden-house.

Jenny knocked at the door. It was opened by the brawny farrier. "Mr. Morgan," she said, "I've brought two men who live over the water."

The man scrutinized Richard, then Digby, with shrewd hard eyes. "I do not know them," he said shortly.

The girl was unabashed by his terseness. "I said they came from *over the water*. I might add they live at Bennett's Welcome."

The man said nothing, staring at them. His rugged massive features showed nothing, and his eyes remained wary.

Jenny went on: "Indentured," and after a long pause she added, "Worcester."

The farrier's face broke instantly into a broad smile. "Enter, men, enter and have a mug of ale with us. Worcester is as good a password as there be anywhere. Enter, my lads. You'll find like company within."

Jenny said, "I'll bring a bit of hot cheese when I fetch more ale. Thompson's treating today, as well as the new governor."

"When'll the oxmeat be ready, lass?" a man called out. "I'm fair starving, I am."

"Be patient, Benny. You'll have your share."

"I dunno. Now that gaol has been emptied, there mayn't be food for honest folk."

The girl laughed and ran off toward the house. Richard walked in and stood with his back to the fire, well aware of the scrutiny. He realized that they were among King's men. How Digby had managed this he did not know or question.

After a time a brawny chap moved up to Richard and spoke in broad Scotch. "Did 'ee ere hear of Boscobel?"

"Yes, and of five brothers."

"Dost recollect their names?"

"Yes, Penderel, and one of them Trusty Dick." He smiled a little at the obvious questioning, so he added something for good measure. "And a long march from Stirling." No one spoke, but the silence was filled with expectancy. "Aye, I recall too a bonny lad with long black curls riding a great black horse."

"And where was that, maybe?"

" 'Twas near a city gate . . . and near by was a sly fox named——"

"Name no names."

Richard persisted. "Do you recollect a man named Leslie?"

"Aye, I do, the scoundrel! He nae moved a step but sat his horse like a wooden image, he and his men."

"But they rode north." Richard took a long pipe from the rack. A man sprang forward with tobacco to fill it. Puffing, Richard looked about the room. Face after face he gazed at. After a time he said, "He is over the water. My friend Digby here found that out in Devon."

Digby said, "That I did. 'Twas a merry chase, but the fox got away." The men settled back; the tension relaxed.

The Scot said, "Your name, if you care to speak it?"

To Digby's surprise Richard said, "Monington, but here I am Richard ap Richards."

An older man, obviously a gentleman, with a heavily lined face and slim delicate hands, said, "Monington is a Herefordshire name."

Richard nodded. "Yes, close to Ledbury."

The gentlemen smiled and said in dialect, "Today's a proper rawdy, fiddles squeaking, folk in the fields a-dancing, lassies with ribbands flying—aye, and the constable and the churchwarden having a peck of trouble over a net to catch crows and other vermin." He looked up expectantly.

"A chafnet," Richard filled in, "and instead of a crow catched me a hoop's head and a furchett's head."

The Scot slapped his leathern-clad thigh. " 'Tis a Herefordshire man, nae doubt of that, as Herefordshire as cider when it frets. Have nae fear, me lads."

Richard leaned forward. "Didst read ye in *Fergus' Letters* the true relation of the infant child found in the field near Leominster last July?"

"Nae. Nae, I never did."

"The infant spoke and declared strange words. It said great things would come true—in three years the destruction of Parliament and the crowning of young Charles."

There was a long silence. Men pulled at their pipes and blew great clouds of smoke until the small room grew heavy with the tingling, acrid vapour.

"And since you test me, I'll tell you another Herefordshire tale. When Charles the First, the Martyred King, was prisoner in a manor-house in Stratton, an old man, the parson of the parish, uncovered, lifted his cider cup to drink His Majesty's health. 'God bless our Gracious Sovereign!' says he. He was about to put the cup to his mouth when a miracle occurred. A little swift flew in, perched on the cup, put his bill into the cup to drink, then flew away. 'Even the birds,' we say in Herefordshire."

A gentleman said, "The test is ample. As for me, I was with Scudamore's Horse—" Digby's ears pricked up—"when old Hopton and his Parliamentarians chased us out of Ledbury. Humiliating, that was; a fair humiliation, and I know everything this man says to be true."

Richard frowned. "Have done with questioning. I am what I say I am. I was taken prisoner after Worcester, indentured and shipped out of Bristol. I take it that you are all . . . ?" He raised his brows.

"Aye, but do not name it. We're in Virginia now."

The farrier said, "Sir, by your speech you were an officer."

Digby answered, "Aye, that he was. And I was a dragoon in Scudamore's Horse. He will not allow me to say 'zur' to him."

Richard grinned. "In Virginia all men are equal."

"Like hell!" someone muttered.

The farrier said, "Do you not think wrong. We are not conspirators. We accept what comes, but . . ."

The Scot said, "The governor lives at Green Spring, not at Bennett's Welcome—just the same as the King is across the Channel, not in London."

" 'Tis true, so let's drink." Every man rose to his feet.

The Scot said, "To a wee lad who's never the chance to sit on his rightful seat, except for a brief time at—" he raised his tankard high—"Scone."

His cup raised, Richard replied, "Love Charles to the heart!" and sat down, feeling that he had wiped away some of the depression that weighed so heavily on him.

The farrier said, "I think 'ee should ride to Green Spring."

Richard shook his head. "We go aboard the sloop at midnight." He sat down at a table. The Scot, whose name was MacInlesher, sat by him. They talked in low tones of Worcester and the lost battle. Richard said never a word about his share in the King's flight. The men looked honest, but . . .

The old gentleman with the delicate hands joined them. "I've been here many years," he said. "I've all but forgotten the green meadows, the orchards and the hop-picking. I'm from the west, close to the Marches of Wales, sir." He looked down at his hands. "I'm an Ancient Planter. My name is Matthew Caswell. I like it well here, but sometimes I yearn for a sight of the mountains and the high green valleys."

The girl Jenny came in with toasted cheese on bread and a jug of ale. "The ox is roasted in the pit, sir. They say it's fair good." Several of the men left, nodding farewell to the new-comers, casually, without suspicion.

The Scot ate his cheese, finished his mug and left. The farrier followed. "You'll hear from us from time to time," he said to Richard. "If you come to Jamestown, a word with Jenny will fetch us."

Digby went outside, walked under the grape arbour with Jenny to the door of the ordinary. Richard heard her laugh at some sally of the dragoon's.

Caswell said, "I live up the James. I have a holding there, left to me by my uncle who was one of the shareholders of the Virginia Company. Come to me, if you need help. Anyone in Jamestown knows my plantation, close to Jordan's Journey and Flowerdew Hundred."

"Thank you, sir. I imagine I won't have many opportunities to get away from Bennett's."

An enigmatic smile came over the man's lips. "I know many a sea captain, sir. A wide acquaintance with seafaring folk is not too bad these troublesome days."

Richard thanked him. After a pause Caswell said, "I saw you in the lane a bit ago. I am not an eavesdropper, but I could not help being on the other side of the hedge. Newcomers are carefully scrutinized in Virginia. Nicholas Holder is known, and his wife also. . . . But do you know her maiden name?"

Surprised, Richard answered, "Kathryn Audley, ward of Sir Robert Harley. I knew them in Herefordshire."

"Audley? I might have known she wouldn't bear her own name."

"Her own name? What do you mean, sir?" Richard spoke quickly, roused by the hostility in the man's voice.

"Her rightful name is Bradshaw."

Richard started to rise, then sat down again. To every Royalist that name was a by-word and a hissing. "Bradshaw? Are you certain?"

"I have reason to believe it, Mr. Monington."

Richard repeated the name, his voice deep: "Bradshaw the Regicide?"

"Aye, the traitor. Not his daughter, but of the blood of that man who presided at the trial of Charles the First, of blessed memory, denying him the right to speak in his own defense, and who, above all men, was responsible for his death. You think I am intruding to tell you this? Betrayal is in the blood of the Bradshaws, betrayal and disloyalty. Judas blood! I call it the blood of traitors."

"But, sir, why did she change her name?"

"You'll remember Sir Robert Harley stood for the King at first. He despised Bradshaw for taking the Parliament side. He never could abide Bradshaw's violent ways. When they were children he made Kathryn and her brother Roland take his mother's name. He brought them to Audley Court and gave Kathryn the deed to it and the land around it. For Roland he made other provision. It was all kept very secret. . . . And now, sir, I must be leaving. I am riding to Green Spring tonight." He shook hands with a firm strong grasp and without waiting for questions went away.

Richard's mind was in a whirl. He sat back and looked long into the fire. The desire that was earlier upon him, to drink himself into oblivion, had left. The day had held much to fill his thoughts: the beaten look on the girl Tamar's face . . . the outraged fire in Kathryn Holder's glance . . . the unspoken bewilderment in the minds of Berkeley's conspirators, outthought by Bennett whom they had called a simpleton . . . now this strange revelation about Kathryn.

How could this planter, three thousand miles away, have information that had been concealed for years from Kathryn's neighbours in Herefordshire? He must know more before he could believe it. . . . Still it fitted in with things he had begun to suspect about Kathryn's character.

He walked out into the garden. The glow from the pit where the oxen were roasting showed shadow figures moving back and forth. He heard snatches of rowdy songs and, beyond the hedge, sounds of revelry. It was like a market day in England, a fair, a field full of folk; only the puppet-show was lacking, and the mummers who came on Whitsun Monday to give a little morality play.

He heard a woman's shrill laughter and Jenny's gay voice. "I says it the same to all of them. Digby, keep your hands off me. A kiss or two is no harm at all, but no hands roaming over me body."

Digby laughed. "A kiss then, me lass, and another for luck."

Smothered laughter of men and women came to Richard. Everywhere was the sound of carefree gaiety and rejoicing. He did not heed. Caswell's words were in his ears, beating through his brain, words that burned like fire. He was insensible to the jollity around him. "Judas blood—that's what I call it—the blood of traitors."

CHAPTER 18

Money Crop

THE weeks that followed the Governor's Day at Jamestown passed quickly at Bennett's Welcome.

The governor came and departed at frequent intervals, taking his family and Stephen with him on his sloop, visiting the counties, talking tobacco curtailment. Making friends for Cromwell was his object, working for the good of the people.

Since there was no paper-work to be done, Richard was sent by the overseer to the tobacco fields, while Digby went to the forest with the wood-choppers, to clear more land.

At sunrise, hoe over his shoulder, he joined the indentured men on the way to the fields. Two Negroes went with them, carrying baskets of tiny tobacco plants pulled that morning from the seed-beds. The men chaffed and told tales, for the overlooker was not present. They tried to engage Richard in their loose talk, but after a civil greeting he remained silent.

"A morose fellow of ill humour," a red-headed bondsman said loud enough for Richard to hear.

"Let him alone," an older man said. "He's new from home. Recollect how you were when you first came, damning and cursing. You can laugh now. Six months to go and you'll get your fifty acres along some creek."

"No creek for me. I'm going south to get my land on a deep river. I've signed with Clerk Greene. I'll get a hundred, maybe two," said Redhead.

"What 'ee talkin' about?"

"Ha'n't ye heard? Mr. Greene, he got a grant from Sir William for ten or eleven thousand acres in the south, if 'e gets a hundred settlers."

"Whatever! Ten thousand acres?" The older man was sceptical.

"Yes, and rivers still open. A man don't have to take to the miserable creeks, with the Ancients and the gentry taking all the good river land around here. Where you been, man, that you haven't heard of Mr. Nathaniel Batts's grant, right where two rivers form a monstrous river that ends up on the Island of Roanoke?"

"Never heard a word," the older man grunted, "never a word."

"If you'd hang around the office after work with your long ears cocked, instead of spending your nights lying in with women, you'd have something."

The laughter that followed this sally was loud and raucous. The older fellow was known to be under the spell of Meg the weaver.

Richard listened. This was not the first time he had heard talk of the land to the south, the richest bottom land, where there was no tobacco cessation in effect. . . . What if one stole off in the dark of the night?

They had come to the field to be planted. The long rows were already ploughed, hilled and ready for the young tender plants to be placed in the earth. The overlooker rode up astride a white mule. The talking ceased. Each man leaned on his hoe, waiting.

The overlooker, whose eyes were bloodshot from a night's secret debauch, barked out orders. "Eph, go ahead of this fellow with the poking stick and make the holes. Puti, you follow and pour water where the plants are set. Don't drown them or you'll get ten of the finest." His sharp light-blue eyes went up and down Richard's tall figure. "So you're a field-hand now, my fine fellow. Well, see that the plants are set properly, and no fudging or loitering! The whip would whine pretty on those broad shoulders of yours."

Richard boiled but said nothing. He took the basket of plants a man handed to him, and started down the field. If the rascal was trying to goad him into anger, let him try. It was back-breaking work, straddling the row, bending to place the plants in the holes Eph made with two sticks tied together. Eph would press them into the soft earth, draw them apart slowly, making a puncture of just the right depth and size to receive the young roots. How uniform the apertures, how skilful the young boy was in keeping the line straight, the holes at proper distance! Richard knew himself the awkward one, as he endeavoured not to damage the tender plants, to keep the delicate tendrils of the roots straight, to press the earth gently with his fingers, so that when Puti poured water on each plant, the little mound of earth would cling and not be washed away, leaving the plant to bend over and wither.

By the end of the first row Richard was working more easily. He wondered how long it had taken to plant one long furrow. He glanced at the long field, girded by the deep woods of the swamp. . . . A hundred rows . . . a thousand. How long had it taken him? . . . A shadow fell over the ground; he smelled mule sweat. . . . "Too slow by half, Richards. Speed up!"

Richard moved up to the next opening. The overlooker raised his voice. "Speed up I said, Welshie. And look at me when I speak!"

Richard raised himself and looked up at the "Fox," as he and Digby called the fellow secretly. Unconsciously his hand went to the small of his back.

A thin smile crossed the man's face. "Aye, more wearying to the back than bending over office books, but healthier. I don't doubt me that the red on your skin will flame in your sleep tonight. Now step up. You've thousands of plants to set in the ground the next three days. Do you want the Nigras to set a pace you can't meet?"

Richard didn't care whether a black man or a white man beat him at his task, but he returned to work. He pressed forward more rapidly. The second row went better. When the sun was at the meridian, a bell rang. The hands in the north field, who were chopping the grass in the bean rows, planted their hoes upright and sprinted to the edge of the field. Richard finished a row and eased his tired back. Eph and Puti went tracing down the field.

He saw Angela and her helpers with baskets and jugs, doling out food and drink. He had no wish for food; he walked over to the side of the field and sat down with his back to a wild mulberry tree. His eyes closed. He knew nothing until he felt a tug at his sleeve. Puti's voice said, "Buckra, buckra, buckra, buckra." The boy was grinning. In one hand he held a packet wrapped in a napkin, in the other a stone mug of sour milk. "Angela sent. She say, less you eat, less you work."

Richard unwrapped the cloth—a chunk of warm meal-bread and a bit of yellow cheese. He ate the coarse bread and drank the milk. The cheese he gave to Puti, who ate it hungrily.

"Angela, she say I'se got hollow legs." Puti showed his strong white teeth. "Hongry all de time. Ready, sar?"

Eph was ahead of them, pressing little openings into the ground. He now had the basket and laid the plant beside the hole, so that Richard's only task was to set the plant. The lad was helping him, making his task lighter. That was because the overlooker took a nap after his heavy dinner.

It was sundown when the bell rang again. This time the hands did not run away. They stood in the fields, their hands clasped in the attitude of prayer, their heads bowed. The plantation bell became the Angelus. Richard remembered a visit he'd once paid to the Low Countries and the people praying at sunset. A new thought came to him: We are pagans. We face the morning sun like the old Picts. We say farewell to the departing sun at eventide. . . . Nevertheless, his lips formed the words, "O Lord, give me strength to bear my afflictions!"

He made his way to the little cottage. Digby had not come in from the woods. A tin of steaming water was on the hearth. He stripped off his clothes and sponged the sweat from his body—honest sweat from honest toil. How often had he heard the words without understanding their true meaning! His face was hot and burned like fire, and his back flesh seemed to throb under the hot skin. The pressure of a clean shirt was unbearable. He put on clean cotton underdrawers, allowed him by his master, and threw himself onto his cot. He was asleep when his head touched the rough pillow.

After a long, dreamless sleep he awoke. He heard Angela's voice. "Lightly, son, lightly, lessn you break a blister."

He sat up. Puti was bathing his back with water that stung. "Master, 'twill burn, that old vinegar, but 'twill ease, and tomorrow the red will be brown. Always like this, first time."

Richard had the wit to thank them, then fell back on the pillow, fast asleep.

He was still asleep when Digby returned from his supper. When he awakened, it was morning. Digby was smiling broadly at him from across the room where he was pulling on his shirt. "All night you slept without moving, zur."

"Without dreams," Richard said, wonder in his voice, "without dreams."

" 'Tis as it should be. You will be stiff in the muscles and the sinews, the thighs and back will groan, and so the arms, but in a day or two you will not notice."

"My fingers are stiff as though they were frozen," Richard said, "and there is Virginia earth under my finger-nails."

"Zur, you are no longer a gentleman!"

Richard sprang out of bed, but his hand went to his back with a groan.

"Easy! Easy!" Digby cautioned. "Here is Puti with your ration."

"And yours?"

"Hours ago," Digby said. "Come. Hasten. That devil 'Fox' will be in the field before we get there." He made a gesture of cracking a long whip; he clacked his tongue.

The second day was easier. Richard got onto the hang of the thing; there was a rhythm to it, like the long sweep of the scythe or the turn of a sickle. How often he had seen field work go on under his eyes without knowing what effort lay behind hop-picking or binding sheaves or loading corn into a cart!

That night again his sleep was dreamless. The heat went out of his skin; the red turned to brown.

In the morning Puti brought him a braided straw hat with an ample rim. "Angela say she make up out of reeds, jus' lak San John's." He pushed a wet cloth into the tall crown. "He keep out the strong sun."

The tobacco was set in all the fields by the end of the week. On Sunday a gentle rain fell, just right for the plants. Warm, sunny days followed, growing weather. The Fox passed him by. The third week he sent Richard out with the choppers to cut weeds from the corn. Here again was rhythm—short sharp strokes of a dozen hoes in unison. Negroes and whites moved along the rows. The Negroes sang as they worked, not from overflow of cheerful feeling, but to time the stroke. The song they sang, set in a minor key, buried itself in his consciousness: "Bird of freedom, you have sold me, sold me."

Digby still worked in the woods. He liked that; there was clear time during the day without the overlooker. The men talked and he gleaned tales and rumours, which he repeated to Richard at night after Thomas Chapman had gone to his bed. The Old One came every night and sat a spell on the bench by the side of the door. He talked of old times, especially of the massacre of '22, when dozens of good men and women on the south side of the James had met their death horribly and in frightful agony. He was saved, he told them, by hiding in a hollow log, a bee log, he found out, but his fear was so great that he had no sensation of being stung until the next day when his face was bloated to double size.

He talked of Governor Yeardley, whom he greatly admired, and of his wife, whose name was Tempérance Fleur de Dieu. He gave it the French accent. She was a pretty young girl who lived at Fleur Dieu Hundred with her family. Yeardley was the Captain of the Guard, an upstanding young fellow. He wooed Mistress Tempérance ardently, but she would have none of him. "Go home to England and get yourself made a knight, and I'll think on it."

And so he did. He became Sir George Yeardley and came back Governor of the Colony, and young Tempérance was "My Lady," which pleased her mightily.

"There is a Yeardley in Jamestown now," Digby remarked, knocking the dottle from his pipe.

"Aye, Argoll. 'Tis the governor's son. A good fellow, but not so strong as his father. In truth, the young men these days seem to lack strength. They're weaker. Things seem to grow too easy. No warring Indians . . . no dangers to face. I tell you, young sirs, a man was a man in those days of Captain John Smith and Newport and John Rolfe."

"And the Princess Pocahontas?" Digby asked slyly.

"Yes, and Pocahontas. Though you call women weak, she had the heart of a lioness." He sighed and rose stiffly. "I'm mighty old," he mumbled as he walked away to his cottage.

"Perhaps the Old One is right," Richard said as he smoked his bed-time pipe. "The planters early in the century weren't so strong as the Elizabethans, we're not so strong as they, and so it goes. Where will England end, if each generation finds us weaker?"

Digby did not reply. He had come to know that these little comments that Richard made about life, or people, or politics, required no answer. But he was pleased that the captain took to work so readily. "It's the Devon in you," he said one day when Richard made some remark about the soil and the growth of crops. "Devon is a good country. Even the rocks be good for field walls."

"Herefordshire is pastoral also," Richard reminded him.

"Zur, there's naught like Devon, yet I note that the land here is fertile. The bog, which these quare folk call a pocosin, is fair overrun with berries and with grape-vines that have trunks as thick as my arm and height to the top of a tall tree. There's wine to be made in the autumn." He smiled a little. "The indentured can make it if they like. The next plantation down-river has vats and all."

It was late May. The daylight was longer now and the days hot; but at night a breeze came off the river, strong enough to blow away the buzzing, biting flies. The crops were all set. The May pease were ready for the picking. That was women's task; they walked down the rows and squatted on their haunches, filling their reed baskets.

The manor-house was closed. Digby reported that the governor had bought Sir William Berkeley's house in Jamestown. The State House, it was called, and all the governors from bad Sir John Harvey down had lived there—until the seasoning fever came in the summer, that is. Then they moved down to the shore at Kiquotan.

Richard had not glimpsed Stephen Bennett for some weeks; rumour had it that he was building a new house on his plantation because he would be wed in the autumn.

One day Digby came in with a packet in his hand. His eyes were bright, his smile was broad. "It's good news. I bring letters, no less." He handed the packet to Richard. "Luck was with us when I went out to meet the sailing ship that tied up at our landing to unload goods from England. 'Twas a good Devon man who captained her. I had heard that he was inquiring for one Richard Monington. I said I knew not that name on the river, but I managed a wink, and he invited me to his cabin for a dram. Once behind locked doors, I told him the tale. 'Twas good, was it not, that he did not go shouting your name in Jamestown?"

"Very good indeed, Digby, and I thank you." Richard broke the seal. " 'Tis from John Prideaux."

"Aye, now that Master Willetts knows all the facts, he will doubtless send some word to your lady mother when he returns to Bideford."

Richard rose to his feet. "I must get to the office for quill and ink and a bit of paper, to write to my mother."

"Read the letter, zur. The ship has sailed to Jamestown Island, but the master will stop when he comes down-river a fortnight hence. So read your letter, zur."

Digby left the room. Richard broke the last seal with nervous haste. It was a long letter, closely written. John wrote that he was at New House in Cornwall. He had not seen Dame Monington for weeks, but from friends heard she was living in the Dower House at Buckland Brewer and was in good health. He continued:

Our friend Phil Blount has departed for Virginia. You'll remember him from old days in the West Country. He has some relatives at Blount Point on the James. Perhaps you have already seen him. He knows you are in Virginia and will search for you. We have had no news since you were deported from Bristol.

As for affairs here, they are not to the liking of all people. My brother and I are sailing our boat along the coast. The fishing is not too good, but we hope for better luck. There is talk of war with the Dutch. One cannot be sure. Some say we are in bad state. Pirates roam the seas and engage our commerce. The wars have made the people so poor that the prisons teem with debtors. A man may now be hung for the theft of six and sixpence. But the army flourishes. They say we have thirty regiments of Foot and eighteen of Horse, plus the dragoons—more than fifty thousand men in all.

The unhappy Royalists are crowding the Tower. Lawyers who negotiate for them are in ill favour and clapped into prison.

The Lord General is very gentle, yet firm in the plan to dissolve Parliament. I hear that the Council is planning great things for Virginia, to bolster trade, which is very low at this time. We do not have many friends on the continent. . . .

A query that puzzles all: are we to have foreign wars? My father says, 'Foreign wars and great changes at home do not march hand in hand.'

Some of the disgruntled soldiers have presented petitions to the government asking about the promised reforms; and they want their pay. Some say Oliver will be crowned King before the year is out.

I am sending this by an honest captain from Bideford. I
pray you are in health, my friend, and in good heart. The
man at Boscobel has been heard from. The tree has not been
cut and the branches are still spreading.

>   With affection, your cousin,
>   J. Prideaux

To
Mr. Richard Monington
in the Colony of Virginia,
at Jamestown

Richard reread the letter before he put it down. He understood the allusion to the spreading oak to mean that the
King was safe and that the Royalists had not given up hope.

Strange how far away it all seemed! It was as though a
curtain had dropped on a stage, and a new act was being
played. The past month he had not given heed to anything
but the work he was doing. The daylight brought thought
only of the plantation work. At night he came home too
weary to do aught but seek his cot and sleep as one drugged.

Lately he had gone direct from the fields to supper with
the other indentured men. This was Digby's plan. "It's best
not to be apart from them. The time may come when help
will be needed." Digby talked constantly about escape on
some ship. But how was that to be accomplished when every
ship was searched before it sailed past the Capes?

The money was safe. Digby had built a little box on top
of the king beam. So skilfully had he hidden it in a little
hollow that no sign of it could be seen from any place in
the room. With enough gold broads a captain might be
bought, who would pick them up somewhere along the beach
after the ship had passed through inspection at the Capes.
This was Digby's idea.

Every day Digby had a new scheme for getting away, but
none with merit. Richard had no hope of escape. Instead,
he was trying to adjust himself to an indenture of four
years. They had learned in Jamestown that four was the
limit now. The old seven-year term had been cancelled. Four
years were not too long, and in the meantime something
might happen in England to change the situation.

Strangely enough he had thought little of his encounter
with Kathryn, or the momentary shock of finding that her

true name was Bradshaw. More often he thought of the meeting in the garden-house behind the tavern. He felt no obligation or loyalty to Governor Bennett or Stephen. He had not been badly treated so far, but if the Fox ever had full control at Bennett's Welcome, he knew things would be different. The low-caste man would delight in holding the whip over his betters.

He had learned many things from the Ancient Planter, who despised the Fox. "A lecherous beast," he called him. The Fox bedded with the indentured women, who were afraid to complain. A woman had a right to go to court if she was with child by a master or an overlooker, but the Quarters Court was not likely to take the word of an indentured woman against her master. Usually they gave the woman some stripes and ordered her sold to another master. But few complained, leastwise at Bennett's Welcome. There were heavy penalties against runaway slaves, black or white; sometimes the indenture term was doubled. To try to run away was not worth the risk, Richard thought. At that, it was better in Virginia than in Maryland, for the runaway could be executed in Maryland or branded with an "R" on the cheek.

No, the only hope was a ship's captain who could be trusted; or a recruitment, like those that took place in the West Indies, where the Navy pressed any servants they liked, indentured or not, in spite of the violent protest of the planters who had paid cash for them.

Richard had just secreted the letter in the sea-chest Digby had made for him, when he heard Thomas Chapman step onto the rough planks of the piazza. Digby, who was outside, said, "Sit here, sir. There is a gentle breeze from the river." The chair creaked when the old man seated himself. Richard stepped out and laid a hand lightly on his shoulder. He had become fond of the cheerful sightless man, who had developed such a fine philosophy of living.

"Good evening to you, sir. What news have you for us the even?"

"Not too much. Only that young Master Stephen will be with us soon. 'Tis said that he will wed in the autumn when the work of the plantation is slack and his new house is finished."

Digby got a pipe, filled it and handed it to the old man. The

Ancient Planter took a puff or two. " 'Tis strange, but when one is blind, smoking does not taste so favourable as it once did. But in spite of all, I still say, 'God bless Sir Walter Raleigh!' "

"I thought it was Sir Richard Grenville who took the weed to England," Richard observed.

"Now that is singular. Tom Blount, down at Blount's Point, always said the same thing. But Tom, he be a contentious man, keen to argue a point. A body never knows whether he believes what he is arguing or no. 'Tis said he's got himself a grant of land in the south, though what he wants with more than he's already got is beyond me."

"An Englishman always wants more land," Digby said. He had seated himself on the steps, his back to a pillar that upheld the sloping roof. "Leastways that's so in Devon."

The old man nodded. "It's a hunger, land is, a great driving hunger that has got many a man into trouble. Take here in Virginia. The people who came early got the choice parcels along the great rivers. The late ones get only the creek lands. Now they talk about the bottom lands south on the Chowan River and on the great sound that they used to call Raleigh's River. I don't quite know what they call it now."

"How far away is this south they talk about?"

"Nigh a hundred miles, about the space across the waist of England."

They all smoked in silence for a time. Then the Ancient Planter spoke. " 'Tis said that our governor has turned the keys and opened the gaol, and the felons had spilled out all over the town."

"An old custom when a new King is crowned," Richard said.

"Aye, and a bad one, turning 'em loose on the respectable citizens, to plifer and commit crimes. They let out Jennie Vose. She'll be thieving and cheating. She's not lost her old pranks because she's been a few months in the gaol at Jamestown. She's wheedled many a young fellow to her bed, she has." He turned his sightless eyes to Digby. "Didst hear if they let Tamar out?"

"The girl the crowd was stoning?" Digby asked. "The poor frightened lass with dark hair and great eyes?"

"Stoned her? The rascals! The villians!" The old man half

rose from his chair. Then he sank back again, a look of despair on his face; his whole thin body shaking.

Richard said, "Digby, get wine for our guest." Digby went inside and returned with a stone jug of Madeira he had got from somewhere. Richard never questioned him in these matters. He knew he would get one answer: "An old dragoon knows how to forage for himself and his horse." The Ancient Planter drank gratefully and wiped his lips with a kerchief he carried in the sleeve of his coat.

Richard said gently, "Tell us about Tamar. Who is she? Where does she belong?"

"To the first question I say truthfully I don't know. She came on a London ship with a load of indentured last year. A pretty young thing, I could tell by her voice. Then trouble came and they took her away. I missed the girl. She had been kind to me, used to give me a helping hand. Gentlemen, there was no harm in Tamar. But she wouldn't tell."

Digby asked, "Wouldn't tell what?"

"Who the father of the child was. They made her stand before the court while they crucified her with their serpents' tongues. I was at the trial. Our parson stood by her and pleaded for her, but they wouldn't heed him. They made her sign a paper, poor frightened, friendless thing! I remember how it read, gentlemen. Men without eyes sharpen their memories as well as their ears. Want I should say it for you?"

Richard started to protest, but Digby, leaning far forward not to miss a word, had already said yes.

". . . humbly sheweth that I, Tamar, have now the misfortune of an illegitimate child, which I am very sorry for, and by God's grace I hope I shall never be guilty again. I do declare to Your Worships in this petition that the father of my child need not be made known and it will be sufficient without publication of the name of anyone else.

"I must beg Your Worships that I cannot pay my fine, for I cannot get security. Neither have I any ready tobacco or money. I hope Your Worships will take this into your grave and wise consideration, to use me kindly. I must stand to Your Worships' clemency."

"How piteous!" Richard exclaimed, remembering keenly the girl's tragic eyes. "How full of pathos!"

Digby said bluntly, "They gaoled her? In with the drunken rascals, the thieves and convicts and the loose women?"

"Aye, that they did. A poor friendless thing! None from here went to stand beside her save the parson from Benn's plantation and me. We stood with her. He made a plea. It did some good. They did not lash her or put her in the ducking-stool or the stocks."

"God blast such wickedness! Where was the man that he did not stand forth?"

Digby looked at Richard in surprise at the outburst.

"None knows," the old man said, fumbling for his stick. "I miss the girl. She was of great kindness, not wickedness."

Richard asked, "Was she afraid to tell the name of the man? Or did she love so deeply?"

"Sir, I don't rightly know the answer to your questions. They took her away from here and I did not hear her speak again. If I had heard her, I would have known, I think. The timbre of her voice had many variations. She must have betrayed herself to me, her friend." He got to his feet. "I do not like to leave you with sad thoughts. Hark, do you hear the mocker tuning up? The bird knows it is the full of the moon." He paused at the edge of the steps. "What a glorious madrigal! The world must be beautiful to him in the moon-light." At the foot of the steps he paused again. "If the bird keeps you awake with his blithe song, he will stop if you shake that little saping where he is poised."

Richard undressed and went to bed with no words other than a brief good night to Digby. He was greatly shaken by what he had heard. Thought of the girl Tamar's desolate tale crowded out other thoughts. Kathryn Audley, born Bradshaw, did not trouble Richard Monington's sleep that night.

CHAPTER 19

Seasoning Fever

AUGUST brought intense heat and the beginning of the seasoning fever in Jamestown. The new governor had taken firm hold of the reins and had a strong seat in the saddle. The tobacco rationing had been accepted by the majority of the large planters. Grumbling persisted, but many of the more thoughtful had accepted the new laws that Cromwell had laid down. The enforcement of the Navigation Laws was the most difficult. The planters evaded by sending their exports of lumber, pitch and naval stores to the Indies, thence transshipping them in Dutch or French vessels to be sold in European markets.

The seven hundred soldiers had been divided. Captain Denis had sent some numbers of them to Maryland, where there was trouble. The billeting of the remainder was a hardship on the people of Jamestown, who were for the most part artisans, craftsmen, glaziers, seedsmen, brewers. Bakers, coopers and gardeners had come on the last few ships to augment the workers, such as joiners, brickmakers and farriers. Only the taverns benefited by the presence of Cromwell's soldiers.

Sir William Berkeley stayed quietly at Green Spring, making no move to secure a ship to transport his goods and chattels or his servants outside the colony. Instead, he set out more trees in his already large orchards—apples, pears, peaches and small fruits.

Many of the Royalists were opposed to Berkeley and wished he would leave the country. They did not forget the boisterous manner in which he had behaved himself in some of the General Court sessions, nor his refusal to allow the lawyers at the bar to conduct themselves according to custom. Sometimes, he had fallen into great passions and used abusive language, even to fairly elected judges. In all this he had defied the laws from the time of King John establishing freedom of assembly and of trade, and trial by jury. He had ignored these primary laws, but been adamant on collecting taxes and quit-rents and on enforcing the old London Company rule that every planter set out six mulberry trees for the development of the silk industry.

He had put gentlemen into gaol without fair trial or just complaint. One day stood out above others, when he had taken a King's attorney by the collar and shaken him, shouting that he was not to follow the laws, but heed only the governor's command.

'Twas said he had taken the tithes from the college land, and that once he had shouted to the governors of the college fund that they were dogs and their wives were bitches. He had ordered his henchmen stationed at the mouths of the rivers to break open private letters, with the result that the planters were in terror of the loss of their invoices and accounts.

These offences outweighed some of the good he had done, such as capturing pirates and levying taxes on tobacco for the government, though many planters thought the money received went to England and found its way to Berkeley's credit in some London depository.

Living now like a country gentlemen or even a feudal lord, he made no move to disturb Bennett. Indeed he was friendly, with a serpent's guile. He got a good price for his town house, for he knew Bennett must have suitable housing in Jamestown. Bennett would have preferred Secretary Richard Kemp's house, which was reckoned the fairest that ever was known in the country for substance and uniformity. It was built of brick and would have suited the governor's purpose well. But it was politic to buy the Berkeley house, since every governor since Sir John Harvey had resided there.

And so Berkeley sat in his manor-house at Green Spring, caring for his crops, making ready to harvest his apples and make wine of the wild grapes, slaughter his kine and store his food—enough, the rumour went, to withstand a two-year siege, if necessary, or until Bennett was no longer governor.

He continued to make out grants, signed by his own seal, to the land of the south, and it was said he supplied arms to the Wiccocomico, who dwelt in the forest of Northampton County.

Governor Bennett pondered over these things, for, like

his master Cromwell, he had a good service of intelligence. It supplied him with much information, not only about his Royalist rival but also about the state of feeling in the colony. The Navigation Act, designed to force a rebellious people to the new government, was resented by all. He had other concerns—the trouble in Maryland for one, and the trickle of emigration to the Chowan River region for another. He blamed the latter on Nathaniel Batts and on Roger Greene, with his talk of carrying a hundred colonists to develop the eleven-thousand-acre grant of land on the Roanoke River, lying to the south of the Chowan. Then there were the pirates off the Capes, and the long dry spell which withered the corn and seared the leaves of tobacco plants before their time. It would be ill luck to lose a tobacco crop this year.

Francis Yeardley and his brother Argoll were expending over two hundred pounds sterling for exploration down the Chowan River, desiring to purchase land from the Chowanoke Indians—a good land, free from the nipping frosts of Virginia.

Perhaps it might be well if he himself furthered expeditions and did not allow Sir William all the credit should the settlements prove successful. Already a few Quakers were settling along the Perquimans River, a goodly stream that emptied into Roanoke Sound, not far from Raleigh's Island of Roanoke.

At his office table Governor Bennett rang a bell. Stephen came in and sat down on the opposite side prepared to write. But the governor was slow starting to dictate. He looked out the window, absently tapping on the table with an ivory papercutter, his eyes fixed on the far shore of the river. "Are the tobacco barns at Bennett's Welcome in good order?" he asked.

"Yes, sir. The old ones have new clapboards, and the new ones are completed."

"Are they picking?"

"A few of the lower leaves have turned, but not many. The middle of the month they'll be ready, the overlooker tells me, if we don't have rain."

The governor nodded absently. After a time he said, "I am thinking about sending some men south to give me a report on the country. I have a request here from Richard Bland, our Virginia merchant, who wants permission to send men to discover the value of the Chowan River region. It is addressed to Sir William, but he sent it to me. Here, read it."

Stephen read. It was dated Fort Henry. Bland wanted a pass for himself; Abraham Wood, Captain Elias Pennant and Sackford Brewster, Gentlemen; four men; a guide named Pyancha, an Appomattox war captain; two servants; four horses—to advance from Fort Henry and to travel southward.

"What do you think, Stephen? Shall I give permission for Sir William's men to make the exploration, or shall I refuse and send my own men?"

Stephen thought a moment. "Why don't you grant the pass, for September, say. That is a good travelling month and the crops will be harvested. Say that you will send two of your own men with them. You would then accomplish two things— please the merchants and have a report to file for future use. Should you not ask for a list of every man in the colony?"

The governor nodded a couple of times. "Yes . . . perhaps that would be wise—a sort of Domesday Book. . . . But whom can I send on such a venture?"

Stephen pondered, turning the feather quill in his fingers. "Why not send those two men I bought, the Worcester prisoners?"

"Royalist prisoners? Are you willing to take the chance?"

Stephen shrugged his shoulders. "Where can they go, if they do escape? There are only a few yeoman planting along the rivers and a Quaker family or two on the Perquimans. I'm sure they won't attempt to run away, with the strict laws and severe punishment for runaway slaves."

The governor got up and walked about the large room. Stephen thought he looked out of place among the ornate furniture left by Berkeley. Richard Bennett was more at home in simple surroundings. The silky velvet hangings, the brocade chairs were not in keeping either with the man or the hot humid day.

"Write the letter granting a pass to Bland and his associates, but telling him that we will send two men with the party. No, don't write now. Later. I have an important letter to write to my uncle, to go on a ship that sails at sunset. Then Madam Montague wishes to wait on me after tea."

Stephen reddened. "Now what does she want?"

"I do not know. I fancy something to do with her ward's dower rights."

"Mathilda is not Mistress Cecily's ward. She's Peter Montague's ward."

"No matter. Mistress Cecily will attend to the details, you may be sure. She is a fine, shrewd woman, and Mistress Mathilda is fortunate to have her interest. But we waste time in words. Take up your pen."

To my excellent Uncle:

From you out of the Virginia Adventure, by way of Spain and the Somers Islands, God be thanked, I have now to acknowledge the receipt, in good order, of:

 19 butts of excellent good wine
750 jars of oil of olive
 16 bbls of raisins
 18 bbls rysse
2½ hogsheads almonds
  3 half hogsheads whale (one of white was salvaged out of the sea)
18 hogsheads olives
 3 firkins of butter
 2 bbls of candles

 and three packets of linen cloths marked with my mark
All goods came safe and well considered into my hands, the best I have received since I came to this land.

I make no question but to get for you, by God's help, a good profit.

The year being well in mid-season—summer of the highest sun, the Indians say—the ship has gone forth to fill with fish. Newfoundland fish as 30c. per cwt. Dry Canada, ten pounds sterling. Wet cheaper.

My family stands well in health. I hope to make a good crop, both of tobacco and corn.

I hope you will receive a good parcel of tobacco. Pray forget me not to my brother and his wife and our uncle.

Thank Mr. Browne for the cheese he sent me.

       Your loving relative,
       Richard B.

To Edward Bennett
Merchant in Bartholomew Lane
London

Stephen's pen scratched. He wrote swiftly, almost as fast as the governor talked. He had about finished when a servant

entered to say that Madam Peter Montague waited on His
Excellency in the great room, with Madam Bennett.

The governor smiled. "Perhaps I wronged the lady and it
is a social visit. Join us at tea, Stephen, when you are
finished."

When the governor entered the room, the company, including his wife, rose. "Be seated, please," he said graciously.
Mistress Cecily, knowing her manners, made a low curtsy,
her pale pink mull skirts spreading about her, the ribbands
on her little rose-coloured bonnet fluttering. Mathilda and
Sibyl also hastened to curtsy, Sibyl a little awkwardly, Mathilda with grace. Madam Bennett was dressed sedately in grey,
with white collar and deep cuffs of the plainest swiss. She
was pale and of very sober countenance, for the heat troubled
her.

Mistress Cecily, having shown that she knew her manners,
forgot them, and began to talk about the weather. "We are
on our way to the sea. I declare we were perishing with the
heat, the biting flies and the burrowing bugs. My young ladies
are not accustomed to such temperature. They are wilting
like lilies on the stalk."

The young ladies didn't look withered, the governor said.
He thought they looked quite fresh and charming—Mistress
Mathilda particularly. "You remind me of a sweet garden
pink."

Madam Bennett smiled a little and glanced affectionately at
Mathilda. "The governor is quite right, my dear." Mathilda
blushed delicately and looked more like a flower, so Stephen
thought as he entered the room. He kissed Madam Montague's hand, bowed to the young ladies and made himself
useful in passing tea and little seed-cakes to the ladies.

Madam Montague set down her tea-cup. "If you have a few
minutes, Your Excellency, I would like to discuss a matter
or two with you concerning Mathilda's dowry. Her poor
lamented father confided in me and I know his wishes. I presume you are acting for Stephen."

Mathilda's cheeks flamed. It embarrassed her to have the
question of dowry brought out so frankly. Madam Bennett
suggested the garden for the young folk, while she looked
after some neglected household matters. She watched them
stroll down the garden path toward a bench within a circle of
box bushes. Her face was set to sadness. She sighed deeply.

She had no will to live in elegance, nor did she like the power that now lay in her husband's hands. She was a gentle, dovelike, mournful person, but very understanding. Her life was bound up in her two daughters and her sons.

In the governor's office the talk was spritely. Cecily had no intention of indulging in a long parley. She leaned a little forward in her chair, with her handkerchief, small bag and fan in her lap. "I've been talking to Peter," she said without preamble. "I have suggested to him that he make an exchange, through Mathilda's barrister in London, of some of her land in Somersetshire for some of Peter's acreage in Nansemond. He has something like five hundred acres, in small parcels, not too far from Stephen's holding in Isle of Wight County. It would be better, don't you think, for her to have land that Stephen may plant?"

Richard nodded, but he was cautious in his answer. One never knew about women. "I should think so, but I don't know all the circumstances. Shouldn't the decision be Mathilda's? She might want a home in England."

"Oh, this would not be the manor-house at home. That is to go to both daughters, so Sibyl shares ownership in it. This is a smaller farm."

"Suppose Peter and Mathilda decide this, Cecily. I do not feel that I need act for Stephen in this matter. Besides, I don't know the value of the land. Why not ask your relation Tom Parker? This land of Peter's must lie somewhere near Macclesfield, Tom's manor-house. You can trust Tom to know the value of land."

Mistress Cecily pursed her lips; her eyes brightened. "We'll have time before the wedding to settle the point. Well, that is enough of business. This is the question I really wanted to ask you: Is Sir William actually banished or are you going to allow him to stay on here to be a thorn in your side?"

Richard Bennett smiled. "You do ask flatly. Well, I will answer flatly. I don't know."

"I hope you make up your mind. If you don't, Sir William will make the decision."

"And what will that be, do you think?"

"Why, he'll stay—to annoy you for one thing, and for another, where is he to go? To England under Cromwell? Never. Spain? No. France? No. He was in trouble with the

French once over their merchant vessels, which he called pirates. He will stay here, if you allow him."

The governor looked at his hands, which lay clasped on the table in front of him. "Which side are you on, Cecily?"

The question was abrupt. It startled her, but her smile was full of mischief. "Why, I don't know. Sir William has entertained so beautifully. He is an interesting conversationalist, with the knack of making one feel important. You were always a little sober, Richard—dour, I might add—while Sir William, in spite of that terrific temper of his, can be gay. Still, in all, I don't believe a word he says, and one is obliged to believe what you say. Truth is in you."

The governor's stern features relaxed. He seemed pleased at her words. "Thank you, Cecily. You couldn't have said a kinder thing."

Cecily absently tapped at the arm of her chair with her almond-shaped nails. "I worry sometimes lest you haven't enough guile, so forthright you are. And if I may say so, you Puritans have a genius for wearing the hair shirt!"

The governor smiled. "I've been recently accused of much guile concerning the opportune arrival of troops at Jamestown."

She smiled back. The little crinkling lines at the corners of her eyes showed plainly. "It was *too* dramatic, Richard! I declare, that morning was like a play by Mr. Chapman. Would it be *Eastward Ho* or one of the tragedies?"

"I cannot answer you. It might turn out to be either tragedy or comedy."

"Be on your guard, Richard! There are many who wish you evil in the colony, not on your own account but because of the man in England—Oliver Cromwell."

The governor nodded. "History must be his judge, Cecily. One day fair-minded folk will say he gave England—and Virginia—their first real freedom. He is a great man, greater than his times. As a general, that is already proved. Now he must prove himself the statesman. He is one man who sees clearly. He believes firmly in the sovereign people."

" 'Tis said that the poor fared better under the Stuarts and the Crown than they do under middle-class Puritans. Do not take that as my belief," Cecily added hastily, fearing she had been too frank.

But Bennett did not take her words badly. "Our duty is to

afeguard Parliament and give it the power that kings held
s their absolute right. The right of free debate and the con-
rol of taxes. Cromwell has said, must be in the people's
ands. We must watch jealously against any usurpation.
Neither must Church rule, nor royal person. Only the people
ave the right."

Cecily rose. "You have noble thoughts, Richard. Watch and
e wise, that conspiracy may not flourish." She looked at him
houghtfully. "Sometimes I wonder how a Christlike person
an, with clear conscience, keep white men in bondage." The
governor stiffened in his chair. His eyes gave her a bleak,
almost hopeless look. "Your ideals and your acts clash, do
hey not?" she added shrewdly.

She gathered her small belongings and made a deep curtsy.
Before she left, she added another word. "One must have an
iron soul and much humility to meet one's responsibilities,
or—" her flashing white teeth gleamed behind her red lips—
"or solve the riddle of the worth of Oliver Cromwell."

Long after Cecily Montague had left the room, Richard
Bennett sat thinking over the rapierlike thrust of her words.
Drat her! That worldly woman to pretend to be the guardian
of his conscience! No doubt she had an ulterior purpose. But
she could strike home. White men in bondage . . . He crossed
the room and took the Bible from the locked box. He must
clear his mind. Surely there would be something in the
Scripture to ease it. . . . White men in bondage . . . her words
were worse than a rapier thrust. They were a brand, to burn
and sear.

Mathilda came reluctantly at Mistress Cecily's call. Sibyl,
who had been catching insects to throw into the fish-pond,
came more readily. She watched Stephen detain her sister
for another embrace, hidden, as he thought, by the boxwood
bushes. It was all so strange! Mathilda had changed much in
these weeks. She went about in a daze or sewed on petticoats
and ruffles feverishly. Every night she opened the camphor-
wood chest and counted the growing piles of dainty white
undergarments. Or she knelt before the window, gazing out
at the river in the moonlight. Sibyl was glad they were going
to the sea. She could walk along the beach and gather shells
to trim the garden paths. She hoped there would be other
girls. The governor would be moving down, and his secre-

tary. That meant that she would see nothing of Mathilda.
Stephen used to be so nice. Now he sat and gazed at Mathilda
like a calf. People were strange. She wished she might talk
to Richard again. She had talked with him only that once.
Uncle Peter had told her that Nick Holder and Kathryn had
gone to Maryland with Mr. Secretary Claiborne.

One thing pleased her. She thought of it as they walked
toward Uncle Peter's Jamestown house. When Mathilda and
Stephen were married, she would live with them, either at
Bennett's Choice, Stephen's manor in Isle of Wight, or at
Bennett's Welcome in Nansemond. Then she would be near
Richard. Even though he *was* indentured, she would seek
him out. This thought cheered her and gave more life to her
step. Now if Richard didn't get married . . . The thought was
distasteful.

"Can an indentured man marry?" Sibyl asked Peter Montague that night at supper.

Cecily said, "Whatever are you talking about, Sibyl? What
indentured man? Marry whom?"

"Why, no one," she fibbed, "no one in particular. I just
wondered if they could. Do they have to select indentured
women?"

"Of course they can marry. That answers the first question. And who would marry an indentured man but an indentured women? That answers the second."

"I did not know. There must be some nice indentured men.
They can't all be rogues."

Cecily laid her knife and fork on her plate. "Sibyl, I don't
want you to get any wild romantic notions about bondsmen
into that silly head of yours. They're all rogues or thieves."
Cecily fitted her notions to her audience.

"Aren't there any Royalists out of King Charles's army?"

"I said, No silly romantic nonsense!" Cecily turned to
Peter. "I think we had better ask your nephew down to the
shore this summer. Where is Sam Bridger? Still on his plantation at Woodmancote? And John Boddie or Weyland Driver?
They're good lads, well landed. They all live over there on
the south shore." She looked at Sibyl steadily, without seeing
her.

Peter said, "Now don't begin thinking of marriage for
Sibyl. She's much too young."

"Nonsense!" Cecily spoke impatiently. "She's older than I

was at my first marriage. She's not so well developed. That's why you say she's too young."

Sibyl said, "I don't want to marry—ever. I want . . . I'd rather be a nun or a martyr, like Saint Kathryn."

Again Cecily said, "Nonsense! You don't know what you're saying. Peter, let's walk in the Parade, to see if we can pick up someone for a game of trump. Young ladies, do not wander beyond our garden ledge. It isn't safe. I saw half a dozen Indians at market today."

Sibyl watched them walk away, Cecily hanging on Peter's arm and looking up into his face, laughing lightly. That was love, too. It wasn't the kind that caused a maid to blush or a grown man to stammer. It was more comfortable somehow. She sighed. She didn't understand any of it.

She walked to the garden. She climbed up into the apple-tree and looked over the wall. The moon was bright. She could see the people strolling along the Parade. Last year Mathilda would have been up in the tree with her, her back against the trunk in a nice comfortable position. But Mathilda had gone inside to read French. Lighting a candle would bring in those little hard black insects and the tiny midges that got in one's hair and eyes.

People walked along the path under the wall. A lover kissed a lass. She laughed and said, " 'Tis sweet—but you kiss other maids. Some say you are the man whose name that evil girl Tamar would not disclose."

"That's a lie. I never bedded with the wench. I tried to kiss her once, but she raised a welt on my face with the back of her hand. She was fiery, even when they had her in the stocks."

"You love her. That's black-hearted. She's a witch."

"No more a witch than Holder's wife, who goes galloping about the mainland on her black horse as though old Beelzebub was after her."

"She's fair a beauty, she is. Witches ain't blonde. They're black-eyed and black-haired, and if you throw them in the water they won't sink."

"Silly. . . . Come close, my girl. How soft your body is!"

Two rollicking soldiers came along, singing a gay ditty. They did not linger, but passed on before three men, who had been walking one behind the other, forgathered below Sibyl. One was the big smith who had shod Madam's horse a fortnight earlier. She did not recognize the others. The farrier was speaking. "I went there yesterday. We are commanded to do nothing, nothing at all. He says soon the soldiers will leave."

"He may wait too long," the short man said. "Now is the time."

"Have done! You're always averse to whatever he says."

"Has he seen the fellow from across the water?" the third man asked. "The one who was at Worcester?"

"No, but he wants him to wait on him at Green Spring."

"Fool, name no names! Come on. We'll be late."

After they were out of earshot, Sibyl slid to the ground. She had been eavesdropping and that wasn't fair. She walked slowly across the lawn. The shadows were dark and heavy, and the moonshine was very bright. The smell of jasmine filled the air. She puzzled over what the men had said. They must have been talking about . . . the fellow across the water . . . Worcester . . . Could that be Richard? Should she tell Uncle Peter? . . . But again if they were conspiring, would it mean Richard would be haled up in the Quarters Court? How did they punish slaves? By whipping? She shuddered. That would be too horrible. No, she would say nothing to anyone, not even to Uncle Peter, who was so kind and understanding.

Mathilda was in bed. Sibyl groped her way into the room and undressed in the dark. She gazed a moment at her sister, sleeping with the moonshine falling directly on her. Sibly drew the curtain. Everyone knew that evil spirits could enter a body if he slept in the moonshine.

Richard woke at three. The moon was bright. He felt cold. He was shaking in a fit, and his bones ached. The cold fit lasted for an hour. His tongue was dry and his lips parched, and he went from the cold fit into a fever.

Digby was terrified at his captain's condition. He sent Puti for Angela, who shook her head, muttering *ipa . . . ipera.*

Puti said, "She say bad, very bad."

Angela spoke rapidly to Puti, and left quickly, running along the path to the kitchen.

Puti said, "She say she get snake-root and stew in wine and water; make big sweat. Cover now with blankets."

Higgins the overlooker came to the cabin while Angela was pouring the drink down Richard's throat. Richard flailed his arms about wildly, turning his head from side to side, the drink running out of his mouth to his chest.

Higgins grabbed one arm, Digby the other, while Angela put the mixture into a covered spoon with a hollow handle and blew the liquid down his throat. Higgins said crossly, "Half the hands are sick of the fever. I've sent to Jamestown for a doctor. May as well have him bleed the lot of them. Get him on his feet by tomorrow. Damned bad luck I'm having with the whites." He went out of the room, shouting over his shoulder, "I want the fellow in the fields by tomorrow. I'm short-handed enough."

Angela said to Puti, "*Mabisalia, Samza.*"

Puti looked at Digby; he spoke with some hesitation. "She say, get witch-doctor. He make him vomit. Get well, maybe? Black man cure . . . no white man."

Digby answered, "Get your witch-doctor. Let him weave a spell."

Puti still hesitated. "No tell? *Chikoti*—whip—no like witch-doctor. He beat, and makes water come at corners his mouth. He like much to use *chikoti*—we afraid of *Nkandwe*."

"What do you mean?"

"His name we call the Fox."

Digby stared. The black man used the same name for the overlooker that the captain used, the Fox.

The boy pulled at his sleeve. "*Mabisalia*, sar?"

Digby looked at Richard. He was still now, too still. No sweat showed on his skin in spite of blankets. "Yes, yes, get your witch-doctor. Run, run, get him quick!"

Puti went to the door, bending his head, listening. He held up his hand. Digby listened. He heard the tap-tap-tap of a drum, far off, through the forest.

"*Mabisalia, Tanga Ku.* The witch-doctor sets off to come to the one in difficulty. He beats the small drum tap-tap-tap."

"Where is this man, the witch-doctor, Puti?"

"Next plantation below, sar. Down-river."

"How the devil does he know to come?"

"He know when you say words, 'Get witch-doctor.' He know. He hear." Puti made a sweeping gesture with his arm, as though sweeping the sky. "He hear. He come at his own will."

Digby heard a slight sound, as though the leaves of the sycamore tree were moved by a slight breeze. When he turned, a dried-up, weazened black man was crouched on the floor near the fire, tapping a small drum, which was suspended about his neck with a leather thong.

He was naked except for a loin-cloth. About his ankles were circles of small shells. Two long strings of shells circled his neck, from which hung a crescent of ivory, with strange signs cut into the bone and filled with some red dye.

The candle had gone out. The room was in darkness, save for the moonshine which cast a light on the sick man. Dark as it was, Digby could see the black man clearly. Digby stood as though rooted to the spot, unable to move. Puti crouched on the floor, his face hidden in his folded arms.

The witch-doctor lifted a pouch which hung from his loin-cloth, and took out a string of beads on which dangled a little tube, the size of a large spool. This he twisted and the top came off. He took out a small collection of objects which he spread on the hearth. Then he began to tap a slow rhythm, so faint it was almost like a ripple on the water, the wind in the reeds.

Digby was impelled to turn his eyes to the cot where Richard lay. His heart pounded, then almost stopped. He saw the shadow of the long body rise, move out and float into the moon shadow which poured in through the window, until it merged and was lost. The faint tapping was faster now—faster—faster—faster—until the sound seemed to whirl and eddy about him. Then there was silence.

Digby looked toward the spot where the witch-doctor had been an instant before. He was gone.

Puti moved. He sprang to his feet and ran to the cot. "Sar, look. He sleeps quietly now. He is strong again." He pulled the blankets aside. Richard was sleeping quietly. His skin was natural to the touch. His breath came normally.

"In the morning he will rise. He will know nothing of illness. Better you forget what you see this night, sar." Puti went out the door quietly and disappeared into the night. The mockingbird began his moonlight song.

Digby pulled a chair by the cot. He was too troubled by what he had seen to sleep. Magic. Devil's magic? Or was it magic for good? Had he seen a man's soul leave his body, or only the evil of fever depart at the bidding of a tiny drum? It was all too confusing. After a time his eyes closed, his head fell forward and he slept.

When the doctor came in the morning, Richard had already bathed in the creek and was dressed. The doctor grumbled because he'd had to come to the cottage. He was weary. Twelve bleedings already and as many vomits. He sat down at Richard's invitation and filled his pipe. The seasoning fever was violent this year, he complained. The pox had appeared in a few cases along the river. He was a small man worn beyond his years.

He talked until the plantation bell rang and Digby and Richard departed for the fields. Doctor Thorpe watched them go. There was something about Richard that disturbed him. He was obviously a gentleman.

In the fields the Negro slaves were singing as they chopped the hills of beans. A leader sang in solo, the chorus followed, keeping time with their chopping hoes:

> The bean pods rattle
> Like the legs of a dancer.
> I fear the rhinoceros
> Lest he eat me.
>
> I fear the Fox
> Lest he beat me.
> Oh, bright are the fir-tops!
> Bright, bright are the fir-tops!

They watched Richard walking toward the field. Every Negro slave knew that the white man had been visited by their Great One. He was now set apart, to be guarded and protected. They sang about him. They had given him a name, Mtengo, the tall tree where the spirits of the great, great dead rest and watch.

As for Richard, he felt wonderful. He whistled as he walked to the tobacco fields. He could lift mountains, he told Digby.

Digby said, "It is a fair good day, zur." But in his heart he was uneasy and disturbed.

In the morning Richard had found a little pine tree, delicately carved in ivory, on his pillow. It was suspended by a small braided string of silk thread. "What is this?" he had demanded of Puti, who looked at the object in Richard's palm, his eyes wide and startled.

"Wear it around your neck, sar. It is a good omen. Very, very good, to keep away evil spirits."

Richard laughed, but he put the string over his head. The ivory tree fell against his chest. It was cool and pleasant to the touch.

"Mtengo," Puti said. "A tall tree. Mtengo."

Richard repeated the word, "Mtengo, tall tree."

The child clapped his hands. "M-ten-go, Mtengo, very good you say our words."

Digby stood by. The wave of fear came over him again. He devoutly hoped his captain was not saying witch words that would bring the devil and all his evil hosts rolling about them. But nothing happened.

Richard said, "I must learn more about these Negroes' language. I never thought of them as having a language, or songs either. Did you, Digby?"

"Zur, I don't think about them whatever. They be proper heathens, with strange and direful doin's." Digby rammed tobacco into his pipe and lighted it with a splinter of lightwood flaming from the small fire under the pot.

Richard didn't notice his companion's agitation, nor see how his hand trembled. He was intent on his thoughts. Strange. Very strange indeed. He wondered that he had not thought of it before. The great houses where the planters lived; the cottages that were assigned to the white slaves; the huts in the compound that housed the black men—they made three castes, as distinct as the castes at home. None of the three knew the thoughts or feelings of the others. Three groups, living within a stone's throw of one another—here they were close, eating, living, on one plantation, yet they were as far apart as Africa was from England, as Virginia was from either country. Strange . . . almost unbelievable.

That afternoon a storm came up. The wind whipped the trees and great limbs broke off the giant oak by the manorhouse and fell on the roof of one of the dependencies. No one was hurt, for all the household had fled and hid themselves in the bricked cellar. All night it rained and hail fell, cutting the tobacco leaves in the exposed fields. Fortunately most of the large leaves were picked and hanging in hands in the drying house.

Richard went to the blind man's door to see that he came to no harm.

It was in the midst of the storm that the girl Tamar sought refuge in the Ancient Planter's part of the cottage. "Hide me! Hide me! Hide me!" she cried. "They're seeking me. Higgins has gone after the dogs." She was shaking with a chill. Her clothes were torn by briers, and great scratches showed on her arms and bare legs.

The Old One said quietly, "Sit down, child. I'll get you a dram of wine. Now drink this, and try to speak quietly and slowly so that we may understand."

The girl fell into a chair. Even in her disarray she showed beauty of face and body. Words tumbled out. "Higgins and the men he stirred up brought me over in a sloop. They were going to put me in a dungeon, they said. I am sick and weak, but I evaded them at the landing."

The Old One said, "We must devise a way to conceal you. In spite of the governor, they may come here, knowing that I am friendly to you. Richard, we must get her to the parson. He'll know what to do."

"The dogs will track her," Richard said, his brows drawn together in anger.

"There is a boat in the reeds. Get her into that and tow up-stream until you are well past the bridge. Go into the swamp. Take Puti. He will know how to cross the swamp. Quick! There is no time to lose." He was putting some food into a little basket, and a bottle of wine. "Quick! I'll tell Digby you have gone. Later we can get her to the church on Benn's plantation."

Richard said, "Come."

The girl shook her head. "I'm too weary to walk. Let them take me. They will only whip me. I can stand that, but not the swamp, all alone. I am afraid of the evil spirits that dwell there."

Richard lifted her from the chair. "Put your arms about my neck. I'll carry you to the boat."

Thomas Chapman said, "That is well. The dogs won't track her there. Quick! There is so little time. May the merciful God protect you both!"

Puti appeared miraculously. He ran ahead and had the bateau loosed from its mooring. He poled the boat skilfully, keeping close to the tall reeds along the bank. A heron, startled, flew up from the water and away, its great grey wings flapping. A blue jay shrilled its raucous cry, but there was no sound of the hounds baying until they reach the small wooden bridge where the paths met. Richard knew those fields which verged at the great dark swamp, but he did not know beyond.

Puti knew. He spoke for the first time. "Want I should pole into the black water, sar? It goes into the deep cypress swamp. It is lonely there. Yes?"

Richard looked ahead and nodded. The cypress was tall and grew deep in the black water. There were juniper and cedar and gum. Vines climbed to the tops of the trees. With his pole Puti lifted a weaving screen of grape-vines that clogged the entrance. The curtain of green dropped behind them, leaving the boat in the twilight of the swamp.

The girl was lying in the bottom of the boat, her eyes and heavy black brows covered with her hands. She was motionless, as though she slept. Richard did not speak. The bateau moved silently along the winding stream. Richard remembered having heard that runaway slaves always sought a hiding place in the heart of the swamp. The black man's haven might prove sanctuary for this forlorn creature.

They came to a small island. Richard would not have discovered it by himself, so concealed was it by the hanging vines. The black water divided here, making two channels. The trees were high and full-crowned, so that the place had a dark eerie appearance. No rain had fallen here. The hard-packed earth under a great spreading sycamore looked as though it might be the dancing place of the strange pagan people. At one side was the remains of a fire, the embers not yet dead. All was greenery, dense lush jungle of bush and vine. An admirable place of concealment. Richard felt uneasiness as though dozens of unseen folk watched from behind the living curtains of green.

Puti brought the boat to the low bank. He searched the forest with his eyes, which seemed to Richard filled with apprehension. "We leaves the boat here," he said, dropping his voice. "There is shelter, and white men does not come."

Richard looked about him. He wished he had a musket or pistol, some other weapon besides his dirk.

The girl still slept, exhausted by her flight. He lifted her out of the boat and carried her to the great tree. Puti stopped him and indicated a little cot, made of saplings. Richard laid her

on it. He took off his jerkin, rolled it into a pillow and slipped
t under her head. He felt a kinship for this hunted creature.
They were both caught in the strong-jawed trap of slavery.

Puti was on his knees, blowing life into the embers. Richard,
without his tunic, felt the chill of evening. He moved toward
the fire, now crackling and blazing strongly. The ivory symbol
on his chest caught the light from the fire. Puti put up his
hand. A small drum was tapping quietly, almost as though it
were a sound of the inner ear. A twig snapped, then another.
Richard turned his eyes slowly. He was circled by black men,
staring at him with solemn unreadable faces. The drum sound
was closer now. Its rhythm quickened. He heard Puti's hard
breathing. Suddenly Puti knelt, his head on the earth.

Richard saw a black man, taller than himself, with heavy,
powerful shoulders. He stood under the great spreading sycamore. He was naked but for his loin-cloth. In his hand he
carried a long stick with a sharp iron tip.

One by one other Negroes, men and women, came silently
from the forest, making a circle about the chief. They, like
Puti, knelt with their foreheads to the ground. Across the
circle the eyes of two men met and held. A knot of lightwood
caught. The flames leaped up. The little ivory symbol on
Richard's chest trembled with his quickened breathing.

How long they stood Richard had no idea. He was conscious only of the drum-beat, almost like the blood pounding
in his temples. It was a test of some kind. He must show no
fear. The hard, almost serpentlike glance travelled down from
Richard's face until it stopped on the ivory symbol.

"Mtengo!" The people raised their heads and sat on their
haunches. The chief crossed his arms across his heavy chest,
bowed his head. *"Nda-m'pasta Moni, Nda m'monika ndi-
mwone."* He turned his head and spoke to his people in
English. "I have given him the Moni salutation, 'May you see
life!'"

Richard remembered then. He crossed his arms, inclined
his head, *"Moni, Moni,"* he repeated. By some strange reason
he had passed a test. Now he knew that the girl would have
sanctuary among these strange heathen people.

CHAPTER 20

The Girl and the Swamp

AN OLD Negress went to Tamar, who still slept on. "Sar,"
she said to Richard, "carry her to the shelter. I will keep
care of her. Sleep and rest."

The shelter was a brush-covered roof, held in place by eight
uprights. Bushes were planted around it like a hedge, giving
some security. The Negroes who had appeared from nowhere
disappeared into nowhere. Only the chief, whose name was
Elijah, remained.

He spoke to Richard when he came back to the clearing
after he had left the girl on a cot. "Better you return in the
bateau, sar. Old Fox liken to whale you if he catch you gone."

Richard said, "The Ancient Planter said to take her to the
church."

The black man shook his head. "Not tonight. Too much
watching. Tomorrow night better, sar. Come moonrise tomorrow."

"But will she be all right here?"

The man nodded. "Sar, she safe with Angela's mama. She
watch over her. The white mistress know Angela keep her
hidden, lak she did before. Old woman very careful of her
all time when she have child coming. No one hurt girl here—
only white man, if he find her."

Up-stream Richard left the bateau and walked quietly to
the cottage. Digby was pacing up and down the room. The
look of anxiety passed from his face when he saw Richard.
"Captain, thank the good God you're safe! But the girl—where
is the girl?"

Richard told him the story, with all its strangeness and
mystery.

"They's heathen. I hope they can be trusted," Digby said.

"I believe so. If the old woman is Angela's mother, she must be trustworthy. I felt she was."

"There is surely something strange goin' on about here. You said a little drum?" Digby glanced at Richard, then looked away.

"Yes, a very light tap, the merest sound. It went on all the time. The thing that puzzles me is why the chief—he was obviously a chief—made the *Moni* salutation. Puti tells me that means an honour is bestowed. Why I do not know, and the boy would not tell."

Digby thought of the visit of the witch-doctor. Perhaps it was because of that. He pointed to the charm that hung on Richard's breast. "Could that not be a symbol he recognized, a sort of password or talisman?"

Richard thought a moment. "It might be. He did call me by the name Mtengo, which Puti says means a tree." He lifted the ivory carving, then let it fall. Smiling a little, he went on: "Puti says it is my African name, 'a tall tree.'"

Digby had held his tongue about the witch-doctor. He didn't like this. An African name . . . a soul leaving a body . . . a prison woman . . . No, it spelled trouble to him. He said, "I'm going to bed. Five o'clock comes early in the morning." He went to the door. The mournful cry of a whippoorwill came clearly through the still night. He heard the far-away bay of hounds tracking. The hunt was still on.

Richard said, "I'll follow you soon. I think I should step over to the Ancient Planter's. If he thinks I did wrong to leave the girl, I can find my way back tonight."

Mr. Chapman had no comment until Richard's story was told. Then he said, "Let be as it is. The black man spoke true. Tonight it is best that you are here. Higgins has not come as yet, but he may come at any moment. Clearly the dogs have not yet got the scent. The girl can stay as she is. I know the woman, Angela's mother. She is the faithful soul who nursed Tamar through her illness. Higgins will not go to the swamp. He is fearful of it. It is an evil place, haunted by strange spirits." Gently his head fell forward, his hands clasped on his stick.

He went on: "It would be foolhardy to try to reach the parson tonight. He is much too far away. Besides, the over-looker will remember how he stood by her. It would be natural for her to fly to the parson in her trouble, and the overlooker would move to intercept her if he could. In a day or two the parson will provide the best refuge, for if Higgins is afraid of the swamp, others will not be. She must be taken to Benn's secretly. But not tonight. Elijah was right about that."

Richard said, "Blast the man who caused this trouble! Cannot he be smoked out?"

"In time, in time. Do not be impatient. Best that you keep free of this trouble."

"I'm already in it. Someone must have seen me carry her off tonight, although I saw no one."

"Only a slave would have seen, and a slave will not tell. I venture every slave on this plantation is within doors. That is what they do when there is trouble. Aye, every man, woman and child will be in the quarters line, well behind closed doors tonight."

"Excepting those who were at the island."

The old one fingered a ring he wore, turning it about. "The people you saw may not have been our people. It may be a gathering from a number of plantations along the river. I have long known they meet somewhere in secret and carry on their pagan rites."

Richard spoke of the thought that was growing stronger in his mind. "We know nothing of what goes on in the minds of the black people who are living here at Bennett's Welcome. They are as foreign to us as though they still lived in Africa. Is it not rather frightening that we are in such close contact, yet each group is foreign to the other? There must be men of ill will among the whites as well as among the Negroes."

"More of them, I'd say. The black people live close to one another. Don't you notice how they work in small groups, so they may talk and sing and laugh together? Our indentured whites are not like that—a man hoes his own row; and thinks his own thoughts."

"I wonder if Governor Bennett understands what goes on here."

"Higgins' conduct, do you mean?"

"Yes. I am told he is cruel and heartless when the masters are away. That is the time he whips with no reason, as though he loved to draw blood."

"The slaves, white and black, hate him, but their fear is greater than their hate. May I advise you to keep clear of him? Give him no opportunity. It would pleasure him to lay the whip over your shoulders."

"Why?" Richard asked.

"Why? I don't know—only we had another indentured gentleman whom the overlooker hated. He whipped him until he was unconscious, but he never uttered a sound. That infuriated Higgins."

"What became of the man?"

The Ancient Planter sighed. "One does not know what becomes of indentured folk. Some run away and get caught and punished. Others are sold to another master. Others still serve out their time and take up their fifty acres."

Richard got up out of the chair. "I must be going. It is very late and five o'clock comes early.

"Come here tomorrow after the day's work. I'll try to get some news of Tamar through my black friends. You have done a fair fine thing this night."

The light was breaking in the east. The whippoorwill's call seemed to Richard to portend some sad melancholy event. No use to go to bed now. Instead, he walked to the creek, stripped and plunged in. The warm soft water poured over him. It washed away the sweat of the fields, the evil odour of dark grease-covered bodies, the stench of fear and cruelty. He thought, There is no escape from persecution, even in the New World.

The day was long. The slaves worked silently, without song or talk. The indentured men were sullen, casting furtive glances over their shoulders whenever a door in the manor-house or the office opened.

One hook-nosed man, with a branded T on his arm, stopped Richard at the end of a row where he was cutting corn and throwing it into a big-wheeled cart drawn by fat oxen. "Have you heard the hounds?" he asked in a lowered voice.

Richard nodded. He did not like this man who was called the Hawk, nor did he trust him, but he knew he had power over the indentured.

"*He's* tracking a white maid, a good innocent lass, but unfortunate. We will hold a meeting tonight after supper behind the tobacco barns. Will you come?"

Richard hesitated only a second. "Yes. But what can we do?"

"Come to the barns. I've already told Digby."

"You speak of the maid as innocent . . ." He paused, leaving a question to be answered.

"Aye, innocent as a virgin, except some man forced her to his will."

"You suspect Higgins?"

"No use suspecting. The maid must be hidden. We must plan."

Richard kept his own counsel. "You know where she is now?"

The man shook his head. "I suspect the slaves have hidden her, but we are not sure. . . . We must be ready." He walked away and was lost in the rows of tall corn.

Richard smiled grimly. He'd come on evil days to be conspiring with a thief out of some London prison. He, the head of the Manor of Coddington, a magistrate in his own right—what strange fortune had fallen on him! Yet he had a glimmer of hope. These people with their sly, shrewd plots might see a way to contrive that girl's escape. It was unthinkable that she should be tied to the whipping-post again, at the mercy of a man who, as Puti said, slobbered at the mouth, like one bereft of his senses, when he laid the whip on the back of some defenceless human being.

In his mind the girl rose before him, slim and supple, her firm breasts, her natural grace, as he had seen her at Jamestown running from her tormenters, or as she had lain limp in his arms last night. He was amazed to find himself almost happy to think he would have a part in outwitting his masters. Let them know that the bodies they owned had sensibilities! Even the Hawk, a thief, was outraged at the treatment of a young maid who had met trouble with courage. Richard was astonished, too, that his sympathies had, in this short time, become so involved. He found himself thinking in terms of lowly folk. What was happening to him?

The night was warm and cloudless. The moon rose, a great red globe, above the spires of the trees, casting a path of gold down the course of the great river. The quarters line was strangely, ominously silent.

At sundown Higgins came riding his horse to the cottage door. "No one will leave his hut tonight," he said harshly. "No one! Do you understand?"

Digby answered, "Zur, we understand."

"Speak for yourself. You, Richard, did you hear me?"

"I heard."

"Heed what I say or it will be the worse for you." He rode off, stopping along the way to repeat his warning at each house where the indentured folk lived, and down the quarters line.

"He's afraid," Digby said.

"He might well be." Richard was thinking of the swamp folk and the angry men who would meet that night behind the tobacco barns.

Digby and Richard found twenty or thirty men gathered when they arrived at the appointed place. A guard had been set, who halted them a hundred feet from where the men were waiting. Satisfied, he passed them on. The Hawk greeted them and waved his arm to a log where five or six men were seated. The rest were in small groups, talking in undertones. A short time later the Hawk mounted a small cutting-block. The men sat on the ground in a semicircle.

The Hawk began at once: "No use tellin' what's happenin'. Every man knows about the maid Tamar, a good maid who has had bad enough treatment already, without being taken again to the post for another whipping and maybe a branding. We must do something."

"What can we do?" a voice asked out of the darkness. "Wouldn't we just lay ourselves open to more punishment, or perhaps make things all the worse for the lass herself?"

The Hawk silenced him. "We are not here to talk about ourselves, Ellery. What say we enlist thirty or forty men from the near-by plantations, get arms and call the white slaves? 'Who's for freedom from bondage?' That shall be our cry."

"What would we do if our masters opposed and set punishments?"

"Let them catch us first. Kill if we must." The voice was filled with the hatred that only the oppressed can feel.

There was an assenting murmur. Richard thought, This is more than the rescue of the girl Tamar. It is the seed of insurrection.

"We have a good master in Mr. Bennett, and the young one too," someone said.

"Aye, good enough, if 'e 'ad 'is mind on the plantation instead of bein' a governor."

"That's so, and Higgins runs the place to suit hisself, he do."

The master's been too much in Maryland to take heed what goes on in Virginia."

"Burn the barns!" another cried out.

The Hawk called silence. "Richards, what do you think?" he asked.

Richard had intended to listen, but not talk. He felt that now he must get these minds back to the girl's plight from wandering off to their own grievances. He stood up, scarcely knowing what he was going to say to men who seemed ripe for some desperate plot to ravage, plunder and kill. He must dissemble. He would draw them out. "The girl Tamar has hidden herself. Does anyone know where?" he began.

"No. She cannot have gone far, with the hounds after her. To the next plantation or the one after. Where can she flee?"

"To the woods, the swamps, the reeds along the river."

"For how long without food?" Richard asked.

"There's folk who will feed her."

Richard said, "Suppose she is ill, starving. She cannot travel."

There was a long silence.

"We can leave food along the little paths," the Hawk said, "clothes too, men's clothes. They will be looking for a woman."

"The dogs pay no heed to clothes."

Richard put another question: "Has she any friends you can think of?"

"The parson down at Benn's place. He is a bold man. Perhaps he would hide her."

"Pity there's no priest's holes in this country," a new voice broke in.

"Well, there's not."

The Hawk said, "Be silent. Let Richards have his word. He seems fair shrewd for a new-comer."

Richard resumed: "Since you ask me, I think this is a matter for two or three men at this time. Let the Hawk select and name the men. Let them meet together and decide on a plan. Let everyone go home, lest we be missed and cause soldiers to be brought from Jamestown. Remember, the governor has seven hundred men at arms, idle, who would like nothing better than quell a riot on some plantation." He turned to the Hawk. "What do you think?"

"Good enough! I name you, Richards, and Scottie the wood-chopper; he's been here longest, knows every path, ever creek, every tree in the forest."

"And yourself," Richard said quickly. "You must be the director. We do not want the plan to fail or endanger any men unnecessarily, particularly those who are near the end of their servitude."

"That's right. No need of whippings, or years added to time."

"Good thing we're not in Maryland. The law there says to execute a slave if he runs away."

Richard said, "We don't want that kind of trouble for anyone. If we can find a safe place for the girl and let her disappear . . ."

"Someone going south could take her to the new country."

The Hawk clapped his hands. "Dismissed, men! Go to your homes by diverse paths, a few at a time, and silent tongues to you all!" Every man raised his hand.

Richard thought it a curious sight: the dark trees, the slanting light of the moon, the hard faces of vagrants, thieves and poor devils of debtors.

The Hawk lingered, signalling Richard and the chopper Scottie to follow him. They walked silently until they came to a path that led to the river. Here under a great tree they came on a little brush shelter the duck hunters used in autumn.

The Hawk said, "You be a shrewd feller, mayhap a gentleman, but you're one of us at that. You give me your gentleman's word that you will not betray what was said this night."

Richard raised his hand. "My gentleman's oath."

"That will do. I'm here because of a conspiracy again' Crummell. The God-blasted conspirators betrayed me. The gentlemen kept their oaths and their silence, but not their heads. They was hoisted on stakes at the Tower gate, along with other gentlemen. So I, the Hawk, a proved thief, know that a true gentleman keeps his word."

"Thank you," said Richard.

The Hawk didn't hear; he went on talking. "I know where the girl is hidden. Never mind how I found out. She can't stay there. Higgins knows there's a swamp hiding place. Even though he don't know where it is, he'll ferret it out."

Scotty said, "He's afeared of spooks and such. He won't go into the cypress swamp."

"Maybe not. But he'll send men in with dogs. Tonight we must get the girl out and on her way to the parson. That's why I chose Scottie here. He knows the Indian way."

"That I do, but it's long and weary, and there be Indians."

"Not a dozen Indians in the whole of this country!" The Hawk rose. "I'll get a boat."

After a time they came to the curtain of green that masked the entrance to the swamp where the creek divided, and found the little island. A whippoorwill raised its mournful cry. To Richard's surprise the Hawk answered, holding the pole suspended. In a little time the bird sound came again. The Hawk thrust the pole deeper into the water and with a long sweep sent it through the tangle of vines.

"Ware!" cried the wood-chopper. "Puff-adder overhead!"

Quicker than the snake could strike, the Hawk brought his pole onto the overhead branch and swept the venomous serpent into the water. They encountered a second adder, which was killed by the heavy blow of the pole. The Hawk stopped poling. He put his finger to his lips and again gave the whippoorwill call. An answer came softly. They were alongside the island now. The old woman came forward, and behind her a man holding a brand aloft. The Hawk put the bateau close to the bank. Richard and Scottie jumped ashore as a young boy ran forward to catch the rope the Hawk threw him. Three shadowy figures appeared to be sitting about a small cooking fire.

"Sir, follow the old woman," the Hawk said. "She will lead you to the maid while I talk with these people."

Richard found the girl seated on the rough cot. A barricade of small leafy trees set upright screened her from the group about the fire. She stood up when she saw Richard and waited quietly for him to draw near. He motioned her to be seated. He sat down on an overturned tree. The old woman squatted on the ground a short distance away. She was grinding corn into meal. The corn was in a small wooden bowl and she used a stone pestle to mash the grain. A heap of meal was piled on an oblong wooden tray, placed on the stump of a tree.

The maid Tamar looked refreshed. Her long dark hair was in braids about her head. She wore men's knee-breeches of brown and no hosen. On her feet were sturdy shoes, with leather-covered buckles. Her white linen shirt, open at the throat, was fresh and clean. A broad beaver hat with a high crown, such as the Puritans wore, was beside her. Astonishing what the Negroes had been able to bring in so short a time! Magical! She looked very young, Richard thought. With the hat covering her braids, and her narrow waist and slim hips, she might readily be taken for a young rustic lad, a yeoman's son perhaps—inevitably Richard recalled the King's disguise at Bentley Hall—or one of the lads the London merchants were sending over as apprentices to the artisans.

He said to her, "You are improved in your health. I am very glad."

"I am quite strong again. . . . Thank you for your help. . . . I was terrified." She spoke with some hesitation. "You must think me a ninny or a fool."

"Neither. It was a bad moment when the bay of the hounds sounded."

"I did not hear them. I do not know why I swooned. I never swooned before. . . . I cannot think what came over me."

He glanced over his shoulder. The old woman was occupied in pouring water over a small mound of grain, stirring it with a stick, then making it into little flat cakes, and laying it in the embers.

"She is making appones for me to take with me—" Tamar patted a little leather pouch at the belt that held up her breeches—"on the journey tonight."

"So you know the plan."

"Yes, Elijah told me you would come and take me to the church at Benn's plantation."

Richard thought, Was Elijah at the barns? Did he overhear me at the brush shelter? How silently, with what incredible speed, he moves and sends his messages!

"Oh, sir, do you think the parson will aid me?"

"The Ancient Planter says he will."

"It would be the parson's wish—that I know—but he has a vestry. Vestries have power, much power. They do not hold with immoral women."

Richard leaned forward and took her hand. He noticed her fingers were long, slender and well-shaped, but hardened by work, doubtless in the fields. The calluses on the palms would be from the handle of a hoe or sickle.

Her dark eyes regarded him anxiously. "Sometimes I think I had best go back and let Higgins have his pleasure in laying the whip on my back. He has sworn to make me cry out . . . give the name of the father . . ." She put her hand to her throat as though unable to say more.

Richard laid his hand over hers. He felt the small movement of her fingers within his own. It was like holding a frightened bird in one's hand. He said, "We must not have fears tonight. The Hawk and Scottie are planning. I am useless because I do not know the old Indian traces through the forest. But Scottie knows. We must trust him to get us to our destination."

She cried, "You must not go! You must not suffer for me. Please. Please!"

"Only part way tonight. They think it best that I return before daybreak, lest I be missed and they raise a great hue and cry. That would mean more hounds and more beaters in the forest."

The Hawk joined them. "I've talked with Elijah. He will go with you to the next plantation, Tamar. There you will be hidden for the day. Richards will go as far as the broad creek, where he will find a boat to return to his cottage before daybreak. Scottie will go all of the journey. It is arranged that each day you will be hidden in some safe spot, and another will join Scottie as a guide across his territory."

Richard asked, "How is this amazing thing to be arranged?"

"Elijah. God knows how! He says the drums will speak their warning. That is why there must always be a black man with you who speaks drum-talk."

"When will we start?" the girl asked. Her voice was firm, without a tremor.

"When the drum speaks," the Hawk said. He glanced at Richard and answered an unspoken question. "We have no other way. We must trust them . . . this drum-talk . . . I don't know. . . ."

Even as he spoke, a sound broke, a great vibration, not loud, but it seemed to roll through the earth at their feet, to throb in the air, to fill the forest, not with a definite noise, but a long rumble. It had no relation to the little tapping drum, or the long roll of the English parade drums.

It sounded three times in this manner. Then another drum sounded, sharp, staccato, with intervals of different length.

The old woman looked up from piling the little cakes on a large leaf. "The speaking drums," she said tersely.

Tamar ran to her. "What is it? Are they calling people to capture me?"

"No. Do not fret, little one. No one can tell the direction of the drum-talk. It rises, goes out on the air like a cloud of smoke from a cooking fire and spreads across the tree-tops."

The staccato beat continued.

"What are they saying?" the girl cried. "Tell me! Tell me! I am afraid."

The old woman shook her head. "Only those who know the drum-talk can tell. When the drum speaks, *Ng'oma* has many voices. *Kunta,* the big one, spoke. It calls the people to listen. It is a warning, not large as war-drum. Now the *Mpange.* It makes words; they are speaking words now."

Richard got to his feet. To the Hawk he said in an undertone, "I don't like this. Suppose they are telling where the maid hides."

"Again I say we must trust them. There is no other way. Come! Elijah is beckoning."

The old woman put the appones in the leather bag. A bottle, tied around the neck with a thong, she gave to Richard. He slung it over his shoulder. Wine or water, he didn't know or ask. They walked out into the open place under the great sycamore. The other Negroes had gone; only the drummers remained. Two men were sitting astride a great log cut to a six-foot length. They sat back to back, each at an end. When he drew near, Richard saw that the ends were covered with skin, drawn taut—a hollowed log, a great drum to be beaten by two men at the same time.

The Hawk said, "They do not beat. They rub the sound from the drum with the heel of the hand. That is the great drum. The speaking drums are in the woods—I don't know the direction."

"Are they saying words?" Richard asked, a feeling of uneasiness showing in his voice. "God's truth, this is witchcraft!"

The Hawk shrugged. "Come! Elijah is beckoning us to follow."

The Negro carried a small lanthorn, which threw a dim light down onto the track. As he walked, he made signals with his great hands, pointing to a hole along the path, or a root that might trip the unwary.

The Hawk left them at a fork in the path to return to the

boat. To Richard he said, "I see you have your dirk. It is well. Scottie will tell you when you are to return and will lead you to the hidden canoe. Your going will give the girl ease of mind for the first miles. After that she will not be afraid, with Scottie and Elijah."

Richard thought, God protect her!

Surprisingly the Hawk said, "Go with God, Maid Tamar!"

"Thank you," she whispered. "Thank you, Hawk. Some day . . ." Her words were cut off by the roll of the great drum. Was it a signal, a word of encouragement . . . or an alarm? The forest received the sound and absorbed it and carried it onward until it became the wind passing across the pine-tops. Richard thought, Whatever it is, we are committed to the task.

For two days after his return Richard's mind was in turmoil. He neither ate nor slept properly. Digby watched him, fretting over him, unable to rouse him from the gloom into which he had sunk. The incidents of the past few days hung over him, causing the darkest despair that had come to him since the tragedy of Worcester. The girl Tamar rose before him until he bestowed martyrdom on her. She became a symbol of the horrible tragedy of white servitude in its most noxious form. There was tragedy in black slavery also, but not the poignant, weary heart-break he saw in the girl, try as she would to conceal it. What was to become of her? God help them, what was to become of them all, from the despair of the young Stuart King down to the lowliest African slave!

After supper Richard walked out to the north field to look at the tobacco. He felt a curious proprietary interest in the plants he had so carefully placed into the ground in May. He had watched the growth with increasing interest through the blossoming season. He found himself worrying when the days were cold and when the rains came too frequently, hoping for warm sun and growing weather. He watched each leaf as it turned from green to brown. He had helped with the picking from time to time. He had watched the small Negro boys pile the leaves in rush baskets and carry them off to be tied in hands by the women and hung on poles to dry.

The season's advance was measured by the growth of the tobacco. It was a late season, two weeks behind time. Now if the good Lord would only hold off the rain until the leaves were picked and into the drying sheds!

The leaves were prime, the Hawk told him. The Hawk had learned to be a tobacco-man. A tobacco-man held a certain place of importance among the workers, for tobacco was the money crop. It was used as currency by the planters to pay free men and women for their work, to pay the parson and the artisan, and even to pay the taxes and quit-rents.

It crossed Richard Monington's mind that he had seen many fields planted at the manor, watched crops grow, witnessed many harvests, but never had he felt the pride of possession that he felt now. This was his planting, his growth, his harvest. The toil of his hands, the bent back, the sweat, the weariness of his body was here, here in these denuded stalks, stripped of leaves to the top palmlike head.

Now he understood the yeoman who, dressed in his best clothes on a Sabbath or holiday, walked in his fields or leaned on a wall or a gate to watch the slow progress from planting to harvest; understood the old gardener smoking his stump of a pipe, walking amongst the beds of flowers or vegetables, bending to pluck a weed or turn a leaf to look for devouring insects. How strange that he had seen planting, growth and harvest all his years, not once knowing the joy of fulfilment that every farmer, every yeoman, every gardener was experiencing all about him! He knew now why the pagans celebrated the harvest with dance and song and festivities. It was the season of accomplishment, therefore of rejoicing.

This was the thing that made a man great. He thought then of his father. How often he had heard him quote, "To the soil accrues what is planted in the soil!" He had never understood what his father meant by the words until now. It was a fundamental thing—the continuation, the changing seasons, the rich development. Kings came and departed, men were born and lived and died, but here before him was the eternal thing—God's promise continually renewed, eternal as the rise of the sun and the moon and the stars, as strong as the ebb and flow of the tide.

He walked slowly in the gathering dusk, his mind and heart at peace. He knew tonight that only through these continuous all-enduring wonders did man find his affinity to God.

CHAPTER 21

A Fire-Brand for Tobacco

THE governor's shallop put in at the landing near sundown. The ship carried a number of guests on their way to the seashore for the remainder of the summer, there to escape the heat and the summer illness at Jamestown Island. Madam Bennett had been at the seaside for a month, but the governor had been delayed by a meeting of the Council about tobacco curtailment. Bennett was disturbed. He determined to have a meeting at Bennett's Welcome before he went to the shore. He invited the planters from the southern side of the James to consider what was to be done. The tobacco was late because of a cold spring. Instead of July picking, they began stripping the first of August on his plantation and others along the river. Rumours were coming in from London on every ship that the market was breaking. The reports from Spain and Turkey were that the crops there were heavy and of excellent quality. London merchants, merchants from Bristol and Bideford were asking, nay demanding, graded leaf, or they would lose their markets on the continent.

On the sloop Governor Bennett had as his guests Cecily and Peter Montague. Cecily would stop a few days while Peter visited his plantation. Sibyl and Mathilda were with them, and young Stephen Bennett. With these was also Philip Blount, who had come over from England a few weeks earlier. Now he was on his way to Blount Point to visit his Uncle Thomas. The shallop tied up first at Stephen's plantation, Bennett's Choice.

Stephen was excited and eager to have Mathilda see the new house, which was almost finished. The carpenters, joiners and plasterers had promised to be out of the place by September, so he might bring his bride home directly after the wedding, which was to take place in Jamestown.

Cecily had planned everything. The wedding at the church

was to be very simple because, in deference to the governor's and Stephen's religious views, they would be obliged to have the Puritan minister, Mr. Thompson, whom the governor had brought down from New England to be his chaplain—a nice man, but the ritual was as bare as a scraped bone, according to Cecily's way of thinking.

She would give a large garden party after the wedding. She wished she might have it at Green Spring, at Sir William Berkeley's Great House, but she supposed that would create talk, and she doubted the propriety of such a move. In truth, when she mentioned the subject to Peter, who usually smiled at her vagaries, he frowned and set his foot down. Cecily, who had more latitude than any other wife in Virginia, knew that, when Peter set his foot down, it was time for her to turn about. Still, a party in the governor's lovely garden, with little tables set under the apple and peach-trees, would have been delightful.

Mathilda's wedding garments were ready. Cecily had given her a bolt of fine white satin brocade for the bridal gown, which she had from France, and a long piece of lace from Spain. She had already planned how she would arrange the bride's blonde hair, high, with a comb of carved tortoise, over which she would drape the lace, as the Spanish women wore their mantillas.

Cecily was thinking of the event as she sat on the after-deck of the shallop under the gay canvas awning that had been stretched to keep the hot sun from blazing down on them. Stephen and Mathilda were seated as far from the others as possible. Peter talked with the governor and Matthew Caswell, who had come down from the upper James and was crossing to one of his plantations on the south shore.

She turned her eyes on young Blount. A little spark glimmered. A well-favoured young man, tall, personable, with the deep-set eyes of the Blounts. He was marriageable; he belonged to a titled family; Sibyl could do no better than marry a Blount, even if he were a cadet. Old Tom had a good plantation, and so did his brother James. Surely they would see that he was well set up in Virginia. She must write to the Heralds' College and find out to which family of Blounts he belonged.

Peter came over to speak to her. Bending down he said,

"I know by the sparkle in your eye that you are up to mischief, my girl."

She put her hand over his, which he had placed on her shoulder. "Peter, which Blount is this Philip? Is he of the Courtney family or the Devon branch?"

"I thought so. Matchmaking! You are incorrigible."

"Well, what's wrong with wanting to find a suitable husband for Sibyl? She'll need a strong, firm hand. The girl shows signs of character I don't like."

Peter asked, "What, for instance?"

"Well, she won't sew a fine seam, or knit a sock, or learn to keep house properly. All she wants is to ride a horse or fish. Last week I saw her shooting from a musket."

"If the Indians ever come to attack us, every woman should know how to fire a musket."

Cecily said, "Mathilda is so satisfactory."

Peter walked to the stern of the boat to watch the sailors getting ready to unload empty hogsheads, designed to hold tobacco bound for London.

Sibyl turned away from Philip Blount to watch the shallop tacking so that it would make a clean landing. The tide was running out, a strong current. To land without banging against the pilings of the dock required some skill. When they made the tack, the sails hung slack for some moments before they caught the down-river wind. At that moment the clearing cut into the forest stood out. In the center was the new house, new and bright.

Mathilda got to her feet, went forward to the rail, Stephen following close. The girl's blue eyes were fixed on the building which, in another month, would be her home—a gracious home, a compact structure of red brick, with a sloping Dutch roof. The glazing of the small panes was already finished. One-story wings on either side gave symmetry and dignity to the whole building.

She turned to Stephen. "It is *so* lovely! I did not dream it would be so lovely."

He put his hand over hers on the rail. "I am glad it pleases you, my sweet girl. It is built something on the order of the new one at the Rolfe plantation, but not alike in all particulars. This house is no copy. It must be different, for you alone, a lovely setting for a lovely maid."

"How sweet you are, Stephen! How very sweet!"

He pressed closer to her, until their shoulders touched. "I love you very much, my dear, more than anything in this beautiful world."

She looked up at him. Neither moved, but in that moment deep love flowed between them.

The governor's voice broke the spell. "I do declare the work has gone swiftly."

Cecily cried out, "How delightful! A perfect little gem of a house! I cannot wait to see the rooms. Come, come, let us hasten and examine it from end to end."

Sibyl alone had nothing to say. It was a little house, not so large as the gardener's home at Coddington Manor, but indeed very pretty, set on the high bank with the broad James as foreground, and with the tall pine trees and spreading oaks for background. It represented the end of something important in the life of the sisters. She felt strangely alone.

On the way up the steps cut into the steep bank she found Philip Blount beside her, his strong firm hand under her elbow to give her the support she did not need—a courteous gesture on his part, which she should meet with equal courtesy. She would have liked to run to the crest of the bank, find her way to the comforting shadow of some wide-spreading tree, lay her head against the rough bark. She wanted to be away from the sound of voices . . . from people. But she held herself in check, walking sedately, listening without hearing.

Presently, when the others were moving from room to room, Sibyl slipped away. She found a tree, the heavy crown of which cast a great dark shadow. She could not lay her cheek against the bark, for it was not smooth like a beech or a cherry, but rough, for it was a poplar, the tulip flowers already faded. She sat with her back against the trunk, thinking her urgent thoughts of what the future might bring. Tears came to her eyes when her mind turned to Coddington Manor. It was so far away, like a dream only half remembered. How desirable it was—Dame Margaret quiet, serene; Cook beating eggs in the sweet warm kitchen; the hunt and the baying of hounds; the church bell at evening!

"Oh, Richard," she whispered, "my dear Richard, if only I had your shoulder to rest against!" Then a cheering thought came. Richard was at Bennett's Welcome. She would see him, no matter where they kept him.

Someone spoke her name. "Mistress Sibyl, do I intrude?" It was Philip Blount standing beside her and looking down from a great height. She thought, I believe he is as tall as my dear Richard. She said, "Please sit down."

"You ran away, so I ran after you." He threw himself full length on the mossy ground beside her. "Why did you run? Didn't you like the new home Mr. Stephen Bennett has built for your sister?"

"Indeed I did. It is very pretty, small and cozy like a little nest. But I was tired." After a silence she said, "The river is beautiful from here, so strong and quiet."

"Yes, of course. How aptly you describe it! You are different from most young maids, but I expected that."

She lifted her eyes. "I don't understand."

He laughed a nice young laugh. "John Prideaux told me I would like you. He said Mathilda is blonde and delicate and haughty. But little Sibyl is all life and gaiety, as full of swift movements as a bird."

Sibyl gazed at him. "You know John Prideaux? You have seen him since . . . Worcester?"

"Yes. He was visiting us in Cornwall, and I was at his home New Place."

"You must have seen Dame Margaret, my dear, dear Dame Margaret, and Cook Ellie. . . ." She was all life now, and questioning. The lonely mood had vanished.

"I saw Dame Margaret two days before I sailed from Bideford. She was in good health, but sad about her son. She had heard nothing from him since he was spirited away from Bristol. I have been searching for him, but no one seems to know anything about Richard Monington. I've come to believe he must have been transported to one of the isles in the Indies, Somers or St. Johns or Barbados."

Sibyl picked a blade of grass with a little blue flower. She did not meet his eyes. She was afraid they would tell a secret, and Richard had warned her. She asked a question, instead of answering one. "Have you seen Nicholas Holder or Kathryn his wife? They both lived near Coddington Manor before they were married. They might know."

"The Holders are in Maryland, I was told." He rolled over on his back, his crossed arms beneath his head. Sibyl was glad she didn't have to look directly into his dark lazy eyes. She spread the skirts of her yellow frock so that her sandals were hidden. She twisted the locket that hung from a black ribband around her neck and tucked a heavy lock of hair behind her ear. Philip was quiet, watching an eagle planing in the blue sky. The voices at the house were faint.

She asked, "How did you happen to come to Virginia?"

He rolled over so that he might look at her. "It's a long story. Some day I'll tell you all about my grandfather, for whom I am named, and how he came out in Sir Richard Grenville's ship on a great adventure. That was in Elizabeth's time, the great, great days of Elizabeth."

"Oh!" she cried. "Did he sail to Roanoke Island for Sir Walter?"

"Indeed yes, and what adventures he would tell us! When I was a young boy, I was determined to come to Virginia to have adventures of my own. But—how sad!—the Indians are friendly, no longer enemies. People dwell in houses and are quite civilized. I lived too late for the great days."

Sibyl said, "So did I. I would have loved to sail out onto the great Ocean Sea with Sir Humphrey Gilbert or Drake or Grenville."

"Strange talk for a little girl!"

"I'm not so little. I'm as tall as Mathilda, and well over fifteen. Aunt Cecily was married when she was my age."

Philip teased, "Don't tell me you are thinking of marriage!"

"Indeed not. I'm never going to marry. I think I'll be a nun."

Philip laughed. "It's unthinkable."

"I don't know why. There are many nice nuns . . . or do you think they wouldn't have me?"

"If I looked into the future, I'd say you'd marry some nice strong man, who understood that a restless horse should be handled with a light hand on the rein, light but firm."

Sibyl joined his laughter. "No one takes me seriously," she said. "I think I see them going to board the boat." She got to her feet easily, without help from Philip.

As they were walking to the bank, he spoke again of Richard Monington. "It is known to a few in England that he was with the King during the escape. It is well if he remains unknown to Cromwell's men."

Sibyl did not trust herself to speak of Richard. She asked Philip if he was going to stay long at Bennett's Welcome.

"A few days only. I'm on my way to visit my uncle at

Blount Point. He is coming to the meeting the governor has called."

"I did not know about any meeting."

"Yes, tomorrow; it's about tobacco. I believe most of the planters along the lower James are summoned. When that's over, I'll go away with my uncle."

"I mean, are you going to stay in Virginia?"

"I don't know. It seems to me very crowded, with all the good land taken and the poor left. I've been talking to Mr. Woodward about the land in the southern part of the colony. It's heavy, rich bottom land, he says, and there are great rivers. I've a mind to go with him when he makes the survey. He is going clean down to the farthest south, along the Great Sound and on to Roanoke Island."

Sibyl's eyes twinkled. "Perhaps the Indians are wild and savage on Roanoke Island."

They had come to the top of the bank. As they started down the crude log steps, he said, "John Prideaux told me I would like you, and I do."

She felt herself blushing. She was sure that with her dark skin it would not be a delightful moss-rose blush, like Mathilda's, but an ugly cabbage-rose red. She was angry with herself, but she answered calmly enough, "I thank you. I value friends, particularly friends of John and Richard." She hesitated a moment. "If I hear anything of Richard, I will inform you." She hoped she spoke casually.

"Please do. I know he would be eager to have news from Devon and Dame Margaret's messages."

The wind had died to a mere whisper. The sails flapped. In some way the tobacco hogsheads came loose and rolled about the deck. All the men, including the governor, sprang to the assistance of the watermen in their endeavour to lash them fast again.

It was almost two hours before they reached the landing at Bennett's Welcome. The governor's servants and two overlookers were at the landing. In the manor-house there was a great bustling and running about of maidservants under the skilful direction of the housekeeper. Only white indentured were allowed in the house.

The governor made an excellent host. He apologized lightly for his wife's absence. He showed the men to their rooms. The housekeeper said, "Madam Montague, will you come this way? I have given you the west room, so that the sun will not disturb you in the early morning, with a room across the hall for your maid."

"I did not bring my maid. She has gone ahead to the shore house. Where are the young ladies?"

"In the east wing, madam. Your husband's room is next to your own."

Cecily laughed. "We still occupy the same room. That is old-fashioned, is it not—but a good idea, especially in winter, don't you think?"

The housekeeper, a prim creature named Pritchard, smiled thinly. "I couldn't say, madam. I've never been married."

Cecily stared at her a moment. "Perhaps you've escaped some annoyances, but again you have missed some pleasures."

The woman's smile broadened a little. "My sister has eight."

"Good God, woman! I've had only four."

"I mean children, madam, not husbands."

"You comfort me. I couldn't imagine twice my number. Eight children! Well, I've had four of them too—different fathers—but they are all gone from the nest."

"'Tis a pity, madam."

"Yes, I suppose so, but that's the world. I'm glad they are having their own lives. I hope theirs will be as joyous as my life has been."

"Perhaps you make your own joy, madam."

Cecily smiled broadly. "My good woman, you're a diplomat."

Pritchard took Madam Montague's light taffeta wrap and little Italian straw bonnet. She hung the cape on a peg under a curtain of rose-vined chintz, and put the little bonnet on the top shelf of the armoire. "One learns to be observing, madam. I'll assign one of the maids to wait on you. She will bring hot water for your bath at once."

Cecily sighed. She longed to stretch out on the high comfortable bed under the canopy netting, but she supposed she had better bathe while the water was hot. Anyway, sailing across the river was not so heating as a trip by horseback or so dusty.

Sibyl flopped onto the bed as soon as she got into the sisters' bed-chamber, but Mathilda ordered her off. "In your gown, and on that lovely counterpane! How can you be so careless? Take off your dress and put on a wrapper, and roll back the quilt." She came over to examine the handiwork. "A rose, the Tudor rose pattern. I must make one for that little pink bedchamber with the dormers. Don't you think the house is a love, Sibyl?"

"It's charming, but isn't it awfully small?"

"Indeed it isn't! It's quite palatial."

Sibyl looked to see if Mathilda was in earnest. She must have forgotten their home in England and the great rooms at Coddington Manor. "Of course I was teasing, Sis. The house is a gem, and such a setting!"

But Mathilda was not listening. She was bending over the pink and white quilt, counting the patches. Sibyl thought, She's an old married woman already, talking about patching quilts. One thing I'll never do is sew blocks to make quilts. I'll have Holland blankets two inches thick. Sibyl kicked off her buckled shoes and loosened her bodice so fast that two buttons popped off.

"Oh, Sibyl, you're so rough—just like a boy!"

Supper was at five. The sun was still high when they left the table. Sibyl said to the governor, "May I walk about the garden, sir?"

"Certainly. But don't venture beyond the hedges, or down toward the compound where the slaves live. They don't appreciate people watching while they eat."

Sibyl went out through a side door and into the trim garden enclosed with holly bushes and little conical cedars trimmed into neat patterns. She wondered where the indentured folk lived. If the slaves were in the direction of the fields and tobacco barns, the white folk must be in the opposite direction. She followed a path to an arbour on the verge of the bank. There was a little thicket of trees, beyond which she caught a glimpse of small cottages. She would walk that way. The governor had said only not to walk toward the slaves' compound.

After she had walked five minutes or so, she came on the first cottage, which was unoccupied. There were two others near together beside a tall sycamore tree. She saw a man sitting on the piazza, an old gentleman with a beard pointed exactly like a portrait of the King, the old King. She went closer. "Good evening, sir. It is a lovely evening."

The man turned, holding his head slightly sidewise like an inquisitive bird. He was very thin and had a gentle look.

"I do not know your voice," he said. "Step closer, little miss. I am blind and I must hear a voice distinctly to know the speaker."

"I am Sibyl Jordan. I came in the governor's shallop with Uncle Peter and Aunt Cecily."

The old face brightened. "Cecily Jordan . . . or is it Cecily Montague now? It is many years since our paths crossed. You are young, mayhap thirteen or fourteen by your voice, and you are tall for your years."

"How can you know that if you are . . . that is, if you can't see?"

He laughed, a sort of dry cackle. "By the height the voice comes from, of course. There is no magic in that, only reason."

"I'm over fifteen," Sibyl said. "And I am almost as tall, excusing a little, as my sister Mathilda."

"Mathilda? Ah, young Stephen is going to marry Mathilda Jordan."

"Yes. My sister."

"Ah, well, well. Is she as nice as you are, child?"

"Oh, much, much nicer. She can sew and she knows how to supervise a cook and make quilts and . . ."

"And you, child, can you sew and make quilts?"

"No, sir. That is, I make quite a mess of my samplers, and I'm very awkward, but I can cast a line and shoot at a target."

"Ah, yes, a boyish girl."

"Well, not exactly. I don't look like a boy."

"Tell me what you do look like. I want to see your countenance through your own eyes."

"Well, sir, I'm tall, and my elbows and knees are knobby, and my arms and limbs are too thin, and my hair is brown and an awful chore to dress because it is too heavy, and my skin is dark too, and my eyes. But Mathilda has a fair soft skin like a rose petal, and her hair is yellow, and her eyes are blue. She is beautiful."

"Now you've told me many things. Where are you going?"

Sibyl had moved, restless. She wanted to walk on the next house. "I am taking a little stroll, sir. I was sitting still for so long in the boat."

"Walk past the next house. You will find a pretty little path that leads to the creek. You may see herons and waterfowl.

Look out for snakes when you get to the reeds along the bank. August is the time they change their skins. But you are not a timid child."

"No, sir. Thank you. I will take the little path to the creek."

She walked along slowly. She saw no one in the next cottage, but evidently someone lived there. There were dusty boots by the door and a coat hung on a peg. She was almost at the creek when she saw Richard. He was casting a line in among the reeds. She stood very still, watching. She must not cry out her joy, nor rush to him and throw her arms around him, as her heart longed to do. One must not disturb a fisherman.

After a moment he had a bite. She could tell by his still, taut body. He gave a quick jerk and a silvery fish made an arc through the air and landed almost at her feet.

The fisherman turned. "Sibyl!" he exclaimed. "Little Sibyl!"

"Oh, my dear Richard!" She flung herself at him.

"Steady, now. Steady!" He laughed. "You'll be tangled in the fishline. I don't want you on a hook." He dropped the pole and put his arm about her shoulders.

She kissed his cheek vigorously. Words tumbled out of her mouth. "Please, may I tell him about you? He saw Dame Margaret just before he sailed from Bideford."

"Who, Sibyl? Who has seen my mother?"

"Oh, I *am* sorry. I forgot. Philip Blount is here. He's over there now, at the governor's. We're all there. He's been looking for you in Jamestown. I didn't tell him, because it was a secret."

"Good girl! Run back to the house. Tell him to walk down through the tobacco field, back of the storehouses, early in the morning. I'll be working down there. Now run back to the house."

"I'm so happy I could sing for joy."

Richard patted her arm. "What a dear, dear child you are! Now run, before you are missed. Remember, I am not Richard Monington, but an indentured man who does not speak with ladies from the Great House."

"Oh, Richard, now I want to weep!"

"Run, run and keep your tears for some other and more suitable occasion, such as losing a five-pound fish off the hook."

Sibyl laughed, gave him a resounding kiss and ran away.

Richard's expression changed. Phil Blount, with word from his mother—that was news to give him a quiet night and a swift rising at sun-up.

Digby came in before he went to his cot. He had other news. The girl Tamar was at the third station. He said he had it from the Hawk; the evening signal drums had brought the message. "Captain, I don't like it, messing around with slaves and drums that talk and swamp spirits. May the Lord protect us from Beelzebub and all his black hellions! I don't like it."

"Nor I, Digby, but let us keep in good cheer." He told him then of the child Sibyl and Philip Blount. "By morning we'll have news of Devon, my man."

Digby raised his head, listening. Through the quiet night the throbbing of the drums came clearly. "I don't like it," he said again. "It's witch-work, it is. Last night I woke and thought I heard old Satan riding through the tree-tops."

Richard got into bed. "Pull the covers over your head. You won't hear the drums or the devil riding."

"Hist! Don't call his name aloud or you'll bring him to you." Digby did as Richard suggested. He crawled into his cot and burrowed under the covers. In a moment he was asleep, breathing heavily. Sleep did not come to Richard so readily. It was a long time before he composed himself, and when he slept, he dreamed that the girl Tamar rescued Sibyl from a serpent's fangs. The serpent changed suddenly to Kathryn Holder. She stood beside the two maids, laughing, laughing.

Philip Blount was waiting in the field when Richard, hoe over his shoulder, came to the place of meeting. The two men clasped hands firmly and stood in silence for a moment, looking at each other. They were old friends from holidays together in Cornwall and Devon.

"You are thin as an August pilchard," Blount said. "And who marked your cheek?"

"No matter who. I'll settle that later! If I seem thin, I'm all muscle and sinew. I've been working for six months, Phil; working with hoe and rake and scythe. Man, I never knew what work meant before. But I'm alive, and not too bad off either."

"When the maid Sibyl told me about you last night, I couldn't believe my ears. Why, I'd talked to the little fibber in

the afternoon; she hadn't heard a thing about you, and all th
time she knew you were here, the little rogue!"

"She was bound by a promise to me."

"Mayhap, but I've never seen anyone lie with quite such
guileless face. I don't trust that maid. I think I'll woo and wee
her one of these days."

A strange, unaccountable anger came over Richard. "How
can you talk that way? She's nothing but a child, a little girl."

Philip laughed. "A child that is bursting the bounds. Did
you not notice how her body pressed against her bodice unti
the buttons were like to burst?"

"I did not."

"Well, you didn't look. And her round hips . . . In another
year she will be in bloom, or I miss my guess."

Richard changed the subject abruptly. He didn't like Philip's
words or the implication. He said, "You have word from
my mother?"

"Yes. There was no time for her to write. I happened to
glimpse her on the quay at Bideford. She was going to London
to see if there was anything to be done about getting the
Lord General to release Coddington Manor. I doubt if she
will have success. Royalists are in ill favour these days. It's
God's blessing you are here in Virginia. In England, if Cromwell knew you aided in the King's flight, he'd have you drawn
and quartered."

Richard grinned. "So John Prideaux wrote, but I'm here,
so I'm safe from danger."

They walked to the verge of the field and sat on a log.
Richard turned so he might watch through the rows of corn,
lest the Fox catch him idling. It was good to talk with Philip,
one of his own kind. It was good to have word of his mother,
to hear about the way she was making a new life.

Philip was disturbed by the situation. "I'll get my uncle to
buy your indenture!" he exclaimed. "I've the money."

Richard shook his head. "I doubt if Stephen would sell me.
He thinks I'm developing into a tobacco-man, and good
tobacco-men are scarce."

"Damn tobacco-men! The idea is intolerable that you should
be the servant of a Puritan farmer. Why, it's like being let out
to one of your own tenants! And his wife a woman who has
been like a foster sister to you! Your mother will be in a high
fury."

"It is rather silly," Richard admitted.

"Silly! It's unthinkable. Look, we'll get Uncle Tom to buy your time. Then you'll go south with me and take up land in the new country. What do you say to that?"

Before Richard could answer, they heard a bird-call, the gay lilt of a mocker, mimicking some song-bird. "Listen! That is a signal. It means the overlooker is on his way to the field. Walk along the path to the right; follow the creek; it will take you to my cottage. From there you will see the house."

Phil said, "I'll come to your place tonight after dark. We must devise some way . . ."

But Richard had disappeared, moving silently through tall rows of corn. Philip Blount watched the approaching figure of a man on horseback. He lingered long enough to observe the overlooker, his lowering brow, the cruelty in his angry face.

"God's death!" he muttered, then he, too, moved silently into the shadow of the forest. In a few minutes he was at the bank of the stream. He turned and followed its winding flow until he was in sight of the houses. He knew he must keep his own counsel. It would never do for the governor to know that he was harbouring a man who had helped effect the King's escape from Worcester. It was a heavy secret for a young girl to carry. She must be trustworthy and have wisdom. He thought of the bland, childlike expression on her face when she told him that if she heard any word of Richard, she would inform him. "The little minx," he said, smiling at the remembrance. "The little minx!"

Philip Blount did not go to Richard's cottage that night. All morning boats sailed up to the Bennett landing. All afternoon horsemen rode in from near-by plantations. By afternoon twenty or thirty had gathered in answer to the governor's summons. They wondered why he had called them at an interval between the Council meetings. But it was August and the plantation work slack, a good time for a visit. Then too Bennett's Welcome was more pleasant in the summer than Jamestown, with its fevers and its plague of insects. "Bug nights" were more frequent on the low land of the island.

The planters moved about, joining one group or another, seating themselves on the piazza or in chairs on the lawn under shade trees. Servants were busy, some fetching chairs and a table for the governor and his secretary. Others served sillabub or wine made from the dark luscious grapes which grew in abundance on the place. Little rustic tables were placed beside the chairs so a man might rest his pipe, his pouch of tobacco and his glass. Quakers from Chuckatuck, Phillips, Jordan, Tomes and Robert Lawrence, sat stiffly to one side, their broad high-crowned beavers set firmly on their heads. Presently the glasses were removed, pipes lighted.

The governor took a seat at the table. Stephen opened a bundle of papers and spread them out so that his kinsman might refer to them without lifting them from the table. After a short prayer for guidance, the governor opened the meeting.

He said he had called them together to discuss some important matters which concerned every planter in Virginia. Dispatches had come to him from England that the Lord General had the affairs of the colonies foremost in his mind. The situation in Virginia had been discussed in Parliament at various times and it had been resolved to bend every effort to strengthen trade.

In so doing it was thought well to concentrate on the commodities most needed in England and in Europe, and those items that would bring the largest reward in money. Endeavour should be made to raise a high grade of tobacco. The Spanish leaf was the best, and the Spaniards were seeking trade in France and the Low Countries.

The governor paused. The men moved uneasily in their chairs. George Durant whispered to Catchmead that something disadvantageous was coming. A man from Lower Norfolk exchanged glances with the men from Chuckatuck. Matthews beckoned a servant to fetch a lightwood splinter, so that he might relight his pipe. Mr. Boddie, whose land lay north near the old Rolfe plantation, said aloud, "I wonder if they will insist on our planting indigo and ginger root again."

The governor took a sip of water. He read from a page: "It has been suggested that we be more selective in the sassafras root we send to England, and that the pitch be clean, without twigs and cones. Why not try another method of burning charcoal? The London merchants want walnut lumber, not pine."

The governor went over the list. Every commodity was inferior in quality to the Spanish competition.

"I don't believe that! . . . Pardon me, Your Excellency, but I'm sure our pitch and tar are equal to any. As for our lumber, it is superior. I can't see why the Board of Trade tries to discourage us. We are not competing with England."

The governor raised his eyebrows. "But they do want to encourage us, Mr. Martin. I think you misjudge the instructions."

Martin shrugged his shoulders. By half turning his body he could see across the James to his own plantation, one of the most successful in the colony.

"Now we come to the tobacco problem. Really it is our first problem, but I have left it to the last." The governor looked for a paper which he could not find. He spoke to Stephen, who rose and went into the house.

The dark-eyed, thin-faced Durant leaned over his neighbour Catchmead to speak to the Quaker gentleman who had left Chuckatuck to plant in the south along the Perquimans River, the lovely stream which flowed into the Sound of Roanoke. "You should be happy that you are beyond all crop regulation and restrictions, Phelps."

The Quaker nodded. "I and my neighbours the Joneses have discussed *that* matter a number of times with the Relphs and Colonel Henderson Walker. I might say we are well beyond taxes and quit-rents, for no collector visits us."

A second Quaker, Joel Ricks, said, "But they tax us extra on all our tobacco that we send on ships sailing from Jamestown. I don't know why."

Durant said, "Because your leaf is prime. That's why."

"We grade," Mr. Ricks answered concisely.

Philip Blount, who had taken a seat at the outer ring of the circle, looked about him to study the faces of the Virginia planters. It was easy, he thought, to pick out the large landowners with Royalist tendencies. They had an easy assurance of success. The small landowners were not so well dressed. Their expressionless faces were like those of yeomen at home, men of independence, who stood with sturdy, almost stubborn independence on their constitutional rights.

The governor's voice broke in on Philip's musings. ". . . to limit the number of plants per head to be cultivated, counting the leaves per plant that are to be cured . . . tobacco viewers and sworn officers to consult with planters . . . one hundred seventy pounds per pole for two years . . ."

Philip felt the change that came over the group. They had been interested listeners. Now hostility hung in the air like a menacing cloud. A number of the men sprang to their feet. Philip was in no mood to listen to harangue or argument. This was not his affair. He left his seat and walked away. As he reached the corner of the house, he paused. The governor had raised his voice. "By an Act of the Assembly of 1640, I have the power to order all the bad tobacco destroyed, and half the good."

A dozen voices of irate planters rose to drown out Bennett's voice.

The sun had set; dusk was falling. Slaves carrying lighted pine torches were standing about the long supper tables in the garden.

The heated discussion went on. Planter Caswell shouted above the clamour, "Gentlemen! Gentlemen! Let us listen to what the governor has to say. Surely there is some solution of our difficulties without giving way to anger."

"That's London merchants' talk. We'll not abide with their interference any longer. We've been silent long enough."

Caswell answered, "Who will buy our tobacco if we do not sell to London merchants? Bristol? Bideford? You know they haven't the money. The money is in London. Let us listen to Governor Bennett." He might be a Royalist conspirator, but he was a fair man.

The governor was standing quietly, the papers rolled in his hands. He looked about him slowly. Then he said, "Gentlemen, I see that supper waits us in the garden. I propose that we partake of food. Let further discussion come later."

Someone laughed. "I second the motion," said Durant. "I've had no food since morning."

They moved across the lawn to the garden, following the governor's lead. A small group held back but were urged on by the others.

The moon had risen and hung like a globe above the dark of the forest, the red harvest moon at the full.

With the first mouthful of turtle soup anger subsided. Let business wait! There was time enough for arguing the governor's suggestion point by point.

Richard Bennett said to Caswell who was seated beside him, "Thank you, Mr. Caswell. Raising your voice gave me a breathing spell."

Caswell said, "I believe in every man being heard, but I reserve the right to disagree."

The governor smiled. "We are in perfect accord on that." Then he turned to Edward Digges who sat at his right. Digges had been an onlooker. He raised mulberry trees, not tobacco.

On full stomachs after the meal the arguments rose and fell. Sometimes the governor all but had the whole group with him, until a dissenter raised a vital question, when the dispute began all over. For an hour it went on, then another hour until the moon was high.

The smoke from the pine torches made a clean and pleasant odour. In the background the slaves moved about, ready to substitute a new torch when the old one died down.

It was approaching midnight. The strain of constant bickering showed on drawn faces and in tired eyes. The men who would sail home that night were getting restive, but not giving way to the governor's plea to destroy half their tobacco crop.

Bennett realized they were beating him down. He did not wish to invoke the Act of 1640 and destroy by force. He had been a planter for many years, a governor only a few months. He listened sympathetically to the objections, but on the other hand his orders from London were definite.

Finally Matthews, from across the river, rose. "You talk about burning our tobacco. What about yours, Governor? You have a big yield of prime leaf this year. What are *you* going to do?"

This was the question for which Bennett had waited. "I have already destroyed some—the lower leaves that showed signs of rust or mildew. Come, gentlemen, do me the honour to step to my tobacco houses. There is something I would like you to see."

The men arose with alacrity. Bennett had always had good tobacco. His houses were large and he made good money. They followed him along the path, slaves holding torches to light the way in the shadows under the trees.

Philip Blount wondered what was coming.

A small Negro boy tugged at his sleeve. He said his name was Puti, and that the "tall tree man" was waiting for him near the tobacco houses. The lad led him through the kitchen garden to a shaded spot behind the sheds.

Richard greeted him. "Stand well in the shadow, Phil. I don't think anyone will see you. Something is up. We were all called in to weigh tobacco and change the racks about. We don't know what it means."

Philip said, "Nothing important. The governor is going to show his tobacco to the planters." He glanced about him. The moonlight disclosed slaves and white men in groups and ranks.

"Everyone on the plantation is here," Richard said.

A dozen slaves were moving about, thrusting pine torches into the dark places beyond the sheds. The rows of hanging hands of tobacco were illuminated. The poles were in ranks, with little aisles between, wide enough for a man to pass.

The governor had arrived. The planters crowded to the poles, exclaiming over the quantity and quality of the leaf. It took some time for the examination. When it was complete and they stood in groups at one side, the governor said, "Mr. Matthews, will you repeat the question you asked me a little while ago?"

Matthews' address was formal, as formal as though he were speaking in front of a Grand Assembly. "Certainly, Your Excellency. I repeat the question: What do you intend to do with your crop?"

In the silence that followed the governor walked up to the giant Negro, Enoch. He took the fire-brand from his hand. "This is my answer, gentlemen. I set the brand to my surplus tobacco, as required by the laws of the Commonwealth."

A protest rose from the throats of the planters, a deep agonized groan from the slaves and the white indentured, whose labour had produced the great yield.

"God in Heaven!" exclaimed Richard, as the flames crackled and roared down the rows of dried leaf. "That is why he had us bring sand buckets and water."

"Watch that shed!" a cry went up as the sparks rose and spread. Slaves ran forward with the buckets, swarmed onto the roof of a small shed that had caught fire. Rows of fire lighted the horrified faces of the planters, the sullen, rebellious faces of the white workers.

The Hawk came close to Richard. "It's evil, it is, to burn a man's labour. I feel my vitals burning with every leaf that the fire licks into its red maw."

"And I," Richard murmured. He turned to speak to Philip,

but he was making his way toward the frightened group of women who stood watching. Richard saw Sibyl, hands tight against her throat, her eyes open wide in horror; Mathilda's pale face, as she clutched Stephen's arm. Someone wailed. The Negroes were swaying back and forth. Some of the white women knelt, their hands lifted in prayer.

"God will smite us down. Oh, my little tender green plants!" a woman's voice cried above the crackling of the fire. "My pretty little plants!"

Richard thought he could not bear such destruction. Digby was cursing silently beside him. The Hawk's eyes were glazed with the light of frenzy. He tried to beat out the fire with a tobacco stick, but it was too late. When he snatched a bundle of leaf from the blaze, he had in his hand only the ashes.

Tears from smoke were in the eyes of helpless onlookers. Mayhap tears came to the eyes because of something deeper, the destruction of man's labour, the waste of Nature's lavish growth.

The governor's face was white; his eyes filled with despair. He raised his head, as though seeking guidance. Every face was turned toward him, waiting.

Breaking the long silence, he spoke quietly, with a sort of peaceful serenity in his tired voice. "Gentlemen, there will be no more burning of tobacco as long as I, Richard Bennett, am Governor of Virginia."

CHAPTER 22

Tamar's Tree and Kathryn's Purchase

THE effect of the tobacco burning was far reaching. Work went on at Bennett's Welcome, but there was no spark, no urge behind the daily tasks. There was no singing as the men cut corn or finished stripping the stalks of the tall tobacco plants for the last leaves.

Amongst the slaves there was no singing in the fields, but the drums tuned up at night in the compound. Strange dances that belonged to pagan harvest festivals took place, but no white man saw these rituals.

The indentured men were irritable. There were fights and loud words and uneasiness. The manor-house was closed. The governor and his family took their rest at the shore through the long hot days. No news came from across the river. No ships lay at the wharf. No word came from Tamar. Yet unrest was everywhere.

Richard Monington shared the unrest that blanketed the whole plantation. Digby was on edge. He swore dragoons' lusty oaths—at flies, stinging insects, small insects that burrowed into the skin, causing irritation and incessant scratching. Only the blind man remained placid and serene. He told Richard, "The seasoning illness can be of the mind as well as the body. I've lived through many a season since I came out here a lad of twenty. That was just after the Good Friday massacre of '22."

He folded his hands over the knob of his stick. Richard settled himself, his back against a pillar that supported the piazza roof. Angela had given them a good supper of fish and fresh beans. The air was humid and heavy. The sun was low, setting red. A storm was in the making.

"Yes," he said, "I've lived through fevers and agues aplenty, over there at Jamestown, when I think back, but none so bad as ship fever, when I came over in the *Abigail*, a little ship that rolled and tossed, full of people and goods and sickness. We grew accustomed to seeing a body sewed up in a strip of canvas and tossed overboard. After a time there wasn't even a canvas.

"The governor's wife, Lady Wyatt, was on the ship. A well-favoured personable woman she was, working among the sick, not sparing herself . . . a personable woman."

Richard asked, "What did you find when you landed at Jamestown?"

Mr. Chapman shook his white head. "Little to comfort a young lad stirred by keen desire to be a Drake or a Cavendish or a John Smith. The massacre had put fear deep into the hearts of the settlers. They drew close together. Some abandoned their farms. Fields were cultivated only as necessary, with one man ploughing and another with a musket guarding. Immigrants were crowding into Jamestown Island. Planters hurried down-river to seek the safety of numbers. I recollect meeting George Sandys, the treasurer who wrote verses, in the churchyard one day. 'The living can scarce bury the dead,' he said. He was shaking with the chills at the moment."

"You've seen many governors in your time, Old One."

"Aye, that I have, good ones and bad. Sir George Yeardley came next. He had been governor once before, you recollect. I told you how he won his knighthood in order to win the maid he loved at Flowerdew Hundred." He chuckled. "A man will do strange things for a woman now, won't he? Glad I never had one to pull me about on a string like a jack-a-monkey. But that was long, long ago."

Richard asked another question. He wanted to keep him talking of the old days. "You say you had good governors and bad. Who was the worst governor?"

Without hesitation the Ancient Planter answered, "Harvey, Sir John Harvey. Maybe we thought him worser than he was. You recollect when James was King, he was a-fighting with the London Company. Some say he and the Earl of Warwick were siding with the Spanish King, wanting to let Florida swallow up Virginia to please Philip. I don't know. Only there in London they were pulling and tugging in the company, Sir Edwin Sandys against Warwick. Finally the London Company's Charter was annulled. That was in '23. Harvey came in the spring of '30 under the first Charles. He was a Royal governor, and he acted that way. He used to go down to the wharf to meet the captains of foreign ships. We had many Dutch and French ships, aye and Spanish, those days, trading and carrying off naval stores when the planters ventured into the woods. Well, Sir John, he always moved in style, with an escort of halberdiers and musketeers and he entertained right royally."

"Why was he always called Bad John?" Richard asked when the Ancient Planter fell silent.

"Because he was bad—cantankerous. He angered his Council from the beginning. He was too sociable and friendly toward Lord Baltimore, letting him make a colony out of North Virginia. Then he acted arrogant, opening the Councillors' letters to the King. There was a revolt, and he was shipped back to England."

Richard asked, "And King Charles sent him back to Virginia again?"

"Yes, with more power than ever. Much good it did to revolt. But we did have a little fun. We had a fight with Maryland. I remember well, we called it a naval battle. Captain Warner and Councilman Cornwallis commanded. We were fighting over the possession of Kent Island in the Chesapeake, I recall."

Richard slapped a biting fly on his arm. Digby came over to join them. He carried a little pan in which an old piece of woollen had been laid over glowing coals. It was smoking heavily and let off a rank odour.

Thomas Chapman said, "Digby, your smudges are evil-smelling, but they are better than gnats."

"Zur, I'm fair bleeding with their bites."

Richard said, "He's telling me about Bad John."

Digby lay down on the floor of the piazza, his face buried in his folded arms. The Old One was silent. The mocking-bird was tuning up in the west. From time to time there was a glow of horizontal lightning. After a while Chapman said, "I recollect that was about the time Richard Kemp started to build the brick dwelling. I helped make brick, wanting to learn the trick, so I could show my boys how to burn them."

"Harvey came back?"

"Yes, yes. What was I saying? Yes, he came back, but he ended in beggary, so many defrauded folk got judgements against him. He did encourage building and many, many servants came out during this time. But he persecuted folk and gave away great grants of land to his friends."

"And who came next?" Digby asked.

"Wyatt again. Did I say that he was a good one? First time, he formally gave us our Civil Constitution, started by Yeardley with the first legislature. Well, he came as governor again, and then Sir William in '42. He was good at first, all full of desire to make a rich and great colony under his direction. He was a fine figger in those days. He wrote a play called *The Lost Lady,* which was on the stage in London, they say. He was a zealous man, but irritable when crossed—specially after the Holy Thursday massacre in '44."

Digby questioned, "I never heard of Holy Thursday. Was it a bad one?"

"Bad enough. Three hundred settlers murdered by that devil Opechancanough—him that led the first massacre. But Berkeley marched out and captured him and put him in gaol in Jamestown. Somebody murdered him, but it was good riddance. . . . Yes, I've seen many a governor and many a governor's lady, too. Some were good and gracious, some ambitious, loving power; some liked Virginia, but more hated it, wanting to get back to England. But never have I seen one like her." He nodded his fine old head in the direction of the manor. "So quiet she moves through life, she is little more than a shadow. But she has power—not noisy or splashing, but steady, quiet like a small stream."

The Ancient Planter yawned. "I've talked too much," he said. "A garrulous old man is what I am, talking, talking."

Richard said, "It was the story-tellers and bards of old who kept history alive."

"Aye, like Homer. 'Twas my kinsman, George Chapman, who put Homer into English." He rose slowly, using the strong hickory chair for support. "I thank you, young gentlemen for listening with such courtesy."

As Digby assisted him to his room, the old man said, "Sometimes in the night when all the world is still, I worry about Tamar."

"And I too, zur. But they say, 'No news is good.' "

"Aye, no news. Wherever she is, I hope the kind Lord will protect her. Good night, good sirs. You have been indulgent. It comforts an old man to talk of the past."

"And it helps young men to listen," Richard replied from

the doorway. "Perhaps it will rain before morning and clear the air, so that you may have a pleasant sleep."

The storm broke about midnight, a torrential rain, blown up from the Caribbean. The thunder was a bombardment, the lightning almost a continuous flash. A tree close by was struck, and the limbs carried St. Elmo's fire from the tips of the branches until it glowed like a great candelabrum.

Richard got up and slipped on his breeks and shoes. He stood at the door watching the fury of the storm in all its diabolic majesty.

Digby buried his head deeper in the covers. "Godamighty, you will be struck!" he cried out. "A feather-bed's the safest place."

Richard did not heed. He stepped out onto the piazza. He had seen something disturbing. He waited for another flash. Now he was sure. A boat in the small creek . . . a bent figure rowing . . . two others silhouetted darkly. The rower was struggling, bent almost double. One man was bailing. The boat must be half swamped. The creek was deep there. A tangle of reeds made it impossible for a boat to reach the shore except opposite to the landing. Calling to Digby, Richard ran down the path. In the boat-house were ropes. He might be able to get a line to the exhausted oarsman. As he ran down the steps he heard Digby's bare feet hit the floor.

The wind had churned the usually placid stream, each gust sending waves into the boat. When he reached the boat-house he found a coil of rope. Running to the end of the wooden wharf, he shouted, trying to attract the rower's attention, but he did not succeed. There was naught for him to do until the boat drew nearer.

Every flash showed the desperate struggle, until a flash came when he could see nothing. The boat had disappeared completely. Digby shouted in his ear, "Over there, by the snag!" Digby was kicking off his shoes.

Richard restrained him. "I'll go. You stand by with the rope." He knotted the rope about his waist, kicked off his shoes and went in. It all seemed silly, but the quiet stream had a strong current, pulling toward the James, and perhaps none of the three could swim. He floated down to the spot where the boat had disappeared, marked by the white snag.

A head loomed out of the water, a coloured man, with a white man on his back. "Catch the rope!" Richard cried. "Go in by the rope." He managed to get the knot loose and tied the rope about the black man's middle.

"There! There, below the snag in the rushes!" the Negro shouted as Digby began to pull.

Richard swam on, shouting. Presently there came an answer, a woman's faint voice. He trod water at the edge of the tules. "Get your feet down," he cried out. "Bottom." The lightning was at longer intervals now, the thunder rumbled not overhead but toward the river.

He caught sight of the girl, the white blur of her face. A moment later he had her under one arm. The up-stream pull was slow, for she was a dead weight. He was glad when he heard the sound of oars in their locks and Digby calling his name.

Digby hauled the girl into the boat. Richard swam alongside. The pull of the current was strong. After a time they came to the wharf. The waterman, Enoch, was kneeling, reaching his long arms out to bring the boat alongside.

The girl began to squeeze the water out of her sodden skirts. The white man was sitting up, his back against an empty tobacco hogshead. It was the parson from Benn's. The girl, then, could be none other than Tamar—Tamar, thin and worn, looking a ghost of herself.

The parson spat water. "We were on the way down-river when the storm broke. We tried to find a place to rest the boat, but there was nothing but reeds and marsh."

Richard said, "Higgins and his men are still searching for her."

"I know. You must hide her for the rest of the night, and all day. By tomorrow night I will speak to Governor Bennett. She decided to come back of her own accord."

Richard said, "The governor is not here. He is at Kiquotan."

"That is unfortunate. I am sure Governor Bennett would grant my request to take her back without punishment, even though I am not of his faith."

"It is the overlooker we have to fear," Richard said. "She must be hidden from him."

The parson shrugged his shoulders. "I'm helpless. I do not know the country hereabouts. If you can get a boat, I can get her to Norfolk County."

Digby stepped forward. "Reverend, we had better handle

this. If it is found out that you aided and abetted, it will go hard against you. Suppose you go to the Great House. The housekeeper will put you up for the night. Best that you know nothing about what goes on."

Richard said, "Well spoken! Digby is right, sir. Enoch will show you the way to the house. Then come back here, Enoch. We will plan what is best to be done." The minister followed Enoch up the path.

Digby said, "I will waken the Ancient Planter."

The girl sat on a coil of rope, leaning against the side of the boatshed. Her voice was flat and weary. "It's no good. I may as well give up. Once I thought I would get away and travel to the south where no one would reach me. It's no use. One cannot run away from punishment." She got to her feet.

"Where are you going?"

"To Higgins. Let him beat me! Let him wear out his wrath on my shoulders!"

"Sit down!" Richard spoke sharply. "You will do no such thing. We will find a way out for you."

Enoch and the dragoon came back together. "The Ancient Planter says to bring the girl. She will be safe with him. They have stopped searching around here for her. Come, Tamar. Let me help you."

Richard did not know that Digby could be so gentle. The girl went off with him, walking slowly, staring straight ahead, almost as though she were in a trance.

In the morning, the minister had departed. When he went to the forest with the wood-choppers to cut cordwood for the winter, Richard found that the restless, sullen mood of the men had given way to a secret exultation. The girl was back, unharmed. She had escaped the hue and cry, the hounds, the diligent search for her on four plantations.

The Hawk gave Richard the news as they went to work. They were carrying a saw to cut a huge cypress that grew at the edge of the backwater. The timber would be used to make shingles to send to England in the early autumn. The Hawk grinned sardonically. "We have a line now. A man can get away, with hiding places ready. Scottie worked it out. Elijah took the girl through to the chapel."

"Then why . . ." Richard stopped. He was anxious to see how much the man knew.

"Some notion that she must come back and give herself up.

Perhaps some of the Reverend's doing. Anyway she was safely carried off and hid for 'most a month. A *man* could do better than that." He looked at Richard with his shrewd little eyes. "Want to try runnin'?"

Richard shook his head. He thought of Philip Blount's saying that he was going to buy him off. "No, not yet. There may be other ways."

"You mean a general rebellion?" The man's voice was sharp in his excitement. "I'd like that. I'd like to pay back some old hurts. Higgins—leave Higgins to me." The Hawk's looks and his voice were filled with venom.

"I know nothing of a rebellion," Richard said.

The Hawk's expression changed to one of lethargy. His hands dropped to his side. His eyes were fixed on the ground. "No. No," he muttered. "No one has courage, no one—not even me. It's the green forest . . . choked by green vines . . . sleeping on the green earth alive with creeping things . . . No . . ."

He turned and shambled away. Presently he came back. He lifted the saw onto his shoulder. Richard followed him along the old Indian track to the backwater of the swamp. The axe-men had felled a tree at the very edge. It lay in the ooze, wedged in among the conical cypress knees. A tough bit of sawing, Richard thought, as he stepped into the soft mud.

"Better you go in barefoot," the Hawk muttered, as he took off his heavy shoes.

Richard said, "I'd rather clean mud off my boots than step on a poisonous water snake."

The Hawk laughed. "Snakes are as scared of you as you be of them."

"I still do not like serpents," Richard took hold of one handle of the saw; the Hawk grasped the other. They set a straight line across the log and settled down to work. It was quiet in the forest save for the sound of birds and the occasional plop of a fish jumping. The whine of the saw was rhythmic, no shriller than the cry of a blue-jay.

After a time the Hawk stopped and stood erect, his hand pressed to the small of his back. "Time to stop for a pipe," he said. He searched about until he found dry sticks suitable to make a spark. With rapid rubbing the spark would ignite a bit of cotton which he carried in the pouch that swung from his belt. Richard sat down on the log and got out his clay pipe.

"It's good to be far enough away from Higgins to sit a spell," the Hawk remarked. "He's takin' to trampin' the woods lately, his long nose sniffin' and smellin' like a blasted hound."

"Do you think he has a suspicion that . . ."

"No, I don't. Not yet. He's edgy, he is. He knows there's something afloat. The fellow scents things out like a ferret."

"Perhaps someone tells him."

The Hawk shook his black head vigorously. "I'd break every bone in the body of a tellcat. Every man knows that. They be scared of the Hawk." He spoke with some pride.

"Do you know where she is?"

The Hawk shook his head. "No, but she's safe for the time being. Best that we don't know the spot. I've seen that devil-spawn draw a whip over a man until he had no will left. That's when a man will talk. So the fewer who know, the safer she is."

Richard said, "Suppose she remains hidden for a few months, what then? You can't put her on a boat for England—or even New England."

The Hawk lighted his pipe with a twig. "She might go to the south the next time there's anyone fleeting."

Richard looked into the dark, twisted face. "You thinking of going out?"

"No. Not me. I talk like it at times, but I haven't the courage. Besides, I'm near the end of my time. By January I'll be a free man."

"Ready to sail for England in the first ship?"

The Hawk shook his head vigorously. "Not me. I'm goin' to stay—stay and plant my fifty acres. You're surprised? I can tell it by the look on your face. Well, I've been thinkin' a lot. The first few years I was ready to bolt at every opportunity—and did—only to be brought back and have time added to my indenture. Lately I've been thinkin', what chance is there for a man like me in England? No chance but the gaol. Here I can be my own man with fifty acres, maybe a hundred. That's why I've made myself a tobacco-man, as good a tobacco-man as any around these plantations. I'll stay in Virginia. Not here along the James. I'll seek new land along the Chowan or the Great Sound of Roanoke. I'll go to Rogues' Harbour, as they call it, because other fleeing men have found haven there. Fine bottom land's to be had along the rivers and the creeks. No, I'll never see England again. Small riddance say you? Mayhap, but I'm a worker. In a new country I'll keep free of gaol."

There was a sound of a twig snapping. Both men silently took their places and began sawing. One never knew whether a broken twig meant a deer or a bear—or an overlooker on the prowl.

Shortly before quitting time the Hawk went off, following the path toward the south. Richard, to ease his tired back, lay flat on the ground under a maple tree. Little shafts of sunlight played about the spreading crown of the great tree. A red-headed woodpecker darted among the branches, and a grey squirrel peeked around a limb, watching the man below with sharp bright eyes. The sky, seen between the gentle fluttering of the green leaves, was incredibly blue. Richard thought, A tree is like the Frenchman's idea that a road is two roads—one to go on and one to return on. So a tree is two trees—the one you see when standing on your feet, and the one you view lying on the ground. The latter was the better, he thought, the more friendly tree with its great spreading arms and its leafy protection. When you were standing, it was one tree among many. When you were looking upward, it became individual, casting its own shade, giving its own shelter to bird and small animal, shade for the weary traveller.

Richard's thoughts were interrupted by the Hawk. His breath came short and sharp-drawn. He had been running. "The hounds are out. Let's be making for home."

Richard said, "What are they tracking? The girl?"

"Don't know. I'm off. We'll do no good here."

"Leave the saw. I'll bring it." Richard did not move. He sat quietly smoking, listening to the far-away baying of the hounds. Presently he heard a splashing in the stream that flowed through the middle of the swamp; an otter or a beaver, he thought. He looked up and saw Tamar. She was wading down the middle of the creek—the old and tried method of throwing the dogs off scent.

"Good girl!" he said aloud. She raised her head, startled at the sound of his voice. Richard glanced at the limbs of the maple tree that hung over the water. He was thinking of Boscobel and Charles's oak. "Can you catch that branch and pull yourself up into the tree?" he suggested. "You'll be well hidden from the ground and have a chance to rest."

The girl looked up, selected a large limb that grew

well out over the water. Gauging the distance, she jumped. She grasped the limb and came forward hand over hand until she reached a saddle near the trunk. After a few minutes, during which there was rustling and agitation among the branches, she said, "Sir, can you see me?"

Richard looked upward into the leafy green canopy. He walked slowly along the path in both directions. "No. You are completely hidden. How did they track you?"

"Sir, I don't know. Perhaps it was accident. I don't like to think that anyone told."

Richard thought of the lunch he had not eaten. He went over to the stump and picked up the parcel Angela had given him at breakfast—appones, a cold potato, an early apple. He climbed to a lower limb and handed the package to Tamar. Her face was strained, weary. The dark smudges under her eyes made them look enormous. He talked to her about the King hiding in an oak.

"For a whole day? Did the King hide in the oak all that time?"

"Yes. He said he could have stayed longer, that he was perfectly comfortable. But now I remember he had a cushion to sit on." He balanced himself straddling a limb and took off his leathern jerkin. "Make a cushion of this." She protested but Richard insisted. Finally he had his way.

"The hounds are closer," she said. "Quick! Get down."

Richard slid from the tree and walked over to the saw log. When the dogs and the keepers came, he was sharpening the saw. The dogs paused, circling about, then made for the stream, lapping at the water with their long red tongues.

Higgins came up shortly. He was winded and sweating profusely. When he saw Richard he stopped. "What are you doing here, Richards?"

Richard glanced at the logs and at the saw in his hand. "Getting the saw sharpened for morning's work," he said.

"Seen anyone go by?" The overlooker was cautious.

"No one went by here, sir."

"Who's working with you?"

"The Hawk. He's gone home. It was my turn to sharpen, so I stayed."

"Sure no one went down the path?"

"No one, either way, sir. Exercising the hounds?"

Higgins glanced at him swiftly. Satisfied by what he saw in

Richard's face, he said, "Yes, exercise. Heard there was a big fox somewhere about." He kicked a cut of the fallen tree. "Hunh, cypress. That's good. We're short on shingles for our next shipment." He went to the creek, scooped up water in his cupped hand and went on.

After a time Richard said, "I'll bring food tomorrow. I think you are safe here. He won't come back tonight. Take the scarf off your head and tie yourself to the tree trunk."

He heard the girl laugh. "You think I'll go to sleep?"

"I hope so. You'll need rest." There was no answer. Richard waited.

Presently she said, "Tell Angela, please. No one else."

"Right. God with you!" Richard shouldered the saw and went down the path. He thought he had put Higgins off, but one never knew. Best to go about everything naturally. He stopped at the plantation kitchen. Angela was alone. He gave Tamar's message and explained the location of the tree where he had left her. Angela listened without comment, nodding once or twice. Richard thought, She is a smart, quick woman; already she has some plan in her mind. He walked slowly to the cottage.

Digby had just come in from a bathe in the creek. He said, "The hounds have been running."

Richard nodded. "I saw Higgins. He said he was hunting for a fox."

Digby grinned as he slipped his tunic over his shoulders. "Did he say a fox or a vixen? Whichever, he came back empty-handed, his face as black as swamp water."

The next morning Richard found his leathern tunic hanging on a limb of the fallen cypress tree.

The Hawk said, "You forgot your jacket last night."

"Yes. I went into the creek for a bathe."

Nothing more was said. The Hawk's eyes followed him as he walked around to his side of the tree. Somewhat later in the day, he said, "You are a good man, Richards. Trust no one. That's the best motto to follow." They walked home in silence.

That night Angela was at the kitchen door. She came down the path on her way to the herb garden. As she passed them she said, "Sirs, fine day."

The Hawk answered, "Aye, fair day and fine for every-body."

Richard glanced from one to the other. He could not read either face, the black or the white, but somehow he knew a message had been spoken. Tamar was still safe.

The fortnight that followed was uneventful. Richard's task was splitting shingles in the Bear Swamp, sometimes with one partner, sometimes another.

Scottie came one morning, whistling a doleful lament. " 'Tis me bagpipe I'd be havin', so's to pipe out a real lament."

Richard said, "Why, Scottie? Why? They haven't found the girl now, have they?"

"Nay, 'tis not that they be findin' anyone. 'Tis that they all come back to Bennett's Welcome. The great ones will arrive on Thursday from their sojourning at the seaside, taking their ease in the cool ocean breezes."

"I thought for a moment they had found Tamar," Richard said.

Scottie shook his head. "No, not that, thanks be to the good Lord! But the manor-house will be swarming, same as it was a month ago, only more this time—Mr. Secretary Claiborne down from Maryland, and Mr. Peter Montague and his house-hold—and all in all Housekeeper's flopping like a chicken that's had its head on the block. She's no time to say a civil word to a mon."

Richard stared.

Scottie explained. "A mon must have a way to know what's going on, and who knows more than Housekeeper?" He raised an eyebrow and grinned. "She's a fair fine bit of a woman, and she'll say a word or two after she's had a wee drap."

"Do you think the girl is well hid?"

Scottie scratched the back of his neck and produced a bear tick between his thumb and first finger. "Beastie!" he said with disgust and proceeded to mash the insect between two pieces of wood. "They bite, and red swellings and fever comes—that I've noticed."

"Do you think the girl is well hid?" Richard repeated.

"Well enough if that devil keeps the dogs off. Otherwise I don't know. We did wrong to take her to the Reverend. He's a good man, but he persuaded her to come back."

"He says she returned of her own accord. She spoke as though she had. But at any rate he must stand for law."

"I suppose so, but what's a mon to do if he believes the law is wrong? Take Mr. Caswell now. He's a law-abiding mon, yet he's helped many a poor devil get away." Scottie stopped suddenly, aghast at what he had said.

Richard said, "Do not worry. I shan't disclose anything. You are not the first to tell of Mr. Caswell's good deeds."

The Scot's face cleared. "Thanks be to God! I should have had my tongue pierced by an awl for speaking and mentioning names. We've few enough friends. It used to be that Mr. Bennett would close his eyes, but now he is the government."

"And must uphold all the laws, good and bad."

"That's the truth. . . . But come, we must split more shingles or we will get a few of the finest for malingering."

"You think a man might have a chance to get away, down south say?"

"Aye, if he can fend for himself in the woods. We've got it easy for a man now, but a woman—that's different. A man can trap a rabbit for a stew, or net a bird, or fish out of a stream. A little corn to carry, and he can fend."

"Then you believe the girl——"

"She'll get tired and give in, that's my thought. Ah weel, we've done what we could. But there's some that's against her for having a bastard child. One of them might give out talk that would lead to her."

"You think the blacks might betray her?"

"No, no. Never the blacks! It would be one of our own, perhaps a woman, a jealous-like woman." He shut his lips over his pipe and hit the log with his froe. "De'il take them all if they let the girl be took!"

When Richard got home that night, Digby was important with news. "They say Tamar has been seen here and about, that she never got away at all. They say too that the governor and his family will be sailing up the river on Thursday. Holiday time is fair over. September be upon us, and all the visitors coming back—Madam Montague and my little friend Sibyl, aye and others besides—Mr. Claiborne and his secretary Mr. Nicholas Holder—" Digby paused and looked quickly at Richard—"and Mistress Holder."

Richard's blank face showed nothing of his thoughts. So she

would be here at Bennett's Welcome—Kathryn Audley . . . born Bradshaw, according to Mr. Caswell. After supper he went down to the water. The old skiff was tied to a piling. He rowed up the creek. The news that Kathryn was coming disturbed him. Days had gone by with no thought of her. Suddenly she intruded herself into his mind. Bradshaw . . . Sir Robert Harley would never have persuaded her to change the name if she hadn't been shamed by it. Since then Sir Robert had become a staunch follower of Cromwell, but Richard knew he had not approved of beheading the King. Many of Oliver's adherents had not—Lord Fairfax for one, and the Lady Fairfax who stood up at the trial and made a brave protest in the name of her sick husband. Kathryn of course shared her guardian's view. She was not responsible for the blood in her veins. Yet surely the blood connection with the violent regicide explained many things in Kathryn's nature. He could not blame her; he began to feel a sort of sympathy for her.

Poor, restless spirit seeking a haven! Would she find peace under Nick Holder's roof, or would she be always one of the uneasy souls, pursued by the furies?

Sibyl was the first passenger ashore when the shallop tied up at Bennett's Welcome. She sped up the log steps set in the bank, and ran toward the house. The housekeeper was waiting on the piazza, and the house was lighted with many candles, for the sun had already disappeared; only the afterglow remained in the evening sky.

"The governor and Madam Bennett are not coming until tomorrow," she told the housekeeper. "Madam Bennett said please to inform you. There was some sort of meeting with men who came on ships. Mr. Claiborne has not arrived yet either, or Mr. Nicholas Holder, but Mistress Holder is here. Oh, it's so nice to be here! I like it better than the shore."

The housekeeper patted her shoulder. "It is nice to have you here, child. You have the same room, with your sister. And Madame Montague? I suppose she is here?"

"Yes, and Uncle Peter, Mathilda and Stephen." She made a little face. "He won't leave Mathilda's side. Are all bridegrooms so silly?"

The housekeeper laughed. "Take your bed-candle, the stairs are dark," she called after Sibyl. She turned to greet the others. The housemaids appeared, and porters with valises and boxes and bundles. "Supper in half an hour, madam," she announced to Cecily.

Sibyl was downstairs before the others had started up. "I'm going to walk in the garden, Aunt Cecily."

"Mind you aren't late for supper."

But Sibyl was already out of doors. She walked sedately down the path to the far garden, then through the little gate in the hedge. Once out of sight of the house, she darted to the path that led to Richard's cottage.

He was sitting on the piazza when she arrived breathless. She did not throw herself upon him in her old exuberant manner, but held out her hand with quite a young-ladyfied air.

Richard put his hand under her chin and raised her face. "What does this mean?" he inquired. "No kisses or fond greeting?"

Sibyl said, "I've been having deportment. I'm not to rush about kissing my friends. I must make a nice curtsy and extend my hand for the gentlemen to kiss. Don't you see, I'll be Miss Jordan in no time now. So I must have manners and not act like a hoyden."

"I thought your manners perfect as they were," Richard observed, sitting down beside her on the steps.

"I can stay only a moment, for the supper bell will ring. Kathryn is here."

Richard said nothing. Sibyl looked up at him. "Nick isn't here. He has stayed behind with Mr. Claiborne and Governor Bennett. They will come tomorrow." There was a silence. Sibyl got up and stood before him. "Kathryn knows you are here. She saw you in Jamestown and traced you to Bennett's Welcome." She leaned over and put her soft cheek against his. "Dear Richard, don't grieve. She's not nice, as you are. You'll find out one day." Suddenly she threw her arms about his neck and pressed her soft lips against his. "Dear Richard!"

Richard got to his feet, his pulses pounding. Sibyl turned and rushed down the path. Richard did not move. He stood looking after her until her white skirts disappeared in the dark. What had happened? Suddenly the child had grown up. Surely no child kissed as she had kissed him! What had awakened her? A memory of Phil Blount standing beside her the night of the tobacco fire, his arm thrown about her shoulders. Had Phil been the one? A feeling of uneasiness came over him. He did not want Sibyl to change. If he had godlike power, he would make her the eternal child, with her gladsome ways, her child's laugh, the provocative smiles about her fresh young lips. . . . Or would he?

He lighted a pipe and strolled down toward the water. He gave no thought to Kathryn Holder or her nearness. Sibyl occupied his mind. Here was something to think about—his little Sibyl slipping across the threshold of childhood into young womanhood.

Sibyl was wakened by the long, mournful bay of the hounds. She sat up in her bed. Mathilda was sleeping peacefully. Sibyl slipped out of bed and crept to the window. The first streak of light lay along the eastern sky. False dawn and a cock's crow gave her the time of day. The hounds' baying was from the direction of the forest. A few servants were moving about near the cook's quarters. Smoke was rising from the chimney of the great kitchen. She strained her ears to listen. The hounds' voices seemed farther away. The morning air was chill, so she slipped back into bed and pulled the covers up, wondering why the hounds were loose so early. She tried to sleep, counting crows, sheep jumping a gate, a flight of wild geese, but she could not sleep. She heard a man's step in the hall, and the narrow stairs creak. Some time passed. She decided to get up and dress. She would run down to the kitchen. Angela would give her a cup of tea. Sibyl quietly opened the door a crack. She saw Kathryn, fully dressed, going downstairs. She tiptoed after her, so that she would not waken Aunt Cecily, who slept lightly.

No one was about, Kathryn had disappeared. Perhaps she too had been wakened by the hounds and had gone for a walk along the shore. Sibyl ran along between the high hedgerows that led to the kitchen. As she passed the office door, she heard Stephen Bennett's voice saying, "The transfer is all ready. Are you sure you don't want Digby too? The two seem to work well together."

"No. I want only one more indentured man. One will do nicely for my work at the plantation."

"I thought you wanted him for Jamestown."

"No; for my plantation north of Green Spring." There was a rustle of paper.

Stephen said, "I have signed the transfer. When the governor comes, he will sign."

"I thought it must be made legal by a notary at Jamestown."

Stephen answered, "The governor's signature will be sufficient. It is a fair exchange—three men for one. You're sure that you will be satisfied? That Nicholas will be? You know how I stand with him. It was your suggestion, you know."

"I'm quite sure I shall be satisfied. I vouch for Nicholas, but I count on you to say nothing about this for the present, Stephen." There was a note of triumph in Kathryn's voice.

Sibyl stood, unable to stir. Fright held her immobile. She shivered as though in a chill. She understood now. Kathryn Holder had bought Richard's indenture. She must find Richard at once. She turned and went quietly down the path that led to the cottages.

CHAPTER 23

The Whipping-Posts

TAMAR came into sight as Richard was stacking the last bundles of shingles before quitting work for the night. She was running, Enoch close behind her. The Hawk saw her first.

"God's death!" he cried. "They'll get her now. The dogs are on her trail. Listen. What are we to do? For the love of God, Richards, think of something."

"The tree! The tree!" the girl panted. But the tree would be no use this time. She had come down the path, not the water. The dogs would track her. They were in full cry now, giving tongue as they always did when the quarry was close at hand.

Richard said, "Get her to the compound, Enoch. Get them to close the doors and refuse to open. We'll try to hold them here."

Tamar paused. She was breathing heavily. She was almost spent.

"Good girl! Only a little farther," he said. "You can make it. Leave the path. Go through the woods—through the woods, Enoch. Throw them off at the creek."

A hare jumped up and ran along the path. "Delay them as long as you can," the Hawk called. "Stamp out the tracks about the tree. There are no tracks on the leaves. I'll go with them to the compound."

The hounds drew near, noses to the ground. Catching the scent of a hare, they paused, circling confusedly. One bitch picked up the scent and cut into the forest, but the others ran about under the tree. A second hare that had hidden in a hollow log near the path bounded out and fled down the path, the dogs after it. Richard breathed a deep sigh. "God is good," he said.

When Higgins rode up a few minutes later, Richard was stacking bundles of shingles. Higgins pulled up his horse.

"Where did they go?" he shouted. His face was red, dripping with sweat.

Richard said, "Down the path, sir."

"Why didn't you stop them? God's death to you!"

"Stop the hounds, sir? Why, they were in full cry after a rabbit."

"God's curse on you! I mean the girl and the runaway Nigra."

Richard shook his head. "The hounds were chasing a rabbit when they passed. Listen, they've got him."

Higgins shouted. "The girl Tamar! Where is she? The hounds are tracking the runaways." He glared at Richard, suspicion strong in his black beady eyes.

Richard repeated, "The hounds were after a hare, sir."

The overlooker snatched his whip from his belt. Richard stood looking up at him. For a long moment neither man moved, then Higgins kicked the mare in the ribs and galloped on.

Richard waited until he had made the turn before he dropped the bundle of shingles and took the narrow path through the pines that led to the west corn-fields. From there he could reach the slaves' compound unobserved. He had no illusion now. The chase was almost over. The girl could not hold out much longer. That was certain. Unless the Hawk or Scottie had devised some hiding place on the plantation, tonight would see the end of the hunt and Higgins would be the victor.

The Hawk met him at the gate of the compound. "I took her to your place. We waded down the creek to throw off the dogs. Only one followed. I choked it to death and threw it into the channel. It will drift down to the river."

"Did anyone see you?" Richard asked.

"Everyone on the place knows by now, but none will tell."

"Not even under the whip? I saw Higgins. He will not give up now."

The Hawk said, "He won't dare whip tonight with the governor here."

"The governor is not here tonight."

"God in heaven, then we are outdone!" The Hawk looked as though he would drop.

Richard said, "Something will turn up. . . . Find Scottie . . . a boat . . . down-river . . ." He walked rapidly away toward his cottage. He stopped at the door of the kitchen. "Will you send some food over by Puti?"

Puti followed him. "She is there . . . food . . . wine. Puti show opening, your chimney. *He's* looking, looking, beating dogs because they jumped hare and got off track."

Richard nodded. "God bless the little animal!" he said.

Digby was sitting on the steps, smoking a pipe. The Ancient Planter sat in his usual chair.

Richard laid his hand on the old man's shoulder. "Go home. Sit on your own piazza." The Ancient demurred. Richard was urgent. "We will find a way tonight. Best you are at your house as usual—if *he* comes this way."

"*He'll* be searching every house."

"But quietly. *He* will not want to make a disturbance while the guests are at the manor. Let everything be as usual. . . . Digby, go to early supper call. I'll go later, when you return."

The others left. Richard went into the cottage. He looked up at the ceiling. There was nothing to show where a trap-door was save for a few prints that might be from the palm of a hand or a ladder—nothing that would be visible in the dusk or by candlelight.

He bathed his face and hands. While he was putting on a fresh cotton shirt, the overlooker came to the door. "Oh, you here?" he said gruffly. He looked around the room. Seeing nothing suspicious, he went out on the piazza and stood leaning against the rail. Richard thought, What is he up to? He hoped devotedly that the girl would not turn or make a noise.

Higgins said, "Sorry I was gruff, but a man's fair out of his wits with these runaways. See here, Richards, you're a cut above the others. You must understand what it means to have one's authority scoffed at by slaves. It can't go on. As long as there be runaways unpunished, we'll have trouble. There's trouble enough at some of the other plantations— actual rebellion up on Pagan's Creek. You see why we can't have trouble on the governor's plantation."

Richard said nothing. He waited for what he knew was coming.

"As I said, you're a cut above the others. I've had my eye on your work in tobacco. It was good. I've been thinkin' maybe I'd make you a foreman next spring. Of course that would mean you'd help chase down these runaways."

Richard took a step forward. His voice was low, controlled. "Get out before I kick you out!"

Higgins' hand went to his pistol, but he backed down the steps. He raised his voice angrily. "You're a fool, Richards. You've had your chance. Now watch out."

Richard did not answer. He moved a step closer. "I said, Get out!"

"Damn you for a fool! You'll get no favours from me. If I catch you meddling, you'll get the whip, same as the others." The Fox turned and walked toward the office.

Digby came back from supper. "You surely riled him, Captain. I don't know what you said, but I saw his face when he went by me like a bat out of 'ell."

"The swine! He offered to make me a foreman if I would ride with him and capture runaways. Swine!"

The two men sat in silence for a time. Then Digby remembered something. He dug a folded paper out of his jerkin pocket. "It's from Mistress Sibyl. She's been wanting a word with you all day, she says to me. You went off to work before cock-crow."

Richard went inside and snuffed the candle to make a stronger light. The hasty scrawl was difficult to read. "Kathryn has your indenture papers. She bought them from Stephen."

"Anything wrong?" Digby asked after a long silence.

"Enough to make a man run away. It seems that Stephen Bennett has sold me to Mistress Nicholas Holder. For what sum of money I know not. If it's true, Nick owns me now."

"God's death, and may the devil blast them!" Digby said.

Richard shook his head, pointing to the ceiling. "Not so loud!" He motioned to the door. Once outside, he said, "Go to the quarters. Find the Hawk. Tell him to be at the boat-house on the river. The only chance we have is to get her up-river to the plantation on Pagan Creek, then make for the Blackwater."

"There's Indians."

"Damn Indians! Begone with you! I'll get the girl down within the hour. We must get moving before morning."

Digby lingered. "Sounds as though you were going, Captain. If you go, I go."

"Do as I say. I am giving *orders* now."

"Aye, zur, aye."

He watched Digby disappear into the darkness. Then he

closed the door, bolted it and blew out the candle. He moved over to the chimney and tapped several times on the ceiling with a stick. After a time he heard the girl's voice.

"Tamar, will you be ready to leave shortly?"

The trap opened. He saw the white blur of her face in the darkness. "Must I go? Can't I stay and take punishment? I'm so weary of running."

Richard thought of the young King. "Weary of running"—those were his words.

"I'll get a ladder," he said, hardening his heart to her plea.

"It's outside the window in the vines," she said. He leaned out the window nearest the chimney and felt amongst the vines. The jasmine gave off a sweet, almost cloyingly sweet odour. He pulled the ladder in and set it against the brick chimney.

Tamar came down after closing the trap carefully. "I'll go out through the window," she whispered. "Place the ladder, please." She had reached the ground and hidden the ladder by the time he had walked around the house. "Where are we going?" she asked.

"To the boat landing on the river. Best go on alone and wait hidden in the bushes until we come. Half an hour, or an hour. Can you do that?"

"Yes, sir. But why do you bother and get yourself in trouble for me? Everyone who helps will be punished. Let me go give myself up."

He knew she was weeping. He shook her shoulder gently. "Do what I say. No more talk of giving yourself up to that brute. The Hawk will help, and Scottie. Trust us, will you?"

"Sir, I will, I will."

"Good girl! Now walk slowly, as though you were one of the maids strolling to the garden. Go along the outside hedge. Stay on this side of the boat-house. Don't go near where the shallop is tied up. There may be a watchman on board. Understand?"

"Yes, sir."

Richard went back into the house. He sat down in the dark. He hadn't any great hope they could get the girl free, but at least they would try.

In a short time Digby returned. "The Hawk's outside with Scottie. They're waiting for your orders. Where's the girl?"

"She's gone to the boat-house. Tell them, if they can get a small sail-boat, we may make it, with the wind from the sea." He belted on his dirk, the only weapon he had.

"There's Indians, naked red Indians," Digby repeated when he came back in.

"Hold your tongue! There's no more than twenty Indians in the whole county. The Hawk knows where they are. They're friendly."

They closed the door behind them and made their way to the water. From there they would steal quietly down to the mouth of the creek and so reach the river.

Half-way down they heard a woman scream, Higgins' brutal voice saying, "Shut your foul mouth! You can't get away now. There's ten of us here. Thought you'd come this way, seeking a boat." There were scuffling and grunting. "Tie her up, boys. Take her to the post back of the barns. We'll see whether she'll talk now."

Richard let go his hold on Digby's arm. "No use going down. There's ten men all armed—too many for us. Softly, man! Back to the house, in through the window. He'll send a watch to find if we're all in bed."

They had no more than thrown themselves on their cots when a loud knock came at the door. A voice called, "Richards! Digby!"

Digby answered, throwing open the door. "What's this, wakin' a man?"

"Where's Richards?"

"In his bed, where he belongs to be."

Richard sat up, cursing.

"All right, all right. Orders, that's all." The man went off. They heard him pounding at doors along the quarters line.

"Now's the time. We skirt the field and come in back of the barns and wait our chance. I wonder where the Hawk is, and Scottie."

"Maybe Higgins got them first, Captain. Maybe they told Foxie."

"Not they! Come on. I'll go ahead. You stop and tell the Ancient Planter. He heard all the racket and will be worrying."

Digby hesitated. "You won't get yourself in no trouble, Captain?"

"Not I. But I've a feeling that trouble will come to some-one tonight."

Digby was at the Ancient's door when he saw Sibyl running as fast as she could down the path. He turned to her. "Now, little maid, what would you be doing about so late?"

"I want to find Richard. Where is he? There's danger about. I heard that horrible man talking to his foreman. They intend to whip someone, some runaway." She caught her breath in a sob. "I thought it might be Richard."

"Not he, little maid. Run along home."

"I'm afraid for him, he's so reckless."

"He's well enough, and he's mighty cautious these days. Run home."

"No. I'll sit here on the stoop until he comes back."

"It might be some time. You'll go to the house, won't you now?"

Thomas Chapman came out. He added a word: "Your pres-ence might get Richards into trouble, you know. Digby is right. Run home and get to bed. It's near midnight, if I feel the wind rightly. Digby will walk to the gate with you."

"All right, sir. But I do feel danger." She went reluctantly.

Digby came back after he had taken her to the kitchen gar-den. He told his story quickly. "I'm like the little one, zur. I smell danger. I've no idea what the captain has in his mind. I'd best be on hand if he gets into trouble."

Richard moved cautiously through the corn rows. He was glad to find that they had not yet been cut. He came to the open space behind the barns. Well cleared it was, since the governor had burned the leaf and the racks. The old whipping-posts stood in the shadow, but there was enough light to see them.

The compound near by was unnaturally quiet. No dogs yapped, nor fowl cackled. Presently men came in sight—ten of them. The overseer said, "Tie them to the posts. Put the girl at the near one. I'll see to her first."

Richard moved closer. The men were tying the Hawk's hands to the cross-rod. He was struggling violently. The Hawk's back was turned toward him as he crouched at the end of the corn row. Since he uttered no sound, Richard knew he was gagged. Some distance away, on the other side, three men were engaged tying up Scottie. The others joined them. Richard slipped down the row and with his dirk cut the

Hawk's thongs. "Stand as you are, until I signal," he whispered. "I'll cut the gag so it will fall away."

The Hawk nodded. Richard retreated down the row. He dared not walk across to where the girl was until he had released Scottie. Then they would be three against ten—ten with weapons.

He moved silently to the end of the row, crossed over a dozen rows until he saw Scottie. He edged his way down. The men went into a group, talking in whispers, some fifteen feet away. Luck was with him so far. He cut Scottie's bonds, repeated the same warning.

It was more difficult to get near the post where the girl stood. Crossing the field, he saw a shadow moving as cautiously as he. He stopped, watching. Then he recognized Digby and waited. There were no words spoken. Digby fell in behind him until they stood at the edge of the corn.

Someone had brought a torch. The men who stood behind the overlooker were strange to Richard, men the Fox must have brought in because he was afraid to trust the plantation people to help him in his awful act.

Higgins' voice was low. Richard thought, He doesn't want to rouse the house. This is his private vengeance.

The overlooker stood near Tamar, asking questions. "Who?" he said. His voice sounded like a file. "Who? Who? Who fathered your bastard?"

The girl was silent.

"Tell me, or I'll lay on the whip—forty lashes that will sting and smart and tear your back to ribbons." His voice rose.

There was a murmur among the men. "Too many. Nay, ten will do it."

"Dammit to hell, this is *my* punishment! The girl's a bastard maker! She's run away twice—a gaol breaker. She's wicked as hell itself!"

A man laughed shortly. "What's wrong, Higgins? Did she repulse you?"

The girl spoke then, clearly. "Aye, I did, the foul-mouthed drunken coward! Binds me to a post, afraid to risk letting me stand and take punishment. He must bind me, a helpless girl, before he dare lay a whip on my back."

Richard crouched, ready to spring. Surely she would goad the fellow into bestial rage by her words.

Instead, Higgins stood before her, his legs spraddled wide

to keep his balance. "You lie, like the witch you are." He said to his men, "She's a black witch. We threw her into the water and she wouldn't drown. She puts a spell on good men. Do you think I would cozzen a witch woman?" And to Tamar he cried, "Stay there! Watch what I do to the men you have befuddled."

He started across the open space toward the Hawk, then whirled and ran back. Under the taunt he couldn't leave Tamar. He raised his whip and struck. *"One for luck, and another."* Twice the whip curled through the air and wrapped itself about the girl's shoulders. He leaned forward and ripped her bodice down. *"Hide to hide!"* he shouted. *"Snake's skin to viper's skin!"* He was a madman in his fury.

Suddenly a drum sounded in the forest, a sharp staccato beat. A second later, a great vibration seemed to tear the air about them. Once, twice, thrice it sounded and was still.

The overlooker turned to attend to the Hawk. His arm came down. The Hawk whirled and sprang, but stumbled as he reached for the whip. He fell defenceless at the feet of the enraged man.

When the first blow fell on the Hawk, Richard sprang to the girl. "Cut the cords," he whispered to Digby. No one was watching them now. All eyes were on the Fox and the Hawk. Scottie hesitated between running to the Hawk and fleeing through the corn-brake. He threw himself at Higgins and hung onto his arm. He was no match for the overlooker, who flung him off, knocked him down and whirled the whip viciously at him. So the cruel whip fell, now on the Hawk, now on Scottie. The new-comers looked on, making no move.

The great drum boomed out again. Richard stood in front of the girl while Digby worked. "It's not thongs. Her arms are locked over the brace, and her feet are chained."

"Get a chisel or a maul or a sledge-hammer. Quick!"

The insensate overlooker, angered and defeated because the Hawk and Scottie did not scream, turned back to the girl and found himself face to face with Richard. The indentured man was standing tall and very erect, his arms hanging beside him, his hands empty. There was contempt in his face, scorn in his eyes.

"Lay down your whip, Higgins. If you're a man, you'll fight a man's fight with bare fists. I challenge you for the right of punishment. If you win, you punish me. If I win, I'll punish you in whatever way I choose."

"You're mad! I'll punish you as I see fit. Stand aside, Mister High-and-Mighty, Mister Cock-of-the-Walk. I'll beat you till you cry for mercy."

Richard did not move, nor take his steady gaze from the bloodshot eyes of the overlooker.

"I'll lash——"

"Did you not hear the signal drums? The great drum? Look down the long rows of corn. What do you see?"

The man swivelled his head. They were surrounded by black men and white, standing in the long rows of corn, motionless, waiting.

"Give me the whip!" Richard said.

"God's curse on you, no!" Higgins raised the whip. It curled itself around Richard's shoulders. Richard struck when the overlooker's arm was raised and caught him off balance. He grasped the whip handle, wrenched Higgins' arm back, lifted his knee, lunged, threw the wretch prostrate.

He raised his voice. "How many?" From the circle surrounding them came the cry, "Forty and one!" Richard tossed the whip to the Hawk, who had struggled to his feet. "Do as you will—but first get the keys from his belt."

"The ten strangers were edging toward the barns. The plantation bell began to ring quickly in alarm. Fumbling, Scottie got the keys from the fallen man's belt and set the girl free. She sank to the ground.

Higgins tried to rise, cursing, tugging at his pistol.

Richard said, "You've no fire. You waste yourself. You'll get whatever these men say."

"Double for each lash, and triple for the girl—aye, for the girl."

The Hawk kicked Higgins to his feet. "Against the post. Tie him up." The whip sang through the air. "This for the girl ... and this ... and this."

There was a sound of voices, of running feet. Richard turned. Men ran from the great house carrying muskets and pistols, Stephen Bennett leading, women in disarray following.

"Hold!" Stephen shouted. "Hold!"

The Hawk did not hear. He went right on with the steady,

methodical movement, the rise and fall of lash on bare back. "For Scottie . . . for the . . ."

Stephen rushed over. He snatched the whip from the Hawk's hand. "This is *insurrection!* Do you know the penalty for insurrection?"

Scottie came forward. His shirt was riddled. "Not insurrection against the governor, sir. Justice to that carrion!" He spat at Higgins.

Stephen said, "What is this? Will someone tell me?"

Richard stepped up. "The man has blood lust in him. The girl Tamar—he would have beaten her until she spoke the name."

Stephen whirled. He took a step forward. Tamar stood leaning against a post. Her torn bodice showed her firm white shoulders and breasts. Her tangled hair hung over her face. Her eyes were glazed. She raised her hands as though to plead for mercy, then dropped them again.

"God in heaven!" Stephen murmured.

The strangers crowded forward. "You must punish the ringleaders. If you don't you will have a slave rebellion. Look in the cornpatch."

Stephen raised his head. There were no Negroes or white men among the corn. "I see no one. Someone take Higgins down. Take him to his house. Angela, take the girl." He moved over and laid his hand on her shoulder.

Higgins, on his feet, shouted, "She's a runaway! She should be branded. See, 'tis all ready in the smithy. Brand her!"

Stephen did not answer. He indicated the Hawk and Scottie. "You and you, to the quarters, on bread and water!" He turned to Richard. Looking him full in the face, he said, "I expected better from you after your treatment here. For you, full confinement, slaves' dungeon until Quarters Court. The Assembly deals with insurrection. They can pronounce the death sentence on leaders. That is the law."

The womenfolk had drawn closer. At his words Sibyl uttered a cry, "Richard! Richard!" She ran across the open space and threw herself into his arms. He patted her shoulder.

"Sibyl!" Cecily Montague cried, horrified at the girl's action. "What are you doing? Come here at once."

Mathilda walked over to Richard's side. She faced Stephen. Her face was very white, but her head was high. "Richard is our very dear friend, almost our brother. I did not know you were here, dear Richard. Surely Stephen will hear what you have to say."

Stephen watched them, his brows drawn together. "You do not know what you say, Mathilda. I suggest you go to the house. This is no place for ladies."

Again Cecily cried, "Sibyl, Mathilda, come to the house at once!" She herself was walking rapidly in that direction.

No one moved. Mathilda and Stephen stood facing each other. In the glare of the pine torch the picture took on a strange, frightening significance. Stephen was stubborn. Mathilda's little chin was thrust forward. Her voice was controlled. She paid no mind to the others. They might have been alone. "I said, Stephen, that Richard is my friend, my brother. His mother gave us a home, two motherless girls. I ask for this man . . ."

Stephen held his anger. He too spoke quietly. "You do not know what you ask. An insurrection is a serious thing under our law, and severe punishment is demanded. We are within the law——"

Sibyl broke in suddenly. "I have not heard these men speak, nor tell their story. My father did his share of writing laws. I have heard him say that every man has his rights under the common law. I have not heard from *them*." She turned quickly to the Hawk, who stood gaping at her. "Is this an insurrection?"

"Ma'am, no. Only justice for Tamar, and justice for Higgins. No insurrection against Governor Bennett."

She questioned Scottie. "Godamighty, ma'am, we've nothing against the governor, ma'am, nothing at all! Just this swine."

She turned to Tamar. "Why did you run away?"

"I ran from the dog yonder, the drunken, lecherous dog."

"They must be punished," Stephen said stubbornly. "Insurrection is a serious crime under the law."

Kathryn Holder walked over to where they were standing. She was dressed in a long white robe, which she lifted out of the dust with one hand. She moved deliberately until she was close to the little group that held the centre of the stage. She carefully avoided Richard's eyes. Addressing Stephen she said, "I do not understand talk of insurrection and punish-

ment. It is my understanding that I bought this man's indenture—or am I mistaken?"

Stephen's face grew red. "I had forgotten," he muttered.

Kathryn's voice was impatient. "Please speak out. Do I or
do I not own the indenture of one Richard ap Richards?"

"You own him," Stephen said, his voice betraying his anger. "But whoever owns him, he has broken the law."

"I own his indenture," Kathryn corrected, "and only I could
bring a charge against him. There will be no charge lodged. As
for the others—the girl and the two men—that is your affair."
Without a glance at Richard, she took Sibyl's hand. "Come,
Mathilda, Madam Montague is calling again. She will be
angry."

The three walked away. Mathilda, her head high, looked
directly past Stephen. Sibyl waved to Richard, whose face
was as glum as though he had been condemned to the block.
He said to Stephen, "I am ready to take punishment, sir."

Stephen gazed at him gloomily. "Did you see how she
looked through me, as if I did not exist? Dammit, go to your
cottage and get ready to depart on the shallop. It will leave on
Thursday. I might have known better than to buy a war
prisoner. They have no loyalty save for their king."

Richard thought, Mathilda has hurt him cruelly. A man
must not be made a fool of before others, least of all before
servants.

Digby, returning with a chisel, had seen how things were
going. Why involve himself? What purpose would that serve?
He had kept discreetly in the dark. Now he said, "They're all
gone, zur. What next?"

"You heard what he said. It's true the lady's bought me."

"And you will bow your head to her will. In Jamestown
they call her a witch—the golden witch."

"I will bow my head to no woman," Richard said fiercely,
"nor any man either!"

They had reached the cottage. The Ancient Planter was
seated on the piazza, and with him was Mr. Caswell.

"My boat put in an hour ago," Caswell said. "I saw that
young Stephen was having a difficult time. That little one—
how bravely she talked out about a man's right under the
law!"

"I'm disappointed in Stephen," the Ancient One said. "It's

time he understood that he can't run a big plantation from the seashore. I'm surprised he is so bitter against you."

Richard puffed a pipe. "It isn't me, or the likes of me, that worries him. He's confused. In the old days every plantation was a kingdom in its own right. A planter was the law. This is the view Kathryn Holder took, and Stephen Bennett submitted to it. But he is worried by the new idea—that the law is a central thing, seated in Jamestown. He feels responsibility. Now Richard Bennett is governor, is he not the law? If so, Stephen must be the law here in the governor's absence. In the old days he would not have been so perplexed."

"You're right, Richards," Mr. Caswell remarked. "The responsibility of law sets heavily on his shoulders, and the ladies did not help him!"

"What's this about his selling you to Mistress Holder?" the Ancient Planter inquired.

"Ah!" Caswell broke in. "I'd heard Stephen was indebted to Nicholas Holder for one thing and another." He smiled thinly. "People are idle at the shore . . ."

"You mean gambling?" Richard spoke sharply.

"So they say."

"May I be everlastingly damned if I'll have my body thrown on the gaming tables!"

Mr. Caswell tapped his pipe. "Good! And well spoken! Then you will be open to a little plan I have in mind."

"I'm agreeable to anything that takes me away from here."

"Right! Get some sleep, lads. We will make plans tomorrow night."

Sibyl lay wide awake for a long time that night. All her thought had been for Richard in the distressful scene by the whipping-posts. But now a face haunted her, and it was not Richard's. Where had she seen it before—those great dark eyes, those heavy brows that seemed almost to meet, that hair like a rook's wing? Out of a vivid experience—so far away, so incredibly far, in circumstances how different—it flashed on her suddenly. It could not be and yet it must unmistakably be. This was the angry girl who had so frightened her when she went to Goody Heskett's for a silly love potion.

Now those fierce eyes were glazed. Nothing to fear from that forlorn yet still lovely creature of the forest! Life and the whip had tamed what Sibyl would have thought untamable. Only pity was in her heart for Tamar.

Her thoughts did not end there. What had she overheard about Tamar? That she was being punished because she would not tell the name of the father of her still-born child?

Sibyl thought she could guess the name. She had seen a man in the thatched cottage. But she would never reveal her suspicion. Sibyl could keep a secret.

All knew Richard was taking flight that morrow night. Puti came to him at dusk, while Richard was digging in his little garden. "The swamp at the third hour."

Richard said, "We'll be there."

He sometimes wondered how news on the plantation spread from the house servants outward in an ever-increasing circle, from the field hands to the quarters, to the compound. So it was now: Everyone knew—everyone but those who lived in the Great House. Bennett's Welcome was no different from other plantations along the James. The planters were last to know what was doing on their own acres.

By ten o'clock the quarters were dark and unoccupied. The swamp was heavy with life. There was a great press of people when Richard and Digby, poling the leaky boat, lifted the green curtain. Tamar was there. For the first time Richard saw her smile. She was happy. Why? The people all knew. By arrangement between the Bennetts and the Montagues she would go off on Thursday with Mistress Cecily to be taught to weave and sew and brew—woman's work. Stephen undertook to engage the governor's pardon for her. Later she would go to Bennett's Choice when the new mistress came in charge of the household.

"What will I do now that I no longer have to run before the dogs?" she said quite seriously to Richard. "So long I have been running it is a habit. Now that I have found a haven I am at a loss." There was only happiness in her face. No lines of pain showed there. Angela had covered the cruel, broken welts across her back with some soothing unguent of her own making.

After a while, when the moon was low, the Hawk came, and Scottie. For time to say good-bye the Negroes had freed them from close confinement. They had word of Higgins. *He* had been taken to Jamestown for a doctor's medicine. It had been said *he* was fair weeping with pain of the beating the Hawk had administered with such vigour. *He* would not come back the Bennetts had had enough of *him.*

One of the indentured said, "Young Bennett is as bad. As these two friends well know, he punishes by clapping men into the black room with bread and water for food."

Faces were turned to Richard. "Tell us, wise one, what shall we do? Run away? Revolt?"

Richard got up from the log on which he had been seated and moved near the fire. Standing with his back to the mighty cypress tree, he began to talk. Words flowed from his lips; inner thoughts found their way into the open air and spread for all the indentured to hear.

They must not run away. They must not revolt. They must not shame the good governor before all the people. If there were insurrection here what would people say? If he could not govern the folk on his own plantation, how could he be fit to govern a colony?

"The young one is quick and impetuous, but his heart is kind. The memory of last night will sink into him and make him kinder. He has rid you of the Fox. He was doing what he thought was right. Punish the wrong-doer—that is the law of the colony. Do you not see that here, first of all the plantations, law must be upheld?

"Since I've lived amongst you these months, I've had deep thoughts, rebellious thoughts, as you all must have had at one time or another. I counted the days until I could go to my home and take up my life. Those were wrong thoughts. My life could never be what it was before, even if I were in England. Other folk walk my ancestral halls and plough my fields. What matter? The fields are ploughed and life goes on.

"Here in Virginia we must cease to think of going home and begin to think of building a new, firm world where soil is rich and pure and fertile. Think about that, my friends. Build as our forefathers set about building a new nation after William the Conqueror came. After the barons wrestled liberties from a stubborn king, a new nation grew in time under Good Harry, and a New World opened to us under Elizabeth. Freedoms we had as gifts from those who went before us. We lost them in the misfortunes of civil war. As Englishmen we will regain them under the law. Then stand boldly and build to greater freedom still. Plant and harvest and trade. Our wealth is not pearls found in oyster-shells, or little flakes of gold hiding timidly in a mountain brook. Our wealth is in the broad land, in our spreading forests and in our great rivers."

"But if they burn our tobacco?"

"That is wise. We must sell in the markets only the *best* Virginia leaf, superior to Spanish or Turkish. Make this our pride."

The Hawk said, "Well spoken, Richards! But we must flee, Scottie and I—must flee and find some haven. Tonight we are taking flight."

Richard turned to the speaker. "No. Hawk. No, Scottie. Think you of fifty acres of land, or a hundred, in a few months' time. Think of security for yourself and your family. The governor will deal gently by you."

"But I want to go south. Thirty or forty men have already taken great plantations. Soon it will be like the James, with the few holding everything."

Richard shook his head. "A few months—then go. Wait out your servitude. Do not throw away your years of work and your future security."

The Hawk was silent for a long time, his lips moving. "January, and I'll be shed of this."

Richard smiled. "You can work for wage then, or have a lease as well as your own land. Eh, Hawk, good man, what say you?"

The Hawk put his great paw into Richard's. "Aye, for you are a wise one. I say 'tis a pity we don't have you for our master."

Richard's face sobered. "Comrades, when I was master, I was termed good enough, kind to my servants and my tenants. But I knew nothing of the land, except that the harvest brought wealth. I lived by their work and the work of the land, not my work. Today I know that lesson. When I make wealth again, as I certainly shall, I will know what it means to plant and cultivate and reap. It will be the work of *my* hands. And the work of hundreds and thousands of others like me will build a great world here in this virgin land."

A voice out of the dark asked the question: "But *you* are going away?"

"Aye," Richard said. "Aye."

"The golden witch bought you. You will go with her. She will devour you."

"Nay, I will not go with a woman. I go on my own and my

own way, southward to the Chowan River, to join the pioneers—'They of the South,' the Indians call them."

A clamour rose. "And yet you tell us to stay until our service is over!"

"Aye, I tell you to stay. Your service is short. Mine is long, only a year finished. Nor will I be owned by that woman. Here is an old tale, my friends, that belongs to another world where once that woman lived and I lived. She does not buy me to work, or for freedom, but to use me pridefully, a slave to her whims. Therefore I go southward, to make the way clear for others who will come. Let me be among the first to cut the forest, to make fields, to lay seeds in the rich bottom lands. Some of you in good time will follow, part of a great host.

"But I have talked too long. You may forget all else, but remember this: *a man may be a slave in his body, but no one may enslave a man's soul.*"

He moved abruptly, throwing out his arms. The front of his shirt came apart. The ivory tree on his breast shone white.

An old man, small and weazened and very black, came forward out of the dark forest. He began to tap a little drum. The slaves came after him in a long line, each one with his arms folded, touching head and breast as he passed by. Richard knew it was a salute of honour. How had he deserved it? He felt humbled by the unexpected tribute of these pagan folk.

When they had disappeared into the forest, the white men came and took his hand, some diffidently, without words. "Go with God!" came most frequently. "Go with God!"

That night, while the guests at the manor walked in the moonlight under the great trees after supper, a boat set out, keeping close to shore. Toward morning, when the wind blew up-river, it crossed the full waist of the mighty James to a landing.

Digby jumped first, securing the boat. Matthew Caswell followed. As Richard stepped ashore, the first rays of the September run reddened the eastern sky. He stood quietly watching a clear sunrise heralding a new day *It was a year to the day from the tragic Battle of Worcester*

Mr. Caswell looked over his shoulder. "Come, let us make haste. The governor has long waited to welcome you to Green Spring."

CHAPTER 24

Green Spring

SIR WILLIAM BERKELEY sat in his high-backed elbow-chair at the head of the supper table. His guests, summoned from their plantations on the James, the York and the Northern Neck, were drawn from gentry loyal to the Stuart King. A faint smile showed on his thin lips, but his prominent pale blue eyes did not reflect even the faintest smile.

Footmen in Berkeley livery removed the dinner plates while he waited for the butler to bring the fruit.

His eyes turned to his orchards. The apple-trees were heavy with fruit, so heavy that the gardeners had propped the limbs to keep them from splitting. He was proud of his fine gardens, his orchards; proud of the tobacco leaf now in hogsheads ready to load on the ship that would moor at his dock in the morning; proud of his house, the finest Great House in the colony. His thoughts turned from his possessions to the large bowl of fruit the servant placed before him——the last of the late peaches, red and golden yellow; the deep purple plums, the first from the new trees; the amber and the wine-red grapes.

It was one of his customs to serve the fruit himself from the blue and white Holland bowl; with his long thin hand lift each separate peach or pear or plum and lay it on the blue and white plate. The lace ruffles flowing from the brocaded satin sleeves of his coat were part of a studied pattern of elegance which had become habitual during his years as governor.

More royal than royalty, Richard Monington thought as he watched the governor's hands moving gracefully, performing the task of host, fingering the stem of his wine-glass, making vague gestures to illustrate some idea. One might think the man a fop, a cockscomb, at first glance, but his chin jutted, and his eyes were cold, betraying nothing of the inner man.

He leaned back to enjoy the ejaculations of wonder from his guests. "Peaches! At this time!"

" 'Tis nothing. I put them in my ice-house. They ripened slowly."

"Does your ice last this long? Mine gave out weeks ago!" a guest exclaimed.

The governor said, "I keep my ice in a very deep pit, well covered with sawdust from my mill. The pit is near the spring-house, so I manage. 'Tis nothing."

The sun set. The room grew dark. The servants fetched candelabra—four to the long table, two to the mantel-board, flanking a large mirror with a heavy Italian frame. Other candlesticks were set about the room, an illumination of twenty candles, displaying the rich colours of the men's coats. The draperies were drawn, the fruit was removed and decanters of Oporto were set beside Sir William. A wine-glass with twisted stem was placed before each guest, and a long clay pipe beside him. Leaf was put into a silver bowl on the table. Then the servants left the room.

Richard noticed his host glancing at the mirror above the mantel from time to time—why he did not know, because it did not reflect Sir William or his end of the table.

The governor filled his glass and pushed the decanter to William Woodward, who sat next to him. The decanter went around the table, each man filling his own glass and pushing the decanter to his neighbour. The governor rose and walked to the mantel. He set his glass on the mantel-shelf and moved one of the arms of a candlestick, until it was in perfect aline-ment, before he turned to face his guests.

"Gentlemen, several matters of interest to us all have come up in the recent weeks which I am sure you will wish to dis-cuss, and about which make some decision. However, that will come later. Before we drink the toast there is something I wish to tell you. A ship came in from France. In it was a present from a friend whom we all admire and love—this mirror, which once graced the walls of the Doges' Palace in Venice."

The guests all turned to admire, with exclamations of "Beautiful!" . . . "Extraordinary!" . . . "Fit for a king's palace!"

Berkeley smiled. "Aye, fit for a king. Well spoken, Major Beverley, well spoken indeed!" He lifted his hand and felt beyond the frame. "A mirror sometimes reflects a face that is not there." He found the knob, pressed it, and the mirror swung back.

Looking out from the old gilt frame was the young smiling face of Charles the Second. For a moment there was a stunned silence. It was as though the King himself were looking at them, framed by a window. In an instant every man was on his feet, his glass raised. Sir William gave the toast: "The King! Gentlemen, the King! God keep him!" The toast was drunk solemnly, not gaily as Charles would have had it. Richard could almost hear him say, "Why so sad, my good gentlemen? Let us drink, dance and be merry."

Seated directly opposite the King's likeness, Richard could not escape his mocking eyes, his too gay smile. Richard remembered him otherwise—a tired, bewildered lad struggling to be gay. A strange abstraction beset him. He stared at the table in front of him. He heard words passing back and forth over his head . . . Governor Berkeley explaining . . . a letter secreted in the ship . . . a greeting to his loyal subjects in Virginia . . . a little time and he would return . . . do not forget that a Stuart will return . . . "My loyal Berkeley, look forward to the day when we shall set our foot on English soil and ride north and be crowned King in our good City of London."

"Does he say aught of Virginia?" asked Thomas Woodward.

"Naught save to be ready when the time comes. Is not that enough?" Berkeley answered.

"We'll be hard to find after this year is passed," said Miles Cary at the far end of the table.

Mr. Caswell said, "God's pity that he did not fly to Virginia on the ship that waited for him at Cardiff! All Virginia would have risen to his standard."

Richard found himself saying, "Neither Herefordshire nor the north counties rose when he marched from Scotland."

Cold eyes were turned on him. Questions followed. They had heard this before, but found it hard and distasteful to believe. How did he know? They looked at his sombre dress, his close-cropped hair. There was a long silence. Then Mr. Caswell said, "Mr. Monington was at Worcester."

"Worcester? . . . You were in the battle? . . . Tell us . . ."

Sir William caught the attention as it was slipping from

him. "We were planning to ask Mr. Monington about the battle later, but perhaps it is as well now. First, gentlemen, fill your glasses for another toast. Do you know the day? September fourth—a year and a day after Worcester. I ask you to drink in silence to the martyred men."

After a decent pause, Sir William went on: "I presume you have wondered who our guest Captain Monington is, and how he happens to be here. He was indentured to the Bennetts on the way out, I believe. He has been living at Bennett's Welcome. Am I right?"

Richard inclined his head. No need to mention Holder. He wished he were anywhere but here, with curious eyes fixed upon him. How could he tell them of a battle they had never seen and could not even imagine? These men who would look at him with solemn eyes and say, "How dreadful! How shocking!" but never know the keen hard thrust of a pike, the din of cannon fire, the terror of the onrush of Oliver's cavalry or the groans of the dying?

The floor of Worcester Cathedral came before his eyes . . . the cries for water, for God to come to them . . . Mother . . . the blood . . . the white drawn faces of pain . . . the smell of fear.

He lifted his eyes to the mockery in the painted face. There was no mockery in the King's countenance that day as he galloped down the streets crying to the men to rally, to advance. There was no mockery at Boscobel.

He felt the power of men's eyes turned to him. He heard the governor's voice, but not the words. Mr. Caswell, touching his arm, said, "Can you tell us anything of that day or has it cut too deeply? Tell about the King. Did he give a fair account of himself?"

"Aye, he fought as a Stuart should fight, fought until no one stood amongst his Scots to stop Oliver's men. Aye, he fought as a brave leader—harder and longer than his followers."

"Mayhap he had more to lose," someone muttered.

"That I wouldn't say. A man can lose his life—and what more?" He leaned forward. The decanter had come to him. He poured the ruby wine and pushed the decanter along. He got to his feet. He bowed to the governor.

"Sir, may I make a toast?" He faced the painting. "To the Man on the Tower! To the Man in Perry Wood when the fight was thickest! To the Man riding from the city at sunset! To the Man fleeing on the country road at midnight! To the Man hiding in the greenwood and in priest's holes, a country lad in rough clothes, in heavy shoes that burned and blistered! To the Man who hid by day and rode by night before the blood-hungry pack!" He raised his glass slowly, looking steadily at the picture. As he stood they were eye to eye. "To the Man whom each day brings nearer to a throne! Gentleman, I drink to a King!"

The faces around him lost identity and became one inquiring face. He turned to Sir William. "Your Excellency, I am drunk—not with your good wine, but with memories. I beg leave to retire."

Without waiting he walked from the room. Before the door closed Mr. Caswell said, "You have had your answer to the question of the King's courage at Worcester. Aye, and after. I deem the flight took more courage than a battle."

His discomfiture on the day Richard Bennett was elected governor was on Sir William's mind, but his voice was composed when he said, "You all know that I would have fought off Captain Denis and his squadron of war, if it had not been that Denis tricked me by taking a great parcel of goods aboard which belonged to two members of my Council. These brave gentlemen would not give up their belongings, even though I had the help of Dutch vessels. They felt constrained to call for submission. They broke our solid ranks by giving in to Denis' strategy. We could withstand Bennett and Denis only if we clung strongly together. Need I say that they are not with us this evening?

"They call me a furious man. God's death, I am that, when I am interfered with in performance of my duty to my people! And the people forget the part I played in the capture of the greatest enemy of the colony, Opechancanough."

"Nay, I remember," Mr. Caswell said, as Sir William paused to sip his wine. "I remember the old man of great stature with slack sinews and macerated flesh, who could not see unless his servants lifted his heavy eyelids. I rode with that party of Horse when Your Excellency seized him."

Berkeley looked down the table. "So you did. You will bear witness that I made a peace which has remained inviolate; a happy peace. And if I ordained severe laws against the Puritans, that was their desert. Were they not in rebellion against our good King? Did they not behead him?

"So I am a furious man, am I? Aye, furious against usurpers and—but now, I pray you, guard your acts and your tongues and build for a day that is to come."

He bowed his head toward the painting. "For return he will, by the grace of God and his loyal subjects! One thing we may think of pridefully: we Virginians have held out longest for the Royal family. Let the Roundheads strut and make laws. Their hour will be short.

"Perhaps it is time to give you an answer to the question that is trembling on your lips. I do not intend to leave the colony. The year of sufferance is almost over, but I shall not take goods or chattels and move to New England or Maryland. I shall remain here at Green Spring.

"Here I have built a home that could house a king. It may be that our King will come and set up a Court here. We have invited him. It may be that if he tires of France he will seek a haven here until Oliver's time runs out. It is rumoured that the Protector has quarrelled deeply with General Monk. If that rumour be true, it is good news for us. Yes, I shall stay and wait."

Someone asked, "What if Bennett sends Denis and his soldiers?"

Sir William said, "He won't. He wants no fights. He is an elder of the Ancient Church, but he is more like a Quaker. He won't fight. I shall stay here at Green Spring, living as I please. I shall obey the law in other matters. I advise you to do likewise—plant and cultivate and grow your crops."

"Are you sure Bennett won't banish us?" one timid planter asked.

"Positive. I banished him to Maryland, did I not? Does he hold a grudge? No. 'Turn the other cheek' is his watchword. Pah! It sickens me, this sanctimonious folderol."

Someone, Cary or Beverley, said, "Sir, you are right. We will stay. Where could one go? Not to England or the islands of the West Indies. They say Cromwell will be at war with the Dutch before the year is out."

"There's France," Ralph Wormsley suggested.

"Who wants France? I'd rather follow the sun westward to the mountains. Byrd is making a fortune trading in that direction."

The governor filled his glass. "If I were going away, I'd go south. There is a great country, an easy climate. The Indians are friendly. . . ." His eyes dropped a little. His head fell forward and his chin sank against his fine waistcoat.

The guests looked one to the other. Beverley pushed back his chair. "It is late, gentlemen. I suggest that we ride to our lodgings in Jamestown."

One by one they went away, taking their lanthorns from the footmen at the door, until only Matthew Caswell was left. He went back to the dining hall. He stood before the painting for a time. He shook his head slowly, murmuring, "You Stuarts, you tragic, unhappy folk, how long will the curse hang over you?" He made a gesture of salute with his right hand and closed the mirror into place over the living likeness.

He called a servant then, and together they got Sir William into his bedchamber. "Undress him and put him between the sheets, Grison. Yon's an unhappy man, for all he holds his head so high."

"Yes, sir. Those Roundheads cause us trouble, sir. Purely troublesome they be."

Early the next morning Caswell came to the garden-house where Richard lodged. He looked at the younger man quizzically. "I see nothing of the indentured man about you this morning."

Richard grinned. "Digby has been working on me, trimming my hair. Somewhere he found this shirt and these breeches. He says they're a loan from the butler or Sir William's valet. I don't ask questions when Digby goes on a raid. He says the women are washing and mending my old ones, if there's anything left to mend."

"He has probably visited the weaving house and drawn an outfit from one of the pretty young women. The governor always has good buxom wenches about." He paused significantly.

Richard reached for a hunk of bread and took a long swallow from a mug of small beer.

Caswell filled a pipe and settled back. "There are things to talk over. First, there'll be a ship sailing for Maryland tonight. The captain is safe. He sails for Bideford with only one stop

—at the Somers Islands. I'll send down writing sheets and ink. You may write a letter or two if you wish."

"Thank you. I'll write to my mother. She'll be wanting news of me."

"Second: Mr. Claiborne is in Jamestown, and with him his secretary, Holder."

Richard's eyes narrowed. The little line across his cheek seemed redder. "Yes?"

"I was talking with Holder in Jamestown day before yesterday while you were on your way here. He's annoyed that his lady has bought you. Of course he controls his wife's property. It's really his. He could annul the purchase, but he'd be embarrassed to do so. Very annoyed, I should say. He would be glad to find a way out. I think we can arrange something." He turned his keen eyes on his companions. His thin face had no expression. "I can buy your papers. The price is high, but we can manage it. Last night before dinner the governor talked with me. He has had word from home—from his brother Sir John, I presume. The letter came in some secret fashion—I think by way of one of the northern colonies. He wrote of you in a guarded style, but I understood."

Richard glanced at the thin aquiline nose, the long jaw, the long slender hands. He had not realized how tall Caswell was. He had thought of him as old—from the grey hair perhaps. Certainly his body was fit and strong. He wondered about him. Almost without thought he said, "You are always well informed."

Caswell nodded. "So I am. I have ships. My captains report to me. Then I have my sources at home. They are my private service of information." He smiled and he leaned forward in the chair. "My father was a shareholder from the first day of the Virginia Company. He used to boast that he attended every meeting. If you read the records in London you'll find his name over and over on important committees. He stood by Sir Edward Sandys against the Warwick faction. Yes, you'd find his name over and over—*Mr.* Caswell. Strangely enough, that is what I am called, not Matthew, nor Caswell, but *Mr.* Caswell."

Richard thought, He has explained to me how he knew about Kathryn Bradshaw. He said, "You are a Stuart man, that I know. But you visit Governor Bennett."

"I've done business with the governor many a year. Trade

knows no religion or political differences. We buy, we sell—we do not ask who purchases our tobacco, only that our notes of exchange are deposited promptly with our London agent." Richard said nothing. "Yes, I'm a King's man, I have served him faithfully, though not in the spectacular manner that was your happy circumstance."

Startled, Richard said, "You know?"

"Yes, and Governor Berkeley knows also. That is why we want to help you to buy your papers from Holder."

Richard sprang to his feet. "By God, no! I'll not have it. I will myself settle with Nicholas Holder." The anger left him as quickly as it came. "I'm sorry, Mr. Caswell, sorry indeed. You and Sir William are kind. I cannot be beholden to anyone for my body, nor for my soul. Do you understand?"

"Yes, I think I do. But let us pass on to another plan. You are quite safe here. Governor Berkeley says you're to stay as long as you will. In a week or two we are sending men to the south under Captain Abraham Wood, master of a bark, at present in Maryland. They will arrive off Fort Henry within a week or so. Berkeley gave Bennett a chance to approve this venture. He has not acted. We will steal a march on him.

"Plans are made for a strong sail-boat to be ready for the party at the Blackwater River. The Indian, Pyancha, has been secured to guide you down the river until it reaches the Chowan. There you will leave the boat and travel by land, always close to the river. The boat will keep pace with you. The gentlemen, Mr. Pennant and Mr. Brewster, go to visit Mr. Nathaniel Batts, who has made himself a governor in that southern country, in order that they may contract for his tobacco. They say it is of prime quality."

Richard listened with growing excitement. The way was made clear for him. He could scarcely believe that Fortune, having played so many scurvy tricks on him, should now turn her eyes to him with favour. "When did you say they will start?"

"Mid-month will be a favourable time. The moon will be right, the days cooler for travelling, the nights not too cold. Will you go?"

Richard asked a question: "Digby also?"

Caswell laughed. "Certainly, certainly."

"Then you may tell the governor I accept. Why not go at once?"

"Steady, steady, lad! There are things to be done. One

doesn't set off on a three months' venture in the twinkling of
an eye. First, we will talk with Mr. Woodward the surveyor—
he knows the country—and then with the Reverend Roger
Greene."

Richard raised his brows. "I understand about Woodward,
but why Greene?"

"Governor Berkeley granted him ten thousand acres of land
and permission to import one hundred families. The old grants
and boundaries stand. Bennett acknowledged that in his speech
at the opening of the first Assembly. Your part will be to
locate desirable tracts of land, suitable for tobacco and corn,
and for orchards."

"Will three months be long enough?"

"I think so, but you may take longer if you like. The captain and his men will not go all the way. You will—to Batt's
place on the Great Sound of Roanoke, and from there to
Roanoke Island, sheltered from the Western Ocean by long
banks of glistening sand."

"Roanoke Island?" Richard's face lighted.

"You know about the island?"

"Who doesn't? My mother was from Devon, sir."

"Ah, of course. 'Tis a tradition in Devon and Cornwall
since Grenville's expedition in the days of Elizabeth. But we
will discuss details another time, when Woodward is here and
we have maps before us."

"I must thank Governor Berkeley at once," Richard said,
starting for the door.

"He left early this morning on a little trip up the river to a
plantation he owns. He will be back by Thursday. Write your
letter, lad. Be cautious. We know the master of the ship is
trustworthy, but perhaps his hiding place may be discovered."
Caswell moved toward the door. "You won't consider allowing us to buy your papers?"

"No, no. That is a matter for me to settle as I will."

"But don't extend yourself and run into trouble. You don't
want to miss this venture."

Richard was not listening. A week and then southward.
There were things to be done, Caswell had said. Aye, things
to be done that wanted careful planning.

A servant brought paper, quill, ink and sand. Richard
thanked him and sat down at the stout table under the window.
He looked idly out the small panes. He saw Digby leaning

against the trunk of a tree, watching a buxom maid hanging clothes on the hedge. The girl lifted her head and laughed.

Dibgy caught her about the waist, causing her to drop her reed basket. The dragoon was no novice. The girl struggled for a moment. Presently she put her arms about his waist and pressed his body against hers, swaying slightly. He let her go. Then, catching her wrist, he moved off swiftly down through the orchard toward the woods along the river.

Richard grinned and dipped the quill into the ink bottle. Life was simple for Digby. One fought, slept, ate, and took a woman for an hour of pleasure. He hoped there were no poisonous snakes by the river, or little red worms that burrowed under the skin.

It was some time before Digby returned. Richard was folding the letter into a square. He glanced up. Digby stood at the door, half a dozen red apples in his hands.

"I've been viewing the orchard and the harvest fields," he said. He glanced at Richard out of the corner of his eye.

Richard did not look up again. He was busy melting wax. "Viewing the harvest, you say? I thought you were sowing seed for spring planting."

Digby's face wore a silly grin. Nothing more was said. Richard applied the red wax, stamped it with a plain seal. The dragoon was chuckling quietly as he washed the apples and arranged them on a plate. " 'Twas an apple that caused all the trouble in the garden," he said. He left the room whistling a gay tune, something about "Welcome to town, Tom Dove, Tom Dove the merriest man alive . . ."

About sunset Digby came back and found the captain reading from a folio. He shifted from one foot to another until Richard glanced up. "I've off and been to town, zur. I walked about the long way and fetched up at the tavern where we met one eve when we were first here. There I found the farrier. We had a mug of ale together and fell to talking. He told me tales. He's restive, he is. Sir William won't let them take up and fight. They must wait.

"There's news too, Captain—the Holders are going home to England soon. And there's talk going on in the town about a wedding. Mistress Mathilda will be standing up before the Puritan Reverend and making marriage with Mr. Stephen Bennett on Thursday next at eight of the clock." He had Richard's full attention now.

"So there will be a wedding. And where will the ceremony be held?"

"At Mr. Peter Montague's, below the State House where Governor Bennett lives, zur. They say it will be a great wedding, with the planters from up and down the river. Puritans and Royalists will eat and drink together, the farrier says. That's Madam Montague's notion—a great fête, with dancing out of doors, and little lanthorns hanging in the pine trees, and plenty to drink, and punch. John Morgan the farrier says all the town will attend—some inside the fence, dancing and making merry; others standing outside, looking over the hedge."

Richard laid the folio on the table. For a long time he sat looking out the window. Presently a smile came to his lips. "So all Jamestown will go to the wedding?"

"Zur, all. It will be like the great market day, with jollity and free drinking for those outside the fence, and a great ox roasting."

A light came into Richard's eyes; a smile touched his lips. "Ah, Digby, what you say pleasures me. Tell me, do you not think that we should join the wedding guests, and drink a toast, and perhaps tread a measure?"

Digby dropped the mug he was holding. "God's mercy, you never will!"

"On Thursday night, you say? We have time to devise a suitable habit for the occasion. Digby, where is our golden hoard?" Richard smiled to himself at the irony of this use of Kathryn's money.

Digby's surprise gave way to a look of grim determination. "You never will be spendin' the broads to buy raiment? And me saving them to buy your papers to get yourself free!"

"I've another plan, Digby. Another plan to gain my freedom."

"You are gay, Captain. Laugh before you weep. They're looking everywhere for us, e'en now, and you talk about rushing into the crowd of them."

"Where can one lose oneself best? In a crowd, my friend. Let them look. They'll not find us. I promise you that. Thursday, you said? Only three days from now."

Digby retired to the kitchen, rattling pots and pans, and making a delirious noise to show his disapproval. When everything was going in their favour, why should his captain suddenly tempt fate?

CHAPTER 25

The Dark Garden

SIR WILLIAM returned to Green Spring on Thursday morning. With him were Thomas Woodward and Mr. Caswell. They lunched under the trees in the orchard, with small black boys standing behind the chairs moving boughs of the honey tree to drive away flies and merrylegs.

Governor Berkeley was in the best of humours. His tobacco from the upper plantation was all packed in hogsheads and loaded. The ship now lay in plain view at the Green Spring landing. By nightfall the last of the tobacco would be stowed in the hold, bound for Bideford in Devon.

Richard's letters were in the captain's care—one for Dame Margaret, one for John Prideaux. He had talked an hour with the master, charging him with oral messages for his mother. His mind was at rest on that score. The plans for the night were on his mind. A feeling of anticipation pervaded him, giving him a strange exultation.

After the port, the table cleared and the servants gone, Mr. Woodward unrolled his maps and spread them on the table. For an hour he talked. Strange names rolled from his lips— Indian words musical and unfamiliar, Currituck, Perquimans, Pasquotank; the Indian villages of Chowanoke and Catokinge.

Mr. Woodward rolled up his maps. Before he left he said, "I heard in Jamestown that Mr. Philip Blount was going to St. Johns soon. He plans to stop at Roanoke Island for a few days. He longs to see the island where his forbear spent a year with the Grenville expedition." He turned to Richard. "Perhaps his visit there will coincide with your own."

Richard made some suitable answer. The mention of Blount brought a picture to his mind: the night the tobacco was burned . . . Phil with his arm about Sibyl's shoulders . . . her face hidden against his coat. A slow anger overwhelmed him. Yet why not? Philip Blount and Sibyl Jordan, a uitable match. But she was too young—far, far too young. Somehow this thought was not comforting. She was not too young. He remembered the sweet pressure of her lips against his—not like Kathryn's lips that night at the inn near Bristol, hard, demanding, as though she would draw his soul from him, possess him and his body, but give no return. Kathryn would allow a man to love her, yet hold herself aloof. Sibyl's lips were soft and warm and fragrant, like the essence of her, all-giving.

Mr. Caswell's voice brought him back. "Something pleasant occupies your thoughts, Captain?"

For a moment Richard was confused. Thinking quickly, he answered, "Yes, a pleasant thought. I mean to attend a wedding feast tonight."

Sir William turned in his chair. "What's that? What's that?"

Richard repeated, "I thought I would attend a wedding feast tonight—the uninvited guest."

Mr. Caswell said, "Are you mad, sir?"

"No, not mad." Richard turned to Sir William. "Pray, may I borrow a long cloak from you, sir—something to cover my clothes, which do not appear to fit a festive occasion?" When it came to the point he could not bring himself to use Kathryn's money for fine raiment. The notion that had momentarily amused him stuck in his craw.

The governor began to laugh. He banged the table with the flat of his hand. "By the eternal gods, this lad is after my own heart! What do you aim to do, sir? Carry away the bride on a milk-white charger?"

"Sir, no. Tread a measure, perhaps. Perhaps glimpse my new owner . . . and an ancient enemy."

The governor tapped his lip with his finger thoughtfully. "A cloak, you say? Nay, my lad, a whole costume, complete with wig, and perhaps a little black mask added to give mystery. Come! We will go to my dressing-room." He raised his voice. "Grison, call my valet! Tell him to unlock the painted armoire where my choice clothes are kept."

Richard exclaimed, "That I cannot accept! The clothes might be stained from . . . wine, the fine brocaded coat rent."

Mr. Caswell protested. "I do not like this, Captain. The danger is too great. Holder will have you slapped into the gaol. How would you like to sit in the stocks, or stand in the pillory, or even be branded on the cheek with an R for Runaway! All these things he can ask by law. It's danger. Danger!"

Sir William, who was hurrying down the hall ahead of them, turned about. "Cease, cease, Mr. Caswell! Let youth blaze and burn. Let him have his way. I confess the idea makes my blood run a little faster. Let him alone. The whole idea pleases me. A bold plot, sprinkled with danger. Man, have you come upon the cautious years?"

He opened the door to his bedchamber. His valet had unlocked the doors of the apple-green armoire, hand-decorated in roses and little cupids. There were racks of coats, plain, brocaded, silk, velvet, twill and linen; rows of saddle-boots and buckled shoes; doeskin and satin breeks. One side had shelves with perukes set on egg-shaped wooden moulds. Cloaks and great-coats, armour and uniforms were in a companion wardrobe on the opposite side of the room.

"Let me see. We are near a height, but your waist is trimmer. I must remember to eat more fruit and less heavy food. . . . Here is the trick—dove-grey, braided in silver thread, with a white and yellow waistcoat and satin small-clothes; a decent stock of Venice lace, and cuffs, silken hosen and buckled slippers—nay boots, soft as doeskin—and a wine-red cape.

"Ah, step into the bathing cabinet, Captain. Henri will bring proper garments to wear under, and bathing water. When you are attired, come to the great hall." Sir William rubbed his hands together. "I declare, Mr. Caswell, we haven't been as amused as this for many a day. What do you say we keep this Captain Monington with us here at Green Spring?"

"But whom would you send to the south, Your Excellency?"

"Yes, yes, I had forgotten. We must send a man of spirit on the southern venture." He left the room with Mr. Caswell. Richard followed the French fellow into the bathing cabinet.

Dressed, even to a hat of finest Italian felt with a sweeping brim over a curled wig, Richard presented himself. Sir William was playing a game of draughts with Mr. Caswell when he entered the great hall.

"Jove on Olympus, I swear it is a changeling!" Sir William studied Richard Monington's face intently. "Is it the fading light, or do I see a likeness to the Royal Stuart? What say you, Mr. Caswell?"

"Passing strange. I had not seen it. The clothes do make the man."

Sir William said, "Has this likeness been commented on before?"

"Sir, yes. And once it stood the King in good service, when his pursuers followed me for a day and a night."

Sir William left his chair. On the table were sword-belt and sash. He took up a sword with a hilt set with damascene. "Buckle it on, lad. You need not worry. 'Tis not a presentation sword, but a good Toledo blade." He bent it and made a forward thrust, stopping inches short of Richard's breast. "Strip off your coat and waistcoat, down to your fine linen shirt. Off with your Venice stock! Let us try our skill. Mr. Caswell, you will find the mate to this sword, and the buttons, in that cabinet. Let us walk into the garden before the sun dies."

Sir William was swift, his wrist was supple, but Richard could have had him a dozen times if he would. Panting from the exertion, the governor cried quits. "Damme, Captain, you are not heaving! You have not even got your wig awry. You are polite. You could have disarmed me, but you had the grace to play along." He threw himself onto a garden bench and mopped his forehead with a white linen square. "Aye, sir, I feel for the man you challenge tonight. Tell me what his name is—no, do not tell me. I will wait until you come back to report."

"I shall not fight tonight." Richard sheathed his sword. "I could not be so crude as to spoil a wedding feast."

Sir William laughed. "A daybreak duel has its points, but remember the grass may have the morning dew on it. I remember one morning in Hyde Park when a man's foot slipped and he impaled himself on his challenger's sword."

Caswell said, "I swear I don't like it. The Puritan will use the laws against duelling. Why rush into trouble, lad? Haven't you had enough already?"

Richard said, "Not quite. I thank you, Sir William, for the use of a noble blade and for the wedding raiment. If I spill ruby wine on this fine waistcoat——"

"Humph! Don't give it a thought. We still have French ships tying up at my landing. I see food is being served. Let us sup and talk of pleasant things. What time do you propose to make this excursion?"

"Near the midnight hour. It is the feast that I will attend, not the wedding."

Digby was waiting when Richard came out the door. A groom held the bridles of two good mounts. Richard swung up onto his horse. Followed by Digby and the groom, he crossed the Back River to the horse ferry at Friggett Landing by the pitch-and-tar swamp and rode slowly down the Back Street to the Montague house beyond the fort. The place had once belonged to Bad John Harvey, and it was bounded on the east by Nicholas Holder's land.

The street near the house was lighted by ships' lanthorns, and a great press of people were outside the hedge looking over.

"Will you enter by the lane behind the house or from the street?" Digby asked.

"In these fine clothes, the front door of course."

"I don't feel easy, Captain, that I don't. The groom and I will be at the back wall beyond the orchards. Whistle, and I will be over the wall."

"Not at all, Digby. This is my occasion, remember. Stay behind the wall, if you must, but no raising the battle-cry, no rushing into the fray with claymore and lance, shouting, 'A rescue, Monington, a rescue!' "

Digby laughed. "You are one for givin' orders, Captain. Somehow I distrust your gay mood more than I distrust your dour moments."

Richard grinned. "Listen! The music! The dancing has already begun." He dismounted. He paused a moment in the shadow beyond the gate. There were only a few onlookers at the front of the house. Most had moved into the lane to watch the dancing.

A servant met him at the door, an old Negro dressed in white. "The dancing is in the garden, sir. Want I should lead you?"

"Thank you, no. I'll find the way."

"No trouble at all. There's lanthorns all along the path. Yes, sir, thank you, sir. Wait—here is Mistress Sibyl." The Negro led the way inside. "She will show you to the garden. Gen'man, mistress, arrivin' late."

Richard watched her as she came down the stairs, one hand on the railing, the other lifting her skirts daintily. She seemed to float toward him, her thin white draperies fluttering. She

oked tall and very slender, her bodice laced tightly about her
arrow waist, showing the delicate curve of her breasts. Her
air was bound in a silver fillet and showered darkly over her
are white shoulders. He caught his breath sharply. Her love-
ness was so tender, so moving! How could this happen? Only
esterday she had been a child who romped and raced about
he manor-house at Coddington, ran up ladders to the dove-
ote to feed her pigeons, scampered down to the pool to feed
he ducks and scold the drake for his invasion of their quiet
ool—a child always in swift motion. Did a long gown work
uch magic? How proudly she carried her small head!

He bowed deeply, his wide hat almost sweeping the floor.

She stood at the foot of the stairs hardly looking at him.
"Sir," she said as he bowed, "I bid you welcome for Madam
Montague and Mr. Montague. Will you lay aside your cloak? I
will take you to them." She started toward the door that led
o the garden. The Negro servant had stepped outside again.

"Stay a moment, please."

She raised her head. "Richard!" she breathed. "Richard!"
She did not move. Her slim white hands went swiftly to her
heart. "Richard!" She drew close. He kissed her hands slowly.
"Richard, how come you here tonight? What if they find you?"
Her eyes were very bright.

"Let us think of that later. I want to talk to you." He
ooked about. The old Negro was standing in front of the
stoop, ready to show late arrivals to the garden.

"My uncle's study." She caught up a candlestick. "Come."
She led him down the hall to a little room at the end. One
small candle burned on the mantel. When she opened the door,
he wind caught the flame. It flickered and went out. Sibyl
ut the brass stick she carried onto a stand. She went to a
seat under the casement window. Richard tossed his hat onto
a chair and sat down beside her. He took both her hands in
his. They were soft and warm. A clean, fragrant scent, like
verbena or rose geranium, came from her long hair. His
and shook as it closed on hers.

"You are very lovely tonight, Sibyl."

"Thank you, Richard, you are very kind. Don't talk of me,
ut of you. Why did you walk into danger, knowing it *is*
danger? They will find you, turn you over to the gaoler. Oh,
Richard, Richard, I couldn't bear that!" She was trembling,
her eyes filled with tears.

He held her small chin with his cupped hand. "My sweet you are all enchantment, all beauty. Is it not worth danger to see you, to look into your eyes, to kiss your lips?" He leaned toward her. "My sweet, you are no longer a child, but a woman to be desired." Her cheek was against his. His lips touched hers gently. He must not let her know the emotion that swept over him. "My little lass!"

"Richard, Richard!" She clung to him. "I thought you would never find out."

"Find out?"

"That I was no longer a child. I got over being a child the night you went away from Coddington Manor. A child becomes a woman under grief . . . and I grieved."

"My sweet Sibyl!"

She pressed her cheek to his. "Did you not discern the differences when I kissed you at your cottage?"

"I know I was angry when I saw Phil Blount put his arm about you." He rose, drawing her to her feet. "I must go now, Sibyl. I have a task to do tonight. When it is finished . . ."

"What task? I am afraid. What is it you must do tonight?"

He released her hands from his arm. "You are a little girl turned woman overnight. You must not try to hold me back." He kissed her hand. "Do not follow me, please. I can play the part better if your eyes are not on me." He caught up his hat and went away.

The lighted path led him to the garden. For a time he stood in the shadow of the trees watching the dancers. He saw Madam Montague. Cecily was as radiant as the bride who stood near by with Stephen at her side. He looked about, but did not see Governor Bennett. Doubtless he had left. Nor did he glimpse Nicholas Holder among the crowd about the punch-bowl. His eyes searched the dancers. A great canvas had been stretched on the grass. The crowd was there, bowing, gliding forward and back, curtsying deeply to partners, clasping hands to form a wheel.

Presently he saw Holder. He was standing to one side, talking to Peter Montague. Richard waited a moment to get himself in hand. The encounter with Sibyl had thrown him off balance. He was stirred by the depth of his emotion. Yet there was this other thing that must be done.

He walked over to Mathilda and bowed low before her. "May an old friend wish the bride well?" he said. He was conscious that the talking had ceased. Eyes turned to him, curious eyes wondering who the stranger could be. Mathilda's eyes showed no recognition. "Thank you——" She stopped abruptly. "Richard," she whispered, "how came you here?" She clung to his hand. "Go. Go quickly before they discover you." She turned to look for her husband. Stephen had stepped to the dancing pavilion.

Cecily came forward. "May I be presented to your guest, Mathilda?"

Mathilda thought, Cecily is short-sighted. She does not recognize him. She saw him at the whipping-posts, but, to be sure, it was dark and he wasn't dressed like this or wearing a wig. " 'Tis an old and dear friend of my childhood, Captain Monington."

"Monington . . . of course. We have heard much of you and your mother Dame Margaret. Welcome to Jamestown. Will you be with us long?"

"Only a few days, Madam Montague, until my ship sails."

Mathilda touched his arm. "Come, Captain, I want to present you to my husband." She moved slowly through the dancers. "You are mad, quite mad. Someone will recognize you. Go down the path. It leads through the Montagues' and the Holders' gardens down to the end of the island. Oh, Richard, it is all so terrible! I could weep."

"Weep on your wedding day? Never! A good man you have, and God be with you!"

He kissed her hand and strode off. He had no desire to meet Stephen. He saw Nicholas and Peter Montague walking ahead of him down the path that led to the little gate in the wall. This was the time! He stepped along briskly. The men had gone through the gate into the dark garden when he overtook them.

He stood directly in the light cast by the high lanthorn at the gate and called, "Nicholas Holder!"

Holder turned abruptly. He too stood in the light. The garden behind him was heavy in shadow.

"Nicholas Holder, I have a word for you." He stepped across the intervening space.

Holder's face changed. He drew back abruptly. "Monington!"

"Aye, Richard Monington. The word I have to say to you is 'Coward!' "

Holder's hand went to his sword-hilt but he did not answer.

Richard saw Peter Montague's wondering glance go from his face to Holder's. *"Coward!* I repeat it. A man who fights another, weak from long illness, delirious with gaol fever—I say he is a coward." He stood waiting.

Holder's voice was high. "No man can say that to me!"

"I say it once again."

Holder turned to Peter. His face was white. Sweat stood on his forehead and his upper lip. "The man is drunk. Call the watch. He is a menace."

Richard stepped closer, lifted a glove from his belt and laid it gently across Holder's face.

Peter Montague came forward. "This is an outrage. You are trespassing on my ground. I do not even know your name."

Holder said, "He is an indentured man. I do not know where he got the clothes. Stole them, I suppose. I'll call the watch."

"Wait. Let us hear what the man has to say."

Richard said, "Mr. Montague, I deplore the intrusion. Holder is quite right: I am indentured. He holds my papers."

"My wife——"

Richard stopped him. *"You* hold my papers. I have come tonight to make you a wager. I will fight you. Let swords be the answer. If I win, I have my freedom. If you are victor—and I live—I take my punishment. You are the challenged; choose your weapons."

Montague said, "The governor is set against duelling."

Richard replied, "No doubt. Let us disregard the governor. Will you meet me at sunrise, Nick? Or must I mash you with my bare knuckles, like a hop-picker at a market fair?"

Hodler said, "Will you act for me, Montague? . . . I think I hear my wife calling." He turned and all but ran.

Montague looked after him, a puzzled expression on his good-humoured face.

Richard laughed without humour. "This smacks of the theatre, sir. I am sorry to disturb you tonight, but I have been informed that Holder is to leave shortly."

Montague said, "I will arrange matters. Send your second to me."

"I have no second, no friend in Jamestown. . . . Wait, there might be one—Phil Blount."

"Mr. Blount is here. I will fetch him. I think I recognize you now—the indentured man from Bennett's Welcome. Of course." He paused, puzzled. "I do not understand."

"No need, sir. 'Tis an old score that began in England, and this——" He pointed to the scar.

Montague said, "I don't like it. Of course Holder is not called to fight an indentured man. You know that. He would have everything to lose and nothing to gain. But if he had taken your 'coward' before me, he would have confessed himself a poltroon. You are evidently a gentleman. The duelling place is the little meadow to the left of the ferry. At sunrise. Shall I send Blount to you here?"

"Yes. . . . No, it will not be necessary. Explain to him, will you, please? I will be at the duelling place at sunrise."

"I still don't like it," Montague said. He took a few steps, then he turned back. He leaned over until his lips were close to Richard's ear. "I'd have liked to see you give him a sound thrashing." He walked away hastily in the direction of the music.

After a time Richard went back to the company. He bade Mathilda good night. Stephen did not recognize him, garbed as he was, with a wig instead of close-cropped hair. Richard paid his respects to Mistress Cecily, who most graciously invited him to dinner with them before he set sail.

At the turn of the path he saw Kathryn Holder. She was alone. For a moment the two faced each other. Richard had brought the bag of gold broads with him, expecting some such occasion. Quickly he reached inside his coat and dropped it before her. The bag broke open. He bowed and passed by so close that her skirts brushed his sword. He glanced around and the last he saw of her, she was on her knees in her flowered dress groping for coins in the dust.

He walked on leisurely toward the front gate. As soon as he was out of sight he cut down the lane. He found Digby walking up and down near the garden wall.

"Thought you would never come," Digby said dourly. "I was astride the wall, ready for a rescue, but the party was well conducted."

Richard mounted his horse. "We'll get a room at the tavern. Thompson's wasn't it?"

They rode in silence for a time. Digby said, "You'd sleep

better in your own bed, zur. There's plenty of roistering about tonight."

"No matter. I must be in town at sunrise—only a little time off."

"Sunrise?" Digby spurred his horse closer. "Be we fightin' a dool?"

"Aye, a duel. I have a wish to lay a scar on a man's face, Digby."

Richard slept soundly on a hard bed. Before cock-crow Digby pulled the covers from the foot of the bed. Richard sat up and rubbed his eyes. "God's death, but it's no more than ten minutes' sleep I've had!"

"Three hours, zur. I hope your hand is steady. Here is your ale and a chunk of bread. The girl says there's talk about an indentured runaway being seen about the town."

"Indeed? Did they catch up with him?" Richard yawned. "Better roll the gay coat and waistcoat into a bundle and hide them in the saddle-bags. I'll ride in shirt and breeks."

"No need. I've found a leathern jerkin that will fit."

They arrived at the meadow first. They waited half an hour. Richard grew restive. "If he does not get here soon, I'll ride into town and fight him in his own garden."

"Here they be."

Two men rode up, Peter Montague and Nicholas Holder. Nick was sullen. He kept looking over his shoulder. Montague said, "I could not find Blount. Your man can second you. Swords. May I have yours to measure?" He spoke sharply. As he laid the blades side by side he whispered to Richard, "The fellow refused to come. I shamed him into it. Sorry." Aloud he said, "The measure is correct."

Richard said, "It is understood that if I win, I gain complete freedom?"

"'Tis understood. I witness that. Holder, speak up."

"It is understood. Mr. Montague holds the papers."

Holder reached for his sword. His hand was trembling.

Montague marked the positions. He flipped a coin for position. Richard drew back to the sun, a good omen.

Holder spoke to Peter. "Let it be understood that first blood constitutes a finish." Montague looked at him, scorn in his face.

Richard laughed. "Satisfied. I do not want to kill the fellow, just touch him a bit here and there."

The sun showed in the east. Steel struck steel as the swords crossed; thrust and counter-thrust. Holder was tense, his jaw clamped; Richard easy, a sword in his hand and his ancient enemy before him. What a blade he held, delicately balanced, bend and spring back, a dream of a sword! This was good. Holder was not too bad—a little careless perhaps. Swiftly Richard rushed his guard. The point touched a spot over Holder's heart. He turned pale, but Richard put no weight behind it.

He's paying him, Montague thought as he watched. The dragoon stood with folded arms.

Another *touché*. Richard smiled. This time he played higher —at the throat—and scored a little scratch, not enough to draw blood. Holder's eyes were bright with fear. His thrust was rapid, not calculated, easily parried. Sweat came to his forehead. His breath was short.

This was the time. A few moments' feinting, then the tip of the sword followed a line across the temple, a clean, light cut that opened the skin. Blood followed the sword tip.

"Blood!" called Montague. He held up his hand. Obeying the signal Richard dropped the point of his blade. Holder lunged, but Richard was swift. He caught the blade as it descended. The two swords ran their length, one on the other, but Richard's wrist was supple. In a flash Holder's sword made an arc and landed near Montague's feet.

"Dammit, I called quits!" Montague shouted. "A foul turn you made, Holder!" To Richard he said, "Sir, I apologize for my principal."

"Digby will ride with you, Mr. Montague. I'll take it a favour if you will deliver the papers to him."

Montague glanced at Holder who stood mopping the blood from his face.

" 'Not so deep as a well, nor as wide as a church-door; but 'tis enough,' " Richard quoted as the three rode away.

Richard was at Green Spring in time for breakfast. He told the evening's tale. "I swear I felt ashamed of the theatrical part I played. I frightened several people, paid one off—and gave one the scare of his life. Montague said Holder would be bound to send Denis' soldiers to search me out."

The governor sat back in his chair and laughed loudly. "He'll never think of looking for you at Green Spring," he said. "I must say I enjoy a touch of theatre. I wrote a play myself once. Had the devil of a time getting the characters on and off stage. Ever think of exits and entrances, man?"

Sir William would have Richard tell the story over again. "You didn't dance with the bride, sir. I swear I would have led the pretty miss out in a contra-dance."

"She was so frightened for me that I wouldn't have had the heart. And thank you for the sword. It has a charmed blade."

Before night, he had written two letters, which Digby delivered to the Jordan house. One was to Peter Montague. It was short and quite formal, requesting permission to pay his address to Peter's ward, Miss Sibyl Jordan, when he returned from a journey.

The other was to Sibyl herself:

The wonder of it is upon me still. I came to cancel old debts and gain my freedom by my sword, instead of with money. You may think this a hard practice, but a man must stand on his own feet. Once I thought of slashing the other cheek, for Coddington Manor and the good neighbours he betrayed to Cromwell. But I desisted. Now he is marked as he marked me.

But we will forget the unhappy things that transpired last night. Let them fade from memory entirely. I shall think of only one thing—that I have found you. I am sad that I may not see you again. In three months' time I shall return. Three months is not too long, my sweet.

                                        Your Richard

Four days later Richard and Digby were on their way to the rendezvous at the Blackwater River for their venture to the southern waters.

EPILOGUE

Carolina

Carolina

RICHARD MONINGTON kept account of the journey in his note-book at the request of Sir William. "Who knows," Governor Berkeley had said, "but it may be a safe retreat for us one day? 'Tis always best to be prepared for all eventualities. Write a daybook, like a sailor's log, that I may have a complete record."

So on the twelfth of September Richard set down the first record:

Edward Bland, Merchant; Abraham Wood, Captain; Elias Pennant and Sackford Brewster, Gentlemen; Thomas Woodward, Surveyor; two servants and an Indian guide named Pyancha set forth this morning with me and my man Digby on the four days' portage across to the Blackwater River.

We carried provisions for the journey and fire-arms. The two gentlemen rode horses, the others in a carriage. Digby and I, along with the Indian and the servants, walked. I thought it much easier to follow the narrow Indian track on foot than to have branches and thick vines slapping my face and briers scratching.

This morning we passed a branch belonging to the Blackwater Lake. At this point we were obliged to unlace the horses from the carriage, for the great rainfall of the past days made the narrow road all but impassable.

Mr. Bland's servant, Robert Farmer, walked ahead. Near a small river he ran into a band of Indians. I do not know who had the more fear, the servant or the Indians. When we approached, they stood like bronze statues, watching us. Suddenly they all ran away into the woods, followed by their women and children. Pyancha quieted our men, saying it was not a war party, because the women, carrying their small children on their backs, were with them. If they had been out raiding there would have been only men. That was re-assuring, but Farmer and the other servant, being un-acquainted with savages wandering in the woods, fell into the rear, leaving Digby and me to walk behind the Indian guide. We camped for the night in a good spot among pine trees. We named the spot Farmer's Chase.

Second Day.

A small group of Indians came close while we were cook-ing breakfast. Pyancha carried a white flag and, waving it, called out some Indian words that meant "We come in peace." After a time one Indian man ventured into camp. Satisfied that we had no evil intention, he let out a great hallow, and the rest came out of their skulking holes. They remind me of timorous hares.

Third Day.

An Indian named Oyeocker, who said he was brother to the Nottoway King Chounterounte, told us that his brothers and other Nottoway kings were hunting, and Chounterounte had shot one of his brothers in the leg, but they would come, bringing the wounded man. We lingered until almost noon, but no one came. So we journeyed to the Indian town be-longing to Oyeocker.

He proffered to be our guide anywhere we wished to go. This is very rich, level soil, well timbered and well watered, convenient for hogs and cattle.

We came to a second town, Maharineck. A Tuscarora Indian told us that there were many Englishmen a great way off in his country, which was to the south.

Mr. Bland bought skins and a great measure of Roanoke [wampum]. The Wainoake had a feast, and at night there were ceremonies and dancing to entertain us.

We passed Indian old fields, full of great reeds by the river and with very good land by the pocosins, passable, they tell me, to the Meherrin, a deep river one hundred paces wide . . . exceedingly rich land. We had roasting ears and sturgeon for supper. They say that the Meherrin is the other branch of the Chowan, which we shall reach tomorrow.

We saw rich, red, fat land. There was marl at an Indian town.

A strange thing happened the last day before we reached the Chowan River. We came upon a path running crosswise, about twenty yards on each side, with two remarkably great pine trees. Pyancha made a stop here. He cleared the westerly end of the path of brush and brambles until it was smooth. We asked him the meaning of this, but he hesitated, unwilling to answer Mr. Bland's questions. He stood looking along the path, making great signs. We decided to take a rest there.

When Oyeocker, our other guide, came up, he also stopped. He walked away and cleared the other end of the path. He was so serious of expression he caused us to plead to hear why they each cleared one end of the path and stopped at the middle.

Finally he told us this tale as we sat about our fire. Many, many years ago the great Emperor Opechancanough came thither to make war on the Tuscarora in revenge for three of his men, killed earlier by a raiding party. One other was wounded, but he escaped and returned home to tell the story of their tribesmen murdered by the Tuscarora—murdered for the Roanoke they carried with them to trade for otter skins. Several petty kings accompanied Opechancanough. Among them was one king of a town called Powhatan, who had long harboured a grudge against the King of the Chowanoke. They had quarrelled about a young woman, whom the King of the Chowanoke had carried off from the King of Powhatan.

The King of Powhatan, being wily, invited the King of the Chowanoke to meet him at this place. He sent word that he would bring fine gifts of great value. The King of Powhatan embraced and saluted the King of the Chowanoke, then with incredible swiftness whipped a bow-string about his neck and strangled him.

So now it happens to this day that when the friends of Powhatan pass this way, they clear the westerly end of the path; and friends of the Chowanoke the easterly end. Here beside two great trees which sprang up at this place is a memory kept alive.

I thought, Sir William, this story would interest you. I do not know whether this Powhatan is the Indian who so troubled Jamestown, or one of his tribe; a treacherous fellow he was.

And that is not the end of the tale. We had journeyed some distance up the path when we saw a grave on the east side— a great heap of stones covered with green boughs. Oyeocker told us that there lay the great King of the Chowanoke who was strangled. In his honour and in memory of him the Indians cover his grave with these boughs. Whenever they go out to war, they relate the story of the great king and other warriors to their young men. "Go out," they say, "and emulate the king in valour."

This I thought showed something of Indian character that I had never realized.

We are come to the great broad river. Tomorrow our companions leave us and return home without visiting Nathaniel Batts. They say they have seen enough good land for their purpose, which I now think is colonization. They say the Blackwater Lake and the Chowan River will suit their needs.

I think our friends are not at ease about the Indians who follow, paralleling us in the forest. Sometimes we glimpse their oiled bodies, their nakedness covered only with skins of cony or hare. We sleep girt in our swords, our pistols beside us. We lie close one to the other, with a guard always posted.

I will send this back by Mr. Bland. Mr. Woodward, Digby, the Indian Oyeocker and I will continue our journey without the trouble of horses (the carriage was left far back). Tomorrow we will meet the settler who lives on the river. I hope the boat is ready, for I am eager to go deeper into this beautiful land.

Your humble servant,
Richard Monington

To
Rt. Hon. Sir William Berkeley
at Green Spring

The little party reached the settler's house on the Chowan River. The old man met them a mile from his dwelling. They saw him coming some distance away, a tall lean man with long white hair and beard. He carried a musket in the crook of his arm and he was followed by two deer dogs.

"Yes, sir. I've lived here since '44. I was here and had had four harvests when General Bennett came."

Thomas Woodward said, "I had forgotten Bennett and Colonel Dew came down the river."

"As far as Bennett's Creek," said the old man, whose name he gave as Wilson. "That is down the river a spell, as purty a little bit of water as ever was seen—yes, sir, a-bendin' and a-twistin' like a snake's back, with bushes droopin' over to touch the water. Sometimes in spring when the bay trees is bloomin', you can see their white wax blossoms in the water just as clear as they's real."

They reached the old man's dwelling. It was a comfortable house of two rooms, with a low extension at the rear, made of a mixture of earth and oyster-shell—marl, he called it—with square timbers and thatched with reeds. The room was quite comfortable, with crude furniture evidently made by the settler himself, except for one thing—a Welsh dresser of aged oak, with pewter plates, bright and shining, on the racks.

Wilson caught Richard's interest in the piece. He touched the wood, lifted a plate and rubbed away a speck of dust with the palm of his hand. "She always loved it. She would say, 'When a body looks at the fine old dresser, with pewter well polished and bright, he will know that gentlefolk live here.'" The aged blue eyes were sad.

Woodward had gone outside to see that his transit was well cared for. Richard examined an old tea-pot. "Worcester," he commented.

"Aye. She came from Lemster way, herself. She was a gentle body. The forest worrit her—the bears that walked up to the door, and the varmits cryin' out in the night. But she never complained. She used to come to the field while I worked, and sit on a stump, her bit of sewing or knitting in her hand."

"Was she frightened of the Indians?"

Wilson took his pipe, crushed a tobacco leaf in his hand and filled the clay bowl. "No, she wasn't." He laughed softly. "She was a Church of God woman, with the Spirit in her. She wanted to convert the red men, and they venerated her. She was pale of complexion, with hair braids like the silk of my corn. She was a gentle woman, she was, and that is the way she passed out of life ... gently ... at sunset ... holding my hand."

He got up and went to the door. The sun was sinking in the west, a great globe behind the irregular line of the pines on the opposite shore. "She loved the sunset. Every evening we would sit there under the pine trees and watch the reflection in the river until the last light was gone. Sir, it was fittin' that she should go that-a-way—gently, at sunset." He was silent for a time.

"Don't you get lonely?" Richard asked.

"Never, sir, with my fields to plant and nurture and harvest, and my trap lines in the woods." He looked at Richard, words hanging on his lips. Richard thought, The prophets must have looked like this man of lofty brow and long white beard.

"There's boats to be built out of 'jumper' wood, such as you will sail in tomorrow. In the autumn, when my crop is in, there's hunting to be done."

He walked to the dresser, opened a drawer and took out a book, carefully wrapped in deerskin. "She was a learned woman, sir. She taught me to read in the winter evenings. 'Tis her Bible." He laid it on the pine table. Richard glanced at the fly-leaf. "Eunice Whiteley. Written in her year of grace 1644, when she first saw the Light and Peace descended upon her."

The man's hands trembled a little as he folded the leathern wrapping about *The Book* and laid it away in the drawer of the dresser.

He turned suddenly and started for the kitchen. "Here I've been talking like an old gossip, and my venison stew like to burn down." He left the room hastily. Richard's eyes followed him thoughtfully. He saw the symbol of colonization— the solitary cottage, the young fields hacked from the hungry forest, the prowling wild beasts, the lonely woman. Here was fortitude at its highest level. Here was an example of what was coming. He felt strangely moved. How many of his own kind had taken what their forefathers had left them without a thought! Here was a man who builded at the beginning, laid the foundation-stone, took not from his father or his father's father, but drew life from the forest and the river. There was nobility in this.

Richard walked out to the bank and looked across the river to the opposite shore. The water was blood-red from the afterglow. In the forest there were no longer individual trees, but a brooding mass of darkness. For the first time he had a glimpse into the future—a wild land brought to subjugation under the plough and turned into wealth.

Aloud he said, "Pray God that we give to this great country and do not strip it! Pray God that I may be one to help build it into a mighty force!"

Four sat down to a supper of venison stew, cooked with corn and potatoes, and appones cooked in the ashes—only Wilson called them "pones." They ate heartily, as do men who walk through the forest. They drank great draughts of cider from the old man's apple orchard, and smoked pipes of fragrant leaf of his growing."

" 'Tis an easy life," he remarked after the pewter dishes were washed, dried and put into the rack.

"And still you never feel lonely?" Woodward repeated the question that Richard had asked. It was an obvious question.

"Don't have time. Then there's a neighbour—the Jordans down at Bennett's Creek, and the Chowanoke Indian town across the river. Traders come to get my pelts and sell me little things. The river is a highway, sirs. Every week someone goes by and halloos or puts in at my landing. Yes, it's a highway. Nathaniel Batts, he's our governor, though I don't know that he's got proper papers. Nat says that a long time ago, maybe sixty-seventy years, there was some queen's ships sailed right up this river as far as where we sit. Fine big ships they was. They visited Chowanoke-town over yonder and saw the king. It was a big town then. My Indians say seven hundred warriors they could put in the field. They must have had surprise to see men all trussed up in shining armour, walking stiff and slow, while they were running about mother-naked." He chuckled at the thought.

Richard raised his brows. Woodward nodded. "Sir Richard Grenville's men, and Ralph Lane the governor. They sailed up the river from Roanoke Island. That was around 1585, when Elizabeth was still Queen. Raleigh's expedition, it was, though he never came."

In the morning early they stowed their gear in the boat, a long dugout of juniper, made by the settler. "I put in a suit of sail," he told them. "I won't be needin' them until spring, when I'm goin' to take Mr. Yeardley to glimpse the land he's been granted. There's grants here that people haven't seen or cleared—" he laughed then—"and many an acre cleared by them who've got no grants." As he pushed the boat off, he said, "Be sure and stop at Chowanoke-town down yonder on the opposite shore. Tell the king I sent you. He's a friend of mine, and he'll cook you a fish or roast a haunch of venison. There's a town on the opposite shore, down below Bennett's Creek and the island. It's Chowanoke also. They call it

Catokinge. It's the women's town. Keep away from it, or the Indian warriors will be after you with their bows and arrows."

The Indian guide poled the boat out into mid-stream, standing in the prow. Once away from the bank and the cypress trees that marched far out into the water, they caught a breeze. Richard hoisted sail. The river was broad and placid. Only the tiniest ripples showed on the surface. The west shore had higher banks than the east; it was unbroken primeval forest. The east had banks cut in places by lowland bays or marshes, which were called by the Indians pocosins.

By sundown they saw cuts in the forest, the fields of Indian corn. Presently they came in sight of a large Indian town with land cleared on either side, and many huts or houses long, with curved roofs. Smoke from cooking fires drifted lazily upward.

"We will not pause here," Woodward said. "I am eager to get to Batt's house."

"Nor at the women's town, either," Richard said with a laugh. "I do not yearn to have a poisoned arrow in my back."

"Chowanoke be peaceful," the guide remarked, showing he understood English better than he spoke. "Tomorrow a governor's place. Tomorrow before moonrise."

The autumn colours touched the heavy foliage along the riverbank—the brilliant red of sourwood, the yellow and scarlet of maples, the gold of the cypress and sycamore; only the pine and juniper held the dark green of summer. Drifting down-river, they found the day went swiftly. At night they went ashore at a convenient narrow beach. Wrapped in their blankets, they slept quietly.

Richard was awakened by the snapping of a twig. He sat upright. A buck with two does had come to the river to drink. The moonlight shone down on the male as he stood guard, his noble antlered head erect and watchful, while the does drank their fill.

They talked little on the journey in the canoe, each man absorbed in his own thoughts. Once Digby said. "The old man had been a mercenary. He told me that he fought wherever they paid him best. He says the greatest general in all Europe was the King of Sweden, Gustavus Adolphus. I've heard you say, zur, that Oliver learned his lessons in the use of cavalry by reading about that warrior's methods. Does it seem a fair thing for a man to learn his generaling out of a book or a paper, and not by sitting a horse?"

Richard had no answer other than "But Cromwell *did* fight his cavalry, and he *did* win battles."

"I know. I know. I've been chased meownself."

Nathaniel Batts was a sturdy man of sanguine complexion. He greeted Thomas Woodward with great cordiality and extended his hand to Richard and Digby. He said, "The lookout told me there was a boat approaching. I could not think who it could be, unless Mr. Yeardley had sent his men down the Chowan on their way to Roanoke Island. Come within, gentlemen. The midges and biting flies are fierce tonight. It is inadvisable to sit out in the open. But before we go inside, let me show you the most beautiful prospect under the cope of heaven."

They walked on the garden terrace. The moonshine was almost as bright as day. The house was set on a high bank, near the confluence of the wide Chowan and the more turbulent Moratuck. The marriage of the two rivers formed a great sound that flowed eastward to the broad Ocean Sea. At the base of the sound, protected by a long sandbank, lay Roanoke Island.

The night took on a magical dreamlike quality under the moon. Miles on miles of silver water stretched before them, edged by high banks, dark with heavy forests.

"My domain," Nathaniel Batts remarked. "I rule her like a king. I call myself governor of all I behold, but I doubt me if Oliver will uphold my claim to sovereignty!" He laughed a good wholesome hearty laugh. A wholesome man, thought Richard, as they went toward the house; a man of character, but by his eyes a dreamer. He looks on this primeval land and sees an empire yet to be created.

Over a mug of ale the governor and Woodward talked. "Madam has already retired," Batts said. "My man will assign you sleeping quarters. I'm afraid two of you will have to share one room, but the bed is wide enough for four, so you will not be uncomfortable."

In the morning Richard came upon Madam Batts in her garden where she was supervising work. She was a quiet woman, simple and direct in manner. She welcomed Richard with pleasant hospitality. "A gardener must be always alert. Here we do not have to coax the plants to grow, but try to restrain the lush and rank growth. Garden pests are as they are at home. Moles burrow and bite the bulbs. Conies nibble young tender leaves. Beetles and insects destroy. But we are progressing." She pointed to a terrace below. "One day we will terrace down to the water, but I find the lack of stone for a well very trying."

"A green wall such as you have is pleasant to the eye," Richard remarked.

"Yes, but it does not keep out varmints." She raised her eyes and looked down the great expanse of water, as beautiful by day as it had been under the magic of the moon. "It is so lovely. The water and the forests beyond make my walled garden. The trees are a curtain that shuts out the great world." She stooped to pick a withered flower from a bordering plant. "I've the whole of the forest for my nursery," she said as she moved away.

The garden made Richard think of Biggor. How had the old man fared since his mother went to Devon?

All day Thomas Woodward and the self-appointed governor studied maps, Richard looking on. The surveyor was making little squares to show the cultivated fields, little dots to indicate houses. Richard listened to the names that fell from their lips. These are the first, he thought, the very first of this great new empire.

The governor said, "These plantation owners are holding under the old Thomas Heath patents. They are troubled, for as more colonists come there will be legal difficulties. I doubt if Cromwell will recognize old grants—or lands purchased from the Indians either. So surveyed lines will be a blessing."

Woodward said, "I doubt if I do any real survey this time. This old instrument is off. I've sent to England for a new one, but you know how long that takes—a year, perhaps more. Sir William wants an idea of what land is already taken and seated." He turned to Richard. "If you're thinking of taking up land, better pick your location before we settle Roger Greene's hundred families."

Batts said, "Why not south of here? There is excellent timber below the point, and two Indian old fields already cleared. You would have almost the same prospect as you see out that window, and we would not be too bad as neighbours."

"I might go farther and do worse," Richard replied. "May I wait until I return from Roanoke Island before I make my decision?"

Batts nodded. "You are wise to look, but you will return to the meeting of the waters in the end. View the points about the Perquimans River—two fine necks of land. There's Little Creek and the Yeopim River also. Folk are already planting there. Phillips is seated, and the Skinners and Roger Williams have holdings. I've heard that the Battles and Henderson Walker want land. Pricklove, a Quaker, came early; so did Widow Forsten and Robert Lawrence."

"How early did the colonists come to this section?"

"I can't rightly say, Mr. Monington. Some say the first folk came after the massacre of '22, when so many were murdered at Bennett's Welcome and near-by plantations. They are supposed to have settled at Orapeak. I don't know who they were. I have only the names of men who applied for land or received grants under Sir William. Caleb Calloway is one; Edward Smythwick, Stephen Mainwaring, Francis Tomes, the Blounts, John Whedby are on the list for land. Thomas Relph wants the south side of the Pasquotank, near Thomas Keile and Mrs. Forsten."

He went to his cabinet and took out some papers. "William Jennings has put in to patent five hundred and fifty acres on New Begin Creek. I have a letter from John Harvey. He gives his notification that he will receive, or has received, grants of eight hundred fifty acres, near Thomas Skinner. Henry Palin sent men to clear. . . . Robert Peele, William West and Richard Buller . . . West has applied to patent twenty-five hundred acres of land."

Mr. Woodward wrote busily. "What about George Catchmead? He has, according to my record, thirty-three hundred and thirty-three acres on the north side of Roanoke Sound, westerly on the Perquimans River."

"That I did not know, but I did hear from Sir William the last time I was in Jamestown that he favoured a strong settlement there. Tell me about Roger Greene, Clerk."

"He's a Cambridge graduate, took orders at Norwich. He believes in towns and close seating rather than large plantations."

"Have it as you will, by 1660 we will have upward of a hundred families here if all these who have indicated they want acreage take up their land and fulfill the requirements of building, and that will be above the twenty-some land grants issued by Governor Berkeley."

"But many have been here before they had grants?" Richard asked the question.

"Aye, that they have. Some came as trappers and traders, then stayed to lay in a crop. Take Robert Lawrence—he's been here several years without any grant at all."

Woodward got up and stretched himself, manipulating his cramped fingers. "I'm going to acquire land here myself, rich fat bottom land, before the best is gone. As it stands now, my lists say there are twenty-seven families and four hundred forty-seven servants. Quite an estimate for 'Rogues' Harbour.' "

"I don't like that term applied to good worthy folk," the governor said. "Remember, some of them haven't been here long enough to fulfill the requirements."

Woodward smiled. "Who bothers now under Cromwell? We will arrange to have the grants made all over when Charles the Second comes to the throne again."

"I'd forgotten you were such a fiery Royalist. Something for you to remember is that Cromwell still sits at Whitehall."

"Aye, and getting more autocratic and royal by the day. The master of a ship out of Bristol told me, war with Holland is now a fact; the people are uneasy; General George Monk's army wants reform laws, liberty of conscience, more gospel preaching and a new House. Oliver has not kept promises, and he and General Monk are said to be quarrelling."

Batts went to the door and shouted for a servant to bring ale. "Little all that English unrest bothers us. Here we plant and cultivate and harvest. Let them wrangle, if they want. It buys them no winter coat."

"If Monk is restive, it gives us new hope," said Woodward. "What say you, Monington?"

"The man in power needs his army solid behind him" was the only comment Richard made.

The little sloop that Nathaniel Batts had lent them sailed briskly eastward toward the Island of Roanoke. Richard lay on the deck and watched Batts's house, at the meeting of the waters, vanish from sight. It would be good, living on that high bank, water on three sides, the forest on the other. He could lay claim to a thousand acres, adjoining Batts's holdings.

To the left, across the sound, were a little bay and the Indian town of Waratan. That was where Smythwick's land lay, according to Woodward's lists. A house showed now and then on the left shore; two or three set among trees on the necks of land thrust into the sound by the cutting of the creeks, the Perquimans and Pasquotank rivers, broad waterways deep enough to carry ships of some tonnage. It was all good, this vast fruitful land, ripe and waiting.

Roanoke Island lay in view. From a distance it seemed a ship at anchor, closing the sound. As they sailed close, they saw men moving about the island. A sloop, larger than the one they sailed, rested in a sheltered harbour. The sound of hammering greeted them.

They dropped anchor off shore. A white man put out in a row-boat. Richard recognized one of the men on shore. It was Phil Blount, shouting and waving his cap.

Philip introduced the man who stood beside him as Francis Yeardley, on whose sloop he had sailed down from Jamestown. They walked through the sand up a gentle slope; then they came on half a dozen men who were building a house of some size. The large squared timbers were set, pegged to the sills. The king beam, square-hewed, was in place, the pitch of the roof set. Fabric, to cover the walls, was already mixed —sand and oyster-shells and some earth. Reeds had been cut for thatching. The house was placed in a small grove of trees, well above the water.

Mr. Yeardley explained, as they sat watching the artisans at their task. A few weeks back a young trader for beavers had come to him in Jamestown and said that his sloop had gone adrift accidentally at Roanoke Island. He asked for help to recover it, for there was a cargo of beaver skins waiting to be brought out for shipment to England. "I sent some friends and a member of my family with the trader. They sailed ten leagues from Cape Henry, entering at Currituck. They found the great commander of the Indians hunting. He greeted them civilly, showed them the ruins of Sir Walter Raleigh's fort, and the trader brought me a token to prove they had been there."

Philip said, "That is where I had good fortune. I met Captain Yeardley at Madam Montague's. He told me this tale. I persuaded him to bring me down in his shallop."

Yeardley smiled. "He importuned me. I intended to come. I was of a mind to build an English house for the Indian king, so I gathered together six men, one a carpenter. I have two hundred pounds sterling in trust for the king, as purchase money for land and three great rivers."

Phil interrupted. "I wish you might have been here, Richard. We took possession in a solemn manner, just as I had heard my grandfather tell. We delivered to the Indians a turf of earth, by 'turf and twig' in the old way. The commander, with other chiefs, took solemn oath, leaving the lands and the rivers to us."

Mr. Yeardley left to speak with his carpenter. Phil and Richard walked up to the ruined fort that Grenville had built for his company, the venturers who stayed one year, then sailed away home with Sir Francis Drake.

Phil was thoughtful as he walked through the ruins. A piece of armour here, a casque or a breast-plate, a bit of leather half-eaten through, the remains of a small dwelling, all told a tragic story. "It took greatness to make the first venture," he said; "to face the perils of the unknown seas, the danger on the land, the vast unknown crawling in upon them."

"Aye, it took courage to be the first to come, but it takes more to stay and make a colony live. I am glad to stand in their footsteps, remembering the glory of their struggle. They failed here on Roanoke, but success came at Jamestown. You will sail home, knowing that the cycle is complete."

Richard sat long on deck that night. He thought of the Old World and the New, but more deeply he thought of the New. Above all other thoughts, these days of journeying, the picture of Sibyl rose before him—early at dawn and in his last waking hours. She seemed to fit into this background. She would have the stamina to be one of the first.

He decided on the land near the meeting of the waters. There he would build. There they would live.

Sometimes he could see his mother coming across the sea. "For a short time only," Dame Margaret would say. "This ... land. It belongs to youth. But I am old; I must ... the old."

... ght of Coddington Manor. Strangely it gave him

no unrest that Kathryn Holder would walk the halls and the lovely garden. It would be for a short time only. Then, when Charles sat again on his throne, it would be his mother, Dame Margaret, who sat before the fire in the Great Room, and Cook Ellie would be in her sweet, cool kitchen, with old Graves to wait on them.

That was as it should be, for Dame Margaret belonged to the Old World. But he must stand with the New World, with Sibyl beside him.

The night before he started for Jamestown, Digby came to him. "Zur, I have thought long on this. I will be staying here, a-working and building me a little house and clearing our land. By the time you come back, in a few months, I will have the work behind me. I like it well. I'm a free man here, and here I will stay."

The Indian went with Richard, and two men-servants of Nathaniel Batts's who had trade goods to take to Jamestown.

Four months had gone by since Richard had left Green Spring. Now he would go back to some purpose—a man with land, ready to take a wife to himself.

Sibyl, Sibyl, how sweet was the fragrance of your lips! Do you know in your heart that I am coming to you?

The eve of the third of September, anniversary of the tragic Battle of Worcester, Richard Monington and Sibyl his wife walked to their new home from the little cottage where they had dwelt for these several years.

It was a day of beauty in forest and on water. Leaves were beginning to turn; grapes hung heavy on the vine. The harvest was in. Tobacco was in the barns; corn in the cribs; grain in stacks. Digby watched them as they walked along the path, his arm about her shoulders. He thought, A wild country, untamed and savage, wants a woman's gentling. There was the girl Tamar. Mayhap he would take his canoe and paddle upstream. It would be difficult going against the current, but coming home would be pleasant, drifting—and maybe not alone. The girl Tamar . . . He knocked the dottle out of his pipe and went for a walk in the woods. Woods at sunset were soothing to a man's thoughts.

Richard and Sibyl hesitated at the stoop. The sun was low. The cry of a heron came above the still water. An owl's lonely hoot sounded from the forest. Down the long vista of the Great Sound the night was falling on the water, quiet and full of peace.

In London on the eve of the anniversary of the Battle of Worcester a great man or a great devil lay dying. The people whispered, within the quiet of their houses, that tomorrow he would depart this life.

Tomorrow was his day. Two battles had he won on the third of September—Dunbar and his last battle, the Battle of the Crowning Mercy. In his palace of Whitehall lay Oliver Cromwell, the near King of all England, with death standing at his pillow. His massive shoulders were still. His thick brown hair fell on his pillow. The thin nose, the wide nostrils seemed to shrivel. Only the lips kept moving—counting his sins, his enemies said; talking with God, his friends whispered. Once he cried aloud, so that the death-watchers in the adjoining chamber heard his every word. "Tell me, is it possible to fall from grace, Chaplain? Tell me . . . Then I am safe, for once I stood in grace."

The great storm came. The wind moved through forests, leaving wide paths. Noble trees lay overturned in great parks; ships sank at their moorings; dwellings were levelled, and steeples and crosses fell from churches. The fury of the tempest was boundless. For a hundred years past, never had there been such rage in the heavens. The devil was in it. Now the Protector must surely die.

Toward afternoon on the next day the bells tolled. His day of victory became his day of departure.

The bells tolled, but the devil rode.

In Herefordshire the great storm raged. For years after, those who saw it whispered to their children how the devil rode that night. Through broken forest he went, burning the tree-tops with evil fires, dragging Oliver Cromwell behind him, until he came to Brampton-Bryan Park, where dwelt Sir Robert Harley. Rushing through the park, the devil was seen still clutching Oliver's arm, knocking over trees and bushes, until he disappeared at last amid murky clouds of fire in their wild ride downward.